EMMA WILLIS, II

I Can Find You

Joss Landry

Book Beatles Publishing Ltd.
260-2323 32nd Ave NE
Calgary Alberta T6W0C4

This book is a work of fiction. Any names, or references of events,
past or present, and/or to existing people, living or dead, are purely coincidental
and intended only for the message to the reader. All names, characters, places
are the product of the author's imagination and used strictly fictitiously to en-
hance the reader's experience.

Book cover design: Ida Jansson of Amygdala Design.
Editing: Jill Noel of Book Beatles LLC.
ISBN: **978-0-9960441-2-7** (print) ISBN: **978-0-9960441-3-4** (ebook)

Publisher's Cataloging-In-Publication Data
(Prepared by The Donohue Group, Inc.)

Names: Landry, Joss.
Title: Emma Willis. Book II, I can find you / by Joss Landry.
Other Titles: I can find you
Description: Calgary, Alberta : Book Beatles Publishing Ltd., [2016]
Identifiers: ISBN 978-0-9960441-2-7 (print) | ISBN 978-0-9960441-3-4
    (ebook)
Subjects: LCSH: Teenagers--Psychic ability--Fiction. | Astral projection--
    Fiction. | High school students--New Jersey--Newark--Fiction. | Lost
    articles--New Jersey--Newark--Fiction. | LCGFT: Detective and mystery
    fiction.
Classification: LCC PR9199.4.A54 I332 2016 (print) | LCC PR9199.4.A54
    (ebook) | DDC 813/.6--dc23

A VERY SPECIAL MENTION:

I am so grateful for my husband Gilles' devotion. He is stead-fast, a powerful motivator, believes in my stories and helps in the thinking process. In short, he has slowly become the voice that drives me.

My children and grandchildren also drive me ... onward to improve, and not merely to do more, but become more than I am. My very own personal cloud of angels.

Last, but most important, "Thank thee, Rabboni for walking beside me."

***

Joss Landry is also the author of:
Mirror Deep: Romantic suspense
Exhale and Reboot: Romantic mystery
Ava Moss: Romantic cozy mystery
Emma Willis Book I I Can See You. Urban Fantasy

You can reach Joss through the web site:
www.bookbeatles.com or www.josslandry.com
Facebook: http://www.facebook.com/josslandry
Twitter: https://twitter.com/josslandry
Please, if you enjoyed this book, please be so kind as to leave a review, which is the greatest praise an author can receive. Thank you!

A Mystery

"The Most beautiful thing we can experience is
the mysterious. It is the source of all true art
and all science. He to whom this emotion is a stranger
who can no longer pause to wonder and stand rapt in awe,
is as good as dead: his eyes are closed." Albert Einstein

"I wrote the Emma Willis series as urban fantasies
because they are explicable mysteries occurring,
in that they could, they might happen ... mysteries
and if you're quick enough to catch their meaning,
you will find them to be more than reveries." Joss Landry

Prologue

Emma picked up Granny Dottie's diary—the leather-bound collection of her grandmother and great grandmothers' personal writings over a century old. The tome was a treasure trove of their magical powers: how to overcome troubles of the craft and how best to use their gifts.

Not all women had been deprived or ridiculed because of their skills or made to bear a painful life like her granny Dottie had.

In fact, one of her great, great grandmothers had been quite wealthy. Emma couldn't quite decipher her name. The smudges from her ink pen became a blotch over time, a shame since she'd been the only woman to write a name. Since the letters 'ra' remained, from what she could guess, Emma thought of her as Sara. And Sara's father being a Duke, they lived in a castle somewhere outside London, England where she shared her knowledge of how to manipulate time with a select few. Sara also talked about how one might use the portals to choose the time or the realm where one might wish to visit or live.

One of Sara's descendants had the book amended with a gold ring binder mechanism in the early nineteen hundreds. Emma fingered the binder and wondered if the device might be real gold.

The first fifty pages or so were difficult to read and of course, time would only worsen this fact, and Emma wondered if her legacy wasn't to find a way to recopy this whole book and perhaps transform the texts into a digital format.

Her promise to write in the diary long overdue, Emma reached for the smooth, round-tipped pen she purchased for this wondrous occasion. She wrote on a blank new page, the last entry seven years earlier when Granny Dottie, very ill waited to die as one might wait for a cab, with haste and trepidation.

She began writing in the neatest way possible, and Emma decided to pen her name letting go of the fear of being discovered and the wariness of being different.

And since all her powers became possible because of her Granny Dottie, she addressed the message to her. "Thank you for handing me this book when I turned ten, Granny. The diary made me realize I was different from other children my age, and for a long time, I fought to reject most of the gifts mentioned here the responsibility of carrying them too big a burden. Until I met friends who helped me understand the meaning of bravery and the ripple effects of kindness. Friends who taught me each time I reached out to someone in need, a little generosity swelled to boundless blessings for others."

Emma paused before adding, "I'm so sorry, Granny, God rest your soul. Sorry, you had to live in fear most of your life. You lived with ridicule and isolation. Yet, the fact you shared with me your precious secrets started me on my journey. What I do today, I also do for you, Granny. You ignored my daddy's orders not to reveal this to me. You opened your heart to allow me inside yours.

You paved the way for my future. Most of all, in a time of strife and great pain, you overcame your fear and handed my mother the amulet to keep me grounded." Emma fingered the Eye of Horus hanging around her neck. "You were most brave, Granny, and so kind. I miss you every day even seven years after you've left me."

Emma wiped a tear from her cheek. "I think you would be surprised yet proud of the way the gifts have turned out. Remember conjuring you said no one could ever do? Well, I can do this, Granny. Although most of the time the power backfired and created nothing but grief for the people around me, the gift helped me on a few occasions.

I have also learned to use OBE as one of our ancestors taught me. Out of body experience is the most precious gift, I find. I learned how to project myself, and even discovered the difference of propelling my body along with my mind by traveling through portals. Propelling was not something our ancestor managed. She mentioned few people did, but she explained the differences quite well, and I finally mastered the technique. Again, this power was tricky to learn and even placed me in mortal danger once or twice.

Of course, the power of sight is less intrusive now. I considered this a curse for years having to deal with something so elusive. The gift impedes on my life at times—the fact I can turn the visions on or off with the oudjat still my only form of control. One day, I will learn how to make an island of peace and calm around me to avoid having the future or the past sneak up on me unexpectedly without having to wear the amulet. I love you, Granny."

—1—

ASTRAL WORLD

Emma's long hair stuck to her temples and her back in clumps and tangles. A dense fog enveloped her, and though she wore an old style black cloak, the cold mist penetrated her garment and chilled her to the bone.

After walking in this strange land for what seemed like hours instead of the mere minutes she suspected to be the dream's timespan, Emma still ignored why she roamed about the alien land—a strange dream Emma doubted she would fight to remember upon waking—her attempts to wake up ineffective.

A carriage strode by, the big wheel close enough to scrape the side of her leg. A disheveled young man sat hunched at the helm of a horse-drawn cart. He nudged the reins of two black Percherons slowly traveling up a cobblestone road. Shabby clothes, unkempt tousled dark hair, his head followed the cadence of the horses' slow gait, like one of those toys in perpetual motion, and the word mendicant crossed Emma's mind.

She caught a brief impression of his thoughts as he rode passed her, warning her, of what? A sense of danger and doom filled her mind, but his words briefly captured dissolved in the fog and disappeared useless to her now.

An echo surprised her in the distance. Too loud to be a woodpecker, the sound became sharper like the wrap of knuckles on a sturdy piece of wood.

Emma opened her eyes startled by her mom's words through her bedroom door. She stared at the light coming through the window revealing the late hour. She glanced at the clock and clutched her heart from the thump in her chest kicking her out of bed. "I'm up, Mom." Gathering her thoughts along with her clothes, she wondered where the word mendicant came from.

She tripped over a corner of the sheet still caught between her legs and bounced her shoulder against the door frame. Late again, twice in one week to Mr. Wright's class. Her social studies' teacher warned them. He would not tolerate tardies.

"Sorry, Mom. Hope you're finished with the bathroom. Can't figure why I overslept this time," she said more to reassure her mother from worrying that she'd fought all night with frightening dreams.

"I'll use the one downstairs, sweetie. Are you going to be all right to get to school?"

Sensing her mother's question to be rhetorical, the light in those big brown eyes flashing the desperation she would be late herself if she drove Emma to school, Emma nodded with a toothpaste filled smile. She gargled to rinse making her eyes water from the burn of mouthwash and toothpaste. "Go, Mom. Don't worry about me. I'll hop a bus." Of course, since her mom now owned the flower shop, she needed to be there earlier than in the olden days when she worked as a mere employee.

With twenty minutes to spare before she needed to be *butt in chair*, a little math equation ran through her thoughts. *Seven minutes to get to school by car. Dad left for work, and Mom is headed in the opposite direction.*

Emma tugged on her long hair with a quick flick of the brush and applied a little pink lip color. Relentless, the math equation continued. *Twenty-three minutes by bus, plus a walk from the bus to school then to my classroom.* Even saddling her bike would make her late.

Emma caught her mom's cheery goodbye while jumping into her jeans and T-shirt, and the front door slammed shut.

She grabbed her bag, shoved her wallet into the front pouch and realized she didn't wear the eye of Horus around her neck. No wonder sleep came in fitful images.

She rummaged through the little jewelry box on the dresser and reached for the oudjat she slipped around her neck as she lifted the thick curtain of her hair. She thanked her lucky stars she no longer needed to remove the piece of jewelry to travel. She now understood how to project and propel herself even with the eye of Horus standing guard, present these days to prevent her from roaming without her knowledge.

Emma still needed to wear the oudjat though not yet having mastered the tranquility she needed to follow her classes with a modicum of sanity. The city's whines and wails still pounded between her temples without the protection of her pendant.

In the kitchen, Emma grabbed a fruit and a power bar to carry her through lunch. What she contemplated doing weighed on her mind since she still needed to master landing in a tight space, like in a bathroom stall.

Emma sat on the settee in her living room. She closed her eyes and slowed her heart beats. Little beads of sweat appeared on her forehead below the hairline, and she dabbed at them with the tissue she grabbed from the back pocket of her bag. Strapping her bag to her back, she found her center. She crossed both palms on each shoulder and invoked the sentence: Lift me away, oh Universe, lift me away so I may fly to school on time.

As usual, the haze around her thickened and soon, she became airborne and no longer in her living room. Over the years, she became accustomed to identify portals when she traveled—flowered arches drawing her forward to wherever she needed to go. Her surroundings made her believe she floated on wings of gossamer in one of Monet's canvases like the Garden at Argenteuil with its dangling wisps of clouds. The picture portrayed helpful souls eager to lead her home.

Emma stared at the vaulted blue sky as always mesmerized by its depth. Yet this time, a strange path drew her attention. Bordered by dark crimson roses, an arch dripping with begonias and oleanders magnetized her pulling her closer against her will. Indeed, not Monet colors, and even though she realized mere milliseconds flitted by, no time remained to explore this strange, menacing spectacle.

She closed her eyes and called for peace and serenity to pull her where she needed to go. She managed to do so, but not before a firm grip on her elbow tugged on her arm to pull her back.

Emma struggled with panic but drew on calm while applying an extra dose of contentment. She spotted the school yard and realized she disposed of seconds to find a place to touch down before she became visible. She landed behind a parked car and prayed no one spotted her.

Someone called her name. She looked up and caught Tommy

slamming the car door running toward her. She caught his dad's car peeling away from the curve tires squealing against the tarmac.

"We waited for you, but Dad has an early meeting downtown."

"I overslept again. Did you drive here?"

"Of course. The whole point of Dad driving me to school is so I can fit in all the hours of driving practice I need. I refuse to extend the first phase of my GDL any more than I need to—July Twentieth."

"Might not be six months to the day from your birthday." Emma rolled her eyes.

"Oh, yes Ma'am. Not one day more," Tommy stated with a smile.

Becoming more handsome with each passing year—years eclipsed in a blur with so many changes—Tommy wore his hair short these days which showed off a square jaw and the dimple in his chin. Tall too, six foot two or more to her five-nine. Even with a short heel, she still couldn't quite measure.

"For your sake, I hope you're right. I understand how much you want your independence. Did your dad say he might help with the money you need for the car you want?"

They walked at a fast pace toward school. Tommy stopped and reached for the straps around Emma's shoulders. "Here let me. I can't figure how you manage to keep your bag so heavy." Amidst her protests, he slipped the bag off her back to hoist onto one of his shoulders.

Emma appreciated the sudden sensation of lightness and waited for his answer, a touchy subject with Tommy.

"He's going to try. Unlike your dad who struck gold these past five years selling insurance to neighbors, and to families at the second precinct, he still has to work hard. My Aunt Caroline might help."

She didn't want to explain how her father now held insurance policies for more than one police division, she told him instead. "I have a little money saved up if you need some."

"Hey, I'm going to be the one chauffeuring you, not the other way around."

They climbed the few steps to the large terrazzo featuring open doors.

"Such a guy thing to say."

"Stop," Tommy ordered. He drew her close to him with his arm around her waist. He stood perpendicular to her while a quick hand softly rummaged through her tresses at the back of her nape.

Emma fidgeted, uncomfortable with the personal invasion of her space. "People are watching," she commented in a singsong tone.

"I spotted something shiny in your hair."

Emma fingered her amulet against her chest. "My new shampoo."

"No. Shine seems more like a bright light—could send a signal all the way to Mars."

She motioned to pull away, but he barred the way flicking her chin to stare into her face. A few long seconds went by as she gazed into his dark blue eyes.

"Stand still," he ordered, the twinkle in his eyes daring her to move.

She mustered the strength to let out a deep breath, and tear her eyes from his with a show of defiance. She thought of last Saturday night at the movies with Tommy when he'd gently pecked her lips for no reason. Even now, the recall of this sensation froze her into inertia creating a tingling sensation inside her.

Her aunt Franka warned her about a change in Tommy's feelings toward her. Emma thought it strange she managed to decipher Hank Apple's mind along with the thoughts of many others, but could not detect this kind of change in Tommy. Were they too close for her to properly read him? Might he be more adept at keeping his mind closed than everyone else?

"A chain and a bauble are stuck in the back of your hair." Tommy dropped his bag on the ground to use both hands to run his fingers through her hair. An unexpected shyness washed over her as she stood in front of him, unable to move.

"Impossible. My amulet is pinned right where I generally place my locket, close to my chest," she added tugging on the pendant.

"How about I make sure and check," he whispered in her ear.

"Stop," she said without conviction. "We're going to be late."

He stroked her cheek with his index finger. "Relax. You've got another five minutes." He tugged on the chain to pry it loose.

"Ouch!"

"You don't want to spend the day with a piece of jewelry in your hair, do you? Here." He handed her the chain with a couple of her hairs twirled around the locket.

"How did this end up tangled in my hair?" She took the chain from him and wondered out loud. "Must have gotten hooked in my pendant. I haven't thought about this little chain in months." She picked up on his puzzled frown. "The little oudjat I conjured when I forgot mine in your coat pocket five years ago."

"I remember."

"Hank says police can't locate the owner if no one ever reports the piece missing."

They walked toward the doors. "Why not take out an add? Might jog someone's memory."

"My mom did five years ago, and I did again last year and the year before last. Nothing turned up."

They entered the building, and unsure of what to do with the second amulet, Emma slipped the piece around her neck. She glanced at her watch, and Tommy laid a hand on her arm. "Wait a minute. If you overslept, how were you on the grounds before I even got here?" He gave her the narrowed eyes loaded with reproach. "You promised you wouldn't do the propelling shit anymore?"

"I even broke the promise to myself. I didn't want to be late again."

Tommy let go of her arm and took a step back his eyes round with panic. "Who the hell did that job on your arm?"

Sensing a slight burn on her arm from Tommy's touch, she twisted to see why and encountered a red imprint around her elbow, almost like a welt. She remembered the grab while in the haze during the few seconds she used to propel herself and realized something attempted to hold her back or direct her elsewhere. Not some vague impression she imagined, but a real threat.

"Did your dad rough you up? Hank maybe, in his hurry to drag you somewhere?"

"Don't be silly. My dad would never hurt me, and Hank is always a gentleman."

Someone called Emma's name, and she turned to catch Amelia running toward them. Out of breath, her friend paused, bending to haul air into her lungs. "Mom and I stopped by your place to give you a ride." More heavy breaths. "Your mom called mine to tell us she worried about you being late." Amelia checked the time on the clock in the hall. "You almost made me late. How'd you get here?"

Tommy stepped in. "Dad and I waited too. When Dad ordered me to drive on, I spotted her at the bus stop."

"Hello, Tommy." After batting her eyes at him, Amelia addressed Emma. "Come on, Em. Wright is going to cream you if you're late again."

Emma appreciated Amelia's insistence toward her parents on allowing her to attend Belleville High. Especially since Amelia's twin chose to remain in private school, which suited Amelia as she maintained they needed to run solo for a while.

Sensing Tommy's hold on her arm, Emma told Amelia. "You run ahead. I'll be there in a sec."

"I'm sorry," Emma said breathlessly. "This happened while I traveled this morning."

"What?" Tommy's eyes bulged with rancor. "How many times did I tell you not to do this? You never listen. One day you're going to be sorry."

"I thought of you to release this hold on my arm." Emma smiled at him.

"You did?" He couldn't help a faint smile. He smoothed her hair. "Go on. You're going to be late."

While running, Emma looked back glancing at the group of friends surrounding Tommy Carson. No doubt whatsoever, Tommy seemed to be elected as everyone's favorite.

—2—

RECONNAISSANCE

As soon as his last class ended Monday afternoon, Tommy scrambled outside with some of his friends. Amelia joined them and tried to mix in with the tall Buccaneers of the football team. Tommy stared at her and took pity on her shyness. He wasn't used to vulnerability in Amelia. "Hey guys, careful with your language, a lady is present." He smiled Amelia's way and spotted her releasing a deep breath as she gave him a grateful smile.

"Where is Emma?" She tossed a shoulder giving him the big eyes.

Peaceful moment gone, he thought, hating the attempted manipulation Tommy spotted in Amelia. "She'll be here. Dad's giving us a ride home. I'm driving."

"Wow, can I come?"

"Isn't your mom picking you up?" The shyness crept back in, and he came to her rescue once again. "Besides, I'm in the first phase of my GDL. I'm only allowed to have one passenger who is not family along with my dad in the car."

"I understand," Amelia seemed incapable of adding anything else. Instead, she waved when Emma called out to her. "Over here."

Emma reached her and was surprised to find Tommy a few feet from where his teammates stood.

He shrugged. "Keeping Amelia company."

"Wow, such a gentleman," she cooed rubbing his arm. "Listen, I can't go home with you tonight. Hank's picking me up. We're going downtown to do a little recon."

"On a school night? Your parents don't mind?" Tommy tried to hide his disappointment.

"Trust me. Hank needs my help."

"Hey, this means I can drive home with you guys." Amelia gave Tommy a big smile.

"What about your mom?" Emma asked.

"She hasn't left yet. I'll call her and tell her I'm going home with Tommy and his dad. I'm sure she'll say yes." Amelia extended her hand to borrow Emma's cell phone. She walked away already on the phone with her mother.

"You sure you want to leave me alone with Amelia, the minx?" Tommy gave Emma a sour look.

Emma chuckled. "Come on. She's not a flirt. She likes you, and I don't find anything wrong with liking you. I do—like you."

"The difference is Amelia wants to own me."

Emma rolled her eyes, yet refused to be baited into an open discussion Tommy style. Amelia was on her way back when Emma spotted Hank's car coming up the drive. She caught her phone midair and told both of them. "I'll call you the minute I'm home. I promise."

She waved, set her bag down in the back of the car, and sat in front with Hank.

His greeting out of the way, Hank stated. "Hope I'm not taking you away from anything important."

"No, of course not. I'll ask Tommy to help me with math later."

"You didn't mention our covert operation to anyone, I hope?" He turned right on Passaic to head downtown, Newark.

"Of course not, Hank. Tommy never even asked. Neither did Amelia," she added when she caught him about to interrupt her. "Amelia is not aware of our cooperation or my powers, remember?"

"Thank you. This little rendezvous has been weighing on my mind for a long time—years, in fact. I don't want anyone finding out before all the loose ends are tied."

Emma opted to remain silent while staring at the streets going by, a river of cars filing in and out in front of her eyes. Of course, she realized being able to read people's thoughts and ideas did not make her an expert in understanding same thoughts and ideas. Still she found difficult to accept how men, at least some men, believed they needed trickery to impress a woman or demonstrate their love for her.

Five years of hanging around Hank, yet she still did not comprehend many of his decisions. In fact, he still lived with Christina in the same house her mother left her, and he continued to do most of the things he did while he worked as a detective. Some of his duties differed somewhat being a captain now, but he still took care of other people's kids on the weekends.

Of course, Christina was proud of him and didn't object to Hank giving back to the community. Yet, Emma wondered if he continued doing what he did to avoid tackling the subject of his own life. Hank's devotion meant no fun vacation for him and

Christina, mitigated Christmas dinners they shared with homeless people, summer holidays they spent with street kids in city day camps.

"Someone has to do this," Christina would add a tad on the defensive. "Might as well be us." Was this even the type of life Hank wanted? Perhaps Hank hesitated to fashion a new life able to include Christina?

"Here we are," Hank announced. He stretched to put the cherry on the roof of his vehicle to be able to park in a restricted area. "You're kind of quiet. Anything wrong?"

She turned and smiled at him, trying not to invade his thoughts. She did promise Hank she would not read his mind—well, at least when his overworked brain didn't spill goo on everyone around him. Like now, when he stared at her, worried she might be reading him a little too well.

"I'm okay, Hank."

When he swung the door to the tall building on Broad Street, she couldn't resist asking, "You think all this subterfuge is necessary? To please Christina, I mean? Why not share with her how you feel and explore what she wants to do?"

He gave her a side glance with a wry smile. "I knew you berated me in silence all the way here. Thanks to the time we spend together, kiddo, I can pick up on those vibes."

"Only because I'm never this quiet when I'm around you which, by the way, doesn't mean I'm berating you in silence. I have other things and other people in my life."

They made their way to the suite of Martin & Son Jewelers. And Hank stopped before entering. "Not when your first question is about Christina. Well, let's say the shenanigans are for my benefit. They make all this nerve-racking business more fun." His eyes grew big as he attempted to make her laugh. She did, thinking Hank was well-acquainted with her moods as well.

Emma followed Hank into the posh boutique which literally dazzled her the first time she accompanied Christina, a mere week ago. Emma recalled the swell of pride in the fact she and Christina, her former fifth-grade teacher, had become such good friends over the past five years. The tall and lanky brunette filled in as the older sister Emma always longed for.

"You should ask for the owner," Emma told Hank, eyeing all the glitter scintillating in the many rows lined with jeweled coffers. "Christina is well acquainted with him. She came here with her mother when she was a little girl."

Hank turned toward her with raised eyebrows. "She told you about that?"

She nodded. "She asked me what I thought of Luigi." Emma scoured the area to find him. "He seems like a kind man."

"How exactly did you two hook up?"

"Well, after Christina took me to lunch, she said she needed to have her bracelet repaired. Since I remembered you asking me to gauge what sort of ring she might like, I thought what a great opportunity."

"Clasp had to be repaired," Hank added with a big smile.

Emma eyed Hank with suspicion. "Said she didn't trust anyone else than Martin and Son to do the work." Emma paused on her way to the aisle in back. "What did you do?"

Hank's big smile would not disappear. "Found a way to weaken a bracelet clasp."

"Oh, my God! Christina will be so angry when she finds out."

"Considering what I'm about to do, I think she'll forgive me."

"Well, I wandered off toward the engagement rings, on purpose of course. She came to fetch me after she finished, and I told her which ring I liked best, and she told me which ones she liked best."

"You make this sound so easy."

"No. Not easy. We spent an hour here while Christina tried on many, many rings."

Hank grabbed Emma's arm. "Come on. Let's do this. Hope the ring she likes is still here. A whole week went by. Might be gone by now."

Emma followed him and scoured the area to try to find the ring among the brilliant mounts displayed in the cases. "Luigi will be more familiar with the ring she loves."

"You don't remember?" Hank's panic appeared out of proportion.

"May I help you?" A young woman brandished an engaging smile.

"Yes," Hank hesitated. "I am looking for an engagement ring for my girlfriend. I wonder if I may speak to Luigi."

"I'm sorry. Mr. Luigi needed to leave early today. Do you have any idea of what she might like?"

He turned toward Emma, a smile on his face with goofy pleading eyes.

She bit her bottom lip not to laugh and started to explain when a familiar jovial voice resounded behind her. "I'll take over, Miss Latham."

"Mr. Luigi!" She turned toward Hank and apologized. She turned to Luigi. "I'm so sorry. I thought you said you weren't well." She lowered her tone. "I assumed you went home."

Emma expelled a grateful sigh for reinforcements showing up at the precise minute she needed them. Luigi was so kind to her when she visited with Christina. His big head of dark curly hair and his warm blue eyes mirrored such a gentle soul.

Luigi replaced Miss Latham behind the counter and smiled at Hank ignoring Emma as though she didn't exist.

Emma's spirits sank. Of course, a lot of clients were in and out every day, but when she first encountered him, he even made the effort of finding out more about her, mentioning any friend of Christina's was a real friend of his.

When she stepped out of her thoughts, she realized Hank waited for her to talk about Christina's choice of a ring. She glanced at Luigi surprised he didn't seem to remember.

"Well, she mentioned the Purple Oasis diamond. Remember?" She addressed Luigi, "The diamond is accented with a crown of Amethysts and weighs 1.5 ct, also appears flawless with excellent color, if I recall. I don't find the ring here."

Emma glanced into Luigi's eyes and she needed to work hard not to lose her calm and scream. Someone else occupied Luigi's body. No wonder he didn't remember her or the ring.

"I locked the jewel away. I thought she might want the ring someday soon, and items from the Bez Ambar collection sell fast."

Luigi bent toward the cabinet, and Emma caught the reflection of unique traits in the reflective glass used to examine the jewels. Once more, she had to clamp on her emotions not to give herself away. Whoever occupied this body, stood to gain, but what?

Emma elbowed Hank as the man disappeared low behind the counter. She grabbed his hand and held on hoping to impart information. In an interrogation two years prior, across a one-way glass, she managed to convey thoughts to Hank.

Luigi came back up with the ring, and Emma turned to check on Hank's reaction. His rush toward the ring told her he didn't grasp a single word of what she tried to tell him. She let go of his hand and exclaimed on how beautiful the ring was. "This is the ring Christina fell in love with, Hank."

"Wonderful choice," Luigi said.

Emma detected an accent as he spoke even as she concentrated on cracking who the man might be behind the face. She spotted superimposed beady black eyes and gray hair at the temples of an almost bald head. The figure was slight and thin. Emma also found strange the sweet, intense honeysuckle aroma wafting from the man's gestures.

By now, Hank had the ring in his hands subjecting the jewel to different lights to allow the sparkle to catch his eye. After discussing the price with the impersonator, he turned and asked, "What do you think, Emma? This is the ring Christina likes?"

Emma nodded, her senses overrun with the heady aroma, almost as strong as to be debilitating. The scent made her lightheaded and clouded her judgment.

Before she had time to move away, Luigi commented on one of the oudjats she wore around her neck.

"I spot a little pendant. Most unusual this smaller one."

Emma kept the jewelry hidden and wondered how the pendant had sprung to the surface. "Thank you." She needed to work hard not to reveal more.

She smiled and called on all her powers not to add anything else. "I'm not well, Hank. I need some air."

"I will take the ring. Can you excuse us for a moment?" Hank dragged Emma away near an air vent. "What's going on? Are you ill?"

"Did you understand what I tried to communicate?"

"No. I didn't."

"A superimposed image of uneven traits is inside Luigi, and a bizarre expression in the eyes as though they are empty yet focused on a single-minded purpose. Appears as though a walk-in took over in an unfriendly manner."

"Well, this is the first time I learn about walk-ins. But how do you figure this to be hostile?"

"Not too sure about them myself. Yet, what little I did read says these mergers of two physical beings are supposed to be agreed upon by both. Somehow I sense Luigi may not be aware of the merger. As for me, the overpowering scent of honeysuckle went right to my head, preventing me from thinking straight."

"What's he after?"

"I'm not sure." She looked down at her chest and fingered the unknown amulet she'd flung around her neck by accident. She glanced at Hank clutching the little oudjat she conjured by mistake five years earlier. "This pendant seems to be the one he is interested in. I am wearing the jewelry by accident today." *Was this an accident?* First, the dream about the boy with the dark fringed and almond shaped blue eyes dressed like a mendicant but oozing of powers, and now this little fellow with the dark beady eyes.

"Don't worry. We'll find the reason for all this. For now, I need to buy Christina's ring. Why not wait for me outside, get some air? I'll be out in five."

She walked out of the store remembering what she read about

one of her ancestor's adamant warning, to allow spirit guides to go about their business without creating any interference.

She had no proof what this man's end goals might be, yet Emma's thoughts assured her the man masquerading as Luigi held malevolent intentions.

—3—

DECISIONS

On the way home from Martin and Son Jewelers, Emma struggled to remember her dream. Ever since her earliest recalls, deleting the ghoulish images coming out of her visions figured utmost on her priorities. Over the years, she became quite adept at this. To exact as much information as possible from the one picture her dream afforded her in the early morning gave her the distinct impression of climbing a hill, backward—a slow process she would need to exercise until she reconstructed the weird puzzle. For instance, did the young man in the astral world and the old man taking Luigi's place work together? Enemies or friends? The incidents might not even be related.

A glimpse of past centuries in the young man's enormous blue eyes surprised Emma, though she was unable to delve into their depth as long lashes dropped to shield her vision. Seconds had fleeted before she faced his broad back while he directed the cart up the road. Though sporting broad shoulders, while she suspected the young man to be tall, he possessed elfin like gestures similar to those of the older man playing Luigi.

"Quarter for your thoughts." Hank's voice made her jump. He flicked a quarter her way, and she caught the coin. "I told you not to worry. Give me a good description of this man, I'll run him through our database."

Emma chuckled, pocketing the money. "I don't think this man is alive, Hank. Your database would be useless in this case."

"Well if he is spirit as you maintain, he needed to be alive at some point."

"I want to figure this out a little more before I go trying to find him."

"Don't shut me out. Might be related to this damn case my department's been working on. Two years. We've put in two years of sweat, tears, and a huge budget with the FBI on our heels with their precious rules and regulations. Still, I believe we're getting closer." He turned toward her having come to a full stop. "Thanks to you."

Emma smiled back at Hank's wide grin before she stared out the window. "Well, I hope you realize you can count on me, right?"

"Did you give more thought to the FAIT Program I mentioned?"

She shook her head. "Not yet."

"Future Agent In Training is a good base to understand if you'd like the FBI as a potential employer. The course is only one week out of your summer. Might be better to take this now than next year after graduation. You'll need to decide what you want to do as soon as possible if only to ensure time to prepare."

"You sound like my father." Emma smiled to relieve the statement. "Don't misunderstand. He's right, and so are you." She pinched both eyes at the bridge of her nose. "I think I might like to go to Rutgers where my aunt Franka went. She is still a beloved teacher at the University. She maintains the place is a rare combination of sharp and friendly. She hasn't steered me wrong yet." Emma attempted to read Hank's expression behind the sunglasses with his eyes fixed on traffic ahead, and since she didn't want to pry she would need to wait.

"In Psychology?"

"Yes. In fact, those skills would come in handy later if I wanted a career with the FBI as a profiler perhaps."

"Forget the FBI. I would hire you in a heartbeat."

She laughed. "Yes. This is what I mean. A university degree would give me more options. I'm sure to be accepted. My aunt will give me good recommendations, so will most of my teachers."

They arrived in front of Emma's house, and she gazed at the family home which remained unchanged since her granny Dottie's death.

"What's stopping you?" Hank turned toward her to obtain an answer to the often evaded question.

"Well, I would need to earn a few scholarships. Find a part-time job. Be ready to put in a lot of work in the next few years. I guess this is why I don't want to make a mistake. Would be costly."

"Can't your father help you at all?"

"We didn't discuss it. Dad's anxious for me to make a decision, but he might not believe in a university degree. All he achieved is a high school diploma and he did quite well for himself."

"What about Abigail? Your grandmother can afford the loan."

"She can. I don't want to hurt my dad's feelings. Oh, the two made up over the years, but I think this sort of advance would weigh on his conscience. Dad is aware my grandmother would never allow me to pay her back."

"Well, don't let too much time go by before you make a decision."

Emma opened the car door and grabbed her bag from the back. "I won't. Thanks, Hank." She hoisted the bag up on one shoulder and bent at the front window. "What day are you going to propose to Christina?"

"Got to find the best time. I'll call you later."

A little hand wave and Emma waited until Hank drove away. She came to rely on Hank these last five years. In her early formative years, Hank managed to establish himself as the hero who chased all the bogeymen out from under her bed. Now, aside from being a friend, he displayed a keen, efficient method of helping her sort out her priorities. He would make a terrific father.

On the drive home, Emma wondered if Hank perhaps considered becoming a father. Might this be why he wanted to propose to Christina? To start a family with the woman he loved?

***

Tommy and Emma sat in the dining room going over the math problems Emma didn't quite understand. The house remained quiet as her father's meeting with clients ran late. Her mother, parked at her aunt Franka's condo in Soho, babysat little Martha, three years old with blond curls and dark blue eyes, the dimple in her cheeks drawn so deep as to rival Botticelli's paintings. She resembled her aunt Franka at the same age family pictures showed. Not surprising everyone wanted to squeeze her like the sweet, precocious little doll she portrayed.

"Stay dialed in, Emma. Your biggest problem is your mind wanders, and you space out on necessary explanations. Worse.

This year, your math teacher is big Bull Randall, and he rambles on and on and waits for no one. You need to stay plugged in when he talks."

"Yes, You're right, but he's so monotonous. Do not understand how you can stay focused."

"All you need to do is mind the words. Not the tone of Randall's voice."

"His tone of voice is what puts me to sleep." She took the pitcher to fill her glass with lemonade. "Want some more?"

"No. Thanks." Tommy put down his calculator. "Why is your place so quiet?"

"My parents aren't home."

"Wow, and we're allowed to study together?" Tommy's eyebrows traveled in a provocative manner.

"Why wouldn't we be?"

"Oh, come on. This from the person who told me we couldn't study in your room anymore."

"Why would we? We're old enough to use the dining room now. The dining room features a new table, and the place is airy. I mean, sprawled on the bed with our copy books on a mushy surface sufficed when we were little kids. Not anymore."

He smiled, winking at her. "Yeah. Too bad I didn't understand life's grand plan at eleven years old."

"Will you stop with the innuendos, please? This is becoming a constant thing with you."

"Well, kick me in the shins! She is at last conscious of the chunk of change I've been throwing at her." Tommy turned toward the right, articulating, "She is aware folks. Yep, she understands."

"Who are you talking to when you do this bit?"

"The walls. They're more understanding than you are on the subject. Emma, innuendos are only innuendos if the person you're trying to reach responds. Otherwise, those words echo in my head long after I say them and remind me of how stupid I sound."

"I'm sorry, Tommy. I don't mean to hurt you. What's wrong with keeping things the way they are between us? I like the fact we're friends. I don't want to lose our friendship."

He placed his hands over hers and stared deep into her eyes. "Why can't we be both? Other people are. Half the guys on my team are dating a girl who is also a friend. Hell by now, they think you and I are a couple."

"You didn't tell them we are, did you?" Emma pulled her hands off the table.

"I never needed to. Our mutual affection is implied. We're tied at the hip, Em."

Emma stared down at her fingernails searching for something to say. "Yes, you're right, of course." Their devotion to each other rendered their relationship palpable, and for better or for worse, she would fight to keep Tommy's friendship intact.

She raised her eyes to his handsome face, caught the concern in his eyes and added with a little more calm. "I'm just not ready. My aunt Franka thinks," she started to say.

"You discussed this with your aunt before even talking to me?" He pushed his chair away from the table to spread his legs while shaking his head with a grimace on his face.

"Girl talk is all." she objected in a loud tone. "I needed to ask her why some girls understand how to flirt while others don't, and why other girls don't seem to care." She hoisted a shoulder in his direction. "She said not to worry. Butterflies would come crawling soon enough with the right boy, at the right time."

"In other words, you don't care for me, at least not the way I care for you."

She caught him making a fist and hoped he wouldn't smash his large knuckles on her mother's new dining room table.

"Not all true. I did experience something when you kissed me at the theater the other night."

"Yes!" he breathed. "I told you, all you need is to experiment a little, and your feelings for me will mature."

"Not what Aunt Franka said."

"Ah gees! You told her about the kiss?"

"Well, yes. I found myself confused and dazed afterward. Aunt Franka said at this stage, any boy I kiss would give me those goose bumps. Hormones she calls them. She specified the unbalance can occur with certain types of contact." A slight blush invaded Emma's cheeks. She hated talking about the subject with Tommy, not quite an impartial listener.

He straightened and jumped up as though bitten by her remark. "Oh, so my father's right. Your dillydallying is not because of me. You want to go out in the world and experiment."

Emma took time rising, surprised by his bitterness. "No. Tommy. You and I are best friends. I turned fifteen years old six weeks ago."

"April 15—hey, this will be your lucky year."

"Can we stay on the subject, please?"

"Is this about the party I didn't give you? You swore you didn't want any surprise party."

"Tom." she shortened his name to grab his attention. "You're sixteen and a half," she added when she caught him about to interrupt again. "You can't be talking about a lifelong commitment here?"

He stared at their books sprawled all over the table.

Emma got nothing other than a sigh out of him. "Whatever your dad says, our situation is different." She motioned to her and him. "You and I are not the same as your mom and dad. What went on between your parents is not the same as what's going on between us. I don't think your dad's the best person to take advice from."

Tommy turned his back on her and grabbed his book bag shoving his school stuff inside in a hurry.

Emma crossed to the other side of the table and grabbed his sleeve as he made to leave. "Talk to someone else, to another adult who can give you more objective answers."

Emma let him go as he reached the door. "Tommy please, the issue is creating a rift between us and threatening our friendship."

He took a deep breath swinging the door open. "I'll catch you tomorrow, Emma. I'm fine. Need to collect my bearings," he added without looking at her.

Emma stared at the door he slammed hoping he might come back, realize how puerile the words he spoke in anger sounded and admit his mistake.

Instead, her father waltzed in looking drawn with his face colored an odd shade of salad green under the hall light. A redhead with tons of freckles the warmer climate accentuated the paleness of Patrick Willis' skin. "Are you all right, Dad?"

He nodded. "Is Tommy the fellow I caught biking away?"

"Yeah. I am studying for a math test tomorrow. Mom's still at Franka's taking care of little Martha." He appeared more haggard than usual she thought as he put down his leather valise next to the rhododendron. He hung his worn beige raincoat on the hook behind the door.

The plant brought life to a room otherwise furnished with little amenities and in dire need of a coat of paint. Emma eyed her surroundings and wondered where her parents' hard earned money had gone. Without a doubt, both had made some these last five years. Yet the only few pieces of furniture added in the last little while happened to be a second-hand dining room table and the chairs to match.

"Are you hungry, Pop? Do you want me to make you something to eat?"

"I grabbed a sandwich on the way, sweetheart." He smiled as he glanced at her for the first time since his arrival. "I guess your mother being elsewhere is a good thing. I need to talk to you."

The expression from a man who needed to be reminded to say hello and goodbye sounded ominous. "Anything wrong?"

He shook his head and took her hand leading her to a smaller living room affixed at the end of the dining room. Musty from old furniture and infrequent use, Emma pleated her nose as she entered the abandoned room. Emma sat down and smoothed the creases out of a throw covering the tired and faded green settee for three, a token purchase from Granny Dottie's days. Her father took the only chair he angled to face her.

Dottie left her house to Patrick, her only son. A tall standing structure in dire need of repairs, yet the only change Emma remembered, occurred when the roof needed to be patched and tarred last year. Oh, and one of the stairs in the indoor wooden flight of steps needed changing—still the color of the original wood. Patrick promised to varnish the staircase as soon as he got a chance, a few years ago.

His hands steepled and moving up and down as though dispersing his blessing, Patrick began with a question. "Made up your mind yet about what you're going to do in a year's time after you finish high school?"

Emma figured this might be the talk, the chat dads gave their daughters. Mothers gave their daughters the sex talk, although her aunt Franka happened to be the one who did, while fathers spoke of education she supposed. "I'm not sure yet, Dad. I do want to work with people, something in the service industry I guess."

"Rather vague," became her dad's immediate reaction. He interjected as she was about to interrupt. "What you're doing is good. Best not to rush things. I'm proud of you, glad you're weighing your options. Please, don't let anyone push you. This is for the rest of your life, Emma. Deciding on a career at fifteen is a lot like securing a boyfriend at fifteen. Both tasks can be challenging and exciting, yet both can also be regretted. More drama to avoid, huh?"

She realized he referred to Tommy and her father's perspicacity floored her. Her cheeks colored a soft pink as she sensed her head bob up and down while she kept her eyes on the hands in her lap.

Patrick leaned toward her to draw her attention. "Take me for instance. I hated school. Almost dropped out of high school. Nevertheless, I graduated, and when I applied to the insurance company someone recognized talent in me and put me through the training. Well, I love what I do."

"You're good at what you do."

"Yes because this type of career suits me to a T. I enjoy working with people and providing a good product while I convince them to agree with me. Oh, work can be challenging, but three cheers—job's never the same, no monotony as in I don't need to punch a time clock. Over the years, the best thing I grew to appreciate was the one I feared the most, the commission my sales bring me. In the last twenty years, I've earned more money than one of them city comptrollers." He rubbed his face with both his hands. "Hell, received more than a college professor—with tenure." He gave her a big smile.

A college professor with tenure meant her aunt, Franka. Of course, her aunt hadn't taught for twenty years yet, so the comparison might be a little off, but she got his meaning. She nodded realizing her father needed to say more.

"Honey, I'm sorry if all this talk about my job over the years gave you the idea I may consider a higher education useless."

"You didn't."

"Well, your mother says I did, and she might be right. The point I'm trying to make is everyone's calling is different, and you need to find something you will love to do for the rest of your life. Emma, an education would give you more options to grow and diversify your field as you become more accomplished. You might even like to take on graduate studies later."

"I like to help people. Make sure everyone gets their fair share. To me, people society judges as bad, as refuse to be thrown in jail or thrown away are some of those who need help the most. All happened to be children once, and if helped a little earlier in life there is no telling what miracle might happen."

"Wonderful. Like father, like daughter. We both like to help people. Please don't let Hank Apple push you into starting too soon. FBI is an exceptional career. Might limit what you want to do later on, though."

"My thoughts also, Dad. The truth is Hank is presenting the FBI to me as a means of showing restraint in not hiring me himself, right out of high school."

"Hell, he would have hired you at ten-years-old if at all possible." He got up and paced a few steps in front of his chair. "Are you still conjuring?"

"What?" Took a minute before his question sank in. "No, Dad. Conjuring gave me nothing but trouble."

"Well, I've been conjuring." He gave a triumphant smile and laughed outright when Emma opened her eyes wide with surprise.

She wondered if he also possessed some of his mother's powers.

"Six months after the commotion fizzled and things returned somewhat to normal, and after all the sales started pouring in when Hank admitted to the young whippersnapper from the Post I'd helped him on his case."

"The reporter who wondered why Hank came over here so much?"

He nodded. "I secured a loan from the bank to replace the amount I burned. Ten thousand dollars invested in a high-yield interest bearing account, and into which I deposited money all these years." He stopped pacing and sat back down.

Emma got up and kneeled beside his chair, concern on her features. "Is this why you and Mom never traveled? Why Mom doesn't wear the fancy clothes she dreams about or buy the trimmings she would love to pour into this house?"

He smiled, pinching his lip as though tears threatened to spill. Emma learned over the years how her father's emotions plagued him, and how they played a significant role in his renowned volatile behavior.

"How much money are we talking about?" she whispered afraid to ask.

"Two hundred thousand dollars."

Emma's turn for tears. She couldn't utter a single word the lump in her throat humongous and fragile. Her father and mother's sacrifices became apparent, and she cried her head tucked on his shoulder.

Patrick rubbed her back with a clumsy hand. "Too much blubbering," he told her as he prompted Emma to rise. He gave her a hug and added, "Now you go and choose a career right for you, one you will enjoy for the rest of your life. Not sure if this money will be enough for everything."

"More than I need, Dad," she said blowing her nose. "My teachers say my application for scholarships should be granted. Also, Hank is going to hire me again this summer. Like last year, I guess, assigning me gofer office chores, typing reports, getting coffee. I only need a pinch of this money."

"Uses you on some of his cases too. I found out, Emma. Hank told me." Patrick took a deep breath. "Please don't let Hank walk all over you, sweetheart."

"I don't, Dad. Hank is my friend, but I'm adamant about my choices, at least, as soon as I discover what they are." She gave him a big smile.

"My advice also includes staying clear of Tommy's advances. I mean, I like the boy. He shows promise. Rudy said his son is likely going to Rutgers on a football scholarship. One of the best quarterbacks this school has hailed in a long time. All I'm saying is, try to focus on you a little while longer."

"I will, and thanks, Dad. I love you so much."

—4—

Dining Out

Tuesday evening, Christina fingered tears nesting in the corner of her eyes. She and Hank sat in an alcove of the Mas Farmhouse restaurant in the West Village, nestled in a charming wooden structure displaying recessed fixtures and candlelit tables.

"Hey," Hank cooed taking Christina's left hand in his as he kissed her wrist with sensuous lips. He caressed the finger wearing the ring he just gave her. "Had I realized my proposal would make you sad, I wouldn't have asked you to marry me."

Christina brushed Hank's wide grin with a mock scorn. "Sad. You know very well I'm not sad. Tears of shock are what these are," she added brushing away the ones trickling down her cheeks. She needed to toughen a little. She didn't want to ruin her makeup. To tear her mind away from the urge of wallowing in Hank's big arms, she gazed at the most fabulous diamond to ever dress her hand. "Can't believe you got me this diamond. Magnificent."

"As magnificent as though you chose the rock yourself?"

"Are you kidding me?" Christina caught Hank's smugness and the teasing smile he wore whenever he won an argument. "What did you do?" She reached to hit his arm. "Hank Apple! Now that I think about this, you tampered with the clasp on my bracelet, didn't you?"

She detected how he tried to remain detached, but laughter overtook him. As he chuckled, he admitted enlisting Emma's help. "Wouldn't have dared to pick this ring without her."

"Well, why am I not surprised? Anyway, Emma played her role flawlessly—perfect actress."

"So is this diamond, by the way. Excellent color, I'm told."

"I am familiar with the jewel's attributes. I picked the ring out, remember?" Christina hesitated, claiming back her hand. She imagined being at home in Hank's strong arms her mouth propped against the musky scent of his neck and cheek. Five years later and she still courted butterflies around him. "Hank, you're not marrying me because of peer pressure, are you? I mean because you think the time is right?" While she waited for his answer, her breathing stopped. She needed Hank's whole heart to want her not just the practical side of him who might believe this to be the next likely step in their relationship.

"Sweetheart, I've wanted to marry you for the last five years. No other way to save enough money to buy a proper ring. One you might like."

She gave him the skeptical rise of her eyebrows.

"I mean, you're my lady and all, but you've got a hell of an expensive bite."

She let out a gasp of laughter. "I worried about asking how indebted we were after this purchase."

She eyed the waiter approaching the table with their entrées and abandoned the subject to glance at the strange and unusual concoctions on their plates. Roasted Goffle chicken, parsnip purée, grilled onions, & mustard greens. Hank cleared his table space for the Flying Pig Farm pork crepinettes with peas and rhubarb coulis.

The waiter left after recommending a couple of bottles of a light Riesling wine with their food.

Christina looked at the wine pamphlet. "Did he say the wine came from Seneca Lake?" Isn't this upper New York?"

"Yep. Wine trail is near the Finger Lakes."

"I didn't realize they made wine in New York."

"New York State began brewing wine long before California did. New York took a little longer to get it right."

"Where did you learn so much about wine?"

"Matt is a connoisseur and spent years beating my brain with the stuff."

"I'm amazed I can still eat after the smoked trout and the soup," Christina said.

"Well the French portions are tiny compared to our regular American size meals," Hank added.

"Which I find is better. We can value flavor over quantity. Very little is all we need to eat, as health specialists maintain."

"I'm not sure I approve of the small portions." Hank made sure he followed Christina's choice of a fork and tried to figure out where to begin. "I like leftovers for breakfast."

She rolled her eyes making room as the sommelier brought one of the bottles of wine to the table. After Hank poured some in a glass and asked her to sample, she did. "Oh, they got it right, Hank. This is superb."

Hank signaled the man to pour.

Once he'd gone, Christina took another sip and added, "Wait a minute. Hank Apple, how in the world were you able to save so much money in five years?" She brandished eyes on him demanding an explanation. "Without me knowing about this?"

He inched a sheepish smile. "This is how long I've been planning this surprise." He put his fork down to satisfy her. "Listen, we live in a house which is paid for, we don't take vacations, we haven't bought a single piece of furniture since I moved in, and we both make a decent salary. I hope you won't make a mountain out of this."

"Not to mention you never bought the car you wanted." Saying this, she spotted fear in Hank's eyes. He worried about her being angry he'd saved all this money without telling her. "I think you are amazing. I'm very impressed with your frugal skills."

"Well, don't worry. No skimping and saving anymore, I promise. And I won't be spending so much time with the city kids, or force street people on you during the Holidays. I also plan to take us on vacation at least once a year."

"Hank, I'm happy with the way things are. I don't want you to give up on the neighborhood kids."

"I won't be giving up on them. These days, a lot more people want to join our group—kind folk in the community who want to do their part. Most of the cops realize a small measure of kindness to one of these street urchins today might be the gesture responsible for saving their life one day." He took a deep breath. "I thought we might want to start our own family, maybe, if you wish—no pressure."

She smiled and tugged on his sleeve. "I would love starting a family with you, Hank." They bent toward each other and kissed lightly on the mouth.

"Christina," a loud voice thundered with the slightest Italian accent. She jumped, turned and spotted Luigi standing beside their table. "Luigi, how are you?" She showed him her ring and said, "Thank you for keeping this diamond aside for me."

"I thought I'd better do this when I met with you and Emma last week. A rock like this never remains on display for more than a couple of days. I am glad you are the one who's wearing the jewel." He turned toward Hank. "Is this your young man?"

Hank stared at him nonplus. "Luigi, we met yesterday. Don't you remember?"

"No, sorry. I believe one of my associates, Mrs. Latham tended to your needs. I suffered a bout of illness. I left early."

"You are the one who waited on Emma and me. You dug out the ring from one of your drawers."

"You sound like my assistant." He frowned, the broad smile he wore fading quickly. "Perhaps iller than I thought," he mumbled under his breath. Luigi turned to signal to someone sitting in another section. "I am happy you are delighted with the ring, Christina. All my best." A quick salute and he ran away.

"Why didn't Luigi recognize you?" She stared at Hank wondering why he'd gone pale. "He is the one who served you, right?" Faced with Hanks hesitation, she added, "Please don't shut me out. Please tell me what's going on."

"I'm not trying to shut you out, Christina. I can't figure out how to tell you this because I'm not sure I understand what's going on."

Hank repeated what little he'd learned from Emma, continuing to eat as he did. He took a sip of his wine raising his shoulders. "I told you the story didn't make any sense."

Christina had only picked at her food amazed Hank attacked

his meal with such gusto, discussing the subject in the same way he enjoyed talking about the weather.

"How can you eat at a time like this? Emma is clearly in deep trouble."

"I'm hungry, and fasting won't help matters." Hank took another gulp of his wine. "I realize she needs help. All last night I thought of nothing else." He picked up Christina's left hand. "When I got home yesterday, I couldn't even wait an hour to give you this ring, but I kept thinking about Emma alone, potentially in danger and the fact I can't help her."

"What does she say?" Christina rubbed Hank's arm, aware the big lug stewed in his own juices, his brain most likely like overcooked spaghetti by now.

"As stoic as ever. Takes everything with poise. She's amazing. Still hasn't grown out of her childlike innocence."

"I hope she never does." Christina caught Hank's dubious look. "I believe her innocence proved to be her saving grace over the years."

"I remember. You gave me hell when I had Emma pick a Manson look-alike out of a lineup."

"Can we please change the subject," Christina smiled his way. "What do we do about Emma?"

"Hey, keep in mind the two incidents might be related."

Christina rolled her eyes and went back to the food on her plate.

"Won't be able to do anything, sweetheart until she lets me in."

***

Lying on her bed in her room, the phone stuck to her ear, Emma listened as Amelia went on and on about Tommy—the only subject dear to Amelia's heart these last few years. She talked about all the cute things Tommy had said the day before on the ride home.

"He's so funny, Em. I can imagine him performing as a stand-up or something."

Another grunt came out of Emma and a nod, although the nod was more to help her dig deep and find patience. She didn't quite understand all the emotions Amelia related, but she wondered if her own dismissal of Tommy's affection had anything to do with the fact her best friend liked him as much as she did. Emma somehow found impossible to return Tommy's feelings for her. Most likely because she didn't understand them nor did she comprehend how Amelia, an intelligent, strong young woman became so nuts around him.

"I'm sure he doesn't think you're ditzy, Amelia. Tommy is much kinder than you think." Something else Emma found odd: the so-called attraction Tommy exercised on her best friend when Amelia understood so little about Tommy and what made him tick? People called the sentiment love—a mindless pull which grabbed hold of individuals while sweeping everyone off their feet. What happened when the fascination wore off? Did people fall out of love? Moreover, why didn't she understand any of these emotions?

"I'm glad your dad found the money to send you to university," Amelia said after a long pause. "I'm going to Rutgers. Already told my dad."

"Excellent, but what are you going to do? You told me you didn't have a clue."

"Well, sometimes I go with my mom to pick up my brother from school, and he's doing really well, by the way. His autism won't be such a roadblock anymore. He'll be able to live on his own, be more independent. I spoke with one of the counselors, and she said they're always looking for special education teachers to help with the load. I think I would like to make that contribution."

"Amelia, how beautiful. If anyone possesses the strength and the patience to work through this, you do."

"Thanks. A lot of work ahead of me, though. I mean, we still have so much to learn about autism. The science changes every day. Still, they're doing amazing work at the Children's Institute."

"Verona, New Jersey?"

"Yeah, where my brother goes. One of Josh's professors I admire so much got her teacher's certification at Rutgers with a major in Biological Science. This is what I'm going to do."

"Well, brilliant you found your passion. I also stumbled on something I like. I spent the evening last night searching the literature my aunt Franka brought me. I think I'm going to go for the dual major of Psychiatric Rehabilitation and Psychology."

"Ouch! Long road for you too."

"I'm not quite sure what I'm going to do with this yet, but Christina said a dual major will give me more choices when I do find what moves me."

"Yeah, smart. Christina is a smart teacher."

Amelia was interrupted by a loud screech.

"What is that noise," Emma asked, surprised at the sound. "Your brother?"

"No. Emily, nerdy twin. She wants the phone. She's been knocking on my door for the last twenty minutes."

"Emily has friends?"

"Working on a school project with other students—not friends."

"You and your twin are so different, even though you resemble each other. And your mother gave you two such similar names."

"Don't remind me. Thank God, we are different. She is a nerd, a bonafide geek. She has decided on a BSc in physics at M.I.T., and she is lining up post-graduate studies in quantum mechanics."

"Wow, impressive."

"Yeah, now Miss Brainiac got my mother involved to grab the phone from me. I've got to go. Talk to you tomorrow, Em."

Emma fingered the cellular phone her mom and dad gave her on her fifteenth birthday. She loved the independence technology brought her. No more waiting for the phone while her father called clients, although he now owned a cell phone for his business and these days, the cell was all he ever used. With unlimited talk and text, who needed anything else? Being an only child afforded some downfalls, but owning cool, cutting edge stuff was not one of them. Amelia's parents didn't want to spend the money to maintain five cell phones. Amelia would have to wait to have money of her own to buy one.

She got up and turned on her laptop while reaching for her tablet. Emma realized her father never skimped on any of the little comforts brought home for her over the years, the mini tablet being the latest.

A book dropped off her shelf, and a muffled word made her jump. The fear of turning around paralyzed her so real was the noise. She grabbed her amulet around her neck aware she was clueless as to who was in her room. Emma turned and faced the young man she had spotted in her dreams, his presence large and his appearance so much more pleasing than the one she'd caught in her vision early morning. "Who are you? What are you doing here?"

—5—

PATRICK & ELOISE

Christina and Hank spent the last part of their meal ignoring the flambéed, Cointreau-soaked crepes nearby. Instead, they savored each other with hungry eyes, an appetite Christina realized would only be assuaged in Hank's arms. "Let's go home." She smiled misty-eyed and hoping he deciphered her dire need of him oozing out of her pores.

"Yes," he breathed. "Thought you'd never ask."

The tremulous hand on her back as he led Christina outside signified he sensed her readiness and ached to reciprocate. With a gentle touch, Hank caressed the back side of her arm as they strolled toward the door.

"Hank? Hank Apple?"

Hank's shoulders dropped, and he released a long breath having to tear his gaze from Christina's velvet brown eyes.

He turned slowly to encounter Patrick and Eloise Willis relaxing in a booth by the window a couple of feet from the front door. He eyed the door briefly, donned a smile and walked back to their table his arm around Christina's waist.

"Fancy meeting you people here," Hank said extending his arm to shake Patrick's outstretched hand. He saluted Eloise with a nod and a smile.

"Spooky, we just finished talking about Emma," Christina said as she bit her bottom lip.

Hank gave Christina a squeeze to impart the gaffe as negligible.

"Is she in trouble?" Patrick's expression turned grumpy, and his eyes glazed over in distrust.

"No." Christina rallied. "We discussed the promising future ahead of her."

Eloise's big smile won over Patrick's mood. "She is going toward a bright future. We're so proud of her." Eloise brushed at a tear in the corner of her eye. At this moment, the sparkle on Christina's hand caught her attention. "What's on your finger?" Her whole face smiled as she stared at the left hand Christina displayed. "Pat, look at the size of that diamond," she breathed as though unable to hold back the words.

"Whoa!" Patrick exclaimed. He propped wire-framed glasses on his nose for a better glimpse. "Didn't realize a police Captain made so much dough. I'm missing out," he added.

"Patrick," Eloise remonstrated with a smile. "So, you two are engaged. Congratulations." Eloise's smile beamed, genuinely happy for them, Hank thought.

"Five long years with me," Hank nudged Christina. "A milestone that needs to be rewarded and duly decorated."

Eloise laughed. She got Hank's gist better than anyone being married to Patrick Willis. Hank decided to change the subject. "Pat, I wasn't aware you wore glasses?"

"To read mostly. They keep these fancy, schmancy restaurants so dark."

"It's our first time here," Christina added with a big smile.

"My sister Franka gave us a gift card for this place last year, and we've been coming ever since."

Hank held back a remark about the wages of a prosperous insurance salesman but droned instead, "We've got to go, meter running on the car."

Outside, Hank gave them both a little wave as they walked past the window on their way to the car park.

Inside, Patrick Willis perused the dessert menu. He turned to his dreamy-eyed wife with her glance parked somewhere beyond the window. He figured escapism as the most likely reason she always chose a window seat, and why she couldn't quite spend a couple of hours in his presence without needing to bail to her own world now and again.

"You must be wondering why I brought you here tonight," he spoke in a soft tone. He removed his glasses and picked up her left hand stroking Eloise's fingers. "Next week is our twentieth wedding anniversary, and I thought we might welcome the chance to celebrate this year." He sighed a little out of sorts. "I'm afraid I didn't hold up to my part of our marriage vows these past twenty years. No, no. Don't deny what I'm saying," he interrupted the shake of her head. "I realize I didn't need to mention anything about Hank's salary."

"Doesn't matter, Pat. I'm sure he understands you used another form of complimenting him on all his accomplishments."

"My sweet wife, always the diplomat. I'm sorry if my behavior gave you the impression I treated you like a doormat all these years. I want to be clear on this, I never stopped admiring you,

El."

"Pat," Eloise squeezed his hands. "What are you saying? Don't belittle yourself. Hurts me when you do."

"I'm not. I'm saying I admire your people skills. If I possessed half your talent, I wouldn't have needed to work so hard these last few years, or jump through so many hoops all the while smiling when I wanted to scream and stomp out." He relaxed in his seat and asked the waiter to bring the desert tray. "I owe everything good in our lives to Hank Apple. He not only saved our daughter's life, but he also saved Emma from me and my goddamned temper. Hank revived my career. I should have congratulated him, sincerely congratulated him."

"Pat, you might not believe this, but Hank Apple is a lot more like you are than you think."

"Not only Hank Apple. I hate to catch you cringe with worry over what I might say or do following someone's stupid comments. Even so, sometimes I still can't help myself. Always thought of myself as such a failure. Mostly, I never managed to live down the fact my mother passed without us ever having made up."

Eloise pulled a tissue out of her purse. "I'm sure she realized how much you loved her. Now, you're going to make me cry." She blew her nose and tucked the tissue away as the waiter wheeled the dessert cart over to their table. "And people skills aren't simply doing what comes naturally. The skill part is when you can turn your temper around or ignore your dislike of someone to advance your career for the good of your family."

He nodded as both chose the crème brulée, the caramel topping hard yet soft and liquid below the first layers.

Alone again, Patrick continued. "Like your talents at taking the flower boutique and doubling its business during the last five years.

Eloise shrugged at all the success she owned. "The money came in handy over the years."

"Your business became our livelihood." Pat took a sip of his coffee.

"And all your commissions, let's not forget. Your down payment allowed me to buy the shop."

"You would think, right?" Patrick rubbed his fingers on the wet towelette left by their waiter. He reached for his cell phone. Bringing his phone close to the little lamp, he donned his glasses and proceeded to use the restaurant's Wi-Fi Network. "I want to show you something." Once he got what he wanted on the screen, he slid the phone to his wife. "Take a gander."

"A bank account—in both our names?"

"Check the investment side of things." Pat waited for Eloise's expression to change.

"This can't be ours," she whispered.

Patrick made sure she eyed the right place, and he nodded and took the phone back from her shaky hands. "A little over two hundred thousand dollars. This is where most of the money from my commissions went."

"The investment. Your mother's money for Emma."

"Not from my mother." Patrick rubbed his eyes underneath the glasses and released a loud breath. "Years I've wanted to tell you. Never figured out how."

In short syllables, with interspersed undertones his eyes scouring the place, Patrick explained what he learned from Emma on a long ago day in Franka's bedroom.

"Oh! My God." Eloise covered her face with her hands, and Patrick caught her shoulders move forward as she tried to hold back sobs. "I can't believe you've kept this from me all these years," she managed to add.

"I'm sorry. I promised Emma I'd never tell. Please don't make a scene, and please stop crying." He tore open a little towelette and handed it to her.

"Cute. You, asking *me* not to make a scene, and giving me an alcohol-soaked towel to wipe my eyes." She pulled the tissue from her sleeve.

Maybe the expression on Patrick's face or the sweet irony of the situation involved, but when they gazed at each other laughter overtook them both: nervous, can't-catch-your-breath, frenzy laughter which served to bring them closer.

Patrick leaned his forehead against hers. "I never told anyone, my love. Until I did, the magic didn't exist."

"The funny thing is I work so hard—can't keep my fingernails clean. You struggle to catch your breath between appointments, and our daughter performs miracles." Eloise eyed the place around her and lowered her voice to a whisper. "She makes things appear out of thin air." She shrugged shaking her head side to side. "Unbelievable."

"Unbelievable and dangerous. Emma was ten years old, El when she promised me she would never do this again. I prayed every day she would respect her promise."

"Why dangerous?" she mouthed with surprise.

"The darkest hour I ever spent, El: kneeling down in the stupid quarry wearing black as camouflage, my back leaning against a chink metal fence for balance after having dug a hole through a bunch of rocks. Burning ten thousand dollars of crisp new bills when I didn't hold two bits to rub together cut me like a knife." They stared at each other, and nerves once more drew them to laughter.

"Why dangerous?" Eloise brought a small hiccup wiping the tears in the corner of her eyes.

"I told you. The government never distributed this batch of bills. Authorities would have demanded to learn where they came from. Emma scared the life out of me. The hours I spent worrying someone might find me while I burned money, and take our daughter away from us."

When he spotted Eloise not convinced, he added. "All the money in the world is accounted for. Whether money belongs to a corporation, a millionaire or a billionaire, every penny is calculated. If money started disappearing from anywhere, whether from a company or from a wealthy celebrity's personal wallet, wouldn't take very long for them to find out. Authorities would ask questions of the people managing the money. There'd be accusations, charges of fraud. Emma is smart. Made sure she conjured new bills. Only, these bills happened to be a little too new."

"I guess." Eloise eyed her surroundings.

"Every little manmade thing is also accounted for. To just take anything out of the fabric world we live in is tantamount to stealing."

"Conjuring," she mouthed. "Not an exact science."

"Not a science at all. Nor will conjuring ever be. If anyone found out about this, Emma's life would be in danger."

"Is this the reason you didn't want to tell me?"

"Not because I don't trust you, more because the burden of

carrying this secret around is actually painful." Patrick put is fork down, pushing away the remaining sweets. "You can't imagine how many times I woke up, middle of the night, hit with the knowledge of what Emma can do—like a ton of bricks falling on me. I caught myself praying and hoping she never conjured anything else." He pointed to himself. "Me praying—a newsflash."

She chuckled and fingered his phone. "What does this money mean?"

He smiled. "Means I can buy you a better ring," he said picking up her left hand in his.

"Seriously, Pat."

"Some of this money is earmarked for Emma's education. The rest, we can use to fix up the house, take a trip, and mostly not work so hard."

"Emma's going to be floored. She worried about not being able to go to Rutgers."

"She spent all last night going through those brochures Franka gave her. I can tell you. She's very relieved."

"You've already told her?"

"Hank left me no choice. He spoke to a buddy of his at the FBI bragging about Emma's people skills for the job and her police experience over the last two years. He wanted her to join the extended FAIT program."

"He told you this?"

Patrick nodded. "Only, I realized Emma didn't fall in love with the idea. She wants to walk her own path. I like the fact she's gutsy."

***

More guts and guile were what Emma needed about now. Alone in the house, she faced an unknown adversary who did not seem human—too spectacular looking to be of their race, almost resplendent. She straightened with all her height to confront the young man with the red, heart-shaped lips, charcoal black hair, tossed and spiked as though he'd traveled through the wind and a complexion as pale and delicate as though he'd never been touched by the wind, or anything disturbing.

"*My name is Hawke.*"

"No last name?"

"*No. Hawke.*"

He wore a black vest tied at the waist over a white peasant shirt opened all the way down his chest. A pair of cotton pants clung to him, offset by black boots strapped to his knees. "You still didn't answer my question. What are you doing here?"

"*I am here to retrieve something which does not belong to you.*"

This was when Emma realized he used telepathy to communicate. The red lips parted, but no words came out of them. She decided to try the same thing. She formed her next question in her mind.

"*The oudjat?*"

He nodded.

Seemed able to read her as well, yet forming whole sentences in her mind seemed alien to her. "If you are here to retrieve a pendant you say does not belong to me, I'm betting you are not the oudjat's rightful owner."

One side of his mouth curled into a smile, and though the black winged eyebrows framed long lashes of the same color, she spotted the blue of his eyes sparkling her way. His eyes reminded her of jewels.

"Another man is also interested in this pendant."

The young man left the safety of her library shelves and came toward her, appearing even more stunning in the room's light. "His name?"

Emma made out Hawke's voice for the first time. She found the tone deep for someone with his build and elfin attributes. "I am not prepared to say." She regretted the information she'd given him. She didn't trust this young man.

Hawke? Friend or foe? She eyed him without fear. "I'm not going to hand over the pendant to you until I can meet the true owner. So, you best be on your way." Emma spoke the words with force, yet she quaked in her shoes worried he might take the little chain despite her protests.

He bowed from the waist and stared into her eyes as he faded away.

Emma dropped on the bed breathing in and out as though she finished running a marathon. Little beads of sweat trickled at the top of her hairline, and her heart skipped a beat inside her chest. Yet, as she recalled the meeting, a slight smile stretched into a grin, proud, and strangely happy she held her own. This meant she would meet up with Hawke again.

Only took a few seconds for the smile to disappear as a sobering thought clinched anxiety in her eyes. She worried about this young man's powers, although they appeared to be less obtrusive than a honeysuckle aroma, his charms might still find the means to inveigle her senses.

—6—

HANK & MATT

Wednesday morning, Hank paced up and down his office in what used to be Kenneth Riley's workplace. He inherited the space when taking over the Captain position five years prior. Hank needed four years to become comfortable in the large office. As long as he used the place to make calls or hang up his coat, the sense he still chased bad guys took precedence over all his other administrative functions.

Christina helped him redecorate by replacing some of the woodlands and winter-wonderland pictures with portraits of city skyscrapers and big bridges, more to his liking. A new dark credenza storing all his trophies and keepsakes occupied the far wall, and the burgundy vertical blinds she used to dress the window pulled all her trimming efforts together.

Hank held pride in the place now, proud of Christina and of the home she made for them in the last five years, in the house her mother left her, and now in her handiwork shining in an office he never imagined calling his own. The realization a woman like Christina wanted to be his fiancée filled him with contentment.

A deep breath later, thoughts of Christina managed to tone down the rage coursing through him. "How is this possible? No fingerprints on the container? I saw him pick up the icebox with my own eyes."

"Nothing showed up, Hank," Matthew Logan, Hank's old partner grumbled and shook his head. "Hard to believe the man got away with this."

"I don't understand. Emma told us in no uncertain terms where the man stood and what he intended doing—bringing someone a kidney." Hank turned and stared at Matt. He considered Barbara Leclerc for a few seconds and deemed her fit to listen to what he needed to say. "Emma is the reason we were able to be on the premises at the exact time he picked up the goods." Hank banged his fist on the desk the moment of calm he'd experienced all but evaporated. "I witnessed him hold and carry the damn container his bony fingers wrapped around the handle. I should have stopped him right there and then," he breathed.

"That would have given you nothing," Barbara Leclerc answered. "You needed to follow the trail of where this was headed. You did the right thing, Hank." Barbara nodded to emphasize her point.

Hank hung his head and sat on the corner of his desk. "I can still picture his gaunt features and those big bug eyes, like those of a frog behind black square glasses."

"Yeah, and his forehead is like a wall," Matt covered his face with his hands. "Doesn't change the fact, the icebox was clean. Not a print anywhere."

"Did someone switch containers by mistake? They all look the same. Maybe some nurse wiped the thing clean? Disinfected the case before she opened the lid?" He eyed Barbara. "Is this procedure?"

Barbara allowed her short, wiry black curls to grow over the years giving her round face and stout frame an extra gentle out-line—more in keeping with the big heart housed in that formidable bosom of hers. Black curls shook side to side. "Bill Frost suggests we give this one to IA."

Matt who'd covered very little of this case appeared stunned. "FBI Frost? You've got them on board now?"

Hank nodded. "We form a good team, and they've been a big help."

"They're not aware of Emma's talents, are they?"

Hank glanced at Barbara who pulled her hands up shaking her head in disbelief. "I would never give away the child's secret."

"They can't learn about Emma. She'd never be safe. I trust Bill Frost, but can we say the same of all their agents? I don't think so," Hank answered his own question.

Matt sat up in his chair. "Since Frosty suggests you contact IA, perhaps the FBI should do the same, talk to their Principal Deputy Director. They are as involved as you are." Matt punched the back of the chair next to his. "The nerve of the man."

Turning toward Barbara, Hank asked. "When did Bill suggest this? Bill never discussed the matter at our regular meeting last Thursday."

"An informal request this past Saturday. At the Mayoral Gala. Bill and Jeannie both attended. We all missed you, Hank." Barbara stared at Matt and Hank a question mark in her expression. "Frankly, I didn't agree or disagree with him. I said I'd talk to you first."

"Really?"

"Aren't you meeting again tomorrow?"

"We are," Hank confirmed. "I'd like you to be at the meeting, by the way. If you don't mind."

Hank stared at Barbara's head tilt and nod. He'd kept the thought of a traitor in their midst hidden unwilling to examine the implications. Moreover, Hank found the traitor factor difficult to swallow when others aired the subject. "I hate to think of Fred Manson buying one of our own."

Matt snickered. "Man's a billionaire. He can buy me if he wants."

Hank rolled his eyes, got off the desk, grabbed a file and hit the side of Matt's head with the folder while walking to his chair. "I've known you a long time, Matt, so has Barbara. So we laugh at your jokes, but watch what you say around Internal Affairs or they'll be in bed between you and Maria."

"Yeah, well, I'll watch what I say if you watch where you sit."

About to land in his chair, Hank spotted the smart-aleck smirk on Matt's face and realized he sat in something. He turned around and spotted a red ink stain on his blue pants. "Goddamn it. What did I sit in now?"

"The ink pad," Barbara indicated the corner of the desk, her lips pursed not to laugh outright, Hank figured.

"I'll need something to sit on not to dirty my chair," he mouthed out loud.

Matt got up and ran to the little sink and cabinet on the back wall where they kept two cupboards stocked with coffee, cookies, cups and saucers. He threw a roll of paper towels at him.

"Thanks, man."

Barbara checked her wrist and got up like a bullet. "Sorry, Hank. I have another meeting in fifteen minutes, across town."

She walked to the door. "Do you want me to talk to Andrew at Internal Affairs?"

"Not right away. Let's hold off. I'm planning to have a little chat with Dr. Manson sometime today. I'll get back to you."

"Don't wait too long. The waiting period is the first thing Internal Affairs will question. Why we waited longer than is recommended before we contacted them."

Once she left, Matt pushed his chair away from the desk and sprawled his legs in front of him. "Do you think Bill's right? About a stooge helping our guy?"

"Barbara is smart. She wouldn't cover this if she didn't think Bill might be right. Bob Larkin didn't make her Deputy Chief in charge of criminal intelligence for nothing." Hank opened the file he picked up on his desk and spent the next few minutes reading its content. "Only this time, I think she's way off."

"Manson's file?" The wait made Matt antsy. He rolled up to Hank's desk leaning his big arms on a pile of papers, waiting for an answer.

When none came, he questioned. "What are you reading? Talk to me? Why do you say Barbara is off the mark?"

An enormous raspy breath came out of Hank's impatient gasp. The eyes demonstrated to Matt he was still reading. "Aren't doctors required to have their fingerprints taken at one point or another?"

"Not necessarily. This would depend on the employer. A lot of hospitals do warrant fingerprinting of their staff. Why?"

"What are we up to now? Sixty—seventy million fingerprints in IAFIS' database?"

"Another forty million for civilians maybe. What are you getting at?"

"No fingerprints on file for this doctor. Anywhere."

"We've got them now" Matt gave him a head nod.

"Don't you think this is odd?" Hank got up still reading the file, dragging with him the wad of paper towels. He walked around his desk to sit in the broad-backed chair beside Matt after applying a layer of towels first. "Here look for yourself." He handed Matt the file.

"I believe you, man." Still, when Hank shook the file in front of him, he grabbed the folder and yanked the file out of Hank's grasp. "What do you want me to check?"

"Take a look at how he got here."

"From the Ukraine to the United States?" Matt gave Hank a shrug. "Says here through the Members of Professions Holding Advanced Degrees Program. So what? He's a doctor."

Hank shook his head and rolled his eyes. "Yes, but since he came in with a special Visa, you can be damn sure he got fingerprinted. I mean, even truckers need to get fingerprinted to get their bloody *Fast Card* to cross the border."

"So, databank lost them. Out of the sixty million, perhaps they couldn't match his. Don't forget they often need to take special care when they fingerprint physicians. They scrub their hands so often, and with harsh products. You and I encountered this problem before."

"Keep on reading," Hank told him.

Instead, Matt slammed the file against Hank's chest and gave him an evil eye. "You're trying to make a point here. I am familiar with how you operate, my friend. Kindly tell me where you're headed without handing me this bullshit drama."

Hank rolled his eyes and opened the file. "Says here, the man possessed a couple of thousand dollars when he arrived, three years ago. Thursday, I received a letter from research saying the man was worth billions of dollars. Fricking impossible."

"Don't ask me. Ask whoever is stupid enough in research to dig this up."

"You're saying the information they found is nothing but a frame," Hank whispered. Turning toward Matt, he admitted. "I have the sneaky suspicion we are being played. This man isn't who he says he is."

"No shit, Sherlock. A man behind bars lying about who he is— good one. Are these brilliant deductions all you have?"

"Is he even human?" Hank mumbled under his breath.

Matt bounced out of his chair the piece of furniture rolling toward the door. "Have you lost it, man?"

Hank watched as Matt stood with face in hands before he straightened to his full height, adopting the nervous tic of brushing the top of his bald head to a sheen. "I mean, lending this jerk-wad Manson X-factor possibilities is too much of a jump, even for you, Hank. I mean I am well acquainted with your legendary reputation for smelling dirt. But if anyone else caught your last remark, they would put you away."

Hank stood and took a couple of deep breaths realizing his comment was left field. "I realize my suggestion is a stretch, and if someone confirmed Manson happened to be some form of alien I'd be the first to deny the idea." Hank hesitated.

"What? More crap you're not saying, right?"

Hank proceeded to tell Matt what happened at the Jewelers. He recounted Emma's version of the facts. He also told Matt about

Luigi while at the restaurant with Christina and the fact the jeweler didn't recognize him from the day before.

"Frick all mighty—Stupid of me to ask. My fault. I shouldn't have asked. To have this supernatural shit thrown in my face. This crap keeps me up nights." He made a fist. "You can ask Maria." Matt stared down at his shoes for a few seconds. "I never told you this, but when we first met Emma, and we ended up chasing crazy Boleslaw, I thought he owned supernatural powers. I was so afraid for Emma. I'd give my life for that little girl. These last few years, as her powers grew, I tended to relax thinking she would be able to deal with anything she tackled. Now …" Matt let go of a huge breath. "Emma's in trouble again, isn't she?"

Hank acquiesced with a nod. "I think so."

"Goddamned drama," Matt breathed. "But how in hell's name does Emma's problem connect with Manson and his illegal trafficking of body parts?" Matt walked away to stand by the back wall. Hank, stared at the tall and wide built Matt as he glared out the window chewing the inside of his lip.

Hank went over in his head what he told Matt, and even to him, the story didn't make any sense. "I need your help."

Matt took another thirty seconds before he veered and eyeballed Hank. "Don't ask me to do anything illegal, man. Over the years, I've come pretty close to getting the boot after reprimands piled up in my file. Most of them I received while helping you by the way—starting with the time I killed Boleslaw to save your life, pal."

"Hey, I always defended you, Matt."

"Yeah, I'm grateful you did, man. But with Maria back in my life, I would like to settle down, raise a family. I can't ride my career to the edge anymore."

"I have no intention of asking you to do anything illegal. I promise." Hank dropped the file on the desk. "I'm going to interview the son of a bitch this afternoon. I'm going to have him brought to room twelve, the one with the adjoining room and the one-way mirror."

"You don't need me to do anything, Hank. Hell, you shouldn't be doing this yourself. You've got psychology trained police officers to lighten the load. They'll tape the whole thing. You'll get all the juicy details."

"Can't. I want to ask Dr. Manson questions I don't want anyone else to hear."

"What kind of questions?"

"The kind liable to make you jump up and slam your fist into a wall."

"Like?"

"Let's just say where he is from originally?"

"Why do I get the impression you're not talking about the Ukraine? Frickin f! Hank, Brian and I are over our heads with the workload *you* assigned to us. I wasn't even supposed to be here today. I'm on a stakeout the rest of the week."

"You're the only one I can count on—who knows about Emma's story. You and Barbara are the only ones, except for Ken, and he's on an island somewhere." Hank walked over to where Matt remained by the window. "Don't you want to be part of a bigger case? I promise you. This situation is a hell of a doozy—one to bookmark."

"No, thank you. Too much drama for me these last five years. Each time, you come out smelling like roses with the awards and the recognition. Me, they slap with everything from impeding a police investigation to manslaughter in the case of Boleslaw."

"Hey, you ended up winning your case with all the evidence we uncovered."

"Listen, I'm avoiding IA. Besides, you have an army of good officers to choose from."

Matt gathered his jacket and headed for the door.

"None of them know about Emma, and I'm not about to tell them."

"Okay. Why not ask Emma for help? She can read people's minds and tell you who's who." Matt didn't wait for an answer. He opened the door and walked away, one last wave his only salute.

Hank loved Matt like a brother, and he realized the latest tantrum displayed Matt's fear of losing his job. His temper got in the way on numerous occasions, and that was the reason for most of his reprimands. Hank understood Matt didn't fear Internal Affairs—not as anyone might gather from their current discussion—and Hank hated how Matt used IA as a valid excuse to run and hide. He realized he could order Matt be on hand to help, and he'd have no other choice but to obey the chain of command. However, perhaps to ask Emma for help might be the best solution.

He glanced at his watch punching up her school schedule on his laptop as fast as possible. One lab left on her schedule ending at two o'clock. He took out his cell and voiced a text message being careful not to convey any errors. She would at least text him back with an answer.

—7—

EMMA TO THE RESCUE

ednesday afternoon, Emma rushed out of her lab. She received a text message during class while unable to check her cell phone for fear Miss Purdie would confiscate her handset.

"Why are you running?" Tommy asked as he caught up with her.

"I got a text half hour ago while in a lab with Purdie on duty watch."

Tommy chuckled. "Birdie Purdie. What's the head count up to? What does she do with all those cell phones?"

"Gives them back, I'm sure, after an indeterminate period of time. I can't afford to have her take mine."

"So why the rush?"

"No reception in the hallway."

"Text is not from me. Can't be important," Tommy added aiming to grab the bag from her shoulders.

Emma got outside and allowed Tommy to slip the bag off her back as she read and re-read the text message almost wishing she hadn't. She glanced up and spotted a few of the guys on his team with their girlfriends coming toward them. No wonder everyone believed she and Tommy went together. "What's going on?" Seemed as though the gang prepared to party.

"Mom and Pop's malt shop opens today for the summer. We're all going down to grab a freebie."

"Is that today?" She sighed smiling at the group now encircling them.

Tommy yelled raising his fist in the air. "Hey, summer holidays around the corner!"

In the midst of cheers, Emma tugged on Tommy's sleeve. "I have to talk to you." She pulled him away from the group and told him about the text she received. "Hank wants me to go home as soon as possible. He needs my input about an inmate he is interrogating."

"What? Emma, this is a load of crap. He can't order you around."

Emma hushed him as she darted eyes around her.

Tommy lowered his voice. "You're not a police officer, you're just a kid. Does your dad know about this?"

"Listen, he doesn't ask for these types of favors often."

"You've got to be joking, right? How are you going to get home, bus?"

"Yeah." She shrugged.

"No hocus-pocus, right?"

"No. Bus."

"I'll go with you."

"Don't be silly. Go with your friends." She gave him a long sigh. "Why should both of us have to suffer?" This last argument seemed to calm Tommy.

"Okay, I'll bring you something back. Something sweet we

can both enjoy."

Emma didn't respond. She hated Tommy's double entendre jokes because he sure didn't mean he was bringing her back ice cream. She gave him a measure of doubt in her raised eyebrows. She hoped he got the signals she sent him.

Instead, he stared into her eyes as he gave her back her pack-sack full to the brim. Leaning in, he brushed her lips with a kiss. A roar came from the group waiting for them.

"Call you when I get home," Tommy said close to her ear. He left without looking back leading his troops to Mom and Pop's malt shop. She regretted missing out on their little tradition.

A little mutinous, she waited for the bus and commiserated on her lot in life. The cold and blue metal bench did little to warm her disposition. She thought about all those times she closed her eyes alone in the dark and made a wish—a small little prayer she might open her eyes and be normal while all this hocus-pocus, as Tommy called her magic, would cease to exist. She would be ordinary and free to live her life the way she wanted. No matter how many times Emma did this, no one ever answered her prayer. Even now, as she rose to hop the bus coming around the corner, she sensed the energy of the powers she developed coursing through her.

Climbing the stairs, Emma figured ordinary or not, since she decided on a career of helping people, replacing rare pleasures with work and a smile took priority over self-pity.

She hoisted the heavy bag on her shoulder as she dropped her token in the tray. Walking to her seat, Emma kept her eyes to herself refusing to let people's minds throw pictures at her. Someone stood to leave, and she slid through the aisle to occupy the seat next to the window.

She wondered what Hank wanted. He didn't say who he planned to interview, but the interrogation pertained to the two-year case he worked on, something to do with the illegal trade of body parts.

The bus made a complete about-face around the corner and onto the boulevard. The driver stopped at the light. A young girl with curly hair caught her eye. She ran while the bag on her back flopped up and down. She recognized Amelia. She knocked on the window wondering why she ran in the opposite direction of home. Amelia never heard. Up ahead, she spotted Tommy and his little gang stop in their tracks. They waited for Amelia to catch up, and she walked out in front with Tommy.

Emma smiled, a tear forming in the corner of her eye. Although she missed them both, delight took over when she sensed the joy Amelia must be experiencing, after which she rolled her eyes thinking she would hear about this later.

Staring out the window, her previous train of thought came shooting back as she fathomed on the type of people who might stand to gain by marketing body parts—people who made profits off other people's misery. As she thought of this a little more, the group widened to include doctors, physicians, pharmacists, policemen, firefighters, anyone feeling good about some volunteer work they did or money they gave to their favorite charity. What would the world be like if none of the drama existed? Half the people in the world, if not more, took care of the other half in some form or another.

"Anything they want to do," said with precision next to her ear. Emma jumped and looked beside her. The heavy bag no longer on her shoulder, Hawke—the strange young man who refused to

identify himself—sat beside her with her big bag on his lap.

"Where did you come from," she whispered.

"I got out allowing you to take the window seat when you first arrived."

She stared at him. He wore the same peasant white shirt with the cotton pants and the boots laced up to his knees. A brown waistcoat completed the odd ensemble, and his black hair still appeared tossed by the wind. Emma looked around. Packed bus, although she wondered how she missed him when she first took her seat.

Emma turned her head toward the window, her heart beating fast. She spotted people interested in their exchange. She used her mind to talk to him. *"What did you mean by 'anything they want to do'?"*

"Your world is backward in their thinking. Proof of this is where your own thoughts brought you: what would people do without the drama? They would live very well."

Emma stared at Hawke and caught him smiling while he stared straight ahead of him, as though he hadn't piqued her interest.

She wanted to tell him to stay out of her head. Instead, she considered Hawke might not understand their culture. He appeared as though he came from another time. *"Do you originate from the past?"*

"No."

"Are you an alien?" She continued staring out the window her staccato breathing producing little clouds of fog in the glass.

"No. I am an earthling. No more questions. Later."

She stared at him wondering why he decided to clam up. Emma caught a man staring straight at them with a little smile in his eyes.

She wrapped her arms around herself surprised by the invasion. She worried about her thoughts being unsecured wherever she went.

Five minutes later she disembarked on her street, shocked at how little time the ride seemed to take. She got off thinking Hawke would follow, but he didn't, and he still held her bag.

She stomped toward home, angry with Hawke, with herself and with her day gone awry, and when Emma remembered she headed back to help Hank, she ran the rest of the way.

Emma shuffled through the front door and headed for her room. Inside, she found Hawke sitting at her desk going through her books and homework material.

"Do you mind?" She ripped the packsack away from him, scooping up books and copybooks to put them back in the bag. "You have no right to go through my stuff, not without my permission." She sat on the bed, a little out of breath. "And how did you get here ahead of me?" She liked the way he smelled, a woodsy aroma mixed with the scent of wild berries.

He tilted his head giving her a shrewd eye. *"You know very well how I am able to propel myself."*

"You can talk out loud now no one else is around. And why the sudden secrecy on the bus?"

"What you find satisfying about the primitive form of speaking words I do not understand."

"I don't like to yell inside my head. Gives me a headache and somehow, Mister, you can push my buttons. For your information, very little makes me angry. Yet somehow, you do."

He laughed and Emma found the sound delightful, and catchy.

A small chuckle escaped from her pursed lips.

"First, I wish to apologize for going through your personal items. I will not do this again. I promise." He bowed from the waist.

"If you're not an alien, why did you call Earth, *our world*?"

"As confusing as this might sound, I do not have the leisure to give you this sort of information, which is I imagine why I push your buttons? A strange expression I can comprehend nonetheless. You fear me as you do not understand me."

"And if you're not from the past, where are you from? You're not from around here. And why the sudden shutdown on the bus?"

"Well, a man sitting in the front seat perpendicular to our own caught the thoughts we exchanged."

"Yes, I thought so by the look on his face. Although, I found distinguishing his exact thoughts impossible. Of course, I'm wearing my oudjat. Can others listen in to what goes on in our head?"

"I can't give you an exact count. Yet, their number is large."

"How am I able to understand your thoughts while wearing my pendant?"

"When I choose to communicate using mental telepathy, this is not the same as you reading my thoughts."

Emma set the radio-clock as a reminder to do her homework every day at this time, and when the music burst in on them, she remembered Hank. "I have to call someone. Urgent. Still, I'd like to find answers to my questions if only to discuss your theory on life's drama."

"Sometimes a mystery like this one, which is an integral part of the forces of dark energy, cannot be fully revealed."

"Dark energy, the dark matter in our universe. The simplest

possible form of dark energy first showed up in Albert Einstein's cosmological constant theory. He coined the term before anyone else, I believe."

He tipped his head. "Fortuitous you are smart and aware as I am allowed to give you very few explanations. Nevertheless, I will return later. Enjoy your homework." He smiled, the blue of his eyes scintillating as he faded away.

Emma wanted to spend time dwelling on Hawke, and on the current events surrounding him. Even what he would not reveal appeared to be more entertaining than listening to some villain incarcerated for trading in livers and kidneys.

She picked up her cell and dialed Hank's number wondering what prohibited Hawke from giving his reasons for wanting the pendant. Why he would not admit who the jewel belonged to or what he intended doing with the little eye of Horus. Emma thought of Horus, Hawke, and Hank. All started with the letter H and were gruff sounding male names. Gruff like the characters they represented. "Hank? Sorry, I'm late. Class ran a little longer, and I took the bus home."

"Perfect timing, Emma. I hate to take you away from your friends and your time at school, sweetie. But I need help with this mystery on my hands. Going through the files with two of my best men, neither one of us can make anything stick, and Manson's lawyer just called. He's coming down here to have the strange doctor released. He can certainly afford bail."

"I'm so sorry, Hank. I realize how hard you worked on this case. What do you want me to do?"

"I would not ordinarily ask you to do this, but I'm at a dead end here. I'm about to interrogate Manson in the little holding cell, number twelve. You remember, on the other side of the glass."

Emma remained silent. Hank's defensive tone filled her with caution. "What is the problem, Hank?"

"I need you to sneak in here with your mind to catch whatever the son of a bitch is not telling me. You'll be able to hear his thoughts, right?"

"You won't be able to record them, Hank. You'll be in the same catch twenty-two you are now. I can provide you with the information you need, as I did for the bust, but you're unable to take my testimony as a material witness. This is why nothing sticks."

"I understand. How about you listen to Manson and report what he is thinking. I can use the truth to unnerve him somehow, hang him with his own thoughts."

Emma bit her bottom lip. She first wanted to say no. She found difficult to imagine what her cooperation might contribute. However, the thought of Hank accomplishing so much for her and her family over the years brought her around. "When would you like me to come?"

"Can you be here in five?"

She checked the clock on her desk. Being present in spirit meant unperturbed immobility for a while. Hawke mentioned he would return later. Tommy would call her the minute he got home. "I have thirty minutes at the most before people start calling me, and my parents will be coming back also."

"More than enough time, Emma. I'm sorry for the last-minute request. These drastic measures are to avoid our next step of involving IA. I would hate to have them tag along." He paused mid-sentence. "So you remember where to go, right?"

"I do. Hank, are you worried Internal Affairs might find out about me?"

"You picking my brain again?"

She sensed a little rancor in his tone, but she chuckled as she added, "No. I just put two and two together. It's not in the cards for them to find out, so don't worry."

"How do you know?"

After a long sigh, she added, "I just do. We're wasting time. I'll be in room twelve in five minutes."

Emma hung up with Hank and lay down on her bed. Her parents would not disturb her when she rested, but Tommy might still call. She forwarded her cell phone to voicemail and relaxed, letting the room's tranquility fill her with promise. Emma smiled as she draped her arms over her shoulders and prayed to the Universe to come to her aid. She didn't need the incantation as she only projected her mind to the place of her choice. She thought of the little holding cell, of Hank, and at once she was in the room behind the glass.

She called out to Hank to make him aware of her arrival. Of course, no one detected her or listened to what she said except whoever she designated as able do so. Nevertheless, she stayed behind the glass not to distract Hank. She would wait for him to enter the little room.

As per their previous arrangements, Hank reached the interrogation area, and Emma confirmed she was on the premises. He rubbed his forehead to show he understood what she said.

"For your information, my lawyer is on his way down to have me released, Apple." Manson's smirk seemed meant to intimidate, Hank realized.

"I Okayed the process. Judge called me and asked for my opinion. I told him I didn't have enough to hold you."

"Fair of you."

"So, now you tell me. Why would you commit this sort of crime—a doctor? And how did you manage this so far?"

Fred Manson smiled and chuckled. You might be an open-minded individual, Apple. Doesn't mean I'm going to confide in you."

Hank scratched his head, he needed Emma's input.

"Hank," Emma communicated with him. "He thinks you wouldn't understand if he took a hundred years to explain. Too complicated for a human's tiny brain."

Hank rubbed his forehead to show he'd understood, and continued, "Are you an alien?"

Fred Manson lost his smirk. He readjusted his glasses. "Are you reading my mind?" he whispered.

"Me? A human with a tiny brain? I wouldn't be able to understand if you took a hundred years to explain."

Hank caught the doctor change color. He went from pale to white as a ghost as though all color drained from him. "You are an anomaly. You are not meant to be."

A scratch of Hank's head brought forth Emma's comment. "He's thinking that for a man who is supposed to be dead, you are taking up a lot of space."

Hank rubbed his forehead. "Dead, I'm supposed to be dead?" Hank swallowed his shock. Again he scratched his head.

"Can't read him anymore. All I see is code."

Manson got up from the table, as though signifying the end of the interrogation. But Hank could not banish the thought. "Why am I supposed to be dead? Is this a veiled threat? Are you planning to kill me?"

The smirk returned. "If you are recording, you will find I never said any such thing."

Hank picked up the phone to call the guard, trying not to let Manson discover how his hands trembled. "This is not over Doctor Manson. Our paths will cross again. You will need to give me answers."

Emma left the little room to regain the safety of her own room embracing the familiarity of her walls. *How did I conclude IA would not find out about me*? Other answers had become unscrambled of late. Perhaps her fifteenth birthday unlocked some doors or was Hawke's appearance responsible for answers coming at her with frightening speed? She sensed the panic Hank experienced while alone in his office.

She lay on the bed once more to go to him. She didn't intend to leave Hank with tortuous thoughts liable to dig a trench between him and his future. She of all people realized how much doom and gloom weighed—enough to keep a big man down.

—8—

HAWKE

A school bag on each shoulder, Tommy walked toward the bus stop. He shuffled his feet searching the ground for something to kick while he came down from a sugar high having scarfed several treats, and from the rush of being with his friends. Tommy threw a furtive eye at the person walking beside him. He didn't consider Amelia a friend. She reminded him of those suction dolls people glued to car windows, the ones that latched on and never let go. He missed Emma, and he found himself hoping his moodiness showed Amelia he pined for Emma.

The conversation between them broke down. Still, he thought, Amelia wore a smile on her face as though walking beside him provided its own reward. *God, the girl's ditzy.*

At the bus stop, Tommy unloaded Amelia's bag on the metal seat.

"Your dad's not coming to pick you up?"

"No. I'm taking the bus."

"Then I will too. My mom can't pick me up today."

"Kind of a long walk from the bus to your house."

"Nah. I've walked those blocks lots of times."

"I'm just saying because I won't be able to walk you home or anything. I'm going straight to Emma's. She's not answering her phone. She routed her calls to voicemail. Never a sign I like." He spotted Amelia roll her eyes.

"Maybe her phone's off." When Tommy refused to add anything, she continued, "I'm not a baby I can walk by myself."

Tommy caught Amelia's change of attitude. His moodiness reached her, and her smile disappeared. Yet, the smug part of him never showed up. No gloating prevailed when shame surfaced for the mean way he treated her.

He stared at Amelia as she foraged in her bag with a rough hand and pinched lips.

One of her books fell on the sidewalk. A tremulous sigh later, she bent to pick up her math tome, but a young man whose bright blue eyes reminded Tommy of Emma's second little oudjat handed Emma the book.

The young man bowed from the waist when she thanked him, and Tommy couldn't quite understand why he disliked him on sight. Especially since Amelia seemed to be caught up in his charms. He stared at the peasant shirt over cotton pants and the boots laced up to his knees. He wondered if perhaps he was a girl as delicate and effeminate as he seemed to be, or maybe a boy looking to be a girl. The thought helped remove the sour puss off Tommy's face putting a corner smile on his lips.

"Thank you so much." Amelia gushed.

Tommy watched Amelia bat her eyelashes at the new boy and stick out her little hand. "I'm Amelia Swift, and you are?"

"Hawke." Hawke picked up her hand and placed a kiss in her palm.

"Wow, you are charming." Amelia retrieved her hand carefully as though not to lose the kiss. "And your hair. Not a drop of wind today. The style is designed this way, right?"

"You go to Belleville High?" Tommy asked.

Hawke smiled at Amelia but ignored her question.

"Sorry. I didn't introduce you. This is Tommy Carson—merely a friend." She threw Tommy a cursory glance.

Turning his attention on Tommy, Hawke took his time to ogle him. He extended his hand first. "Pleased to meet you." He smiled outright as though he were laughing. "No, I don't go to Belleville High, and I'm not a boy." He waited for the full message of his last words to record shock on Tommy's expression. "I'm a young man."

Tommy sensed his cheeks color as his eye narrowed, and distrust in him grew. This was no ordinary young man. He picked the thoughts right out of his head. "What are you doing here?"

"Tommy!" Amelia shot at him. "That's not very friendly."

Hawke shrugged the incident away. "I'm visiting. A friend."

The bus pulled up, and Tommy hoisted his bag and grabbed Amelia's bag as he stepped inside.

"I hope I see you again," Amelia smiled, raising her shoulders as she climbed the steps.

Tommy spotted her run to the first window seat she could grab to answer Hawke's flick of the hand as they pulled away from the curb.

Dropping Amelia's bag on the seat in front of him, Tommy sat behind her. As he studied her gesture and rapt expression, he complimented his choice to keep Amelia at arm's length. She appeared as fickle as most girls his father warned him about. Like the mother he hadn't seen in years—his memories of her all but faded. He still kept one picture of her tucked away in a drawer, a photo where she and Tommy hugged in front of the camera. Eight years old at the time his father had snapped the picture—a few months before she ran out on him and his dad to remarry some harebrained chump of an actor.

The episode did nothing to alter Tommy's mood. So, when Amelia turned to look at him, he closed his eyes and pretended to sleep.

"I can tell you're not sleeping," she lamented in a sing-song tone, impatient with blame. "And why did you have to be so rude?"

Tommy ignored the question or rather answered with a question of his own. *Why does life have to be so stupid?* He only ever wanted to be with Emma, but she didn't like him, at least not in the same way he liked her. Instead, he had the adulation of some weird, ditzy girl for whom he had no respect whatsoever. No fairness on his plate. All his friends thought he and Emma to be the perfect couple and he allowed them to believe this, better than to gather their pity as a pathetic horn-dog.

Perhaps he should let them in on his secret and put himself on the market and out of his misery. This way, he'd find a real girlfriend and be rid of annoying and pesky Amelia. Why did she keep staring at him? His eyes were closed and in no way was he talking to her again today.

***

Emma found Hank in his office, standing by the window and looking outside. She read the worry from the back of his head his neck stiff and his arms wrapped around each other while his hands seemed to hold onto his elbows for dear life. No doubt Manson's words still trotted in his head.

She entered without permission, breaking her promise to give Hank fair warning. She hesitated on how to reassure him, and she thought by first assessing the situation she might be better equipped on how to bring him around. Only now, a good three minutes later, she worried about how to alert Hank to her presence. "Hank," she whispered not to scare him.

Hank turned abruptly and scanned the office for her. "At least show yourself."

She did, smiling as soon as she appeared on the premises.

"How long have you been here—not picking my brain, I hope."

"Not long. I had to make sure no one else was here with you."

"Well, he's gone. Manson's gone. It's official. The lawyer just picked him up."

"I'm sorry, Hank. You did your best."

"One more idiot criminal walking the streets."

"He's not a criminal." She flinched from Hank's angry eyes. "You were right to let him go," she found the courage to add.

"What are you talking about?" Hank appeared outraged. "The man steals body parts and sells them to the highest bidder." Hank plunked down in his chair. "Who knows how long he's been doing this?"

"Hank, when I became unable to read his mind because he replaced the words with code?"

"Yeah."

"Some of the code filtered through. Manson is an alien all right. He's not even from our Galaxy."

"What?"

"If we were to travel to his planet, we would need one thousand of our years to reach his home."

"How is this possible? How can they take a thousand years to get to us?"

"We calculate space travel at the speed of light. They travel at the speed of thought."

"My God! Is he trying to undermine our world? Did you catch his threat? He said I should be dead." Hank was up again bouncing from his desk to the window, and Emma sensed the helplessness oozing out of his pores. She'd never witnessed Hank so wound up.

"Should I alert the President, the Pentagon, what? I can't fight this alone."

"Nor should you want to—fight this I mean," she answered in a little voice. She came toward Hank and wished she had her whole body with her. Hank needed comfort, and she wasn't sure how to provide him with the reassurance he needed. Emma decided the truth would be her best ally and the tack to take with a man like Hank. "He's not alone, Hank. There are hundreds more like him from the same planet, here on Earth."

"This is unbelievable. Is this an invasion? Is this why they are snatching our body parts? Like a cheap B-movie." In his rant, Hank continued to trash the very notion Emma had mentioned. On and on, he continued to state how impossible he deemed the whole scenario to be. "Perhaps you misread the code? Possible, right?"

Emma didn't want to admit how she started to discover other information as well. Perhaps the less information Hank uncovered, the safer he would be. "They are here on Earth to help us."

"How? How are they helping us?"

"I'm not sure exactly. For now, I understood some of our officials also discovered their whereabouts and fear their intervention.

Of course, not knowing why they are on Earth a few of our elected administrators have attempted to jeopardize Manson and his compatriots' rescue mission."

"I don't understand." Hank took a couple of deep breaths to calm down. "An alien race who allows itself to be discovered?"

"They didn't realize their identity was compromised. These aliens don't have access to the same powers they do back home. Earth's atmosphere impedes their communications. Besides, they've been here for years, decades, although not as many as there are at this moment. If they wanted to harm us, they would have done so a long time ago."

"Why not just sit with them and ask why they're here? What is this rescue mission you mentioned?"

"I'm not sure yet—an impression I will need to confirm. All I can say is authoritative figures believe it's easier to spread fear and command secrecy since they don't have a clue about who the aliens are or what they are doing here."

"Meaning a few of our officials have their own agenda and don't want the rest of us to discover why aliens are here to help us."

She nodded pleased Hank was as smart as he was. "Who first brought this case to your attention?"

"Ah. Pull on the thread and find out from where the first stitch originated." Bill Frost first brought this to his attention, but Hank didn't want to say. "What about the threat on my life, you heard him."

"More a fact than a threat. The proof is although Manson said you are in his people's way, no one has eliminated you. I believe the aliens, as you would say in the digital world we live in, found a way to work around you." Emma laughed at Hank's cross-eyed stare. At least she sensed the relief in him now, her words making sense enough to calm his apprehension of a threat on his life.

"So convoluted," he added with his eyes still crossed.

"If you're not careful, one of these days you're going to stay like that." Again, she laughed as he hurried to remove the posture. He glanced at his watch. "You better run home. They'll be looking for you. Please. Keep me posted—and thanks for the pep talk."

"I will. You're welcome," Emma said as she hurried back to her room.

—9—

TOMMY AT EMMA'S PLACE

ommy stood on the sidewalk with mixed emotions as he spotted Amelia walking in the opposite direction, strapped with a heavy bag on her shoulders. She faced a long walk ahead of her, a couple of blocks—long ones.

He took a deep breath and schooled himself to do away with the pity. The girl needed to figure out he didn't care for her the way she cared for him. Anything he did to be the gentleman his dad raised him to be, she misconstrued. Starting with the first time she asked him to dance and he made the mistake of accepting, to please Emma. He remembered how he grumbled about the dance later. Still, Amelia coveted the foolish impression he liked her for some oddball reason.

He hoisted his own bag and took long steps toward Emma's house. Why would Emma put her phone to go straight to voice-mail? He mentioned at least once a week how this infuriated him. This meant she busied to do something she promised not to do again like propelling herself or some other thing.

When he turned the handle, the Willis' front door opened. *Not smart enough to lock the door after she's in. How many times do I need to tell her?* "Emma?" he called out. *Not downstairs.* He took the stairs two at a time and banged on her room door.

When Emma returned to her room from Hank's office, she heard the loud bang on her door which made her think of Tommy. Her mother and father would never pound their fists on her door. Emma rose to answer, a little anger in her posture. "Why are you banging on my door?"

Tommy appeared shocked by her attitude. She caught him searching her room, what little made available to him from the hallway. "Is someone here with you?"

"No. Tom. I told you. I helped Hank with work."

"So why did you put your phone to voice mail? And I called you from downstairs, and you never answered."

"Why are you here?"

"Your phone—on voicemail."

Emma got treated to his 'dah' expression.

"Aren't you going to invite me in?" He gave her a few eyebrow pushups.

"You are in, and I am submerged with homework." *Left the door opened again.* "Can you lock the front door on your way out?" She smiled up at him trying to appease the frown on his face.

"So it's okay for you to do homework in your room, but not you and me together," he added.

Emma sighed wondering why Tommy seemed to want to impress her, like a rooster facing a hen with a wild fanning of feathers and cocky dance moves. "Tom. You of all people can appreciate how teeny my workspace is. A little square table with a few drawers Grandma Abigail gave me when I turned eleven. The small desk hardly holds my books." She let go of the door handle and stared at him her arms crossed. "What is wrong with you today? In fact, you weren't like this earlier on. What happened at the malt shop?"

"Nothing happened. I'm pissed at the way you treat me."

"No, no. Don't make this about me." Emma left the room door open as she stepped out into the hall. She figured she'd need to walk him to the door, the surest way to make him leave.

Tommy stayed glued to the spot.

"So." She leaned against the stair railing. "Amelia." She smiled. "Has to be. I spotted her running after you guys on your way to Mom and Pops. She got to you again, didn't she?"

"Will you forget about her? I'm certainly trying to."

"Okay. But I'll learn about it later."

"Yeah. You'll hear Amelia is mad at me. Big deal. Maybe now she'll leave me alone."

"What don't you like about her? She's warm and caring. Did she tell you about her dreams of taking up a career teaching mentally challenged children?"

"Of course, she did. Who do you think did *all* the talking *all* the way to Mom and Pops, and *all* the way back? God, she's ditzy," he added under his breath.

Emma shook her head hating the torture Tommy's mother still exhorted having abandoned him at such a young age. "Ditzy? This does not seem like a career a ditz would choose."

A soft, shuffling noise inside the room forestalled Tommy's answer, followed by a whack as though one of Emma's big books had landed on the floor which drew both their attention.

Tommy threw Emma a reproving smirk, and dropping his bag in the hall, he marched into the room followed by Emma who caught the fading outline of dark, windswept hair and a tall pair of boots. She closed her eyes lodging tight fists by her side. Hawke needed a sense of propriety.

"No one in your room, Huh?"

She stared at Tommy uneasy with any sort of answer. A deep breath later, Emma told Tommy the truth. "I didn't realize someone was here. I swear."

"Let me guess. Dark messy looking hair, boots tied to legs as thin as this dude's chances of escaping my knuckles in his face? Goes by the name of Hawke?"

Emma scanned the area where she'd first seen Hawke and a mere pale outline of his disappearing form. "Where did you meet him?"

"Bus stop. Strange how the freak got here before me, but the clown never took the bus. Friend of yours, I imagine, going by the little disappearing act I just witnessed."

"You met him at the bus stop?" Floored by Hawke's gall, Emma wondered about his intrusion on her friends no less.

"He introduced himself to Amelia with a kiss on her hand. She dialed up ditz to a new level, proving my point she'll fawn over anyone who pays her the least bit of attention." Tommy pulled Emma aside as though the invisible Hawke might be listening. "Is he the reason you and I are not," Tommy hesitated. He lowered his voice, "A real couple?"

"Of course not. I don't have a clue who this boy is or where he comes from. All he admitted is he's after the oudjat, the one I conjured by mistake."

"Don't let him take the jewel, Emma. The oudjat might be worth a lot of." Tommy walked toward the bookshelf where Hawke first showed himself. "Why don't you show your mangy self? Scared?" Glancing at Emma, Tommy asked her. "Want me to flatten him for you? Shouldn't be difficult. The guy is as thin as a pancake."

Hawke reappeared, complete with a smirk on his face. "Big man. First, you need to catch me."

"I don't want to fight with you," Tommy muttered fists clenched by his side. "But I will if you don't stop harassing Emma."

"Harassing," Hawke spouted. "What is the meaning of the word? Not one I am familiar with."

"Time to go back to school, chump." Tommy took one step forward.

Emma spotted a gaze in Hawke's eyes she didn't care for at all. What would someone like Hawke do to a mere mortal like Tommy?

She put up her hand to interfere when Hawke chuckled. "You're right, Emma. He does possess a bloated feathers sort of appeal, flapping his wings and doing the rooster dance." Hawke stood to his full height. "For my benefit?"

Emma grabbed hold of Tommy's sleeve and managed to pull him back. "I never said these words, Tommy, I promise."

"Don't worry. I don't believe anything this guy says."

"Please go home and let me handle this. Hawke means no harm."

"Are you crazy? I'm not leaving you alone with this freak."

"The longer you stay here, the longer I will need to be rid of him. And, if I finish my homework fast enough, you and I can go to a movie." She nodded and smiled.

"On a school night?"

"Yes, fewer people."

"Sure." He bent to peck her lips. "You sure you don't want me to stay?"

"I'm sure. My dad will be home in the next ten minutes."

Once Emma hurried Tommy out of the house, she addressed Hawke with hands on hips. "Okay, Mister. Enough with the babble talk. You are going to tell me everything, at least if you wish to obtain the oudjat." A little voice inside her wondered why he didn't take the pendant.

"Unlike you," Hawke answered her silent question. "I can't take the oudjat since I cannot conjure. And, teachers taught me not to appropriate someone else's belongings under any circumstances."

Emma fingered the small pendant she rarely took off anymore. Two of the men she'd encountered lately, in troubling, unheard of conditions, were after this. "I conjured this by accident. I mistook the oudjat for my own."

"I believe you. No need to defend what you did."

Emma acknowledged new beliefs assailing her. Yet her private thoughts were none of Hawke's business or were they? "Are you responsible for the new information I'm receiving?" She hated the way her voice trembled. Yet, more memory flashes seemed to be coming forth, releasing pictures and scenarios in her mind almost on the hour now.

"No." He no longer wore the smart smirk—his trademark since they first met. "What about this other man you said wanted the oudjat? Who is he?"

Torn between trusting him and doubting him, old fears found their way back to Emma's heart. She hadn't sensed such raging ineptness or run up against this much loneliness since the age of ten, stuck in her room without dinner and worried about an image where she caught Tommy breaking his neck in a great fall.

Five years later, Tommy still faced a great fall: having his heart broken into tiny pieces because she couldn't return the sentiment he so needed to share with her.

Emma bit her bottom lip and vacillated under the weight of too many doubts. "Please," she whispered wishing her voice didn't sound like someone crying out for help.

She caught Hawke's shoulders fall, and his head bend as he hid his eyes from her. "I am the one who should be pleading for your help and your forgiveness, for the flippant manner in which I accosted you. Not you begging for mine."

Emma understood their positions had changed, only she didn't know how or why. Her legs weak she sat on the bed hoping he would explain.

He stared at her as he stepped out of the shadows. He sat on granny Dottie's bench his long arms and thin fingers poised on his knees. "The Oudjat is a key."

"A key to what?"

"More like a key fob."

"Key fob? A component one uses with a pin number to gain entrance to what? Is this the reason you want the pendant?"

"Entrance. The smaller oudjat is used to gain access to portals."

"Like the portals I go through when I propel myself?"

"Somewhat. More like gateways to other addresses."

"Not street numbers if you're talking of portals."

"I guess you can call them, IP addresses." He smiled.

Emma thought back to her ninth grade computer class. "The pathway to another computer?" She paused searching for a meaning she might grasp. "Are you saying this eye of Horus cedes entrance to different paths?"

He nodded. "Emma, what do people say about sleepwalkers?"

She sat up on the bed and slid closer to the little bench as though realizing the moment of truth hung close. "Never to wake them. Specialists consider waking them can lead to danger. Although, once they are awake yet still unaware of where they are, aren't you duty-bound to help them find their way back?"

He smiled outright. A beautiful smile, Emma thought. She'd never seen this big or bright a smile before, and the sight warmed her. "Give me facts about your world," he said.

"My world? You said you're from Earth."

"I am from Earth. Yet, not from this particular version of Earth."

She shook her head and rounded her eyes until he repeated his question.

"Facts? Since you're from Earth, you should be aware of what goes on here." When Hawke said nothing and waited for her answer, she added, "We suffered through two world wars, a bunch of ongoing Holy wars, if this is what they are. Five people get richer to every twenty who get poorer. We closed off all our borders while we keep two-thirds of the world at bay living in poverty and filth. Fear plagues our nights and dulls our days. We're quick to talk about love even though we don't often experience the sentiment. Why the question? How many versions of Earth can exist at the same time?" Emma raised both shoulders unable to stop the skeptic smile from rounding her lips.

"Meaning who would want several versions of the kind of Earth you described?"

She nodded.

"Not many, I'm glad to say. In fact, your Earth is part of the worst cluster."

"You're not making any sense."

"Imagine idyllic living conditions, although I understand that to imagine such surroundings is likely impossible."

Emma raised her shoulders in a helpless gesture.

"Well, each one of the decisions we make every day affects the outcome of our world. Each one of these outcomes lives and breathes and forms a different version of Earth."

"Not possible. This would mean billions of versions of Earth in existence."

"Billions upon billions, yes. Now, many of the decisions we make every day don't accrue to provide opposite results, many of them being mere minor adjustments. Therefore, many Earths are quite similar and in time, have formed clusters."

"Like families or communities."

"Yes."

"Do optimal clusters of Earth exist?"

"Of course. Billions of them. In fact, billions of other versions are close enough to be perfect so as to fit into the fold I speak of without endangering any optimal earthlings."

"I find the idea difficult to conceive."

"I'm not surprised. To picture life as wonderful beyond this crude version of Earth is a difficult task indeed. However, a meeting will take place at some point in the future where all the clusters will gather and merge into one new galaxy, a superb area of contentment, peace, and enchantment."

"All of them?" Somehow, Emma knew the answer to this.

Hawke hesitated. "This particular version still has far to go.

Behind in its development, this Earth's inhabitants are trapped in worthless fears and too primitive to ever be absorbed without hurting the others. Some of this Earth's people are aware of what is going on, though not enough to make a difference. Power has been acquired and manipulated on this Earth so as to tie the hands of those who would change status quo and better this planet."

"Is this why you are here?"

"Many of us are here, from other versions of the big Blue to level the playing field. Visitors from other planets and even other galaxies are here also. The merger must take place while including all of Earth's clusters to fulfill its destiny. The union of our worlds will benefit countless of other planets and star systems. All versions of Earth will become one and serve as the doorway to Heaven or Nirvana. We're talking about a galaxy of peace and joy for everyone and everything alive or that once lived at one point in time."

Emma wrapped her arms around herself. A chill took over her slim body. "When?" she breathed.

The shrug of Hawke's shoulders brought back his smirk. Truce over, Emma thought as she eyed his strange mood back to the forefront. "You don't know when do you?"

"No specific date. Cleaning up this cluster is arduous, much more than many of us first predicted."

"So, the oudjat allows you safe passage to and from other clusters?" Emma lifted the little pendant sitting on her chest. "Who did this belong to?"

"Columba held the responsibility of the small eye of Horus. We traveled here together."

"What happened to him?"

"Her. Council pulled her back home when you conjured the oudjat five years ago. No one from my cluster can come here, and no one who is here can go back."

"Wow, five years." Emma fingered the little blue eye, bright as though it shone from within. "I'm surprised your people didn't hand out a new key. What if the pendant had been lost?"

"With no human contact, the oudjat would have deactivated itself. The Council on my planet would have issued a new one." He stood. "Some of the people on my planet thought the oudjat might be in the hands of wizards."

Emma couldn't help a chuckle. "Wizards?"

Hawke stared at her with his eyes somber while his expression mirrored pain. "They are a nation of troubled tricksters now confined to this Earth cluster only, and furious they were shunned and thrown out of all other Earth clusters. An amalgamation of our fears, they thrive on greed and devastation, manipulate people to obtain what they want."

"What do they want?"

"Power to rule and to decide who lives and dies." His head bent, when she spotted his eyes she found hesitation in them. "These wizards are at the heart of all your troubles: fear, greed, responsible for the wars and the hatred."

"So this is why you're helping us. Your rejects found us and made our Earth inhospitable. Won't getting rid of all our negative emotions produce the same results?"

"Only reason they are here is that they discovered hearts and minds in which to thrive. Once kindness and love prevail, the wizards will disappear into nothingness."

"As though they never existed. The memory of all wrong-doing shall not remain, and all of the Earths shall couple and rejoice their inhabitants without any notion of suffering or painful endurance ever having afflicted them."

"Emma, this is the dogma of my high council. How are you aware of this?"

Emma stared straight at Hawke. Another piece of the puzzle revealed itself. "I'm not sure." She stood and took off the smaller oudjat from around her neck. "The jewel is empty. The pendant is no longer active. The Eye of Horus will not take you home." She handed him the small gem.

"How?"

"I'm not sure. I'm not familiar enough with the pendant. A few seconds ago, the jewel became dormant."

"When I first met you, the key was active."

"You're right. I sensed the energy coursing through me when you first appeared." Emma caught him handling the little pendant with a sad gleam in his eyes. "How will you reach your destination?" She sensed how much he missed Columba and wondered about their relationship.

"She is my sister," he answered her thoughts. "I do miss her." He tucked away the oudjat in the palm of his hand then straightened to his full height and gave the pendant back to her. "I will call out through the soul's portals. Some kind spirit will send word to my Earth. In any case, the oudjat having deactivated itself, someone will come to our rescue with a new key in a matter of hours."

"Meanwhile, tell me about the wizards," she said as she took the pendant he handed her.

"First, tell me about this other person interested in the pendant?"

"I can't. Not now. I don't know enough about the man."

—10—

F.B.I. In The House

Thursday morning prior to the meeting, while they waited for Bill Frost, Hank stood by the window in the meeting room beset with a sense of vulnerability so high as to leave him feeling small and inept as he chewed the inside of his lip trying not to let perplexity paint his features. Dapper in a new dark three-piece suit and tie, he drew no comfort or reassurance from the elegant wear.

He worried he might be dropped as a collaborative partner in a case drawing full, international recognition. Ever since an agent at Europol discovered the route of disappearing body parts spanned the distance of three continents, the story gorged more than its share of ink.

Although Hank held a degree in psychology and a whole lot of field experience, he couldn't understand a word Bill Frost used on the phone while speaking French to Guillaume Balay, one of Interpol's undercover agents located in Paris and assigned to the investigation.

A top-notch group of officers and policemen worked on this case, and he thanked his lucky stars to still be among them, although, the thought of summarizing his dealings to write a coherent report for the commissioner humbled him with embarrassment.

On the one hand, he fancied telling the world about Manson being an Alien. In fact, he didn't know how he would keep the words from pouring out during any conversation. On the other hand, someone being able to trace the information to Emma restrained him from spilling his guts as did Emma's admission of Manson being on Earth to help them.

Even as he recognized himself to be a sharp investigator, and the findings he discovered being extraordinary, he realized remaining silent would be his trophy-fight to date. Like an alcoholic struggling with his daily vow of abstinence, he would need to take the vow of silence everyday. Once enough time lapsed without him revealing what he discovered, he would be less inclined to tell—reprisals over his silence likely to be quite severe.

He rubbed his face with his hands a gesture of self-soothing, Christina called it. The woman owned X-ray vision where he was concerned, and this worried him. What would he tell Christina? What sort of alien sustained thoughts in code? The sophisticated ones and the way-ahead-of-their-race sort of alien. Friend or foe?

He tended to believe Emma's claim of a rescue. She never steered him wrong. Yet he doubted anyone else would share the same confidence faced with this knowledge. Tantamount to his first reaction, most people might want to rid themselves of people from another planet.

Hank stared at the commotion in the street below imagining the media's spin on a teenager able to read code in an alien's mind and how much of a splash this might make on the front page of every paper in the world. Never mind paper. CNN would broadcast on an hourly basis, and once the news reached the Internet—no turning back. The planets involved would hear of Emma's talents and realize she might be a threat. They'd find the means to be rid of her—fast.

The needling thought Emma knew more than she admitted also troubled Hank. Without her help and her trust, he would flop in this case, crushed under the weight of a debilitating sense of dread while the acid reflux symptoms he'd experienced his first year on the force returned with a vengeance to plague him without mercy.

Hank jumped at the loud call of his name. He turned to gaze at the group assembled in the meeting room. Two pairs of detectives Hank had invited to understand some of the legwork sat at the table. Barbara Leclerc as well as Bill Frost—FBI agent they called frosty for the cold way he dealt with facts and people. Another FBI agent closed the ranks, Tim O'Rourke.

"Miles away, champ. Trying to tell you this meeting needs to be a private one. I want you to lose the extra men," Bill Frost said.

Hank sighed and nodded. *Best to placate the man.* "Thank you for coming, men." He eyed the four with a smile.

As they left the room, one of them, Paul Larson threw a strange pair of eyes on Bill Frost which Hank questioned. Chairs got hoisted away, and they opted for the small round table by the window.

Tim O'Rourke, a red-hair giant looking more like a club bouncer than an agent remained silent, and Hank would do the same: not ask any questions too fearful of blurting out what he learned about Manson. Bill ran the show, as usual.

Instead, Hank waited for Bill to finish sorting his papers and stop stalling, as he appeared to be doing before he began the meeting.

"Balay just handed me some grim news." He raised his eyes

to stare at Hank. "News as rotten as Manson walking out of this precinct hand in hand with his fricking lawyer."

The dig directed straight at him robbed Hank of words. He avoided the eye roll as he tossed a glance at Barbara. She wrinkled her nose to show Hank restraint, the tremor of her head perceptible only to him.

Hank ran a finger around the knot of his tie threatening to cut off his air supply. Nevertheless, he bit his tongue, and inhaling some of the tension around him, longed for strong coffee. "Would anyone like coffee?" Saying this Hank got up and walked toward the coffee pot still on the burner. He waited by the stove to see a show of hands and brought back three cups of black coffee on his tray, fixings sitting in the center of the table.

Bill took the first sip, and the strain affixed to his body seemed to follow the smoke of his coffee as Hank witnessed the man relax.

"Appalling news indeed," he added. "A worse tragedy than first imagined. The men we were hoping to pick up and interrogate, the ones who contacted us a few weeks ago are dead."

"How?" Hank couldn't help his eyes from rounding.

Bill glanced at Tim who stared at his knuckles. "Secret Intelligence Service raided their place in Warsaw and killed them."

"Under whose orders?" Hank breathed. "Are they allowed to do this?"

"Officially, no. Unofficially, British officers can do whatever they want. MI6 agents have a passport to kill, and they will draw blood if they judge they can't drain anything else out of the suckers. Their motto is to work toward the resolution of any grief-causing situation." Another long sip of coffee and Bill relaxed in his chair.

"Whatever happened to teamwork?" Hank said appalled.

"No team work. MI6 agents don't give a shit about what we do. They've been after this gang of mercs for supplying automatic firearms to the LRA for months."

"Who?"

"A group of terrorists in Southern Sudan."

"Mercs?" Hank barked. "Simple mercenaries wouldn't dip their hand in such different pots, would they? Mercs usually follow a leader, and if this leader is trading in arms and weapons, he wouldn't be trafficking body parts."

Bill eyed Tim who gave him the nod. "Good instincts, Apple. This might explain why the relative of one of these mercenaries contacted Guillaume. Our Interpol friend received a complaint that they were being forced to peddle uncommon body parts under the threat of death to their families."

Hank said, "Or exposure of their arms trading which would mean the overseer might be someone high up and important enough to have his hand in both kettles." Hank took a sip of coffee.

"Meaning?" Bill asked Hank.

"Might be some high-placed rival wanting to eliminate the competition in both trades: weapons and the transaction of human body parts."

Tim's deep voice spoke for the first time. "As simple as shutting these people up might have been the reason for the raid."

"Let's not become sidetracked," Bill barked. "British secret service agents don't go around shutting people up. Mission leader was ignorant of the complaint made to Interpol. We must avoid getting tangled in suppositions and stick to what we understand to be true."

Hank stopped short of calling Bill a liar, but he found himself doubting the honesty of the man he worked with on this case. His gut told him Bill used the shared information as a shield to hide something. What? Hank couldn't imagine. He scratched his head the gesture a nervous tick and wondered why Bill kept him in the loop. Perhaps the dictum held meaning: keep your friends close, and your enemies closer.

"Off topic, but for the record," Bill said his calm returned. "Manson played you. You're not the reason he walked, Hank."

Hank glanced at Barbara Leclerc. She sat with a serene expression on her face confirming Hank's decision to never play poker with Barbara Leclerc no matter what the circumstances. "What are you saying? He put up the elaborate ruse to fool me?"

"Perhaps. I'm not privy to Manson's reason to dupe you. But, the fingerprints we lifted off the case belonged to someone else."

"He faked them?"

"Easy to do," Tim thundered.

"He did. Also, the particular case he carried—empty."

"I saw him reach for the ice and pack the case myself. No way could he dump the article on the way to the hospital." Hank jumped to his feet and began to pace.

"Well, he did. We collected an empty case with phony finger-prints."

"No wonder he walked," Hank whispered.

"Which brings me to the reason I asked you to clear the room." Bill stared long and hard at Barbara and Hank. "I need the name of your Intel. Apparently, whoever gave you this information misled you or managed to warn Manson in the meantime which brings us to the same conclusion: discrediting our efforts and confusing our investigation."

A little smile fleeted across Hank's face. Barbara and he had prepared for this contingency—not to reveal Emma as the primary informant in their case. His department relied on an elderly street informant often enough, and paid the stool pigeon on a regular basis to report to police anything suspicious happening in his vicinity. Of course, Joe lived in the park, his mind gone, and likely to reveal anything he spotted in exchange for a little food and alcohol. This made him a credible witness if they needed to replace the gibberish he spouted with the real information Emma supplied.

Only, as Hank stared at Bill Frost, into those cold eyes, he could not give Joe's name. He sensed the old man's vulnerability were he to reveal his identity to Frost. Might be signing the old man's death warrant. "I'm not authorized to give this information."

Bill rose from his chair. "Unwise to thwart me on this, Apple. So far, I've kept you in the loop. You're smart. I like to surround myself with smart people. But keeping Intel to yourself is dumb, which means I would choose to sail my boat without you and your merry men." Bill smiled as he waited for the information.

Hank preferred having wasted his time these past two years to condemning the old man to his death. However, what if he read Bill wrong? What if giving Bill the name would make sure Joe received protection?

Barbara came to the rescue. She rose pushing her chair back with a lot of noise. Once she secured Bill and Tim's attention, she proclaimed. "Hank Apple is following my orders."

"You? Why would you give such an order?"

"Because of what you mentioned at the Mayoral function last

Saturday night. I paid attention. IA has asked us not to reveal anything about this case until they finish conducting a preliminary investigation."

Hank held back a smile when he gauged how angry Bill appeared to be. Yet, Frost still managed to smile and give Barbara a head nod. "I'm glad you took my advice." He nodded toward Tim, and O'Rourke got up and gathered the files. "Please send me a memo as soon as they are finished."

"What happens now? What about the informant your French Legal Attaché found?" Hank asked.

"Guillaume is not a Legal Attaché with the Bureau. He is Interpol. And the informant was a brother in law to one of the mercs. Also killed. Back to square one."

"Why not ask British Intelligence who they believe holds the arms' contract and you'll find your missing link."

"We'll see." He gave Hank an unctuous smile. "I will keep you posted."

When the two officers left, Hank thanked Barbara. "I guess Bill left us with little choice. We need to alert IA and bring them into this mess."

Barbara fell back into her chair appearing utterly exhausted. During moments like these, Hank realized what a dear soul she was and how good a performance she portrayed when needed. "You realize you've only got a couple of hours to get Joe out of the Park. This is how long Bill will take to find him. He is very astute. In fact, this would not be the first time Bill Frost has asked a question to which he already knows the answer."

Stunned, Hank walked to where Barbara sat and flopped into the chair next to her. "He's done this before?

"He's become an expert at doing this. Don't know how he manages, but he does."

"You don't trust him?" He didn't say the rest, looking around and unsure if he should.

Barbara rose to her feet. "Truth is, might be smarter not to warn Joe."

Hank also rose. He stared into Barbara's big brown eyes and read a cautionary message, a sad one. She never mentioned Emma's name. But he realized Barbara issued the warning to keep Emma free from harm.

Barbara approached Hank her mouth glued to his ear as she whispered. "Keep your enemies close. If he believes he has eliminated your source of information, he will be more relaxed, more apt to make errors."

Hank closed his eyes with the dilemma rising inside him.

"After all, where would the man go? He lives in the park." She walked toward the door. "You might consider keeping your visits to our friend to a bare minimum, not to jeopardize anyone's safety."

Hank scrutinized Barbara's hunched shoulders as she left. He decoded her suggestion he forget about Joe to protect Emma. If Bill thought Joe to be the source of his information, this would avoid him searching for Emma. Undoubtedly, Frost wanted to find the cause of Hank's success over the years which could also be the reason Bill kept him on this case.

Hank changed his mind about walking away from this investigation. Curiosity about the sort of agenda FBI senior member Bill Frost had in mind became too tempting for him to bow out of the fray.

—11—

WIZARDS

After a light lunch on Friday, Hank worked on reports all afternoon going through a mountain of paperwork and making sure he kept busy his back to the small park adjacent to the precinct. He worked hard at not running across the street to offer Joe protection. Best Hank assumed Bill wanted to protect the mole and not harm him as his tortured mind first considered. He ignored the fact Barbara harbored similar thoughts. Hank also considered a small triumph that for the last two days, he'd managed to keep the Manson secret from spilling into his life, not saying a word to Christina. Although he sensed concern in her, he hoped she understood about the rigors of his job, about his need for secrecy when conditions imposed this.

As afternoon shadows deepened, Hank's personal phone with the private number vibrated in his vest pocket, and he thought of Christina as he gave his Bluetooth the command to answer. The sound of his fiancée's voice began the much needed soothing process. "Hello, love. Don't tell me," she said with a smile in her voice. "You're still at work."

"I am getting ready to leave," he couldn't help the long sigh escaping him.

"Hank, what's wrong?"

When Hank couldn't produce an answer fast enough, he bit into the corner of his lip and prepared for Christina's usual doubts.

"You're not keeping anything from me, are you?"

"No." His fault, he gathered, if she still harbored distrust. He'd shut her out of his work in the past, one of the reasons they'd broken up two years into their relationship. Five years later, the question still popped up on her lips now and then.

"We'll talk when I get home, sweetie. I guess I am thinking of tonight's outing with Matt and Maria. Not looking forward to the rich food. My gut is bothering me."

"How about we invite them here, and I cook something like organic chicken, sweet potatoes, some gravy you can enjoy on the side and a salad of mixed greens."

"The idea behind the outing is to get you ladies out of the kitchen." He took a deep breath and added with a smile. "I'll be careful what I order."

Her goodbyes to Hank ending the conversation, Christina flipped the hair behind her ear and tapped the phone with her index fingernail. She loved Hank so much. Yet, Christina sensed he kept vital information from her at the moment. Of course, she didn't need to learn about all the cases he encountered in his everyday life. Yet, every now and again, Hank drifted away. Strange and aloof for the last few days, she prayed Hank would come around during their monthly Friday night dinner with Matt and Maria. She eyed the gorgeous diamond on her finger and smiled playing with the light from the lamp for the gleam to tickle her eyes and relegated the dark thoughts to a deep drawer in her mind. Hank would not have blessed her with this wonderful ring and delightful proposal if he didn't love her as much as he did.

She called The Spanish Tavern to firm up the reservation for the four of them. Maria loved seafood and the Spanish flavor of the place, and they each took turns choosing the restaurant. Fridays were noisy in most restaurants, but she looked forward to the outing. The reservation clinched, Christina stared outside and thought of Emma and how much their friendship flourished over the years. She realized the young woman likely figured at the center of this new complication, and a small prayer rose from her lips asking for Emma and Hank to be safe.

***

Emma and her new friend Hawke sat on the bed chatting away, and Emma found herself questioning Hawke's version of a wizard. "If you say no one can see the so-called wizards which you infer are nothing but remnants left over from your scattered negative emotions, how did you find out they even existed?"

"Take a look at the world around you. Do you really think humans would be as cruel as they are if something didn't drive them to despair, or lead them around by a leash of fear?" He shook his head. "Many thousands of years ago, we shared this same problem."

"Still, who told you what wizards resemble?"

"I don't blame you for doubting me. You are one of the more evolved humans I've met in a long time, but your mistrust stems from what you witness around you. So, you can imagine how a lesser evolved human might find coping difficult."

Emma shook her head still unsure of the message Hawke tried

to convey. "You talk of evolved humans, yet you won't tell me anything about what goes on in your world."

"It's not my place to tell someone living in a primitive version of Earth how people live inside another more advanced version. This would be equivalent to you going to a third world country and telling them how you live here. Most of what you do here would mean nothing to them."

Emma nodded, understanding the comparison. "Yes, first we must accept who we are before we can hope to become a better person, enjoy a healthier life. This makes sense."

"One thing I can tell you. On my Earth, you would not be plagued with Tommy's incessant requests."

Emma's cheeks colored as she remembered Hawke read her mind loud and clear. Then she drew fists by her side when she spotted the smirk back on his expression. "Meaning?"

"Not to make you sad, but on my world, the union of two people is made through spirit and soul, and we don't use the baser need to couple in a physical way. The deep pleasure of two spirits touching and two souls becoming aligned far surpasses the joy anyone can endure on the physical realm." He produced a radiant smile again, one which faded everything around her. "This generates a state of euphoria like none other, and lasts and lasts."

"How would you know—about the comparison?"

"Many of our ancestors confirmed this. And," he continued to forestall her interruption. "Truth with all its simple fineries is not only revered on our planet but also enjoyed. You see, honesty and all its derivatives never fail to steer us down the right path."

"Those ancestors would have to be old."

"Some are. Aside from accidental death on our planet, which is most rare, we can live a healthy life for as long as we wish."

"How do you procreate?"

He hesitated, and she considered he might be trying to spare her. "Thought waves," he said. "When a couple is active and willing, they will lean their foreheads together while they hold hands, and process the thought between them. Energy descends into the woman's womb, and a fetus is present. When the child is ready, the mother picks a moment and an area, and her thoughts bring forth the child into her arms."

"Wow, you're right. Best I don't listen to any more stories of your world. Only make life more difficult to take here."

"So now you believe I'm telling the truth about the wizards."

"Yes, of course. Only I don't understand how you chased the wizards away without being able to see them."

"Wizards didn't exist at first. Not until we identified our negative emotions and decided to embrace change. Our leaders helped by making our primary mission to rid ourselves of all pessimism. To let go of all inadequacies is never easy. We trained in schools, in our homes and after a time, judgment, fear of coping, envy, all disappeared which is when the bulk of our dark emotions took on a life of their own." Sitting on the bed, Hawke wrapped his arms around his bent knees.

"At one point, they attempted to influence a bunch of us, only by now enough humans had purged them that we were able to gather and channel our thoughts to free those who needed to be. This was when we realized this dark force had become a living, breathing entity. For a long time, we remained on our guard for anyone behaving in a suspicious manner. We were not aware that when the wizards walked out of us, the treacherous beings filtered into other versions of Earth. Took us a few hundred years to discover their deception."

Emma got up, walked around her room and paused in front of the window. She tried to infuse numbers into her thoughts so Hawke would not read her mind. *What if Luigi's walk-in is one of these wizards and this is why he wants the key? This might explain why he appeared so strange looking.* She shook her head under the strain of guesswork while keeping the numbers inside her head intact.

"What are you doing?" Hawke rose, and shock replaced the smirk on his face. "You're encrypting your thoughts," he whispered.

"Of course not. I'm running numbers through my head. I don't want you to access what I'm thinking. Don't people value privacy in your world?" Emma tried not to sound peevish, but she couldn't muster the calm she needed to do so.

"So this man who is interested in the pendant." Hawke stared down at the inactive key she still held in her hand. "Are you ever going to tell me about him?"

Emma hadn't mastered the procedure. He could still read something. "You haven't answered my question. Don't you value privacy? Aren't you the least bit ashamed of prying into someone else's thoughts?

"We don't recognize shame in our world. We don't need privacy either. We don't hide because we don't possess any fears." He stared at her, the question repeated in his eyes, one she heard loudly echoing through her thoughts.

Emma took a deep breath and owned up. "A friend of a friend appeared strange when I met him a second time. Barely a week after my friend introduced me to him. I spotted a walk-in controlling his body, his mind. Walk-in played the role to perfection. The person I accompanied, a detective, never spotted anything amiss."

"But you did? Actual, visual contact?"

"Yes. At first, the image portrayed a mere outline. I detected some of the walk-in's traits, small bone structure, and an empty void instead of eyes." She turned toward Hawke as she continued. "I left. Couldn't take the honeysuckle scent. Still, he's the man who asked me about the pendant."

Hawke's eyes bore into hers as though her words came from a great distance, their meaning piercing the fog she sensed in his demeanor. "Honeysuckle aroma? Are you sure?"

"Yes. Made me nauseous and dizzy."

Hawke got up and turned his back to her, as though gathering his thoughts. Once more he turned toward her. "You visualized a wizard." His legs seemed to give way, and he flopped down on Granny Dottie's bench in front of the window. "No human can," he breathed.

"Most likely because he's not a wizard. Just a walk-in." Yet, Emma considered he might be the dreaded evil. This would explain the pale outline of his traits and the deformity of his face.

Hawke shook his head, still at a loss for words. "Why do humans say things that contradict their thoughts. Makes no sense."

Emma began to pace in front of her bed. "Because I don't know what to believe. I'm weighing the pros and cons."

"Well, pro: a strong honeysuckle scent predicts their arrival—the only warning they give."

"So this is how you found them."

"No. Humans cannot detect them through smell or sight. You

are the first."

"The first you encountered." Emma sighed. "Besides, how can you tell about the scent if you can't experience the odor?"

"The people subjected to their invasion remembered being afloat in an intense, debilitating honeysuckle aroma while inhabited by the wizards."

Emma stared at the little clock on her bedside table. "I need to study. I promised Tommy I'd go to the movies with him, and my parents aren't home yet. Strange." She glanced once more at the time. "Besides, I've googled honeysuckle aromas. The oil is said to illuminate mental patterns and invite spiritual growth and enlightenment—a desirable attribute about this particular walk-in."

"Except if he's helping himself to your thoughts using the oil's fragrance to subdue your mental abilities. This would enable the creature to extract knowledge."

His eyes dared her to argue with him. And Emma remembered how dizzy she had become while experiencing the urge to reveal more than she cared to say.

Her cell phone rang, and she stared at the number on the screen. "Tommy," she sighed. "Wants to firm up our date." Turning toward Hawke, she apologized. "I need to take this call. He'll keep calling until I do. I hate to lie, but I plan to tell him you're gone."

Hawke stood with the telltale smirk on his face and faded away. No goodbyes, no mention he would return.

She told Tommy she'd meet him downstairs at seven for the eight o'clock movie. He'd be driving with his father in the passenger's seat so she needed to be prompt.

Emma tried to focus on her studies, but slight hunger pains made her stomach gurgle, and she wondered where her parents might be, at least her dad. Her mom would sometimes work late in the evenings depending on who assisted her at the flower shop.

Then she thought of Hawke's version of the world and how lovely the sensation not to need to lie must be. But her whole life happened to be made up of lies. Not just to protect her reputation from the dubious judgment of society as a whole were they to discover her powers, but even to shield her privacy from friends like Tommy and Amelia who didn't realize all Emma could do.

She remembered Hawke mentioned fear as being the main reason why most people lied. Fear someone might discover what they really thought, or fear of what her powers might do to them. Fear of loss, fear of not being accepted, fear of being ridiculed, a sentiment her Granny Dottie lived with all her life.

She considered politicians and the promises most of them made as they lived with the fear of not getting elected if they didn't. The practice of half-truths and lies, though still covered in disrespect, somehow became accepted over the centuries and ran all the way up the echelons in the task of electing a leader. The fact everyone considered these people wimps or failures didn't seem to make a difference in their life, as long as voters kept their ideals buried deeply enough, these political figures continued to pretend she supposed, comforted instead by the adulation of their entourage, their family, and their friends. Politicians cared little about the corruption they endorsed.

Maybe someday, her version of Earth would advance enough for her to be frank about her talents. Others like her might even be hiding in the shadows making a difference whenever they dared. Her time would come she consoled herself.

The phone rang and made her jump. She checked and recognized her dad's cell phone number. A cold chill swept through her.

—12—

SECRETS

Alive with the scent of delicious food and a slew of avid patrons, the Spanish Tavern welcomed people lined up around the block on busier days. Friday evenings appeared to double the crowd involved. Luis, one of their friendliest waiters, invited Christina Tyler, Hank Apple, Maria Bracero and Matthew Logan to one of the loveliest tables by the window festively decorated with summer garlands.

Sliding into her chair while Hank stood behind her, Christina eyed Maria with a smile. She still did not understand the reason behind Maria and Matthew's separation.

They began dating last year after a four-year breakup. Why Matt chose to end the liaison, no one ever found out. Maria certainly possessed the looks and the body to keep a man like Matt interested. Tonight, her full lips painted ruby red she wore a dress showing off her Spanish figure's tiny waistline and curves in all the right places.

Christina nodded and took the menu from the waiter. She remembered being intimidated by Maria's appearance. Christina always thought Hank's eyes grew a little wider whenever they hung out together. Now, glancing at the ring on her finger, she tossed those old memories aside. The macho, handsome man sitting beside her belonged to her and to her only.

She put her hand on his knee underneath the white tablecloth and squeezed his thigh with a gentle caress hoping her gesture might alleviate his funky mood. His mind remained at work, tangled in some problem he might not want to share with her.

She eyed Matt to ask him the silent question with regards to Hank's mood. She and Matt developed a sort of sign language over the years, quite useful when attempting to discuss Hank without his knowledge. But for the moment, Maria owned Matt's attention as she whispered something against his cheek. When Maria finished, Matt eyed Christina and she understood his girlfriend's words concerned her, or perhaps they questioned the big oaf's silence, the one sitting next to her but miles away.

Matt broke the tension. "Hey, Hank, what's going on with you? Why aren't you strutting with pride, feathering your tail like the peacock you are?" The big smile on Matt's dark face dared him to argue.

Christina caught Hank's irritated expression and thought Matt's brusque manner did not hold the key to his heart tonight.

"This is our first get-together since you and Christina became engaged, man. Why aren't you celebrating?" Matt raised his arm to summon their waiter's attention, and when he did, he ordered a bottle of champagne. "One of your finest." He pointed toward Hank. "For the two of you, man," Matt smiled stretching across the table to knuckle Hank's arm.

Christina sensed Hank's touch as he searched for her hand underneath the table. He picked up the one responsible for caressing his leg and brought the hand to his lips to kiss her fingertips. "Ring looks great on you, sweetheart."

She nodded, smiling back at him her eyes never leaving his.

"True love here, your Honor." Matt raised his bread stick.

"Rough day, huh?" Christina asked hoping the prompt might foster Hank's wish to confide.

Christina sensed Hank's hesitation and worried he wouldn't say anything in front of the other two, not because he had secrets from Matt, but she figured Maria would not be aware of Emma's talents. Christina didn't expect Maria to be familiar with precinct affairs either, any more than Hank allowed Christina to be except Hank sometimes relied on his fiancée's help during a case. She found herself hoping he would reach out instead of maintaining this stubborn silence.

"Yeah, day's been rough." He searched Matt's eyes and glanced at Maria. He couldn't be sure how much Matt confided in her.

"I overheard about Manson walking, Hank." Matt grabbed Maria's hand. "I'm sorry, man. We'll catch him. A waiting game we'll win, don't worry." When Hank would not elaborate, he added. "The man is a creep whose time will come."

Hank stared up at him, no longer able to repress the information he hid inside. "A creep?" he exclaimed. "How about an Alien?"

Hank waited for the stunned audience to be in motion again, to say something—anything to stop the echo of his last words from rumbling back to his ears and mocking his own fears.

Matt recovered first. "Not this again?"

Hank waited for Luis to be done with their water and bread before he explained. Turning toward Christina, he toyed with her fingers while he slid a tentative glance her way. "An alien."

"Confirmed by?" Christina stopped as she eyed Matt and Maria. Hank realized she didn't want to reveal Emma's secret.

"I told Maria about Emma," Matt admitted. "One of Boleslaw's victims five years ago came from her village, the small daughter of a friend of her mother's."

"I told no one," Maria admitted her chin in the air. "I would die before sharing this lovely angel's identity," she added with a touch of drama. "She is selfless and generous, and we need to keep the secret so she may live with a semblance of peace."

Theatrics aside, Hank nodded. He believed Maria's avowal of silence. She resembled a Spanish Franka, Emma's aunt, who would give up everything even their life before parting with Emma's knowledge. "Divulged and confirmed by Emma. No doubt whatsoever."

"She can read an extraterrestrial's mind?" Matt asked.

"Yes, she can. She repeated Manson's thoughts to me which I repeated to him which is when he clammed up. I stared in awe at the fear on Manson's face, Matt. From a know-it-all smirk to the wild gaze of a trapped animal under sixty seconds."

"What else happened?" Christina pressed while her hand squeezed his.

"Communications ceased. Emma told me she no longer read him." Hank waited for the information to sink in. "When Manson discovered my ability to read his mind or rather when Emma read his mind."

"She stood out of his view?" Matt asked.

Hank nodded. "After the doctor's initial shock, the fool encrypted his thoughts—Emma's words not mine."

"Encrypted?" Matt's fist came down to wallop the table enough to jingle the silverware and tip the closest glass to spill water on the white linen cloth. "Sorry," he muttered dabbing with his napkin the water stain around the bottom of the glass. "Still taking anger management," he added under his breath.

Maria gave him a proud and conciliatory smile.

Hank didn't add anything as Luis their waiter held out a wine menu, ready to take their order. He rushed over when Matt's notorious temper flared Luis most likely thinking Matt needed to be served at once.

"Outburst is not due to your fine service," Maria said clutching Matt's arm. "Men are doing the unthinkable: discussing business at the table." She gave Luis her most charming smile, and he ceded a broad smile showing he understood.

The four gave their orders and Hank asked for a bottle of Sauvignon Blanc and Cabernet Sauvignon, both medium white and red wines able to compliment most of what they ordered.

"All good choices, indeed," Luis added as he took back their menus. "The champagne is on its way with some rare and delectable crudities, compliments from the Chef," he bowed with a charming smile for Maria.

Hank wondered if Matt's earlier abandonment of Maria occurred because of the charms she seemed to dispense freely, and perhaps the notches in her belt.

Matt kissed Maria on the tip of her nose showing he appreciated her intervention, and Hank fought hard to keep the surprise from raising his eyebrows. The old Matt would have pouted with jealousy for hours or so before coming around.

"What's this all about, Hank?" Christina asked.

She is one-track-minded, as usual, Hank thought. He hesitated. With a few well-chosen words, he explained what he learned from Emma about Doctor Fred Manson. "Truthfully, I hesitated on whether to contact the CIA or the DHS."

"What is DHS?" Maria asked.

"Department of Homeland Security," Matt added.

"My God, Hank. Told by anyone other than Emma, I would say the intuitive is looking for fame." Christina passed a trembling hand over her brow impatiently removing a wayward curl bobbing into her eye.

"Well, words are from Emma. So the threat is real and accurate."

"Did she say anything else?" Christina smoothed Hank's shoulder.

"Not to tell anyone. Emma said she would provide me with information as soon as she obtained anything more." Hank kept silent Manson's mention of him being dead. Christina did not need to worry about a threat on his life.

"How much longer can we afford to wait, Hank?" Matt seemed edgy and frightened. "I don't want anyone accusing me of withholding information. I can't afford another blot on my record followed by one more investigation."

Hank searched the area around their table and eased Matt's demeanor with the motion of his hand. "Emma seems to think Manson is not a villain. She said he is trying to help the best way he can."

"By stealing our leaders' body parts?" Matt's whisper still drew attention due to clenched teeth and bullet loaded eyes.

A smile on his lips, Hank warned him to remain calm. "Emma is never wrong. She said she will deliver, and I trust her. Now, this is a pleasant place, and we're sitting down to a most enjoyable meal. If you don't chuck the anger, they will ask us to leave."

Matt took two deep breaths and apologized, subdued and contrite. "You're right, of course." He whispered toward Maria staring into her eyes. "I'm sorry."

Crisis averted as Maria nodded, her face still reflecting the hot temper stirring in her eyes, her Latin blood never cool in the least. Whether Maria's anger seethed at Matt for airing his emotions or furious at the turn of events setting him off, Hank didn't care about the reason.

"Don't worry, Matt. Emma will help us figure this out." Christina smiled, putting a hand on Matt's big paw.

"Oh, I don't doubt she will. She's a winner, and I stake my life on her. I don't want to be left holding the short straw this time. Department always finds a reason to come down on me, hard."

"Not this time, Matt. I'll make sure they don't." Hank gave the sommelier the nod to go ahead and pour the champagne he brought to the table.

Hank took the first swill and smiled. "Wow, this is so dry, did not sense any liquid go down my throat." He turned toward the wine steward. "This is excellent champagne. Thank you."

Hank changed his mood in keeping with the beautiful evening ahead of them.

***

After staring at her school bag leaning against her bed, thought of the unfinished homework made Emma squirm. Still, a strong omen running shivers down her back forced her to clutch the bluetooth in her ear. "Dad? What's wrong?"

"I'm at the hospital, sweetheart. Jimmy is in a coma."

"What? Why? How did this happen?"

"A neighbor said he went berserk, chased Franka and Martha out of the apartment with a meat cleaver. Franka screamed so neighbor called the police. This is all I got."

"How is Aunt Franka?"

"She and Martha are with Abigail. Franka needed to be sedated—screaming and going on about Jimmy needing help, yelling he is possessed."

"Why is he in a coma? Did police shoot him?"

"No. When officers got to him, after having the landlord unlock the door, they found him unconscious."

"He adores Aunt Franka and little Martha. He'd give his life for them. He has. I can't accept this kind of behavior from him."

"I agree, honey. This is why doctors are going to check him for any anomalies. They're going to find out what happened, don't worry."

"How's mom taking all this?"

"Crying hysterically. I'm waiting for Franka's prescription at the pharmacy. Your mom's in the car, a nervous wreck. We're driving up to Abigail's place. Are you going to be all right on your own? Do you want me to pick you up?"

"Home alone? Please, Dad. I'm fifteen. I'm more worried about Jimmy. If anything were to happen to him, Aunt Franka would never be the same."

"The sad part is little Martha kept screaming for her daddy. She's daddy's girl and when she found her mother so upset and Jimmy down on the floor, made matters worse."

"Where is he, Dad?"

"First Avenue."

"Thanks for calling me."

Emma found her hand shaking when she pressed down on her Bluetooth. She remembered her dad saying Franka screamed about her husband being possessed. Why would she think this? Even stranger: why would one of the entities Hawke mentioned invade Jimmy? He owned no money to speak of or input into decision-making policies—a regular Jo working hard to make a living and support his wife and daughter.

A small voice crept inside whispering the unspeakable: *evil entities trying to warn me not to pursue my investigation of them. Perhaps these wizards, as Hawke called them, can combine forces for the purpose of working together—one core leader able to organize all their defenses?*

She checked the time and sensed homework would not help her this evening. Emma recalled her promise to Tommy. To go to the movies with him, her pitiful way of appeasing his jealousy toward Hawke.

"Hawke?" She wanted to reach him. She called out for him again, but nothing stirred. "Where are you? You often hang around here somewhere." What she wouldn't give to spot his tossed black hair and riveting blue eyes. Strange how in such a short time, she'd come to lean on Hawke with complete trust. Emma detected strength about him, a most attractive sturdiness.

She had no clue on how to handle this situation when the phone rang and she glimpsed Amelia's home number—a call for help with math.

"Do the homework yet?" were Amelia's first words.

"No." Emma hesitated. "My dad called." Emma took a deep breath. "Jimmy is at Bellevue in a coma."

"Oh, my God! Your aunt Franka must be freaking out. Where are your folks?"

"They're gathering at my grandmother's place, and little Martha is very upset. She's screaming for her daddy."

"Poor little thing. You're not home alone, are you?"

"Yes, of course, I am."

"Truth is as much as I envy you when I think about you being home alone since I never experienced this blissful sensation my whole life, I don't think now's the time for you to be by yourself in your big house. Do you want me to come over, sweetie?"

"No. I need to go to the hospital." The thought, newly formed inside her brain took shape, and although she did not discuss her means of transportation with Amelia, Emma made up her mind. She needed to see Jimmy.

"Emma, this is crazy. How are you going to go to Bellevue?"

"Taxi. I need to go see Jimmy."

"Want me to ask my dad to drive you?"

"I can do this on my own. I'm not a kid anymore." Emma caught Amelia's sigh at the other end of the line. "Besides, you're the one with bigger problems." She couldn't help a little giggle. "You've got to pick between asking your twin for help with your math homework or calling Tommy and sucking up. Tom said you guys got into a fight."

"Yeah," she breathed out loudly to show annoyance. "Tommy is such a dunce. Can't figure what I ever liked about him. He's so, I'm-the-man. So over him." Another sigh came through, and Emma's heart went out to her. "Or ask my sister. I'm telling you if

Emily Swift is wearing her cranky, aspie-riddled brain while she lectures me with a lights-are-on-but-nobody's-home expression, I may hand in the homework full of mistakes."

Emma couldn't help a giggle. "I'll be home eventually. I'll call you before I go to bed and we can match up our answers."

"Don't bother. We'll all be sleeping over here by the time you come back. No way will you be back from Bellevue before eleven, needing a taxi and everything. Can't imagine why you want to go to the hospital. The man's in a coma."

"I'll keep you posted." Emma hung up her cell phone faced with two more calls she dreaded to make.

—13—

EMMA SEARCHES FOR JIMMY

Their meal served, Matt raised his glass of red wine and toasted Hank and Christina's engagement. "Never thought I'd meet the day when Hank, ex-partner and biggest oaf around, would ask a prize catch like Christina to marry him, and she would say yes." He smiled and brought his glass to the center of the table. "Here's to you two, living proof love conquers all."

Hank gave him a loaded stare but clinked his glass to Christina's while pecking her lips, and to Maria's and at last to Matt's. "Crudely put, but correct," Hank added.

A cell phone rang in their midst.

"We agreed on a rule, my friend. No cell phones at the table," Maria scolded Matt.

He shook his head raising his chin toward Hank. "Hank never goes anywhere without his special phone."

"Only a few people are aware of this number, and I too call the phone sometimes," Christina admitted to Maria.

"When did this happen?" Hank asked the caller.

Hank didn't add a word other than a grunt now and again. "I'm at dinner with friends."

"Celebrating your engagement to Christina, I hope."

"Yes, I am. Call me when you return, and let me know what

you found."

When he replaced the phone in his jacket's inside pocket, Christina asked, "Emma?"

He nodded. "Looks like you got your wish, Matt. We might get some answers sooner than I expected. Emma will give me more details later." Hank did not want to say in front of the others. His ears still rang from Emma's words and what she intended to do. He no longer wanted to stay at the restaurant, and it took all his poise and crisis experience to go on with the meal. Hank stared at Christina's lovely profile, and he realized he stayed for her.

*****

Emma prepared her address slip to Bellevue Hospital. No need to dress as though she propelled herself. Emma needed to project her nervous self on the premises to check on Jimmy's coma and scan the energy around him. In the room, she would obtain a better read.

Propped up on the bed, Emma tried to erase from her thoughts the last call she made to Tommy. Tonight, they experienced their first fight, and Tommy calling her a liar because he stated she spent her time deceiving him did not help their friendship—the friendship she treasured more than anything. She wanted to call him selfish when he didn't seem to care about Jimmy, but she understood Tommy was a horny sixteen-year-old buck who needed something she could not give him.

She thought of how much easier her situation would be in a more evolved version of Earth and the thought of propelling herself to the hospital popped into her mind. By riding the waves of the astral world, she might use the portals to try to locate Hawke where she first encountered him.

Propelling meant longer preparation. Forty-five minutes to eat, prepare the backpack, and find the dark color clothes Emma needed. Throughout her preparations, she called on Hawke once or twice. She needed suggestions from him, but he didn't seem to be around.

She made sure to tie her hair in a tight bun with a rubber band rolled around the strands as she prepared for the journey. She sat on Granny Dottie's bench in her room and recited her little mantra. "Lift me away, oh Universe, lift me away so I may fly to best serve a loved one."

She found herself once more floating in the haze of afterlife. Surrounded by the love of gentle souls, Emma skirted the portals she would use to bridge the road to where she headed. She stopped in front of the entrance where she'd first spotted Hawke and called out to him using her mind. No one appeared, and Emma remained close to the archway bordered by dark crimson roses, and dripping with begonias and oleanders. She remembered the burning pull on her arm and worried this might be a direct result of this portal. Emma didn't dare go down the path. Or should she?

A noise startled her, and she turned to find Hawke's double staring at her. This person's long black hair appeared even messier than Hawke's do. Deep blue eyes rimmed with dark lashes gawked at her. Full lips formed a small pout in a porcelain face. Dressed in the same style as Hawke with the peasant shirt, the jacket, and the knee-high boots, Emma thought this person appeared to be a woman—as sylphlike as Hawke only more delicate. She bore the likeness of a pixie.

"Who are you?"

"You know who I am."

Emma smiled, cornered with the same astuteness she witnessed from Hawke. "Columba." Emma caught the oudjat dangling from her neck. "I'm sorry for all the trouble I caused when I conjured your oudjat. I hope you can forgive me."

"Forgiven a long time ago. Conjuring is something we still cannot master, even on our enhanced version of Earth." She came forward and raised her hand her fingers forming a peace sign. "And you're Emma, the one Hawke mentioned more than a few times. He is quite taken with you. You can count on a friend for life in my brother."

Emma wanted to ask Columba if a version of Hawke and Columba existed on this Earth but instead inquired about Hawke's current whereabouts. "Where is he? I've been calling him. I need his advice."

"Hawke is with his betrothed. They lived apart for a long time. They need to verify if they can rekindle what they once shared."

Emma hid her surprise. Hawke had never mentioned anyone special except his sister. "He told me about the wizards, and I need more information."

"I am aware of this. My brother mentioned you can visualize them. Yet, no other human we encountered is able to do so."

"Well, this entity may have been a simple walk-in I managed to grasp, and not one of your wizards."

Columba smiled and winked at her. "Difficult to keep your thoughts on the straight and narrow, don't you find? I understand."

"I'm not lying if this is what you are implying. I need to be certain."

"I believe you, which is why you're going to the hospital to check on Jimmy."

"You know about him?"

Columba smiled and continued to impart her thoughts to Emma without words. "The wizards cannot enter a child or rarely so. They would not live inside anyone who is aware and filled with love and peace. Jimmy, on the other hand, may be an easier target. He worries much about his family and how to care for them. Anxiety will make anyone a prey of the wizards."

Emma found difficulty in forming the correct thought in her mind. "What if a wizard did take hold of Jimmy? How do I prevent this from happening again?"

Columba's turn to depict sadness. "Only the human held hostage can decide his fate. Once a possessed person is freed, Wizards will not return to this human."

Emma nodded and prepared to go when a burning grip seized her arm. "Did you ever try to stop me before?"

Columba shook her head. "No. Although I confess, touch is painful here in this place without walls. The invasion of infringing on someone's physical aspect does not provide comfort. Our magnetic resonance repulses touch by replacing the sensation with an aching burn."

"For you also?"

She nodded. "Good luck. Oh," she hesitated. "You cannot let the wizards see you or they will kill Jimmy. You need to wear your eye of Horus. The pendant will make your attributes invisible to them."

Emma reached for the necklace tucked underneath her shirt happy she remembered to take the jewel before leaving the house.

She closed her eyes and pictured where she needed to be.

The room where she landed appeared dim but not dark—a private room. A small lamp burned near a window. A quick survey of the room and Emma found the door closed. A grateful sigh escaped her as traffic in the hallway sounded heavy. She didn't want anyone to catch her on the premises.

Emma walked into the room, and dizziness overtook her as the scent of honeysuckle surprised her. The odor made more pungent with a mixture of astringent and a twinge of ether became the root cause of her momentary nausea. She put her coat in front of her nose and took a deep breath, found her feet and walked to the bed where Jimmy lay pale and listless, stretched out on his back and doused in a quiet sleep.

The coma rendered him unresponsive, and she wondered where his mind might be trapped and how to bring him back. Emma once took her aunt Franka by the hand to lead her back from a coma which at the time seemed easy to do. She guided her back with love.

Perhaps this might work. Emma picked up Jimmy's hand and became assailed with fear and loathing. She wondered if this portrayed the wizard inside him struggling to maintain his position. Maybe Jimmy strove to kick him out as he fought the evil inside to return to his life. Emma needed to impart love and peace to Jimmy, and the only way she visualized success in doing so was to hold Franka and Martha's pictures in her mind for Jimmy to find and gaze upon.

She applied her thumb to the pulse in his wrist. She found the echo of life faint, but she closed her eyes and followed the tempo to wherever the sound might take her.

She sensed being afloat in the afterworld or somewhere inside the archway of some strange portal, perhaps deep inside the dark entrance she glimpsed on her most recent travels. The gray speckled vault above her, as far as her mind spanned, did not bode well when an overwhelming scent of honeysuckle threatened to have her turn back. Eyes closed, her mind still verified her surroundings and the more she traveled, the thicker the haze around her became, like driving down a small road overtaken by dense fog transpierced with many lit flames, but too numerous to count.

Emma worked hard to stay focused on the pictures of Franka and Martha she branded in her mind. Terrifying notions bounced against her extracting child-like screams from her although she remained quiet. The shrieks sounded like the ones Emma experienced as a child in each one of her nightmares.

Surrounded by total darkness now, she glimpsed the flicker of a candle in the distance and moved toward the faint light. On his knees with his head hanging down, Jimmy appeared drained of any strength from which he could draw.

Emma understood. Jimmy fought the wizard as she captured a whiff of his anger, strong even in his diminished state.

She called to him, and he raised his head slowly. Only one eye opened, the other one obliterated in the fight. He bore no resemblance to Jimmy—unrecognizable.

Emma smiled and focused on showing him the pictures. Once Jimmy caught sight of the photos, he moved them around in Emma's head as though playing reels of memories the pictures brought forth: Franka's smile at their wedding, the birth of Martha, and Martha's first birthday celebration.

She heard him cry out as the love for his wife and daughter

filled him to the brim, and he grabbed her hand and begged her to take him home. Emma spotted black entities pulling at him with vicious anger, but they remained powerless against him now.

As she reentered the room, she caught footsteps coming down the hall. She needed seconds to glance at Jimmy as he moved his head and stirred his arms. Jimmy's movements tracked by a monitor alerted a couple of the night nurses. She hid behind a curtain and left.

Once more in the realm, she searched the pink haze and blue vault and realized she'd been down the path marked off by the begonia dripping archway. She caught the fog escaping from the outer edges, the scent of honeysuckle vigorous and unmistakable.

She wondered if other souls portrayed as flames of a candle were trapped inside like the ones she spotted while searching for Jimmy's light flickering in the night. Did she possess the power to pick out other souls from the dark, dense gap? Perhaps the task to pick anyone out of the fog, once time altered them, might be impossible. Did the faint light die after a given period? Did other souls realize the portal stood in front of them, unprotected yet inviting them beyond its gateway? So many unanswered questions she thought with a full heart.

As Emma continued her way home, the peaceful cradle of her thoughts shifted toward Tommy and at once she found herself near his house. She hovered outside unseen and wondered about the wisdom of going to Tommy's house at this hour. Emma wanted to give him the chance to apologize, and she wanted to further explain why she needed to be with Jimmy at the hospital. She wanted to make her best friend understand.

A light shone in his room so Emma smiled and found a small

corner to land so as not to scare him with her immediate presence out of nowhere.

As she was about to hum a song they both enjoyed, to make Tommy aware of her presence in his room, she heard Amelia's voice. Surprised by her friend's presence in Tommy's room so late, she checked her watch and noticed ten fifteen. Amelia had another fifteen minutes before her dad picked her up. Her friend had decided to get help with math using the less formidable of the two tortures, Tommy versus her sister.

Taking a peek as she was about to leave for home, Emma witnessed Tommy and Amelia in the throes of a kiss. Not a friendly peck on the cheek or the lips, a passionate and forceful embrace which seemed to carry them both beyond all their inhibitions.

She gasped and Tommy, who faced her, opened his eyes and stared at her. "Emma," he whispered. "This is not what you think," the nervous words spilled out of him.

Before Amelia turned and glanced at her, she closed her eyes and left, grateful she had practiced being able to propel herself in a pinch.

When Emma landed in her room, tears ran down her face only she didn't understand why sadness enveloped her. She wanted to be happy for Amelia and Tommy. They'd found each other. Somehow, Emma wondered about the passion she discovered wrapped inside Amelia's arms, and about Tommy stirring mindlessly against her as his need for Amelia deepened. She hugged herself, but this accomplished nothing other than to reinforce the knowledge she was alone.

Emma envisioned packing a few things and going over to her Grandma Abigail. No one would question how she got there.

Grandma Abigail, her folks, and her Aunt Franka were well aware of what Emma practiced. She eyed her cell phone and waited for a ring. Tommy would call, explain and maybe want to apologize for their fight earlier.

She lied down on her bed still in her windbreaker and running shoes with her cell phone on the pillow next to her. But the call never came.

An hour later, the tears continued to pour out of her, and she still couldn't understand why. Served her right, she supposed, for not being ready to accept her friend's advances. She blamed herself for not wanting to experiment, for being so rigid with her ideals. They were young, yes, but this sweet time would never return, and now, no matter what the evening's outcome might be, things would no longer be the same between her and Tommy.

Sleep delivered Emma from the grips of sadness—tightening a band around her heart and squeezing her throat until swallowing ached.

All around her lay meadows of tall flowers and valleys rich with luscious fruit and fields of plenty bordered by bountiful rivers. The sky purple and rose, bounced two suns next to each other while the two took turns to illuminate her world. A euphoric ease washed over her, and when a Blue Jay landed on her hand, she kissed its fluffy head sensing the bird's tremor as though the Blue Jay recognized her, happy to see her again. She'd been to this paradise before, always in her dreams. She formed the wish to be back as soon as time allowed.

Go back where? Emma found herself carried once more into a land of sadness. She stirred and opened her eyes the evening's memories coming back full strength. She eyed her phone and checked the screen for missed calls. None. She closed the lamp, pulled the comforter over her shoulders and tried to find the beautiful haven again.

—14—

TOM AND EMMA

The following Monday afternoon, Hank picked up Emma at school and parked in Branch Brook Park where they might amble without being spotted by other students or teachers. The tall man walked hunched as he bent to capture her words, and Emma imagined herself as slight and small walking beside him.

Deftly, she moved a little branch heavy with blossoms from one of the cherry trees lining the winding paths around the grounds. Emma loved this time of year when the dark pink flowers rendered the area so festive. The gaiety of the place did not reflect her mood today, but she fought hard not to make Hank aware of her sadness.

Amelia had not come to school all day. Of course, without classes Monday mornings this late in the year, she would normally attend her labs, and she never missed her math class after lunch. Emma guessed Amelia didn't need help with math anymore.

As for Tommy, she'd arrived as the bell chimed managing to land in the women's washroom, and headed to class. By lunchtime, he'd called her phone three times, but Emma didn't pick up. She didn't know what to say to him or how to react, time being her only ally at the moment. Since Hank picked her up before her last class, the English class she didn't need, she missed Tommy entirely. Two more unanswered calls later, she tried not to imagine how angry he might be.

Hank shook his head. "We'd make a movie about this one and no one would believe the plot." He directed her toward a park bench next to a light pink Japanese Cherry tree, part of one of the biggest collections in the United States their beauty unrivaled at this time of year. Seemed as though the park wore its most alluring dress to relieve her pain. Why be so upset? Two best friends found each other. She too should be rejoicing, and she would in a little while, she supposed.

"I went to the hospital to see Jimmy this morning," Hank stretched out his long legs in front of him. "He's doing great. Eating like a horse. Didn't stay long. He expected your aunt and your little niece. Didn't want to be in the room when they arrived."

"Why not?"

"They need their privacy. By the way, he remembers you pulling him out of some dark place, only he believes you rescuing him happened in a dream."

"Let's not change what he thinks. Easier." Emma balanced the heavy bag on her lap. Hank reached for Emma's bag and dropped it down beside him on the grass.

"So, you want me to contact Fred Manson." Hank stared at her with a dubious expression. "You think this man can tell us anything about these wizards? If he does, I won't be able to use the information."

"No. But the situation might make more sense solving some of the crimes in this city. He might even be able to help you with your case of trafficking in body parts. How weird is that?"

"A shot in the dark. Like you, I'm sure this guy's motto is the less he says, easier for all of us." Hank seemed to hesitate. "Are you all right? You look a little gloomy today."

Emma smiled. Hank was well acquainted with her mood. "What's going to happen to Jimmy?"

"Don't worry about Jimmy. I spoke to the attending physician this morning. They did a CT scan."

"Don't you mean an MRI?"

"Apparently, this doctor prefers CT scans when they're looking for tumors."

"A lot of radiation for nothing."

"I have had more than one, being in the field of broken bones and everything. The X-rays are much faster these days, very precise. Not any more exposure to radiation than anyone might suffer on a long air flight, a nurse once told me. Of course, they're not going to find anything."

"Does this mean he will be arrested?"

"No. No. This falls under domestic jurisprudence. An officer will talk with him, but the DA won't press charges unless your Aunt Franka insists on doing so. All police are holding on record is a neighbor's hearsay. I guess you'll explain to Franka since she knows about you, doesn't she?"

"Not looking forward to this, but yes. I will talk to my aunt if only to reassure her this will not happen again."

Hank got up and waited for Emma to do the same. He glanced at his watch. "I need to hurry. Attending a meeting in forty minutes."

Hank opened the car door for her. "Anyone else these wizards can infect?"

Emma gave him a shoulder toss and slid inside tying her seat belt. "I suspect they've been doing this for centuries."

Hank put the car in gear. "You are telling me everything, right?"

She chuckled. The Captain's words and their tone tickled her funny bone. "Hank, I'm telling you all I learned, which isn't much I will admit." She turned in her seat to stare at him earnestly. "Listen, I don't blame you for having a hard time swallowing all of this. This happened to me, and I want to pretend it never existed—that's it's all a dream. I want to be a kid again, graduate, go to college, and hang out with my friends."

She pinched her lips and wiped a few tears from her eyes still picturing Tommy's deception. "I guess I burrowed my head in the sand and looked the other way, at least before this happened to Jimmy." She sighed eyeing her house coming up in the distance. "Too close to home, as though these wizards are trying to reach me somehow."

"Listen. Keep the oudjat 'round your neck. Do not take the pendant off for any reason and you'll be fine."

Emma prepared to depress the door handle the car coming to a full stop. "I'm not worried about me, but the people I care about." She gave Hank raised eyebrows and big eyes.

"Emma, that sentence Manson said? I'm not even supposed to be here? A bunch of baloney."

"Do me a favor, Hank. If you ever sense yourself troubled by an idea which is strange or alien to you, don't waste time asking yourself how or why or try to understand as we tend to do when this happens. Picture Christina in your mind's eye, how lovely she is inside and out and how much you love her." She laid a hand on his. "Promise me."

He nodded squeezing her fingers. "I promise."

She took a deep breath and smiled at him. "Bye Hank." She stepped out of the car and Hank called out to her.

"I'd like you to be present when I meet with Manson."

She bent to gaze inside the car. "With you and him?" This was new. Hank didn't usually like to involve her with the criminal types he investigated.

"Yes. You need to tell me what to say to an alien. You're asking me to trust this man. I need your help to do so."

"I'll be there."

Emma turned and walked toward her front door to unlock the bolt, but the door opened. Her parent's cars weren't in the driveway. A small shiver ran through her. She turned to send Hank a signal, but too late.

She hesitated then decided to face the music. Perhaps her mom came home early to go see Jimmy and forgot to lock the door in her haste. Besides, unless one fidgeted with the locking mechanism, the rusted pin didn't always drop into place.

Noise came from the kitchen. "Hello? Who is here?" Emma found her heart hammer hard, but the beats arose from a large pair of sneakers coming at her.

Her mouth dropped when she found herself standing in front of Tommy. "What are you doing here? You just barge in now?"

"Door is unlocked—as usual. And you wouldn't return my calls. What did you think would happen? I live a block away. You don't pick up my calls, I'm here."

He stood mutinous and terribly handsome when his blue eyes sent intense little flecks of light her way. As Tommy stopped in front of her, legs apart, with his football jacket giving him the broad shoulders, she shivered from a strange stirring in the pit of her stomach.

He motioned for her to look behind her with the rise of his chin. "Take a gander at the door." He waited with a smile on his lips.

She turned, staring at her school bag leaning against the door, needing a few seconds to remember she'd left her bag at the Park. "Oh, my God! My bag. I forgot all about my school stuff." Emma ran to the bag, sat on her heels and proceeded to check the content.

"Don't worry nothing is missing. Bag never left my sight."

"God, my wallet, my money all my identification, my books. How did you find my bag?" Emma stood the packsack's strap still in hand.

"When I caught you getting into Hank's car, I followed you. Finished early and got tired of hanging around waiting for you."

"With your dad in the car?"

"No. Dad couldn't pick me up today. I rode my bike."

"You followed us with your bike?" Emma walked up to him still holding her bag.

"Yep—rode in slow motion because of all the traffic from school to the park."

"So you walked behind us." Emma wondered if Tommy had gathered anything from their conversation.

"Yeah. I hid behind a tree when I spotted you stopping. I caught Hank take your bag and dump the thing on the grass. I would have made a small fortune betting on you forgetting the bag."

"You think you're so smart." She smiled and knuckled his arm.

"I am a tad surprised Hank didn't remember."

"Hank has a lot on his mind right now. So, did you listen to what we said?"

"No." He gave her the evil eye. "Wind blew the other way. Needed to be directly in front of you to listen in."

"Well, thank you for the bag. You hungry?"

He stopped Emma in her tracks grabbing her arm as she went toward the kitchen and took the school bag from her putting it down by the stairs. "I want to talk to you about Friday night. I didn't want to call you from the Connecticut compound. My aunt's birthday, we spent the weekend with her."

She released a huge sigh and closed both her eyes. Staring up at him again, she didn't look forward to Tommy's discussion which she spent the whole day trying to dodge. "No need to talk about you and Amelia. Oh, I admit to being a little disappointed, a little disillusioned you could forget about the sentiments you swore you feel for me."

She took in his downturned head and experienced the friendship she held for Tommy rise to the surface. "I'm happy you and Amelia got together. I mean, my two best friends falling in love, wonderful. Doesn't change the fact you and I are friends and always will be. Girlfriends come and go, but BFFs are for keeps."

"Kiss meant nothing. I'm not in love with her. My feelings for you are the same today as they were yesterday and the day before. A stupid testosterone blur. We were arguing about Math. Next thing I know, I'm trying to shut her up."

Emma stared at his face and stroked his cheek, dabbing a gentle finger on a slight blue swell below his left eye. "What happened to your face?"

"Amelia," he enunciated with rancor. "You should have seen the bruise on Saturday. Had to tell my dad I got anointed with a jab at Football practice."

"No way. I caught how she kissed you. No holding back."

"Yeah, well, when I yelled out your name, and you disappeared, she took one step back and slugged me."

Emma put her hand over her mouth to cover the chuckle.

"What was I going to tell her? You appeared and disappeared? She would have hit me again."

"I appreciate you not saying anything."

"She's your best friend—after me—why can't you confide in her?"

Her shoulders slumped. "Not quite sure why. I guess she's my safety-net. When I am with her, none of this crap exists. I don't have to think about magic."

"I think as your powers become more a part of your life, you'll have to work harder not to say anything. But," he raised his hands to reassure her. "She'll never learn this from me."

"Thank you." She smiled. Then she hesitated.

"What? Speak."

"When I witnessed the kiss between you too," she laughed as Tommy rolled his eyes. "I became sort of jealous."

"You did?" He came closer and encircled her waist with his arms. "No need to be. I can reproduce the kiss right here, right now." He grinned.

She stayed still, but moved her head back. "Not jealous of you two kissing. Envious of Amelia's passion. Where do people find this sort of hunger? Where does this excitement come from?"

Tommy let her go and stepped back. "You're just a late bloomer. At least, this is what my dad says."

She smiled. "You still didn't get a second opinion, did you?"

"Nah." He stroked her arm. "Don't worry. A late bloomer is

good Dad tells me. More of a lasting flower he said. He also told me if my mother had been less hormonal when they first met, we wouldn't be in this predicament."

"Yeah, but you might not be who you are." She tugged on his jacket. "I want you to find someone who is hormonal." She chuckled. "Find a girlfriend, and I promise you, this will not diminish our friendship in any way."

He nodded. "I don't think I could ever picture you in the arms of someone else."

"You will never need to. The moment I sense these hormonal urges, passion overriding my better judgment, I will come straight to you."

"What if I'm dating someone?"

"Then I'll wait, for as long as I have to. After all, girls are better at waiting than guys are."

"True."

Emma refused to think of all the problems her proposition elicited. Instead, she jiggled his hand. "How about one of my double-decker ham and pepperoni sandwiches with all the trimmings?"

"Coleslaw and lots of mustard?"

"Yes."

Taking his hand back, he slid an arm around her waist and led her to the kitchen. "You're on."

—15—

DR. FRED MANSON

*E*mma hurried to grab her windbreaker and fastened the jacket's arms around the belt of her jeans.

"Good morning, sweetheart. Did you eat breakfast yet?"

"Yes. Mom, Tuesday, today. You're not working?"

Eloise walked over to her daughter and gave her a hug and a kiss on the cheek. "I thought I'd stay home today and do a little shopping. I'm picking up Franka later, and we're bringing Jimmy home after lunch. Hey, you said you have no classes today. Want to come with us?"

Emma made a face. "Oh, I'm out the door, Mom, sorry."

"No problem. Franka said she had a nice chat with you last night."

"Ah, yes, we did." Her mother understood all her powers, yet a soundless, tacit agreement existed between them never to discuss those skills. Emma always believed worry of what might happen to her kept her mother silent.

"She didn't say much, mind you. Told me you reassured her Jimmy would not experience a relapse."

"Sums it up."

"Where are you off to so early?"

"Hank's picking me up. I'm meeting with him and Christina at their place. Christina has this new recipe she wants to share. You know how I love to cook."

"Okay." She ran a hand through her daughter's hair. "Don't forget to call back Amelia. She called the house phone several times last night while you were on your cell with your aunt."

Emma heard Hank's horn and grabbed her purse. "I told him I could walk to his house, but he insisted." She gave her mom a hug and a kiss. "Don't fret. I'll call Amelia. I'll be back for dinner. I'm meeting Tommy later at the movies."

***

Emma sat quietly beside Hank in his car, in the driveway of the house behind the elementary school she attended as a child. The house where Christina and Hank now lived together, Hank having given up his apartment on Prospect Street.

She kept sliding the ring off and on her finger, the one with her birthstone, a gift from her grandmother Abby on her fifteenth birthday. Unused to the weight of the lovely diamond, she toyed with the jewel when nerves overpowered her resolve.

Hank didn't seem in any hurry to leave the car, and they stayed in the cruiser's sanctuary both unwilling to go inside. Emma figured Manson's vehicle still a no-show, they could remain inside the car a few more minutes.

"So, you think I made the right decision inviting Manson here?" Hank's hands kept circling the steering wheel, and this made Emma realize she was done playing with her ring. She grabbed her purse and turned toward him.

"Yes. I think this is a terrific idea. No witnesses, no sneaky media paparazzi lurking in the bushes or in the precinct hallways." She hesitated. "Is Christina going to attend the meeting?"

He gave her a tentative nod. "Thought Christina's presence would save me from having to repeat everything afterward because she'll want to be informed."

"Of course. Plus she has good people sense and another opinion can't hurt."

"Shall we?" Hank smiled at her before he stepped out and lunged for the front door.

The door opened as they reached the stoop and Christina eyed them with a leer. "What are you guys doing? The man's here already," she whispered. "There's an alien sitting in my living room. How the hell do I entertain him?"

"He's half an hour early." Hank chuckled and kissed Christina on the forehead.

"Sorry," Emma told her with a slight smile.

"Not your fault," Christina said stepping behind Hank to walk with Emma, holding her by the waist. "You're just a passenger. It's this big oaf's fault."

Hank stopped at the French doors giving way to a small living room. Fred Manson sat in the armchair by the window his eyes roaming the view outside.

Emma caught some of his thoughts and trembled. Though encrypted, she still got a harrowing sense of how primitive and inadequate he regarded their society, enough to cause him extreme dread at conversing with them. The sentiment resembled the fear Emma might harbor were she to face a supposedly tamed grizzly bear. Except the fear coursing through Manson ran much deeper than any emotion she ever experienced.

Christina seemed to catch her shivers because she squeezed her toward her in a show of support, and her friend's sympathy rallied Emma to the task.

Emma's thoughts grazed the man because Fred Manson turned and cornered her with those protruding round eyes of an unfathomable color. The doctor did not rise or show the others any attention. His lips were tightly drawn as though he never used his voice, and Emma allowed him to read how she realized Manson not getting up and not giving a greeting only painted him as unused to exercising ordinary social skills.

Manson did rise, still staring at Emma.

"Thank you for coming, Doctor Manson. As I said on the phone, if you and I cooperate, we can achieve our goals much faster."

Hank turned and indicated to Emma and Christina to have a seat on the loveseat.

"I brought a friend along. Her name is Emma." He indicated her. "She is aware of our predicament and can serve as an excellent communicator, if only to bridge the gap between our societies."

Emma pondered how Hank's speech sounded rehearsed. Yet, Manson didn't seem to care.

Faced with Manson's stone silence, Hank turned and grabbed a straight-back chair from the small dining room and hopped a seat in the opposite direction his tall torso leaning against the back of the chair.

Fred Manson remained silent and kept his eyes on Emma while she realized he was computing large amounts of data and not about to be disturbed no matter what Hank said. She put her hand to stop Hank from adding anything else as she feared Manson might become antsy and decide to up and leave.

Only once he sat down did Fred answer Hank's question. "You cannot help me," he mouthed his tone mechanical and slight. "I cannot discuss my goals with you."

"Why did you agree to come here?"

"I wanted to meet the Pathfinder, a myth amongst our intergalactic cosmos."

"Pathfinder?" Christina put her hand in front of her mouth, her eyes apologizing to Hank. She'd obviously promised not to say anything.

"I am not the Pathfinder, so please do not think I am." Emma appealed to this man with whom she sensed protection and respect, if for no other reason than his thoughts seemed to become tamer when he considered her.

He did not smile nor even look at her. "I am also here to correct a wrong," Manson added. "I searched ahead in Earth Optimal. You are present, Apple. Therefore, you are not an anomaly. You were meant to be."

"Thank you," Hank answered his eyebrows up and down apparently not understanding the implication Emma thought.

"Hank has therefore enhanced our Earth, has he not?"

No answer from Manson. Yet, she read he had understood despite the encryption in his mind. She continued with her thoughts. *"This would be a recent development made possible due to your impact on us. You must continue to help those who wish you no harm, those able to understand who you are."* Emma continued with what she sensed to be the battle for their lives as she pleaded for Manson's help.

"How are you aware of what I do? If you are not the Pathfind-

er, how do you possess this ability?"

"*I can read your encrypted thoughts. You come from another galaxy, the Devron System, one thousand light years away. You traveled here in an instant, via a single thought.*"

By now, the hand Emma put up to keep Hank from saying anything popped up again as she continued her silent conversation. Hank understood and waited patiently while Christina stared at Manson, her curiosity making her brown eyes huge.

This time, Manson gazed directly at her and maintained eye contact. "*Where are you from?*"

"*I am an Earthling. I come from here.*"

"*From Earth Refuse?*"

Emma couldn't help a small chuckle. "*I call this place home.*"

"*You are not the Pathfinder. She is from Earth Optimal.*"

"*Yes. Her name is Columba. She also wears the eye of Horus, a little different than mine.*"

"*You have seen her?*"

"*Yes, in the afterlife where I travel. She is not a myth.*"

"*Difficult to believe you are human and not at least a hybrid.*"

"*Hybrid?*" All Emma could think of were the new cars on the market requiring fuel and electricity to function.

"*From the union of an alien and a human, most times an off-spring of parents from two different versions of Earth.*"

"*Both my parents are very much from Earth Refuge,*" Emma deliberately changed the appellation of her Earth and dared him to say different. He ignored her.

"*Are there others like you here?*"

"*Perhaps. Vulnerable people in our world, hiding and lying about who they are for fear of reprisals. Without the intervention of Hank Apple, you would not have found me."*

"Apple can he be trusted? He respects your secret?"

"He saved my life. He not only kept my secret, but he is willing to protect this secret with his own life."

When Emma closed her eyes momentarily during the last statement, the inner strength and congeniality of Fred Manson surprised her. Yet when she stared at him again, the sensation disappeared. Like others in her world, Emma became prey to simple imagery, what he resembled rather than what he carried inside. No wonder so much dissension existed around them.

"I cannot help you, Apple. In fact, to discover more about me would put you." He paused and eyed Emma strangely. "All of you in grave danger. The council I deal with have eliminated those who found out about us."

"Murdered them?" Hank's face depicted his disgust.

"Of course, to keep our secret. We must continue our work in complete anonymity."

Hank rose and walked over to Christina. "My fiancée knows nothing about you. I will not let you harm her."

Manson rose. "You are not aware of what we do here. You and your friend will not be harmed. People we terminate are moved ahead to a much more advanced version of Earth, as are the victims of the very people we are here to help."

"You're not making any sense."

Manson refused to add anything else, so Emma explained. "They are here to help those who tyrannize us." She also rose and stared at Fred Manson. "Tyrants and despots are the ones holding back our version of Earth, aren't they?"

"You comprehend far too much. I cannot vouch for your safety here."

Emma drew a great breath thinking how these all-powerful beings attempted to sort goodness from evil to meet the deadline in the race to merge all of Earth's versions. While on Earth, they sought to enlighten the persecutors and the dictators to free their minds and help them weigh in the balance should everyone in this cluster not become aware quickly enough to beat the universe's clock.

"How are you able to understand all of this?" Manson's smile surprised her with a pleasant and soothing effect lighting his otherwise alien features.

"I'm not sure how I know what I do, but I'd rather we kept this quiet so no one asks me specific questions. Also, if you can alert the Cosmos to the many ways I can help here, I would be most grateful."

"I am a mere pawn in this Universe. I am not a guardian. Therefore, I cannot promise you a stable situation." Manson shook his head, trying to understand. *"Why would you wish to remain here, on Earth Refuse, rather than move on? Your level of awareness would undoubtedly bring you to Earth Optimal."*

"I have a clear impression of being here to help our cause. I can see and smell the wizards."

Manson threw back his head in a haughty manner. *"Impossible, no human can. Even my Devron counterparts cannot uncover their whereabouts while we are here, suppressed by this primitive Earth's atmosphere."*

Emma all at once worried she'd said too much. The boast she'd voiced to gain his support had lost her Manson's respect as he no doubt now thought her a liar. She didn't fudge under his gaze but remained quiet.

Manson turned toward Hank, and the smirk had returned to his face. "I cannot help you, and I would recommend you stay out of my way."

"A threat?"

"Should you attempt to cross me, what you call a threat will become a truth you will not be able to undo."

As he made his move to leave, Manson turned toward Hank and Christina. "Two people you must investigate, Senator Kirk Assany from North Carolina, and Rabbi Minsk from Miami. Out of Miami, the maze will fizzle if you seize all the elements correctly."

He grabbed his bag and closed his eyes beginning to fade out of sight. "Beware of the worm circling the apple, insidious, your worst enemy," were the last words they caught as Manson disappeared.

"Well." Hank rubbed his face with his hands. "This explains no car in the driveway." Hank let go of a huge sigh. "Also explains how he could have gotten rid of the container he held without anyone being the wiser, replacing the container with an empty one on which he left no trace."

"What do you mean, Hank?" Christina searched his face, and she checked Emma's expression for some sort of comprehension.

Emma smiled at her. "Something that happened a while back with a case Hank worked on," she added.

This seemed to satisfy Christina. Yet she collapsed on the sofa, her face in her hands. The soft motion of her shoulders led Emma to believe she was crying.

While Hank paced the small living room floor, pale and absent-minded, she sat beside Christina with her arm around her shoulders. She reached for a tissue on the coffee table beside her and handed it to Christina. "Don't cry. The alien is here to help. He's not here to harm you. In fact, by now, he's forgotten all about you and Hank."

She smiled when Christina took the tissue to wipe her eyes. "What about you? What went on between you two?"

"Never worry about me," Emma stressed. "Worrying will render us both weak and vulnerable." Emma hesitated. "We need to be more like …" She bit her bottom lip delaying the sentence before she decided to cough up her idea pleating her nose as she did. "Like my mother."

Christina chuckled but seemed to understand. "Gotcha. I think." She blew her nose and released a few nervous giggles.

Hank stopped pacing. "And what did he mean by the worm circling the apple?"

Emma glanced at Christina, and both enjoyed a laugh. Nerves letting go. "Or like Hank," Christina added.

"I don't see how this is funny. Yes, it's a play on words."

Christina rose and tiptoed to lay a kiss on Hank's cheek. "Yes, dear. A brilliant play on words." She turned toward Emma. "Come on, I'll show you how to refine the recipe you like so much."

"In a minute," Emma answered as she stayed pat. She realized Hank wanted to talk to her.

Christina left, and Hank shook his head, faced once again with an impossible situation: an even deeper mystery with more questions than answers. "What the hell do I do now?"

"He gave you two hot leads," Emma added.

"Yeah, and the idea of a worm circling me. Who?"

Emma chuckled. "I'm sure he didn't spend all his time in jail either, considering he can disappear at will," she reminded Hank.

"Son of a bitch, you're right. All a big game to him." He released a huge, trembling breath. "Frankly, kiddo, I'm more concerned about his menace to you, about not being able to vouch for your safety." Hank rubbed Emma's arm. "How can I protect you?"

"By doing your job and not worrying. Remember, anxiety brings these wizards about, gives them the strength to own us."

"I'll remember." Hank coiled his arm around her shoulders as he led Emma to the kitchen. "What went on in the silent conversation between you two?"

Emma smiled at Christina who busied herself getting all the ingredients ready. She winked at Hank and whispered, "Later."

—16—

SELFLESSNESS

The clock having struck one, Hank dropped off Emma at the Wendy's near the Home Depot on his way to the office.

"You going to be okay here, alone?"

"Yeah, Tommy's meeting me here. We'll eat something before walking to the Cineplex."

"What movie are you going to?"

"Two thirty presentation of Divergent." She made a face but raised a shoulder to show she agreed with the choice. "The movies he likes, we view at the theater and the ones I like we wait until they come out on DVD."

"That doesn't seem fair."

"Well, Tommy thinks his movies resonate with more action than the movies I like and are best viewed on a big display, which is true. And since neither of us owns a big screen TV or a kickass sound system makes sense to attend the action-packed movies at the theater."

"Well put, Professor." Hank smiled at her. "Listen, I'm not going to worry, at least I will try not to because of what you told me, but please be careful. This Fred Manson doesn't seem to care about anyone but his cause."

"He does, Hank. Deeply so. His mission is a difficult one. Yet I don't think he can express how he feels wearing the body he does. Besides, they aren't prepared to be detected, so his lack of social skills is not supposed to matter."

Emma nudged him with a soft blow on the arm before she got out and waved him off. When she walked into Wendy's forty minutes earlier than hers and Tommy's designated time, she sat at a booth by the window and called Amelia.

"Hey, how are you?"

"Oh, my God, Emma. I've been trying to reach you."

"My mom gave me your message this morning. Why weren't you at school today? And I called you Saturday, but no one was home."

"I spent my whole weekend as a hostage, at my grandmother's house in Ithaca. She's not well, and my father and mother usually leave us with a sitter while they go help her twice a month. This time, they thought it would be good to drag us there with them, to learn a little responsibility."

Emma chuckled at the picture Amelia drew. "I thought you'd disappeared off the face of the earth of something."

"Oh, my God, Emma. I did something awful," Amelia whined. "Friday night, when my sister kept shoving her superior brain in my face, my dad drove me to Tommy's house to get help with math, and then one thing led to another, and we kissed."

Emma closed both her eyes while she juggled with answering that she knew or pretending this was brand new information. She opted for something in the middle. "Why aren't you happy? Isn't this what you always wanted?"

"Yes, of course. But then the fool whispered your name while kissing me. So I slapped him, hard, and I'm so ashamed. I can never look Tommy in the face again."

"Why not?"

"Because I'll be the girl who hits. Emma, I never struck anyone in anger in my life, and not because I never itched to do so."

"Who?"

"My sister. God, she is vile." Emma caught a tremor on the other side of the line. "I don't know what came over me. All I know is I would do anything to take it back."

"Why don't you call him and explain. Just a stupid reflex."

"Yes. This means I'll be the girl who can't hold back a mere reflex. What does this make me? A ditz and a half?" She sniffed her discontentment. "Maybe Tommy is right about me."

"Hey, for the record, Tommy does not think you're a ditz."

"I've heard him on more than one occasion. I'm not deaf."

"Well, that's his stupid reflex whenever he calls you names."

"Emma, what am I going to do? And after I tried to make him jealous with the boy I met at the bus stop. He must think I'm an idiot."

Emma did not ask about the boy Amelia met when she took the bus—too revealing right now. Instead, Emma juggled with a brilliant idea. "Listen, we can't talk about this over the phone. I'm at the Wendy's across the Cineplex. Meet me at the theater at the concession stand. We'll talk more."

"Yeah?"

"Of course. It'll be fun." Emma thought of Tommy and how much he wanted to go to the movies with her. Perhaps he'd be kind to Amelia for once.

"I wanted to review some math. A movie is more fun. Can we

get tickets for Divergent?"

Emma smiled to herself, thinking this happened to be the movie Tommy had scheduled, the one she would rather not have to watch. Her whole life happened to be one big deviation from the norm. She didn't need any reminders staring at her from a big screen with surround sound filling her thoughts.

"Sure. Got to go. My cell phone battery is dying. Meet me as soon as you can." Emma hung up and called Tommy. "Listen, I'm at the theater. Hank dropped me off. Can you meet me at the concession stand?"

"Sure. I took the bus. I should be there in thirty minutes."

"Not a problem." She hurried to hang up afraid to change her mind. She'd looked forward to spending time with Tommy. Now, she would take a back seat to Amelia and share her friendship. Despite what she told Tommy about BFFs being forever, she understood the girlfriend had the first choice and played the lead character in most situations. For some reason, she found impossible to cast herself in the role.

The fact she lied repulsed Emma as much as Amelia loathed slapping another human being in the face. Yet sometimes, Emma deplored her choices. As she took a stall in the women's bathroom, Emma wondered about the paths she took which gave her such limited options. Was she to blame?

Emma closed her eyes and propelled herself to the theater in one of the dark corners nearest the concession stands. Instead, she ended up in the exact theater room she wanted to avoid, catching Beatrice Prior jumping off a building. She moved to the back of the aisle and made a dash for a quiet and unvisited corner near the concession stand to supervise the meeting between Amelia and

Tommy.

Tommy got there first. She spotted him getting the tickets and fidgeting with his jacket as he watched the doors.

Five minutes later, he didn't catch Amelia who entered from the other side. As she walked backward, chewing a wad of gum while keeping her eyes on the door, she bumped into Tommy.

Tommy's eyes narrowed ready to wage war on her. His lips thinned, and as he prepared to blast her as Emma sensed he might, Amelia put her hand in front of her mouth her cheeks coloring a bright pink. "Tommy," she exclaimed. "I'm so sorry I slapped you."

"Slugged me you mean," he spat rubbing the offended side of his face.

Tears rushed out of her eyes and as she wiped them away, more followed fast and furious while she gushed, "I never hit anyone in my life. Not in anger not in frustration, never. I am so ashamed. Please forgive me. I swear," Amelia crossed herself. "I won't ever do that again."

"Well." A huge sigh later he asked. "What are you doing here?"

"Emma invited me to take in a movie with her."

Tommy brandished the tickets in his hand, and both said, Divergent at the same time.

"Where is Emma?" Amelia asked.

Tommy searched the place and allowed his eyes to roam around the area, but Emma, close enough to hear and observe what they did, remained tucked away in a dark doorway.

"Bets are I call her phone, and she sent the thing to voicemail," he muttered.

"Maybe she had to leave because she told me she was here."

Emma realized Tommy got the gist of what she'd done. He put both thumbs down and flashed them around the area then turned toward Amelia. "You want to see the movie with me?"

"It's okay. You go ahead. I'll wait for Emma."

"Voicemail," Tommy shot.

"Her cell phone battery was dying when we spoke earlier. Maybe she ran into some emergency at home."

"I'm sure some unforetold crisis is what happened," Tommy added his face pale.

Emma brushed away the tears with her sleeve. Tommy realized what she did, and sadness overtook her at the sight of Tommy's downturned head. She hated deceiving her friends. This might be what made her cry. More tears followed, and when she looked outside, she couldn't bare the gorgeous afternoon sun. No bus for her today. She would fly home by way of propelling her stupid self.

When she did, Emma never realized the azure dome that normally lay before her extended instead in thick gauze, dense and damp like air heavy with fog before the rain. Shivering from the cold moisture, she wondered about taking a wrong turn.

She sensed she would need to shed the gloom cloaking her in guilt and sadness to get home. She pictured Christina and their friendship, and when this didn't work, she imagined her mother and how her denial portrayed a show of strength, her deep denial of Emma's situation attributed to a decision to pursue their lives with normalcy. This realization cleared up most of the fog until she sensed an intense burn on her arm, this time pulling her toward where she needed to be rather than stopping her in her tracks.

Just as she thought she would not be able to withstand the burn much longer, she embraced her surroundings with a grateful sigh. The pain disappeared, and she drifted toward the lovely lady staring at her with a big smile.

The woman wore an old garment of blue silk brocade with white lace trimming the sleeves and front pinafore. The lady's blond hair combed in an intricate French braid depicted a time long past.

"Who are you?" Emma surveyed her surroundings. "And where am I?"

"I apologize for the burn on your arm. Pulling you became necessary as your thoughts were not going to help you against intruders."

"The wizards?"

"I am not familiar with this name."

Emma nodded to show she understood. She also recognized she took the trip without first securing her mind with ease and cheerful tidings. "Who are you?"

"I'm the one you call Sara from your grandmother's diary. Only my name is Aurora."

"Oh, so pleased to find you here. I'm sorry I called you Sara. I could only read the last two letters of your name."

"I'm surprised to find you in this place. Have you passed? So young."

"No. I'm still alive, but thanks to the diary, I learned how to propel my whole self through the portals to go from one place to another."

"Indeed. Now you need to learn about propelling yourself only under optimal conditions. When you travel with your mind, you leave troubles and emotions behind. Nothing can touch you. Quite the contrary when you travel with the shackles of physicality." Aurora smiled.

"Thank you for rescuing me from my own thoughtlessness."

"Don't worry about the boy. Things have a way of working out."

"You can tell?"

"And don't worry about your dad."

"My dad?"

"Oh, forgive me. You are still in linear time. Once you master the chapter on time travel, you will better understand." Aurora curtsied. "Farewell, little one."

She disappeared, and a few seconds later, Emma landed in her room. She appreciated the door being closed while she recuperated from the great shock of meeting her ancestor. Musings of Aurora managed to pull her out of the pit of depression and helped her recover in a snap. The universe appeared hell bent on lending a hand and showing her the way to go.

Despite the closed door, she could not make out any sounds downstairs. What Aurora had mentioned about her father hit her like a wall. She swung the door open and yelled out her parent's names to locate their whereabouts.

Her mother responded first, an apron around the waist and hands full of flour as she stuck her upper half out of the kitchen. "Anything wrong, sweetie? I didn't even hear you come in."

"Where's Dad?"

"He's in the study. You know how he enjoys takeout."

Emma took a big breath and released it with an even greater smile. Well aware of her father's vernacular, she learned to remain calm over the years whenever he claimed to bring takeout home which was his word for bringing work home.

Faced with the fact her mom and dad were all right, the remainder of her sadness lifted. Perhaps Aurora referred to her father's acceptance of her gifts. Aurora had to be aware of her grandmother Dottie's difficult life.

Emma fingered her phone and decided she would do homework instead of thinking about Tommy. As Emma picked up her bag, a strong scent of honeysuckle punched her in the gut almost making her keel over and raising more fear in her than anything had ever done.

She clasped her oudjat with confidence and pictured her mother and her lovely aunt, Franka. Even as the scent increased, Emma thought of Hawke and the gentle, kind way he'd awakened her to the truth about her surroundings and given her courage to act. She owed him a debt of gratitude, and she sighed as the honeysuckle aroma subsided.

Once she gathered her bearings, still shaky as she sat on the bed, she wondered how this happened. She decided to follow her own advice, the one she gave Hank and made the conscious decision not to fret anymore, about Tommy or anything else. Counterproductive, sad perceptions only brought on despair, leaving anyone unable to solve anything that mattered. "Practice what you preach, dummy." The thought made her smile, and she refused to wonder why wizards had buzzed around her like vultures waiting for the kill. Emma sat at her little desk and attacked the math problems she'd not yet handed in class.

—17—

BARBARA LECLERC

After dropping off Emma at the restaurant, Hank went to meet with Barbara at her request. He'd marked this day off on his calendar not knowing how long he would be with Manson.

Drained, tired and dejected at the recent turn of events, Hank sat facing Barbara Leclerc in her office. Sips of his cold coffee, the gesture mechanical, filled his mouth with sticky, cold syrup. He didn't possess the legs to rise and fetch a new mug after swallowing Barbara's reconnaissance findings, which seemed viler than chugging down bitter cold Columbian.

"Why did we take so long to find out?"

Barbara shrugged. "Joe has no family, no friends. Officers found him dead late Thursday evening. Brought his body to the morgue. No one thought more about him."

"How did you find out?"

"I gave an ally a description of the man. A seventy-year-old hobo with a full head of hair, tall and lanky is bound to draw attention. He called me the minute he discovered the body, tucked away in a drawer, nameless, rope burn still prominent around his neck."

"Deliberate hit."

"His shoes were gone, the jacket also, but I'm not buying the robbery theory."

Hank leaned forward his hands needing to support his head. "We both called this, Barbara. I should have warned him."

"Where would he have gone?"

"Can this be right?" Taking a long breath, Hank got up and walked off shaky knees by strolling to the window. "I mean, there is no love lost between Frosty and me. But the man is not all bad." Hank turned toward Barbara while leaning against the wall. "He is a devoted family man, a soccer coach. Even helps out at the Community Center a couple of weekends a month."

"Hey, I'm as baffled as you are. Perhaps we're barking up the wrong tree." Barbara put up her hand when Hank wanted to interrupt her. "Nevertheless, after your call this morning giving me these two names, I contacted Cyril Platt about my doubts."

Hank straightened, shock making his heart beat faster. "Director of National Intelligence—Lord Cyril Platt?"

"Lordship is an empty title handed down from his family. But yes, Cyril himself. Didn't trust The Principal Deputy Director or even the CMO for the same reason."

"I am acquainted with the Chief Managing Officer, Ben Craig. He's a good man."

"Yes. Dedicated, and most likely a straight arrow. But, Ben's been assigned to the hot issue of complaints of agent brutality at some of our borders. Man's hands are full. Besides, Cyril and I go way back. He owes me a couple of favors."

"Wow, Cyril Platt."

"Hey, Bill Frost is the one who got me thinking about IA. By the way, you never told me where you got your Intel concerning

Rabbi Minsk and Senator, Kirk Assany?"

"Fred Manson gave me the names during that interrogation. I didn't know if they were credible enough to release. Then I figured it might be unwise to overlook them." Hank had prepared his speech, his decision firm not to alert anyone to Manson's mission.

"I'm glad you did. Plus if we can connect Manson to these names, we'll be able to get the DA to reissue another warrant for his arrest." Barbara rose and smoothed her suit. "I never told Andrew Watson about all this."

"You told Bill you put the matter in the hands of IA. You couldn't give him a name until they finished. How are you going to explain this?"

Barbara smiled and left to fetch herself a coffee refill. "I did contact IA—only not the one he thinks." She chuckled. When she sat down again with coffee in hand she addressed Hank with probing eyes.

"I like you, Hank. I do. I pushed Kenneth Riley to give you this promotion."

"You did?" Hank walked over to the nearest chair and sat on the edge, elbows on thighs, peering at Barbara. "He never said, but he spoke of you many times in glowing terms. Ken has the utmost respect for you and your methods, I think he called them."

Barbara chuckled. "Yes, Ken became well acquainted with my ways of lawmaking. The reason I'm bringing this up is I hope you feel the same way about me. That you enjoy working with me and trust me enough to rely on my methods."

Hank cocked his head. He realized Barbara headed somewhere with this preamble.

After exhaling a long breath, she admitted, "Matt came to talk to me."

"Matt Logan?"

"Your ex-partner. He confided interesting information."

Hank sensed dread bringing down his shoulders a peg or two, and he couldn't think of any way to hide his discomfort. Matt's betrayal shocked and dismayed him while the implications weighed a ton. What might become of his career flashed in his mind, supplanted by the dangers to Emma's safety? "Matt Logan had no right to go over my head."

"Before you condemn him, I will tell you something he did that he doesn't want me to tell anyone, and this way you'll be even." She smiled at his up and down eyebrows. "Matt is like the son I never had." She stopped to consider this for an instant. "Don't misunderstand me. I love my three daughters." She smiled. "His mother and I attended Harvard Law together. We became good friends. Of course, we lost touch after we both got married and had families. Nevertheless, she called me one day, worried sick about Matt. He'd built a juvie record, kept getting into scrapes with the law, his foul temper, joyriding and such. So, I had a talk with him and convinced him he would be a good police officer."

"He is. He's an excellent detective."

"We sealed his juvie records, and the rest is history."

"What did Matt tell you?"

"I'm not finished. There's more."

Hank released a huge, impatient breath and gave her the nod.

"Matt accumulated run-ins with the authorities since he became a detective, a few suspensions because of anger, thus the mandatory anger management sessions. However, nothing as drastic as the reprimands he faced five years ago when he shot

Boleslaw to save your life.”

“I understand all this, but please get to the point.”

“Public seemed outraged. They wanted to be reassured we hadn’t shot an innocent man in the back to cover our tracks. Boleslaw never merited so much as a parking ticket. Reporters were livid. They’d been robbed of weeks, months of any progress— mighty news coverage they thought they lost when all of a sudden their man appeared face down in the ground. Worse, no one would ever learn about the reason behind the crime.” She took a sip of her coffee.

Barbara continued. “As the scope of the crime unfolded, people began hailing the two of you as heroes.”

“What I thought. I never understood this trouble Matt talked about.”

“Oh, lots of trouble all right.”

“Wouldn’t be from Ken.”

“Wasn’t Bob Larkin either. He always liked Matt Logan. No. Someone else stirred the pot.”

“Who?”

“A young and upcoming police administrator took matters in his hands to dig up all the records on Matt. He used them to threaten him. He told Matt he would go to the media and turn public opinion against him, after which Matt would need to disappear if he didn’t want to go to jail on charges of murder one.”

“Matt would never agree to this.”

“You’re right. The administrator had Matt checkmated into giving his resignation.”

“This is when you intervened.”

She nodded. “Yes. I made sure the young man got his promotion and sprinkled the event with my own brand of menace."

"I find strange Matt never told me any of this. He doesn't mind confiding in me."

"Matt never chats about anything of matter to anyone. You can imagine my surprise when he came to talk to me."

"What did he tell you?"

"He's scared, Hank. Terrified of losing his job, his girl, the life he's known for the last ten years. He gets how precious this all is."

"He told you about Manson, didn't he?"

She nodded, putting a finger in front of her lips. "I was disappointed the information did not come from you." She put up a hand to stop him from continuing. "However, I understand you needing better corroboration before you can discuss this with me. If you'd seen Matt's face, you would know as I did, he was coerced into coming to see me."

"Maria." Hank paced, unable to prevent his legs from needing to move, to run to hurry and solve this case, but how? He stopped in his tracks and turned to face Barbara. "Wait a minute. A young police administrator trying to obtain a promotion? Andrew Watson," Hank breathed his mind running horrible pictures as scenarios came flooding in. "And Bill telling you to contact IA, the man who gave Matt a hard time. No wonder you're not worried about Andrew Watson's collaboration."

"Irrelevant." Barbara smiled. "With what I told Bill Frost, we'll find out soon enough on which side Watson butters his bread. I suspect he is in with Bill. I might even receive an official reprimand if Bill were to find out I didn't put IA in the picture as I mentioned."

"And if you don't receive the reprimand?"

"Might not clinch the fact Watson answers to Bill Frost. Perhaps Andrew Watson has more favors he needs me to fulfill," she added as an afterthought. "Either way, I'll be hearing from Andrew soon enough. I'll keep you posted."

"You still didn't tell me what Matt said."

Barbara smiled and rose. "Let's take a walk in the park across the street."

They got to the park close to lunch time, and quite a few people ambled by. Barbara brought Hank to a bench where sat a crown of flowers. A small placard across the crown stated the flowers commemorated a gentle Park resident, Joe Smith, who lived here for the last ten years of his life.

"I didn't even know his last name. You did this?" Hank tweaked the corner of his eyes and the bridge of his nose.

She nodded. "Smith is not his last name—might be. Unless someone claims the body, he'll be Joe Smith."

"This can't be why you brought me here." Hank remained standing.

Barbara handed him a card. "These kind folks will sweep your office once a week."

"We hire our own specialists to do this. Not as often as once a week, but on demand."

"Of course, we do. IA supplies them."

"So you did insinuate what I thought you did."

"With what Matt told me about Manson." Barbara kept right on smiling. "IA would hold enough to bring you both down and cause a lot of trouble for," here she covered her mouth before she whispered, "Emma."

She began walking, inviting Hank to follow her. "I devised

meeting points outside the office. We will vary them and make sure no one can read what we say from afar." She looped her arm into his. "My behavior borders on paranoia, I realize this. Yet, we are dealing with an intelligent benefactor whom I am certain will appreciate the effort we are attempting by trying to catch the bad guys in the act."

"You're talking about Cyril?"

She nodded.

"In the meantime, who is going to investigate Andrew Watson?"

Barbara chuckled, the way she did when she planned a little coup. Hank stared at her with a glint of mistrust. He'd worked with her long enough to realize he didn't need to worry about her attitude. Still. "What are you up to?"

"We possess in our midst the greatest secret weapon around. Matt tells me Em reads minds for you."

Hank stopped walking and threw Barbara a hard glare. "You want me to ask Emma to snoop into Andrew Watson's life?"

"And perhaps check out Bill Frost and his acolyte Tim O'Rourke."

Hank let go a huge breath, his head shaking side to side in an angry motion. "No. No way. She's just a kid, Barb. She'll be in the midst of barracudas." He sat down on the first bench he found. "I can't do this to her."

"Hank, I can't come up with any other solutions, can you? We are cornered by the FBI and our own Internal Affairs. Cyril asked what we were doing on our side to resolve this situation. He expects assistance."

"You can't tell him about Emma." Hank's tone rose as he

glanced at Barbara willing to flash angry eyes on her. Right now, Hank fought the urge to strangle Matt Logan for putting him in this situation. He remembered the wizards and the promise he gave Emma. He made a point of calming down.

"Of course not. Hank! I'm not going to tell anyone about Emma."

"This is what Ken meant about your methods. Unorthodox. How do we start?"

"Well, Cyril assigned three agents to me, agents who will keep secret this investigation from everyone else. Two will be leaving for North Carolina to investigate Senator Kirk Assany." She put up her hand to prevent him from adding anything. "They are real investigators who will not be swayed by the obvious. One of them will go to Miami next week to try and locate Rabbi Minsk."

"Where do I fit in?"

"Well, you will need to be the point man here. You'll be working with Emma giving her the names of the people we need to scrutinize."

"I'll establish a pattern of meetings and vary my locations," he mumbled.

"I can help with this. The other thing you're going to need to do is to take some well-deserved vacation."

"What the hell are you talking about? Barbara?"

"You and Christina need a rest. In fact, I've checked your roster and your full vacation allotment of the last five years is intact. Pack your bathing suits and a big beach towel for two. I'm sure Christina would love to show off the rock you gave her to her mom."

Barbara's big smile made Hank chuckle. "You are a wily one. I suppose the point man in Miami understands I'll be working with him?"

"He does. He can manage on his own for now, but he will need our help in the next few weeks."

***

In the middle of trying to solve a math equation, Emma scrunched and threw away the nth piece of scrap paper she cut up from old sheets of homework. The wastepaper basket beside her little desk full to the brim. She refused to give into frustration when she jumped from a piercing, gut-wrenching scream downstairs.

Dad! Noo. She resisted the temptation to propel and flew down the stairs instead. She recognized her mother's scream, although the shriek held such terror she didn't know what to think.

When she got to her father's little office, her mother stood in the doorway paralyzed and unable to say anything coherent.

Emma found him lying face down on the floor. "Mom, call 911. NOW," she yelled. Emma ran to him and turned him around. She grabbed her cell phone and punched 911. Her mother cried in her search to locate the house phone's handset. Emma gave the address and told the operator she suspected a heart attack.

Emma realized this was no ordinary cardiac arrest. The study reeked of honeysuckle, an aroma she dreaded and hated. Her father murmured something so she bent as close as she could to catch what he said.

"I can't breathe. Devils are sitting on my chest."

Emma applied her right hand to his chest and murmured in his ear. "They can only do this if you resist or try to fight. Release all anger. Let go of any regrets. Think of me and mom and how much we love you," she whispered.

Softly she continued to whisper in his ear, wanting to reach him and making her words as clear as possible. "Think of the love you share with us, and allow the sentiment to fill you to the brim." She sensed him relax. When Emma peered into his eyes, she smiled at him, grateful her father understood as his whole body collapsed into one big breath while a big smile released the frown on his brow.

"Dad?" He was out. She took his pulse and found one, weak but steady. She closed her eyes, and as tears rolled down her cheeks she caught the sound of an EMS getting closer. She thanked God for sending them this quickly. Seemed as though she'd phoned seconds ago.

When they wheeled her father out, she found her mother on her knees sobbing and mumbling gibberish. Emma scooped her up in her arms and cooed comforting words rocking her back and forth like a small child, their roles reversed. The tears on their cheeks mingled, and Emma sensed the strength inside her grow to give her courage. With their shared pain, the separation between them blurred and Emma breathed with relief when she realized she'd be able to keep her mother safe from harm.

—18—

CHOICES FOR EMMA

Late Wednesday afternoon, Hank's brain still ran scenarios from what Barbara Leclerc had confided. He stood in front of the office window overlooking the park and wished he'd followed through on his intuition to protect Joe.

Once again, the old bugaboo reared its head back to flog him with doubt: did some people need protection more than others? Aside from age or strength, should one life be more important than another? Did some lives become meaningful enough to take precedence over others?

He hated the fact state officials were blessed with protection ahead of ordinary citizens. No one foresaw the future. Therefore, no person should be allowed to profess one life to be more important than another with any kind of assurance. Emma did predict the future. In his mind, in Barbara's mind, she took precedence over Joe. Emma occupied a choice place in his heart which entitled her to a real part of his life, and this assured her his protection and his devotion.

Barbara mentioned if Hank tried to protect Joe, FBI might go after Emma. This didn't ring true somehow because even with Joe still in the picture, how long would Frost take to discover the improbability of Joe being the informant he sought? However, with

Joe dead, the FBI agent might wonder from where Hank still received his information?

This meant he needed to limit what he confided to Bill Frost. If Barb happened to be right, Hank needed to ask for Emma's cooperation to find out Bill's associations so his crew would not carry the risk of informing the wrong person.

His phone rang inside his jacket pocket, his private cell phone, the one he answered no matter what the occasion as only a few were privy to the number.

"Abigail? Who gave you this number?" When the answer never came, he asked. "Is Emma all right?"

"She is not hurt." In what seemed to be a tired and winded tone, she related what happened to Patrick and how Emma needed his help. "She's comforting my delicate daughter Eloise, her own mother, but she's scared Hank. I caught an expression in her eyes I hadn't seen in five years—the wounded, terrified look of an animal in a trap with nowhere to go."

Before Abigail finished forming her sentence, before tears overtook the elderly woman, Hank rushed out of his office. "Where?" he yelled.

"University Hospital," she sputtered.

He put the phone away and ran toward an unmarked car. He decided not to radio anyone about his whereabouts and drove straight to the emergency entrance flashing his police badge when he entered. "Patrick Willis' room, please."

After the nurse at the desk went through the recent admissions, she asked to see his identification one more time. "I'm sorry, detective. Mr. Willis is in the trauma center. An orderly will need to take you to him."

She pressed a button. Still, Hank counted another five minutes before the orderly reached them. "Please take the captain to Dr. Mendez' quarters in the trauma center."

"Follow me, sir."

When Hank reached Dr. Jorge Mendez's office, he asked about Patrick Willis' condition.

The doctor hesitated. "We're not quite sure. All the signs appear to be a coronary. However, the heart's rhythm is regular, faint but steady. We're still trying to find the cause. From the family's information, we gathered, Mr. Willis does not seem to suffer from CHD."

"Laymen's terms, doctor."

"CHD. Chronic Heart Disease." Doctor Mendez answered.

Hank stared at the man who rose and threw him a nod to follow. He wondered about his skills. The dark curly haired young man did not appear old enough to be a heart surgeon.

"I'll bring you to him," Mendez added. "You'll have ten minutes or so. We've scheduled an EKG and a few other tests and depending on the results, we'll find out what's at the source of his coma."

When Hank entered the quiet room, he found Patrick alone. "When did his daughter leave?"

"Daughter? His wife came with him. She stayed until a sister picked her up, Franka. The sister is the one who filled us in on the family history. Wife too distraught to be of any help."

Hank didn't add anything but wondered what Abigail meant about Emma's presence. He approached the bed as the doctor left, closing the door behind him. Patrick appeared serene and resting comfortably.

"Don't say my name or speak out loud, Hank. I'm here, but I don't want anyone to find me."

Hank pulled up a chair and nodded. He resisted the urge to search the room for the source of the sound. He realized the voice belonged to Emma.

"Try to form clear, concise sentences in your head. I will read them and answer you."

"This is not a heart attack, right?"

"No. My dad mentioned they sat on his chest hampering his breathing, and fighting with him. I told him to only think of me and mom and how much we love him, after which he collapsed."

"Letting go saved his life."

"Before this happened, I arrived in my room to an intoxicating aroma of honeysuckle, so intense. Wizards can't trap me. So instead, they are attacking the people who matter to me."

"Please don't let them intimidate you. This will only make things worse for everyone else."

"They're trying to shut me up. I'm not sure how, but I think these evil entities found a way to band together. They appear to be planning their attack."

The door opened, and a couple of orderlies entered and prepped Patrick to wheel him out.

Hank watched him go and wondered if Emma would follow. She might be anywhere and everywhere she wanted to be. Unable to do the same, Hank waited to hear from her, and when he didn't, he left the hospital.

He unlocked the door to his car, and when he sat down, he jumped hitting his head on the car ceiling. Emma sat beside him in the adjoining passenger seat. "What are you doing here?"

"I'm not really here. Just my mind is. I'm at home, resting. I didn't want to risk possible photographic equipment in the hospital's trauma room. I'm not sure if a camera might pick up my image."

Hank rubbed the top of his head, adding, "I'm sorry about your dad, Emma, but I need your help. We need to discover who we can trust in our division. Barbara and I believe some of the FBI agents may be corrupt."

Hank watched Emma squirm and bite her bottom lip as she did when she wanted to opt out. Familiar with the expression he encountered often enough in the past, Hank worried Emma might clam up and refuse to help as she feared what happened to her dad might also happen to other people she loved.

"Barbara brought in some big guns, and she is having the names Manson gave us investigated."

He waited for an answer, but only the echo of his words bounced inside the car, and Hank worried the vulnerability pulsating through Emma's eyes might make her refuse to help.

"Emma?"

"What if this evil is affecting the people in your division? The wizards will realize I'm helping you. They will retaliate and hurt someone else I love." She turned in her seat to stare right at him. "I need my dad, Hank. I want him back, safe and healthy. You and I both understand the medical profession can do nothing for my father."

"You believe by not fighting for truth and goodness, you can stop these devils from attacking the people you love?"

She didn't answer and Hank experienced remorse crawling up his spine at the sight of frailty enveloping her. He wanted to pull her close and give her a hug, but he stared at nothing more than an image of Emma. He couldn't even hold her hand. "I'm sorry. I understand you're scared, and you need help I can't provide. So, I have no right to ask for your help."

She nodded her lips tight, her frown quickly replaced with a small smile

"What happened during the silent conversation you shared with Manson? You never did tell me what transpired. Can he help in any way?"

Grasping a shaky breath, Emma shook her head side to side. "He's helping people sentenced to die at the hands of murderers."

"The gang willing to sell body parts at outrageous prices?"

She nodded. "Helps the victims stay alive by supplying them with new organs. Manson's race can grow them from the victim's own cells. No need for an endless amount of pills to fight rejection. Sometimes they can't reach them in time, so they relocate the victims to a better version of Earth. He's amassing all good souls, the ones worth saving and sorting the lost ones so they may be reprogrammed or put aside until they can be made aware, at least when the option to educate them becomes possible."

"I'm not sure I understand." Hank thought he might venture a question. "Can he help us?"

She shook her head. "He is—helping us. His powers are limited on this Earth. He and his counterparts are struggling, but they manage to do what needs to be done to fulfill their agenda. Best you don't discover the details about their particular mission."

"I'll understand if you don't think you can help us. I realize your dad means a lot to you. Emma, I don't believe your lack of cooperation with us will guarantee ..." he searched for a word.

"Wizards."

"The wizards—will release your father. No guarantees. Are the wizards purported to play a fair game?"

Emma stared at him, panic in her eyes. "I can hear my mother and my aunt Franka walking in. I need to go home. Can I call you later?"

Hank nodded as Emma closed her eyes and disappeared out of sight. He remembered Manson vanishing in the same way, and wondered if the strange doctor came to his house solely in spirit.

***

Emma came out of her room to go downstairs, and in the living room, she faced her aunt Franka, her mother, and Tommy. "I'm sorry, Mom. I fell asleep. How is Dad?" Since the EMS held one additional place, Emma stayed home to allow her mom to go with him. Her mother breathing out the occasional hiccup made no attempt to hide her eyes swollen from crying.

"Doctors are running tests. This is all I know, sweetheart."

"What are you doing here, Tommy?"

"Thirty minutes into the movie, my dad texted me about your dad. He thought you and I were together. Apparently, our dads were on the phone when yours collapsed. So mine called 911."

"No wonder they got here so fast," Emma whispered. "Where's Amelia?"

He shrugged. "Amelia went home. Said she didn't want to watch the movie alone. She called her mom and waited for her to pick her up. She's pretty worried about you. You should call her. I ran, took a bus and came straight here."

Franka re-entered the living room. "I ordered Chinese food. Hope that's okay." She came up to Emma and gathered her in her arms. "So sorry, kiddo. Don't worry about your dad. He's a trooper."

Emma nodded, her nose pressed against her aunt's shoulder. She pushed herself away slightly to blow her nose. "I hope so, Aunt Franka."

Later, after reassuring Amelia over the phone, alone in her room, Emma called Hawke's name. She needed answers about the wizards and how they worked. Emma remembered the caution her great grandmother Aurora had given her concerning her father and shivered faced with the fact Aurora identified the issue ahead of time. Perhaps Emma should have better prepared him. She also remembered Aurora speaking of linear time and how Emma still followed the straight line. She made a mental note of consulting those pages which appeared as gibberish a few years back.

Then she remembered Hank's question. Whether she knew if the wizards played fair? She realized they did not. Impossible since the so-called wizards embodied all of humanity's flaws and negative emotions flowing throughout the world. Of course, no fairness occurred in anything they did. Her fear of them attacking other people she loved made Emma reject the coincidence notion. First Jimmy, her uncle, now her dad.

On her way back home from the hospital, she tried to communicate with her father. She did not find him anywhere in the haze of the afterlife. Not even down the path she took outlined with begonias and a dark omen. Through the thickening mist and the screams and the taunts, she encountered many little lights, tips of flickering candles, some long and tapered others round and robust. Only none she stumbled upon represented her father.

Tommy left after supper. Franka drove back home to Martha and Jimmy, and after taking a couple of sleeping pills, her mother went to bed.

Still up when Abigail arrived with a small suitcase, Emma ran downstairs to greet her. "I'm going to take care of your mom, sweetie," Abigail said as she gave Emma a protracted hug. "You go back to what you do best, being a kid. You should not have to worry about taking care of grown-ups."

Grateful for her grandmother's arrival, the strong matriarch's presence provided Emma the reassurance and the calm she needed to fall asleep. Yet, slumber still came in bunches of fitful images. She kept thinking she wore the eye of Horus throughout her dream. She shouldn't experience painful, unexplained imagery grotesque enough to prompt her search for an exit.

When she couldn't find a way out of the nightmare, she focused on making sense of the string of events happening before her eyes. She spotted a valley brimming with flowers, and two suns in the distance. She loved this place. Calmness descended upon her, and she caught a glimpse of broad shoulders and a sylphlike outline in the gray foreground of an orange sky.

"Hawke, is that you?"

"Yes."

"I've been trying to reach you. Where are you?"

"On the brim of a few worlds, cleansing, ridding myself of five years of Earth Refuse contamination."

"Columba told me you went to spend time with your betrothed. You never mentioned her."

"We don't generally spend as much time on your version of Earth when we visit—not as long as I was forced to do so. We return on a scheduled basis to cleanse and center our thoughts, our soul. I suppose my communications with Willow became distant and thrust to the background. Your ego-centered atmosphere makes actual memories difficult to seize. In any case, we were unable to recapture what we once shared. I need to cleanse, but also, she has formed other ties."

"I'm so sorry. It's my fault for conjuring Columba's oudjat."

"Every action we take has a productive solution if we dare to examine the consequences. Because of your actions, we discovered you, the one human able to detect the wizards. You can even fight them. This has never been done before."

"They are attacking my family members—deliberately so. This means they can organize and work together."

"This is why this particular world drew me in, to warn you against the wizards. I will not be able to frequent the after-haze of your Earth for a while, and it's important you realize the wizards are now cooperating with each other."

"How is this possible? This would mean they are not pure evil."

"They are. Therefore, the wizards' own mistrust will disband them. You must remain vigilant and not allow their tactics to influence your decisions. This will create mistrust within their ranks. When they fight amongst themselves, they lose ground. This means we go to work and accomplish twice as much in less time."

Hank spoke the truth. Hawke came to word the same thing through different arguments but achieving the same goals: to rid themselves of these wizards.

"I hope to see you again, Hawke. I miss you, your knowledge, your reasoning."

"I understand. I also miss you." He smiled the first one she'd spotted since last encountering him. "Stay clear of Devronairs. They come from a different star system, and they will remove all earthlings who discover their whereabouts."

"Are they xenophobes?

"No. Our belief is they worry about contaminating Earth with extraneous information."

"Thereby contaminating us even more." She smiled back at him. "I met one. He is using the name of Dr. Fred Manson. I read his mind even though he encrypted most of his thoughts."

"You can read a Devronair's mind?"

Hawke appeared disturbed, staring at her with new curiosity.

"Yes. He knows I can. He is also aware I can spot wizards."

"Watch your step. If the Devronair tells his leaders, you may encounter more trouble than the wizards can give you."

Hawke's words echoed in her mind as her eyes opened and she stared at the elm tree tapping its branches against her window. The night was balmy, but the breeze was strong and she sat up in bed wondering if she'd encountered Hawke or if the encounter had been the artifact of an overly active imagination.

—19—

HANK & CHRISTINA

Hank paced up and down his little living room as he waited for Christina to come back from a parent-teacher meeting. He checked the time and wondered why she was so late coming home. He hadn't touched base with her about any of this, not about the wizards or the threats to their lives. She didn't even know about Patrick Willis yet.

He needed to warn her. After all, she belonged to Emma's circle of good friends which meant her life might be in danger.

When the door opened, he ran to the small vestibule and pulled Christina into his arms. "Why so late?"

"Well, I see you missed me." She looked up at him with a bright smile. "Some of the parents pleaded for solutions on the necessary steps to help their child graduate with the others. Three students in my class are having serious trouble, and their only chance will be how well they score on the upcoming board exams. No parent wants to see their child held back."

"We need to talk." Hank hated springing this on her in this manner, but a mighty urgency paralyzed him, and he needed his future wife's wisdom to lean upon.

Forty minutes later, in the midst of their discussion, his private phone rang. "Hank."

"It's me."

He waited, but nothing else came through. "Kind of late for you to be calling."

"I'm sorry."

"No. I meant I thought you'd be sleeping. Christina and I are up. I told her about your dad."

"I'm going to help you, Hank. These wizards don't own me. And I think thwarting them will contribute to weakening their hold on us."

"Good decision." He took a big breath. "I also gave Christina instructions on what to do if she experiences any of those sensations you mentioned."

"The second reason for my call. Had I been more specific with my dad, he may not be in this predicament."

"Don't start blaming yourself. You warned me, and I never really paid attention until now. Don't worry, I'm on board." He stretched a hand to wrap his arm around Christina's waist. "We both are."

***

Emma could not fall back asleep. She walked around her room thinking she should go back to the hospital to visit her dad. Yet somehow with the little she knew about his condition, the trip to the hospital did not motivate her. Too many questions needed to be cleared up before she might hang another left down the forbidden path stretching beyond the strange archway. The sound of those shrieks she'd caught down the gloomy path still echoed in her mind and terrified her.

She remembered Aurora and wondered how she first encountered her: on her way home from the theater after having left Tommy with Amelia. She'd weathered a strange sadness when she left her friends behind, almost a longing as deep as a canyon, and her unguarded thoughts flew her to another set of arches.

She prepared to propel herself in the haze once again, this time attempting to recapture her previous weariness. She hesitated. Aurora and Hawke warned her to only use loving and nurturing thoughts when traveling in the astral world while using her whole body as this rendered her vulnerable and might send signals to the forces of evil.

Instead, retaining only sound, pleasant thoughts, she made up her mind to call her ancestor the moment she reached the clouds.

"Aurora, where are you? I need to talk to you. I need your help. Please?"

She waited with her eyes closed her senses in readiness for any sound or presence strong enough to imprint itself on the mist around her. No one appeared, near or far. She waited a little longer as she experienced many souls with encouraging words passing through, yet no Aurora.

Did she dream about her ancestor being there? A light materialized in the distance, bright and becoming brighter as she stared at the radiance growing from its sphere.

She moved toward the sunlit passage emitting a strange, homey sensation. Like the world with the two suns, this light enveloped her with a great peace.

Just as she prepared to enter the archway bathed in a luminous glow, the familiar burn struck her arm, and she turned to see the beautiful outline of a stranger. The woman from another era wore a smile, yet a strange gleam shone in her eyes.

"Do not enter this archway, my beautiful child."

"Why not?"

"Remember Shakespeare's play, Merchant of Venice: 'Thus hath the candle singed the moth.' Those who enter the beauty within are never encountered again. Some say the gate is the doorway to another universe."

"A more advanced one, I'm sure," Emma whispered under her breath. Worry she would not be able to spot the beautiful doorway again crept into her mind, and she chased the thought away. The pull too strong, now, Emma decided to obey this stranger and leave. "Can you tell me how to save my father? He is in a coma because of the wizards."

No comprehension in the lady's eyes, simply a smile as she faded away. Emma started to move away from the tunnel with the bright light. She sensed the pull on her holding her back. Emma thought of Columba and called out to her in her mind. The Pathfinder appeared as she was about to enter the glowing passageway. "How do I go back? I was told not to go down this path."

Columba smiled as she extended a field around Emma. "Their pull is strong, but you will be safe if you think of home. Do not come this way anymore."

"How do I avoid this path? And where does this corridor lead?"

"Where, is not significant. How to avoid the path? You must not propel yourself inside the afterlife with the sole purpose of exploring the place or its inhabitants. Best to do so without the entrapment of your physical self. When you travel corporeally, you must adopt a loving manner and focus only on where you wish to land, remember?"

Emma nodded. "How do I get the Wizards to release my father?"

"Your father is not under their spell. He is afoot and trapped in a prison of his own making. He carries unresolved issues, and they are keeping him from finding his way home."

"How can I help him? I have searched, but I can't find him anywhere."

"He will need to find you." Columba smiled, and just as her brother's smile did, the bright grin did away with the words and touched the right strings in her heart. Emma closed her eyes and thought of home.

***

Hank slid his bare leg between Christina's silky thighs still moist from their lovemaking. "When I have you in my arms like this, all thoughts of hostility toward corrupt individuals disappear. I'm safe and whole," Hank whispered against her cheek.

She moaned and twisted in his arms, their embrace deepening. "I understand what you mean. I love you, Hank and the very idea of wizards and us needing to tackle this whole world's negativity problem becomes ludicrous." She sighed and bit his bottom lip with a gentle peck as she did to get him aroused, to taunt him into a deep, sensuous kiss.

He pulled away to stare into her eyes. "You understand the threat is real, though, don't you?"

"Maybe," she answered rubbing up against him. "After all, they say what you worry about you bring about."

Hank backed up gripping her arms with his hands to prevent

her from coming forward. "Who? Who says this?"

She shrugged. "I'm not sure. Overheard this somewhere, perhaps at one of my teacher's seminars."

"What about the song with the lyrics you make trouble double when you worry," Hank added as a contribution.

"Thank you for understanding. Hank, you're a police officer or rather the captain of a division which brings all its problems to you. You're in a constant battle for people's lives. I'm a school teacher, in a rough district. Out of the twenty-four students I teach, quite a few excel at pushing my buttons."

"This is Emma. You have to realize the threat is real. You can't pretend that it's not."

"I trust Emma with my life. She never steered us wrong, and she never lied to us even when this meant exposing herself to ridicule and unfavorable judgment. I understand." She let go an enormous and shaky breath. "I have to remain focused on the pleasant times and on the certainty I designed for myself, or I wouldn't be able to cope, not the way Emma does. She has to be the bravest person I know. I, on the other hand, need a little pink in my reality, at least when we're making love. Can you respect this?"

He chuckled softly and gathered her in his arms stroking her bare back with hungry hands. "I understand completely. We'll leave this sort of conversation for later. Better? Hank asked his lips against hers.

She nodded her mouth open and inviting, and Hank delved right in with the deep, sensuous kiss she longed for.

***

A knock at the window woke Emma with a start. She sat up in bed and took a deep breath to gauge the air around her. No honeysuckle aroma, so she attributed the sound to the elm's branches rapping against the pane.

A second knock got her attention, and she spotted a shadow in her window. A shadow she recognized. She ran to the window to slide the bolt the opposite way and faced Tommy his arms wrapped around the main branch. She hesitated slightly before she moved aside to let him into the room. Her father's absence, her mother asleep with a couple of pills and her grandmother also sleeping in the den downstairs, Emma wondered about the wisdom of allowing Tommy entrance.

"What are you doing here?" Emma asked as he jumped from the window sill into the room.

"I wanted to talk to you earlier, and I never got a chance with everyone around."

Emma, conscious of her short nightgown, put on her housecoat securing the belt around her with a nervous knot. "This couldn't wait till morning?" She had taken so much time to fall asleep. Yet, Tommy happened to be the one constant in her life she enjoyed for no other reason than she loved his company. She smiled, glad he returned.

"I needed to say you were right. Amelia is not the ditz she appears to be." Fidgeting while appearing uncomfortable, not in Tommy's nature, when he kicked a box of Kleenex lying on the ground, Emma paid attention. "She dropped the popcorn at the movie and when we both bent to pick up the bucket we banged our heads. Well, one thing led to another and we kissed. This time, she didn't slug me, and the kiss was sweet."

Tommy's words answered Emma's hopes, except Tommy's confession did not make her as happy as she thought she might be. "This is what you couldn't wait to tell me?"

"No. I also wanted to say how sorry I am about your dad. If you need anything, Emma, anyone's help, I'm here for you."

She nodded and didn't pull away when he took her in his arms. He made no attempt to kiss her, and she found this odd. Instead, he smiled and reached for the window sill again.

"Be careful. The climb down may be more difficult somehow. Didn't realize those bottom branches had grown so much in the last five years."

Perched on one of the main branches, Tommy looked at her and added, "Yeah you may want to tell your dad it's time …" He stopped mid-sentence and made a face. "Sorry. I can probably trim the tree for you if you like."

"No. The tree surgeon my mother hired last time warned us not to do this again. My mom will call him."

She watched as he grabbed his bike and rode away. A little piece of her heart went with him, and her bottom lip trembled slightly. "Bye."

—20—

EMMA THE SPY

The next morning, Emma told her mother she couldn't go to class. She wasn't feeling well. "I need to stay home and rest, Mom."

"Sure, honey. I'll call the school. Would you like me to take you to the clinic downtown?"

Her mother's face appeared as though she'd spent the night crying, so she thought the offer brave of her, and Emma rubbed her mom's arm as she answered, "Thanks, Mom. I think after a full day's rest, I'll be better."

Once in her room, Emma locked the door. While she realized her mother would never walk in uninvited, her grandmother, who happened to be a little bit nosier than everyone else, might walk in unannounced to check up on her. In the name of helping Hank Emma needed to go snoop on people, something she hated doing. Lately, she developed a particularly heightened sense when someone approached while she was out of body allowing her to return in time, but she didn't want to be interrupted.

She read the address: Englewood Cliffs, the same area where her grandmother Abigail lived.

Hank had phoned her with some of the specifics he had on Bill Frost. Family life, his wife Jeannie, his daughters, Brittany twelve,

Caroline five years old and Madeline the cute little toddler. When Emma asked how an FBI agent could afford a three and a half million dollar home, Hank had mentioned his wife Jeannie came from money.

She took a deep breath as she landed in the front hallway and glanced at her surroundings. Laughter came from somewhere to her right, most likely the kitchen so she moved toward that area, happy no one could see her.

As she took in the furnishings, she found the house moderately decorated. A room right off the kitchen where wood floors gleamed, and the green and blue window treatments made one think of sky and meadows, owned no furniture.

In a large kitchen, decorated in light oak and dark Quartz, Bill and his daughters sat on stools around a moon-shaped island. Baby Madeline kicked her feet in a high chair facing them and nearby Jeannie busied herself with turning out pancakes and sausages. Every now and then, she threw a pancake in the air, and this made Madeline laugh and giggle. The crescent-shaped counter kept the baby safe from splatters.

Emma wondered if the honeysuckle odor might be overpowered by the delicious aroma of breakfast, made so much more aromatic since she had not eaten before she left.

Two huge bay windows on either side of a large area where a table and chairs might fit framed a lovely garden adjacent to a large in-ground pool. She thought of Abigail's property and compared how this house's yard appeared smaller, without the tennis courts or the other extras. She found her grandmother's house also better adorned, at least more suited to her taste.

Since she came to observe the people, she switched her focus to their actions. She read their thoughts and as she did, found nothing amiss with Bill's mind. Nothing but musings of gratitude for his children and the life partner he loved dearly.

At the moment, no wizard occupied Bill's brain. She would need to visit him throughout the day to check on him in different situations.

Next, Emma visited Tim O'Rourke's apartment near Hank's old place on Prospect Street. She arrived in time to catch a naked woman walking out of bed, and Emma changed rooms. In the washroom, Tim stood at the sink shaving.

"Thanks for coming, Maureen. Appreciate it."

"What if your holier-than-thou partner found out you spend the occasional evening with a hooker? We might both be out of a job."

"You ask this question every time you come here. I told you, my partner ain't ever going to find out. Even if he did, Bill wouldn't care—not the way you think."

Emma tried not to listen to the personal banter, but could not discount the conversation. She needed to report this to Hank. She did not smell any honeysuckle aroma and found no wizards in the area.

Tim rinsed his hand-held razor and turned toward her. "Until they assign me to a post less threatening, I'm not going to entertain a serious relationship with a lady." He smiled. "I told you this a couple of times."

"Yeah, well don't hold your breath. Liaison to a European office in Ireland doesn't come along every day."

He moved up to her and patted her behind, sliding the robe she'd donned off her shoulders. He cupped both her breasts.

"Didn't you once tell me you came from Irish ancestors?" He smiled as he pinned her arms behind her back and prepared to kiss her.

Emma left and headed for Paul Larson's residence on a narrow street in Jersey City, the one who threw Bill Frost a dirty look when ousted from their meeting. She hated what she did and hoped this might lead somewhere.

The man stood in front of his window, chain smoking from the looks of the smoky haze filling the small, unkempt studio apartment. He wore a camisole, baggy pants and had slipped his gun holster around his torso. The gun was on the table next to him.

No wonder Paul seemed to enjoy the view from the window. The small unwashed aperture rendered spectacular views of the Manhattan harbor and the Statue of Liberty, and Paul appeared to care more about the sight outside than he did about his digs. No honeysuckle aroma here, only the vile odor of mildew as she considered mold might be growing in places, but no wizard in sight.

She got out of the place as fast as she could and went back to Bill's house. When she got on the premises, the little girls were hopping a bus parked in their circular drive while Jeannie waved them off, the baby sitting on her hip. "Take care of your sister, Brittany."

Jeannie waved and went back toward the house. Emma followed her inside. She did a quick survey of the grounds and could not find Bill anywhere. Emma made a point to catch him at the office.

About to leave she spotted Jeannie sitting on the floor in one of the unfurnished rooms having a good cry. The baby sat on the ground playing with blocks, staring up at her mother with a little pout and a trembling bottom lip. Emma thought Madeline might cry also seeing her mommy so sad.

This complete change of attitude threw Emma for a loop, and she found herself wishing she possessed more knowledge about psychology. Why did a lovely person like Jeannie, who seemed so happy earlier on, manifest such sorrow? Blond, slim like an elf, possessing delicate features and a small bone structure, she appeared to be a child herself. Thoughts about the woman's family floated in and out of the space between them, and how much Jeannie seemed them and her old home.

The loneliness palpable in the other woman had Emma want to blow her cover allowing Jeannie to see her standing in the room. She wanted to help her and the child. By now, Madeline whaled and appeared inconsolable. Jeannie blew her nose and wiped her eyes and picked up the little tike. She cooed to her wearing a bright smile until Madeline's tears were nothing but breathless hiccups, and the baby smiled as she pulled her mother's hair.

Emma left. That was close, she thought. A few seconds more and Emma would have exposed herself. She needed to leave her emotions at home. This assignment was tough and a sign of things to come if she didn't choose a befitting career. She needed to develop backbone on these missions and not be so wimpy, or she would end up unproductive and useless.

She went back home to recoup, eat breakfast and check up on her mother. Eloise had gone, stopping by the hospital on her way to work.

Abigail, concerned about Emma's health peppered her with questions while standing outside her room.

Emma opened her door to reassure her grandmother. "I'm

resting, Grandma. I don't feel up to going to school. Plus, I have two exams tomorrow so I'm in my room studying."

"With all that's happened, I can understand you needing time off to study. I'll make you a nice lunch, and you let me know when you want me to bring the food upstairs." Abigail smiled at her, passing a hand through Emma's hair.

"Thanks, Grandma."

At a time like this, Emma appreciated her grandmother's attention. With both her mother and father working such long hours, she'd missed the incredible sensation of being taken care of by someone else. One less preoccupation, Emma thought.

—21—

HANK HAS DOUBTS

After Hank's call on her cell, Emma met him in Branch Brook Park by the water underneath the Cherry blossoms. Emma gave him a detailed picture of everything she had encountered along with her thoughts on each person.

Hank seemed most upset with Jeannie's tears, and this surprised Emma. "What about Paul Larson?" Emma said. "He must make a good salary. Why does he live in a rundown studio?"

"He's been through a divorce. The ex-wife sucked him bone dry." He threw a rock in the water. "Some of us chipped in to help him out with furnishings."

"Wow. I wonder if Paul's ex-wife knows how bad he is set up."

"A woman scorned." Hank made the face of someone scared to death. "What do you suppose is wrong with Jeannie?"

"Nothing Bill did, I'm sure." She eyed Hank who gave her his doubtful expression of eyebrows raised high. "His mind focused on how much he loves his children and his wife. He is a proud and happy man. Might be her time of the month." Emma thought back to the heavy sobs, almost the sort of desperation occurring when someone is cornered with no way out. She thought of the fleeting images of loneliness she sensed in Jenny with regards to her family, and raised her shoulders at Hank.

"I want you to stay with her." Hank stopped when unable to draw Emma's attention. "Emma, don't worry about your dad. I realize the medical profession can't do anything for him, but at least specialists monitor his vital signs and take good care of him."

"Thank you, Hank. I'm surprised how my father's predicament darkens my life. I'm struggling to study and to go to class. I can't bear to watch my mother suffer and wait."

"Hang in there, kiddo. Wizards will realize they can't use your dad and let him go."

"He's not held by wizards anymore. He needs to find his way back to us." Emma realized Hank didn't understand, and so she changed the subject. "You want me to give Jeannie priority? I'm writing exams all next week so I need to study, after which I might be able to use parts of Saturday and Sunday before I need to be back in school." Emma gave him the sheepish eyes.

"Do what you can, kiddo. I'm meeting with Barbara later at a restaurant in Manhattan to discuss the information she received on Kirk Assany."

"I've got to go Hank."

"How are you getting home?"

"Same way I got here." She stretched her smile and widened her eyes.

"Aren't you worried someone will see you?"

"Safer than being spotted with Chief of Police, Hank Apple. Since taking the bus takes too much time, and you can't drive me home." She gave him a shrug.

"Where are you going to disappear without being seen?"

"In the little tree grove down the hill. Bye." She waved as she left.

As Hank took giant steps down the meandering paths toward his car, he shook his head as though to rid himself of water in his ears. Emma never ceased to surprise him. He might never become accustomed to her antics. Even after five years, more so in the last year, he didn't understand how all her powers worked.

Spotting his car, Hank found Bill Frost on his phone pacing alongside his police cruiser and seemingly waiting for someone. His first impulse to hide followed by the worry Bill encountered him with Emma forced Hank into the need to confront him.

He walked up the slope to the sidewalk and waited to be spotted fighting not to hold his breath. He smiled the minute Bill waved at him tucking his phone away.

"The man of the hour. Apple, we need to talk."

Hank remembered Emma's details about Bill, and although wizards might not be in the picture, this didn't assure him Bill did not maintain a little crooked business on the side for himself. What Emma mentioned about his big house with the empty rooms, and his wife crying her eyes out when Jeannie thought herself alone in the house, set off a little alarm in his head.

"Sounds ominous." Hank glanced at the time. "I have a meeting in twenty minutes or so."

"Who with?"

Hank gave him the none-of-your-business slant of the head. "What's this about?"

"I have been meaning to talk to you for days now, ever since Joe's murder. This was why I postponed today's meeting." Bill smiled. "An informant in the Park, don't kid yourself, Hank. I knew about him. A slew of people did, I am sure."

"Why did you ask?"

"Testing a theory." He gave Hank a head nod. "Walk with me."

Curious to see where the conversation might lead, he followed Bill down the path.

"I remembered an obscure little article I read five years ago when all the trouble came down with the perp and the kids— well not so obscure. This article mentioned Patrick Willis and his well-deserved accolades."

Hank stopped in his tracks and ignored the heat spreading under his collar as he stared hard at Bill Frost.

"You are familiar with the article, I'm sure. How an insurance salesman helped police solve the case. Now, this Patrick Willis is in a coma, University Hospital. Someone is hitting below the belt."

Hank worked hard not to let Bill catch the shock his words brought nor the slight trembling so he shoved his hands into his pant pockets. "Heart attack. Nothing to do with this case." Hank caught his breath and added, "What are you up to?"

"Hey, I'm not the enemy. I'm here to warn you." Bill sat down on the first bench he spotted. "That was the main reason why I cleared our meeting. Of course, I'm not talking about anyone of inferior rank, but there might be people reporting to others in more senior positions, people I can no longer trust."

Hank hesitated but sat down beside him. Strange how Bill Frost had come to the same conclusion as he and Barbara, then again why not? The man was smart, and while he cataloged twenty-five years of field work with the FBI, he possessed a well-honed sense of people which at least equaled his own. "So, you suspect someone. Who?"

Bill's turn to give him the brush off expression. "Too soon to say." A few seconds passed when Bill added, "When did you first meet Barbara Leclerc?"

The left-field question caught Hank by surprise. He nearly burst out laughing, especially since he and Barbara both suspected Bill Frost. "A few years after I started with the Department. She is a dedicated police officer with a law degree from Harvard." Hank added with a smile he couldn't hide.

"Curiosity—not discounting anyone. And Barbara lied when she said she brought IA up to date with her findings. Watson never heard of this."

"Perhaps she worried about revealing the name of our informant, and perhaps like you, she's not sure about who the players are, at least not enough to bring IA into this mess." So, Bill had checked with Andrew Watson. Would be interesting to compare Barbara's notes about all this. "You don't have to say who, I understand. But, what makes you suspect foul play within our ranks?"

"What I did not reveal at the meeting, Apple. Guillaume Balay had finished negotiating a truce with the gang in question. MI6 agreed to stand down as all weapons exchange with the LRA ceased."

Hank's face flew forward as he extended both arms in a show of shock. "Why didn't you brief us?"

"For the same reason, Barbara lied about speaking to Andrew Watson. Mistrust is setting us back, not the terrorists who killed the people in question."

"So they were terrorists."

"No. MI6. When top brass interrogated the agents concerned,

those same officers became unable to concur on where the orders came from. One man told us he thought the orders came from their immediate superior. When Secret Service attempted to contact Charles Laslow, the head of the operation, they found him hanging from the rafters in his loft."

"Suicide?"

"Murder. Guillaume says this goes all the way up to a higher political agenda."

"What do you mean?"

"Quite impossible to smuggle arms these days. All the popular routes are now uncovered. Besides, impoverished countries are now making their own."

"Poor countries don't own the money to make weapons." Hank wanted to understand Bill's scheme.

"Ever learn of kleptocracy?"

"Yeah. So?"

"Foreign, dictatorial governments stealing money from their constituents. Some of them stash the money away should their reign ever topple, others use the funds to create chaos, from arms fashioning to trafficking in all types of illegal trade, including women and body parts." He took a deep breath. "Thus, the middle class is disappearing. So, we are left with fewer well-to-dos versus an abundance of poor, healthy people the rich can take their due from to prolong their life. Wheeling and dealing in organs is expanding, made easier than any other trade and much more lucrative."

"This would explain the increase in the trade."

"Worse than that, Apple. People needing these organs show no morals, no sentiment for anyone other than those in their immediate employ or surrounding family. If you read the anti-corruption, Germany-based Transparency Report released in 2004, you'll remember talk of the hundreds of billions stolen and stashed by top presidents, in the Philippines, Indonesia, Countries in Africa and the alleged biggest thieves of them all, Russian dictators labeled with over two hundred billion stolen from the people."

"Some of the crooked leaders have more money than our own United States' Government. I am aware of that. So, where are you going with this?"

"Well, when you take this information into account, after which we find someone in a high position like Charles Laslow murdered, we kind of wonder how far up the sewer the trafficking of body parts reaches?"

Hank didn't say anything but nodded as he considered Andrew Watson too low down the ladder to participate and the same true for Bill Frost, unless this intelligent discussion happened to be part of his ploy. "I'm guessing since you are sharing this Intel with me, I'm not a suspect on your list."

Bill smiled. "You guessed right. I studied your file and your accomplishments, Apple. You would be the last person on the totem pole I'd want to bring down. Others, however, never paid their dues in the traditional sense of the word. They relied on their contacts to advance and acquire status. These people, I mistrust." His smile deepened. "I need your Intel, Hank—all your Intel. A sneaky suspicion tells me you're keeping most of what you know under wrap."

This was when Hank worried Bill might have spotted him with Emma. "How did you know I might be in the Park?"

"I recognized your car. Besides, I do the same thing when I

don't want anyone to listen in. Park is the best place to hold a meeting." He searched their area. "You still didn't tell me who you're meeting."

Hank relaxed judging Emma's secret to be safe. "I come here now and again to soothe my troubled soul." He extended his arm. "Walking under the trees while breathing fresh air helps me think."

Bill rose as he prepared to leave. "Don't breathe too hard. Air's not that fresh." A head nod and he left.

Hank got into his car and kept an eye on Bill in his rearview mirror, walking in the opposite direction. His last comment made his breakfast come up in little sour mouthfuls. 'Others, however, never paid their dues in the traditional sense of the word. They relied on their contacts to advance and acquire status. These people, I mistrust.'

Hank thought of Bill's question about Barbara Leclerc and realized Bill considered her to be a traitor. Barbara, a smart and intelligent woman, had made it to the top through the many contacts she acquired and the unusual methods she used to get the job done, like promoting Andrew Watson instead of denouncing him for what he tried to do to Matt Logan.

Still, he couldn't believe Barbara might be the enemy. She knew too much about Emma, and Hank enjoyed working with her.

As he approached the café Barbara picked out for their meeting, he slipped his index between his tie and his Adam's apple for the third time to pull on the damn noose. Either his shirt collar had shrunk, which happened to be the stupidest thing he ever considered, or his neck was swelling. Nerves, fear, ignorance, all contributed to making him feel inadequate and clumsy.

Hank reached Le Bernardin in midtown Manhattan in record time. He appreciated Barbara's invitation, aware of how pricey food and excellent wine fixtures were at the posh establishment. He planned to bring Christina here one day since he received nothing but raves about the place.

Following the seating hostess, he gave Barbara a little nod as soon as he rounded their table. He caught her eyeing the clock on the wall and he shrugged to apologize. "Bill Frost held me up just as I planned to leave."

"Bill Frost? What did he want?" A waiter came with drinks to the table. "I took the liberty of ordering lunch for both of us: surf and turf, so you can pick whatever you like."

Once the waiter took their drink orders, Hank stated. "Bill suspects the same thing we do. Someone on the inside is stacking the deck, and he seems to think this person is someone high up the chain of command."

"He said as much?" Barbara frowned and appeared flustered, something Hank considered a rare occurrence for Barbara.

"He did. Also, knows you lied about going to Andrew Watson."

"Andrew never mentioned this, which means they might be working together. What else did he say?" Barbara took a sip of her water, and Hank noticed her hand shook somewhat—the iron maiden of their precinct, the unflappable poker player renowned for her game.

He hesitated unsure of whether to give her all the information he received from French Interpol. "He stated he trusted me but had begun to suspect other people. He wouldn't say who."

"Typical. Trying to shift the blame onto others. The fact Bill came to you might mean he does suspect you and is trying to lull you into a false sense of security." She paused to accept the dish from the server and waited until he left. "Please take all you need. My appetite is small," she said while digging into the ribs.

Hank reached for shrimps and a small platter of diced, tenderloin tartare to dip in a sauce made of anchovies, capers, and Dijon mustard. "Rich fare for lunch. Hope Christina is not making anything fancy tonight."

"Lunch is my biggest meal. I like to skip dinner—too tired by then." Barbara wiped her hands on her napkin and reached for her bag. "I hope you didn't tell him anything."

"He didn't tell me anything worthwhile why would I confide in him?" Hank realized he was lying to the woman he worked with, and he would likely regret this later. For now, he didn't understand the shift in his plans. He didn't say a word about what Bill mentioned. "I can't reveal the information I received. He would want to know where I got the Intel."

"I understand. Happens to be the first question the agents I sent down to North Carolina and Florida asked me."

"What did you tell them?"

"I said Cyril, and I deemed the matter classified—for now."

"So, what's the info on Kirk Assany?"

She pulled a tablet from her bag, keyed in her password and searched for the folder she needed. "I took some notes while Agent Smythe was talking. We're not emailing on this or, needless to say, texting. We talk on a secure line."

Hank wiped his mouth after taking a sip of his ice tea, his curiosity aroused. "So?"

"Too many facts, searching through to see what is relevant." She smiled and stopped flicking. "Here are amazing stats. The number of people in the United States on the waiting list for an organ donor has tripled over the last ten years." She nodded at Hank's surprised expression. "More than eighty-two thousand individuals are waiting for a vital organ transplant."

"In the United States alone?"

"Yes. In fact, twenty people a day die from lack of a replacement organ."

"How did we get here?"

"Well, don't kid yourself. This is not merely population getting older. You should check out the age of some of the people on the waiting list. Has to do with the food we ingest the polluted air we breathe. Some say GMOs contribute quite a bit to kidney and liver failure, and while all of this brouhaha is ideal for doctors and big Pharma, the policy of, take-whatever-organ-you-can, is now the new designer crime."

"GMOs? Ruining our organs, a fact?"

"By design, genetically modified seeds require pesticides and herbicides to survive. Pesticides interfere with our digestive tract and are known to be carcinogenic."

"Crazy," Hank whispered. "This can only get worse." Hank pushed the plate of food away and stuck to his ice tea. "Where does Assany fit into all of this?"

"Two words: *presumed consent*." She smiled at Hanks expression. "There are a lot of details. The short version is in regards to organ donors. The United States operates under a system of *expressed volunteerism*, with consent received from donors and their families to donate their organs. Other countries such as Spain, Belgium and Austria use what we refer to as an *opt-out* policy to their *presumed consent*."

"What?"

"Means, if you live in those countries and have not registered your name on a National Registry opposed to giving your organs, opt-out solution, once you die you become an eligible organ donor through their policy of presumed consent."

Barbara took a sip of her water and waited for Hank to express something. Only Hank toyed with his fork unable to say a word. Once more, the old bugaboo of who decided on which life counted more versus which life needed to be sacrificed came to stare at him with its one evil, protruding eye. Who made those decisions and what did this mean for all of them?

"You're quiet, Hank?"

"Someone out there decides who lives and who dies."

"I hear you. In fact, in a way we do this as police officers. Ignore one to protect the other." Barbara signaled for the bill. "In Belgium, in 1982, the transplant center of Leuven decided to adopt the solution of *presumed consent*, and by 1990 they had quadrupled their number of donors."

"You mean if someone's name did not figure on the opt-out Register?"

"Yes. The same year, the number of patients awaiting kidneys equaled the number of transplants. Meanwhile, in this country, the number of donors remains stagnant. In fact, these three countries not only demonstrated they saved a lot of lives, but Spain estimates the ten thousand renal transplants they performed saved them hundreds of millions of dollars."

"Yes, when you exact the cost of dialysis. Where does Senator Kirk Assany fit into this? And why don't we lobby for this policy change?"

"Some people did, and still are. Senators from California and elsewhere tried to drum up support to get the bill passed."

"Let me guess, Assany is campaigning against *presumed consent.*"

"Absolutely. The senator states *presumed consent* is a violation of our privacy laws, a government trick to steal the organs right out from under us. Assany campaigned against it, launched rallies, flaunted his political clout to obtain people's votes, even voiced something close to threats I'm told."

"If Government gave people a choice to list their names on a National Registry to oppose giving their organs, if one of theirs showed up in the lineup, this would create a red flag."

"Assany doesn't care about the opt-out Registry. His real beef is more about the threat of *presumed consent*—since few people will ever take the time to put their name on a National Registry to oppose giving their organs."

"Not sure I follow."

Barbara hesitated. "Psychologists have found that although people scoff at giving away their body parts to someone else while they are alive and well, they leave the question open many of them thinking that when the time comes, and they are dead or on the verge of dying, the hot topic will vanish or resolve itself. In fact, in death, they might like to help someone else to live—their last good deed so to speak."

"Ah, dead, they don't care about the outcome. Makes sense. So, the undecided are really a resounding vote of yes allowing the promise of *presumed consent* to work for those in dire need of a transplant, at the same time creating an impasse for thieves who stand to gain from illegal trade."

"A huge roadblock, needless to say." Barbara took a sip of her coffee. "Still, be mindful of the word thieves. Amongst those so-called thieves are doctors, politicians, elitists and la crème de la crème of our society."

"You don't approve of these hooligans, do you?" Hank's legs weakened at the thought of Barbara's nonchalance. Her arguments went one way when her tone indicated another.

She gave him a dubious, expression. "Not up to me to judge. Just saying. I sense confusion in both camps."

Hank gulped the rest of his coffee, more to hide the horror in his eyes. Could he be misreading Barbara's interpretation of the situation? Of course. She was the mother incarnate, her big heart brimming with compassion. No way would she side with the enemy. He got up and dropped some money on the table. "When do you want me to leave for Miami?"

She glanced up at him smiling her big brown eyes little slits. "No precise date yet. Don't worry. I'll give you enough time to prepare."

He bobbed his head and left. *Yes. Always the mother*.

—22—

EMMA AT THE HOSPITAL

Emma walked the length of her little room back and forth until she realized she needed to stop pacing. She removed the plugs out of her ears and listened. All seemed quiet on the home front. Her grandmother had emptied all she thought was wrong with her mother in her mom's face, punctured by Eloise's little sobs and jerky explanations.

To calm herself, Emma sat down on Granny Dottie's little bench and stared out the window, at the summer breeze moving the leaves in the elm tree. Not yet summer, the warm weather nevertheless gave an exciting glimpse of her favorite season rounding the corner.

Conflict upset Emma even as a child. She didn't understand why people didn't get along. When Emma got older, she began to revere her mother as a blissful guru—happy to avoid conflict and remain stoic through any mess. Emma remembered how her mother recovered first from the great shock of her husband lying in a coma, and she played the big sister to Franka when learning of Jimmy's violent episode toward his wife and child.

In fact, Emma believed her mother's stoicism had given her father the drive and encouragement he needed to make something of himself. Yet, with continued, humble dignity, Eloise worked hard without ever taking a bow of any kind.

No wonder she disliked her Grandma Abigail's rants about her mother's ineffectual behavior or mitigated results. How a spitfire like Abigail Tichy might not be aware of the beautiful daughter she'd borne surpassed Emma's imagination. The idea hit Emma how much like her mother she aspired to be—a gentle, kind person who got things done without the need to assert herself as lord and master over everyone.

She rose, closed her books thinking she'd studied enough for tomorrow's exams, as ready as she wanted to be. Then Hank's request glared one spooky eye at her, menacing and disturbing. Spy on Jeannie Frost and report back to Hank. She disliked prying into other people's lives, yet she promised him she would. He counted on her feedback to navigate through the maze of uncertainties he dealt with daily.

She didn't want to leave her mother alone again tonight. She wanted to go to the hospital with her to visit her dad. Emma realized she was the one constant in her mother's life right now, the presence she most needed around her. And although she loved Grandma Abigail, she wished she might go back home to allow mother and daughter to fend for themselves.

Well, she would never be able to tell her to leave, not in a thousand years. Her mother would not either. The only presence able to stand up to Abigail was her dad. She sat on her bed and brushed away the tears soaking her courage to mush. How would she ever be able to bring her father back home? First, she needed to find him.

Her grandma called to her from downstairs. Emma opened her door and stood in the hallway. "I'm not hungry, Grandma. I'm going to the hospital with Mom."

"You can't be serious. Nothing at the hospital for you, child."

A slight pause before she caught Abigail say, "Eloise, talk some sense into your daughter."

Her mother poked her head at her with a smile and eyes all cried out. "I appreciate this honey, but only if you feel you've studied enough," she said with a smile.

"I did, Mom. I want to see Dad."

"Well, that's it," Abigail muttered. "I'm going home."

"Mother," Eloise attempted.

"You gals are fine on your own. Besides, my accountant is expecting me early in the morning. And Jimmy and Franka are going away for a few days, so I am taking care of Martha for the weekend."

Franka never left Martha with her mother for more than a couple of hours.

"And you're okay with this, Mom?" Eloise asked in a small voice.

"Of course. Franka knows she can't impose on you at a time like this."

Emma pondered taking care of little Martha would be ideal for her mother's recovery, take her mind off her husband lying near death in a hospital bed.

Abigail continued. "Oh, she wanted to ask you, but I forbade her. You're not in any disposition to take care of a child."

Her mother ignored the war of words and turned toward her. "I'd like to leave in thirty minutes, Emma. Is this alright with you?"

"I'll be ready, Mom."

By the time Emma and her mother left for the hospital, they caught Abigail boarding a taxi. She was headed for Englewood Cliffs.

Mother and daughter shared a small meal at the hospital cafeteria. Afterward, in silence, they rode the elevator to Patrick Willis' room. Through the hospital window, the setting sun left a trail of hope while pointing out rays of dust scattered over the place. An earthly anointment, Emma thought—a reminder of where life runs to at the end of the cycle, and from where life once sprung.

Her mother read her father a passage from the Bourne Legacy, Robert Ludlum being her dad's favorite author. Calmly and with a soft lilt to her voice, Eloise read on, puncturing the action now and again with her own dramatization.

The hypnotic, soothing sound almost made Emma forget the noisy rush fibrillating outside the room and along the corridors, up and down without ever a sign of ceasefire. Where was her father? What vile trap held him against his will? Since the wizards did not lay claim to his captivity, the prison might be of his making, a trick his lost mind played against him. Yet, even the many times she attempted to read him, she found nothing. No thoughts of any kind.

A stab of light from the sun playing a game of pic-a-boo in the trees caught her attention. She rose and followed the glare to the window. Her mother's drone faded in the background as the pink colored sky taunted her with its beauty, as though someone from the astral world summoned her. She turned to gaze at her dad's sleeping features and wondered if the call might come from him.

She cast her eyes beyond the clouds where the sun created a

splash of colors. She should be out there, combing the horizon to find him, not resting until she brought him back.

She paced with restlessness unable to tell her mother she needed to leave.

Yet, Eloise spotted Emma's nervousness. "Emma, is there something you forgot to do?"

"No, Mom. I just hate to see Dad like this."

"Go home, Emma. Grandma's gone. You'll have the whole place to yourself. You can study."

"Will you be all right?"

Eloise smiled and continued reading.

Not surprised her mom didn't ask her how she'd get home, Emma nodded admiring her mother's sparse use of words—Eloise never one for stating banalities. In fact, as a youngster, Emma thought husband overshadowed wife or perhaps her mother didn't harbor the right ideas to put forth. Turned out Eloise's brain not only came up with all sorts of ripe ideas, her success at the flower shop a small example, her need to brag about them did not exist. "Love you, Mom," she whispered as she kissed the top of her head.

***

The last sliver of sun gone, and alone in his office with lights off, Hank brewed what Christina called a murky soup of burned beans. The street light cast an eerie white glow filtering through his open blind. His back to the door, he stared at the gray and white nebulae streaking the sky as he rocked the back of his chair.

A knock on the door made him jump. He turned and stretched

to light the lamp on his desk. "Come in."

Hank fought to wipe concern off his face, but couldn't greet Matt Logan with anything else than a grunt and a nod. He indicated for Matt to close the door behind him. Hank thought, Matt's attitude seemed poised and relaxed.

"What's the big mystery—don't tell anyone you're coming here, don't even tell your partner." Matt chuckled.

"Did you? Tell anyone?"

"No. Of course not. Maria thinks I'm on a stakeout."

Hank waved his hand toward a chair in front of his desk. "We need to talk." Without waiting for Matt to get settled, he asked, "How well are you acquainted with Barbara Leclerc?"

Matt shrugged as he sprawled his long legs in front of him. "Not at all, I'm afraid."

Hank leaned toward him. "Isn't she a friend of your mother's?"

"They went to Harvard together. That's all I know."

"Is Barbara the reason you became a police officer?"

"Hank," Matt scolded. "Of all people! You've heard me say this a thousand times."

"Yes," Hank added to himself. "You wanted to be a detective since you were ten years old. Stayed out of trouble, refused to go joyriding with your cousins. How did this slip my mind?" Hank got up and started walking in front of his desk. "You never confided in Barbara about Manson or anything else did you?"

"Of course not, why would I?"

Hank dropped his face into his hands and swore under his breath. Hank proceeded to let Matt in on Barbara's musings.

"Well, I'd never screw your balls to the wall by telling someone how much I hate your guts." Matt smiled, and Hank realized he relished the situation. "You asshole," Matt added.

"Well, it's clear and evident how a lack of respect for your superiors brings you grief." Hank gave him the evil eye.

"Don't shit on me, man. What the hell is this about? So, Barbara lied to cover her tracks. This doesn't mean she's up to no good. In fact, did she ever say what I supposedly told her about Manson?"

Hank covered his face with his hands. He took a few minutes to juggle with his thoughts. His head bobbing side to side, he used a handkerchief to wipe his brow and stared at Matt. "She didn't. Never said a word."

"Which means she knows squat about Manson. A fishing expedition.

"Yeah. I kept asking Barbara to tell me what you confided. Why she laid the story on so thick, to get me to give her the information."

"Did you?"

"No." Hank rose and walked around his desk to hand Matt the business card Barbara supplied while they walked in the park. "This is for a company to sweep my office for bugs." Hank took his coffee mug and sat on the sofa across from Matt.

"Why?"

"Barb gave it to me. She asked me not to go through IA."

"What the f? what's wrong with Andrew Watson?"

Hank explained Barbara's comments, her suspicions, and the story she weaved around Matt concerning Andrew.

Matt turned his chair around. "You're starting to scare me, man. Glad I know you, or I'd call you a damn liar to your face." He flicked the card and threw it back to Hank. "Isn't this one of the jerks we arrested for fraud five – six years ago?"

"Yep. They are the same fraudulent organization. Checked them out yesterday. Creep has not changed his line of work."

"Wouldn't Barbara be aware of the arrests we made back then?"

"Why would she? She didn't work with us. She headed SARA division. The Sexual Assault and Rape Analysis unit."

"Still, why would she lie about me? She knows you and I are friends. You can check on what she says anytime you want."

"She told me this in confidence, information handed through the course of an investigation is on a need-to-know basis and we usually don't share. Under normal circumstances, I would not have discussed this with you."

"You're right. Same as I wouldn't talk with Barbara about what goes on during mine and Brian's investigation." Matt leaned in, his arms resting on his thighs. "Why are you checking up on this? I mean, what triggered these suspicions about Barbara of all people?"

Hank told him how he and Barbara had come to suspect Bill Frost in the murder of Joe, their informant from the park.

"I don't trust Bill Frost, buddy. She might be right. You both may be right about him."

"Emma disagrees. She went snooping on Bill and his family, on Parson and Tim O'Rourke."

"And?"

"She says they're clean."

"Eliminating Bill as a suspect doesn't automatically make one of Barbara Leclerc." Matt shrugged.

Hank briefed him about his group's last meeting and about the admission Bill gave him in Branch Brook Park, about Interpol's findings. "Bill asked me in quite a unique tone about Barbara Leclerc and how well I knew her. He seems to think the treason stems from high in our ranks."

"Holy shit this is complicated." Matt rose and walked from his chair to the window, from the window to his chair. Brushing his bald head with his hand, Matt added. "If Joe was killed by one of ours, I doubt whoever killed him did this merely to lay the blame at Bill's feet. Joe might have been aware of main ground information."

"I never considered this. You may be right, but we'll never find out, will we?"

"Talk to the people he hung with."

"Joe lived in solitude."

Matt sat down. "What are you going to do about the two names Manson gave you?"

"I told you about them?" Hank couldn't remember mentioning them to Matt.

"Yeah, and about the worm circling the apple." He chuckled.

Hank recounted Barbara's initiative of contacting Cyril Platt to supply agents to investigate those names.

Matt chuckled and stared at Hank in the eye. "I believe Emma's peeping on the wrong peeps."

"You mean she should visit Platt and Leclerc?"

"Dah." Matt gave Hank a sideways glance loaded with meaning. Then he wrapped his hands around his head. "God! I swear, if Barbara Leclerc so much as touches one hair on Emma's head, I'll kill her and make her death seem like wild dogs did it," he mumbled.

"I hadn't even gone there. Help me God, if Barbara holds the threat of Emma over our heads."

Matt punched his left hand with his right fist. "She'll never see this coming."

"Can't believe she would do that."

"Let's not wait around to find out," Matt whispered between clenched teeth. "This is not going to be a 'Joe' situation. This little girl has been through enough—helping others while sacrificing her wants, her life. She always needs to fret about everything and everyone. No one's going to mess with her, not while I'm around." Matt got up and walked toward the door. "Hope you used someone to comb your office for listening devices?"

Hank nodded. "Someone I trust." Hank looked up at him and caught the worry in Matt's eyes.

"By the way, if you still need my help on this case, I'm available. Rob's back, and he can work with Brian for a while."

Hank rose. "Thanks, Matt. I appreciate this."

"Doing it for Emma," he tossed before he walked out the door

—23—

THE TRIAL

*E*mma stood in the hospital washroom as she couldn't wait to comb the heavens for her dad. Confident, he called out to her, his unanswered pleas tore the heart out of her. She hesitated. Columba warned her not to seek answers in the astral world in corporeal form—flying through the haze of afterlife with her body merely used for traveling from one port to another. Emma realized the dangers far outweighed the results, and gave the adage of curiosity killing that cat definite meaning.

Yet, she was not going to the astral world to satisfy her curiosity. She headed into space to help her father, and the sounds of those pleas, real or imagined, became louder.

Shoving her wallet in her jacket pocket, she closed her eyes and left the rational and safe walls of the physical world for an unknown realm where ordinary laws did not apply, where alone, she would be unable to seek support from anyone.

The antiseptic background of the gray bathroom paled, and as clouds to the other world parted, she caught the sound of voices in the background tied to a series of unrelated events. She witnessed her mother lamenting and screaming out her name. Hank asked her to investigate two new people, Tommy, down on his knees on the school's tarmac crying, appearing inconsolable, her aunt Franka screaming, "No, no. I refuse to accept this." All these comments echoed from different areas confusing her with their imprecision of time and place.

When the haze cleared, she found herself facing a huge room with walls made from an unfathomable substance, without a roof like a coliseum, with rows upon rows of seats arranged theater style. A force continued to pull her down below, further inside the room where a small group of people had gathered.

She sensed the place full to capacity although Emma was unable to decipher any of the faces or even the shapes of individuals assembled. She spotted one face she recognized amidst the invisible crowd gathered in the floor area, and gazing upon his face made her quake in her shoes.

Emma wondered which portal she'd skirted to land under such blurred horizons. The area foretold of trouble bounding her to the spot, and she sensed no invoking of home would set her on the right path.

A hum invaded her ears, her head—not the usual sound of a crowd talking in loud voices amongst themselves. More like thoughts invading her mind, and she covered her ears to create a little silence, but to no avail.

Strange how no one seemed to be present, although the arena shone as bright as day with giant flames and soft lights. Emma figured these graceful dancing flickers might represent the formidable presence from where these thoughts originated.

She found herself seated in the front row, and didn't relish being so close to the little group standing a few feet away, bathed in a stream of light. An animal caught in a trap seemed to be the picture her mind conjured, and she wondered if she might need to chew off one of her limbs to escape.

Only one face was visible in the group standing on the floor in front of her: Fred Manson. He seemed to be the only one in corporeal form. All others were bright pulsing glows which explained why she couldn't visualize their presence. The intensity of light in this cloud scattered brilliance that seemed to rival Earth's sun. This warned her many were present and the menace insurmountable. She remembered Fred's threats saying she should not be aware of what they did. She also recalled Hawke's words cautioning her to stay clear of Devronairs. Too late now. Cornered, with nowhere to go.

The noise bombarding her head ceased when Manson stood and spoke reading from a scroll in his hand. His lips did not move, and the sound of his voice remained silent. She attempted to read his mind through the encryption barring her way to catch all the information she needed.

"We are at this moment unanimous in our decision for Emma Willis, trapped in Earth Refuse, to be sent to Earth optimal where we deem she belongs and will be able to live out a life she can enjoy."

Emma's brain spewed enough venom for Manson to stop and give her the evil eye.

Well, the expression seemed evil to her, perhaps more annoyed than outright mean, yet he did not stop reading because of her intervention. Someone in the crowd prompted him to do so, the brightest light glowing. The good thing about thought communication: everyone listened in and understood no matter how far removed they might be.

Emma used this lull in Manson's reading to spread a little

propaganda of her own. "How dare you pass judgment on my life deciding what is best for me without first consulting me?" She formed sentences and ideas she wished to convey with clarity and purpose, and she realized everyone listened with intent from the silence dropping on the area like a wet fog. Plus, Manson waited for an explanation from whoever had asked him to stop, his emaciated features contorted into an arrogant expression.

"You call humans from Earth Refuse barbarians," Emma repeated what she'd picked from his thoughts. "Yet, as uncivilized as they are, they would never conclude judgment on anyone without first giving them the means to a defense or at least the right to a valid statement explaining their purpose and the reason behind such a purpose. Are Devronairs hypocrites?"

Many clamors assailed her mind, yet she managed to continue. "If I belong in Earth Optimal, am I not your equal? Or do you consider yourselves to be far superior to all of us? Our Earths are destined to form a universe of peace and love reuniting layers of multi-universes including Devronairs."

The clamor stopped and out of somewhere danced toward her the likes of an intense flame, the same who'd ordered Manson to stop. She sensed this flame wished she continue to speak. "I believe I chose to be born here to help the horde of souls, including Devronairs, who sacrifice their time and their lives to come down here and help. I believe this decision to be a conscious one on my part."

She stopped, wondering if the great light facing her could still understand her. She read the flame's nod and continued, "In my family, women throughout time demonstrated special powers during their stay on Earth—this Earth. I used the diary they left as well as their accomplishments to understand and provide an explanation to my own family for all these unusual feats I am able to do. Only, there is no explanation as to how or why I can perform most of the powers I own." The great silence continued. Had the tall flame not faced her, coupled with the luminous quality of the area, Emma would imagine everyone gone.

"For instance, I can detect the evil everyone calls wizards. I can see them, smell their presence, and I stopped them on several occasions."

Emma held her head applying her hand on her ears. The great clamor returned, and the sound overwhelmed her.

A huge call of, "Silence!" surprised her as the last word she caught. A deep breath later, she continued. "Of course, no mention of wizards is scribbled in the diary my ancestors left me. Therefore, I now believe my powers do not come from the talented women who preceded me. No doubt in my mind I chose to be born here, on Earth Refuse, to help and try to speed up the rescue mission. I believe you realize, as I do, this version of Earth will not make the convened deadline. This is why you have begun to separate the tortured from the torturers while eliminating those you feel you cannot salvage by sending them to Earth Optimal where you hope the kindness of this version will heal and correct their path." She waited, worried about saying too much. "However, I also realize as you do, of course, you cannot send everyone to Earth Optimal, and the versions between here and there are not robust enough to overcome the malevolence some of these souls engender. How many will perish? Do you not wish to secure more help—to save errant souls?"

Emma waited for the noisy wave of shock to subside, trying

to catch meaning amongst the many cries assailing her all at once. Manson had not mentioned this to anyone, obviously.

"The process failed twice," Manson said. "We have one last chance to succeed. This is why we are adamant about eliminating all sources of failure, any incomprehension with the risk of causing billions upon billions of planets and hundreds of universes to compromise eternal joy."

Emma smiled. "I understand, yet inside each human being lies the potential for the birth of another one hundred universes, each more blissful than the last. Isn't each and every one of these universes worth saving?"

Manson did not answer, and although Emma understood every human on Earth might not be saved, she wanted him to agree even one more on board ought to license outside help.

"If you are not from here," Manson questioned. "Where do you come from?"

"I don't know. I can't remember. Although, during times of awful stress, only in dreams mind you, I have reached another place where I can converse with trees, talk to the animals no matter how small. A place where I am endowed with great peace, and where abundance is accepted and joy is the norm, a home where the pink and purple sky embraces two suns."

Emma stopped as the tall flame came very close, close enough for her to catch its brilliance and absorb the heat emanating from the fanning glow, as though she'd been touched by a glacial hand up until this very moment. She closed her eyes and sensed her heart bursting with kindness and a great love, the sort of heartfelt sensation you never have to fight or compete with while a sublime moment of ecstasy suspended her in time, one she wished never to end.

Yet the flame left her, and she found herself more alone than she ever imagined she might be. The cold wind of isolation robbed her of the joy which had thrilled her.

Manson's face appeared before her, and she recognized the sentiment of respect he first held for her. "Of course," he bowed to her. "Now we understand who you are and what your purpose is, we will not interfere. We may call on your skills to help, gentle one if you so permit."

"Who Am I?" Emma asked. "What do you mean? Please tell me." Manson's side to side signal confirmed he would not provide an answer.

Best she not push her quest for more answers. "I will do all I can to help, Doctor Manson. Right now, I must find my father. He wrestled with the wizards, and even though they were unable to hold him, I combed the afterworld and cannot locate him anywhere. Did you take him?"

"No. We did not. Your father is trapped by his folly. You need to seek the one who seeks him. This is how both will find peace."

"Who has him?"

His eyes were kind, yet he would not say more. Emma would need to figure out the puzzle on her own.

The exchange ended. Emma sensed and read as much, and she smiled at him grateful for his help. Before she left, a glance at her surroundings told her all lights had dispersed, and they left the place empty. The blue dome returned, yet Emma remained alone with her thoughts. She closed her eyes and found herself once more in her room at home.

—24—

HINT DISTURBS EMMA

Upon her return from the meeting with the Devronairs, Emma lay on her bed realizing someone else had sent her home. Home, she thought. Manson said, "Now we understand who you are." What did this mean?

She shook her head and turned right to catch a glimpse of the little wooden box Granny Dottie carved and painted for her. The coffer usually lay in the bottom of the big treasure chest at the foot of her bed, buried underneath a whole slew of personal trinkets. She had not taken this out in months—years even.

She sat up all at once excited to discover who put the chest on her table. No one else appeared to be in her room, and she scratched her forehead wondering if she'd retrieved the box without remembering? Impossible, she pondered as she picked up the little container. She experienced daft occasions now and again forgetful about homework, or not returning someone's call, but not digging for a little souvenir.

This was the box her grandma Abigail suggested she throw away many times beginning with the day Abigail gave her the bigger sandstone jewelry box. The new box lined with red satin and topped with a strange sort of dog on top, Emma realized Abigail had likely paid a small fortune for the gift. Nevertheless, because of her grandmother's insistence she destroy the old one, she'd buried her granny Dottie's masterpiece so as not to throw it away during one of her daft moments.

She smoothed away the dust layered on the lid, and unlocked the little box with the key hidden on the bottom. Nothing had changed. The weird, misshapen key her granny found among one of her ancestor's belongings—two thin prongs extended on each side replacing the little key's bow. Dottie had engaged a locksmith to fashion the jewelry box' keyhole tumbler to match the cuts on the key. She found the book of poems Amelia gave her on her tenth birthday, old pieces of wrapped chewing gum she kept as a souvenir.

Replacing the key on the bottom of the oddly shaped groove, she put the box away. Emma remembered Manson's words. "You need to seek the one who seeks him. This is how both will find peace."

Was this the hint Manson would not give her? The gift from her Granny Dottie? Her heart beat faster as she got up and walked to the window to sit on Granny Dottie's bench. She couldn't get into her father's mind no matter how much tenacity she used. What if she located her Granny Dottie?

Her cell phone rang and startled her. She slid her finger across the screen and answered the ringtone with the tune of Crazy assigned to Hank.

"Emma. I worried about you. I stopped by the hospital, and your mother told me you went home. I've been trying to reach you for over an hour."

Emma looked at the clock on her desk. So much time had gone by. Time spent in the astral world seemed like mere seconds. "I must have fallen asleep. Where are you?"

"I'm home now. I wanted to stop by on my way from the hospital to discuss certain developments with you. Probably best I didn't. We can never tell who is watching."

"That's true. Would you like me to drop by?" Emma realized Hank got the gist of what she said.

"If you're finished studying, might be a good idea. I'll turn off the back porch light and leave the door unlocked. Can you find your way around?"

"No problem," she answered curbing a tremor in her voice. She sensed her body physically drained since her return, and couldn't quite understand why. Worse, she hadn't so much as cracked a book since returning from the hospital. Also, her mother would be home soon and worry about her.

After leaving her mother a note stating where to find her, Emma sat on the bed, called on some courage and invoked her little sentence. She would once more use the physical portal to go to Hank and Christina's back door. Quick and straightforward, Emma would be at Hank's place in the blink of an eye. Only, she never arrived at Hank and Christina's home.

Emma wasn't earthbound anymore. The dome on top of her head gleamed as dark as night, and even though Emma had teleported at night many times before, the sky's roof always shone a bright and clear blue.

Fear grabbed her as she called out for someone to acknowledge her. "Hello, who is out here?" She heard nothing but her own voice echoing back several times as though she fell into some deep chasm, the darkness evoked by high walls. Her eyes welled up with tears, and she did not understand why sadness engulfed her. Did Manson and his group change their minds and take her from Earth Refuse to go to Earth Optimal? She refused to accept this conjecture. Only a dream brought on by fatigue might elicit this type of dread—a dream Emma believed in this dark realm existed solely in the throes of a nightmare. Indeed, no passageway from one version of Earth to another would display this surfeit of terror.

For some reason, her mind kept spinning scenarios over and over until nothing made sense anymore. Why did she travel to the astral world—for what purpose? And with her body?

Emma kept moving—at least she imagined motion as obscurity, marked with striae of varying shades of black, danced in front of her. "Hello," she cried out again. "Please, anyone. I'm lost and I need help." Still, no answer except her own voice echoing back the same sentence more than once, and she hated the panic she detected in her tone.

Another worry began to dawn. How long could she maintain being in the astral world with her physical self? If the few seconds she endured during the meeting with the Devronairs took one hour or more of Earth time, this wandering she did, which appeared to be minutes in duration would be how long on Earth? Someone would worry about her, she thought. But then, who else might be able to come and save her?

***

Hank waited by the back door behind the curtain for over two hours. He didn't tell Christina yet and wondered how he would do so without alarming her. Emma might be asleep again, at least she admitted as much when he called her. Still, Emma took seconds to transport herself to their house. The only explanation was sleep.

His private phone rang, and he jumped, dreading the call as much as he hoped this might be Emma, stuck somewhere in need of help.

He smiled when he read the number to Emma's house. He answered with a sigh of relief happy to forgive her anything.

"Hank, Eloise Willis. I'm sorry to be calling so late, but Emma left me a note saying she was with you and Christina?"

No words came out. Hank's throat constricted into a knot and panic felled his legs. He collapsed on a kitchen chair. "No. She was due here, but when she didn't show up, I thought she fell asleep. She never made it here."

Eloise's cry of Emma's name resounded with so much pain, she who comforted her husband who lied in a coma in a hospital bed—the sound of her shriek pierced his heart while his mind conducted feverish scenarios of what might have happened.

"Please, Eloise, don't let anyone know about this. Not your mother not your sister, no one. Just take your car and drive to the second police precinct and park closest to the coffee shop. Stay in the car and I will meet you there promptly."

A tearful gulp was the only acquiescence Hank caught before he hung up the phone and summed up the courage to talk to Christina.

—25—

EMMA LOST

Christina sat in Hank's car chewing one of her knuckles. She put her hand down whenever Hank glanced at her, but through the corner of his eye, he caught her draw her hand to her face after he turned to look at the road. Hank didn't remember Christina ever displaying this nervous tic before.

They were on their way to meet Eloise, and because he drove with reckless speed, he activated the flasher without the siren.

When they reached the coffee shop, he pulled up beside Eloise and watched as she got out of her car and ran to his passenger side. When she spotted Christina, she hopped in the back and asked as she closed the door. "Hank, where is Emma?"

Her voice shook, her whole body trembled. Hank cast pleading eyes in Christina's direction, and she got out of the front seat to sit in the back with Eloise. She wrapped her arms around Eloise the minute she sat down, and Eloise began to cry again. "I can't lose Emma," she mumbled through her sobs. "She's my only reason for living."

"We'll find her, Eloise," Christina cooed her eyes imploring Hank for help.

Hank recounted his conversation with Emma and Eloise's curiosity took over. "What do you mean by drop by? What is this code for?"

Hank hesitated on an answer. He felt sure Eloise understood about Emma's powers, but he wondered how deep in denial she might be. "How did she get home from the hospital?"

Eloise backed away from Christina to stare at Hank. She bit her bottom lip and admitted, "We all asked her to stop using the mode of transportation she does. She's young. Always in a rush. Was this how she planned to go see you?"

He nodded. "I believe so. I didn't offer to pick Emma up because we're trying to keep our meetings on the QT. A lot of people are snooping around these days. FBI thought Patrick's coma might be due to the fact he helped us during the Boleslaw incident."

"But he didn't," Eloise said.

"I used this ruse to explain my many visits to your house, to keep Emma away from the media."

She nodded and took the tissue Christina handed her. She wiped her eyes and blew her nose. "This would mean she's somewhere out in space. She's been so determined about rescuing her dad. What if they're both stuck in the same place?"

Hank wanted to reassure her, but he could only add, "None of the ideas I can give you make any sense, Eloise. However, whatever you do, please keep this quiet for a while."

"I can try. Emma has exams next week." Eloise started crying again. "I need to find my little girl."

"Don't worry, Eloise," Christina wrapped her arms around her. "Emma is one of the most resourceful young women I have ever met. If she doesn't find her way home, we'll make sure she does." Christina stared at Hank. "What about Manson? Can he find her?"

Hank thought Christina's question might deal with Fred Manson's threats during the discussion at their house. "I left a message for him. Your guess is as good as mine."

"No. I think since he travels the same way she does, he might be able to help us find her?"

"Who is this Manson?" Eloise asked.

Hank threw Christina a cautious pair of eyes, and he caught the downturn of her head which meant she regretted her outburst.

"He's just someone we interviewed. Emma met him. He is very knowledgeable about OBE. He might be able to help us discover what happened to Emma."

"Oh, please let this be so. I need my daughter with me. I love her so much. Plus, my mother's going to blame me for what's happened."

"You can't tell anyone about this, especially not Abigail." Hank took a long breath to calm down. "Listen, you can look forward to a couple of days reprieve with tomorrow being Friday. Then Saturday and Sunday. I know Emma has exams on Monday. Come Monday, you'll need to call the school and let them know Emma is not well. With her father in a coma, this is understandable if she's had an attack of nerves."

Eloise nodded. "Hank, what you ask is not easy. Emma's good friends, Tommy and Amelia, will want to know what happened."

"This is no different than keeping her powers a secret." Hank stared at Eloise through the rearview mirror. "This *is* keeping her powers a secret."

"What if we can't find her?"

"Let's not imagine this, please," Christina added taking both of Eloise's hands in hers. "Would you like me to stay with you tonight?"

Eloise appeared as though she welcomed the suggestion, but she turned toward Hank and shook her head side to side. "I'm going to take a sleeping pill, try to remain unconscious for a while. I pray Emma will be back by morning."

Christina drove Eloise home while Hank followed her. After one last hug of the disheveled woman, Christina hopped into Hank's car and asked, "How long before Manson's call?"

Hank pulled up in their driveway and turned toward Christina to answer her question. "I dialed the number he left at the precinct. No longer any service at this number."

"No." Christina's long drawn out breath rattled his nerves.

"His way of cutting off all contact with us," Hank answered.

"This didn't go to trial yet, did it?"

"DA wasn't thinking of prosecuting. And, first, we'd have to catch him." Hank passed a shaky hand over his eyes. "Not the first time someone jumps bail—certainly won't be the last. Only this is the first time a son of a bitch robs me of my ideas, of all my courage."

"I'll make some coffee. Hank, we'll put our heads together. We'll figure this out."

Sitting at their little kitchen table, Christina wiped her eyes on a tissue between gulps of coffee. Hank patted her hand. He appreciated Christina's display of bravery. "I think I need to call Tommy."

"At this hour? Almost eleven."

"Thursday night. I'm guessing no school tomorrow. He's sixteen years old. I doubt he's in bed right now."

"Why Tommy?"

Hank let out a sigh as he searched for Tommy's number on his cell phone. "He knows her better than anyone else. He's aware of all she can do and some." He went through the list once again. "Where the hell is his number?"

"Are you saying she tells him things she doesn't tell you?"

"I am sure she tells Tommy stuff she doesn't tell me," he stressed with a sarcastic chuckle. He highlighted the number he was looking for. "She's been rather secretive these past six months."

"You might frighten his dad."

"Calling his cell—Tommy, Hank Apple."

"Hank? Is Emma all right?"

"Yes. Where are you?"

"At a school dance. Emma didn't want to come so I took Amelia. Why?"

"I'm going to pick you up."

"Don't. Amelia's mother is on her way. We both have exams next week. I'll ask her to drop me off at your house."

"I'll be waiting."

When Tommy arrived, he waved off Amelia and her mother and followed Christina to the kitchen.

When Hank glanced at the tall and broad young man, he thought what a credit he was for his school. The best quarterback Belleville had seen in years. He also thought how Tommy tried not to appear moody and worried. Yet he didn't manage to pull this off.

"Something did happen to Emma. You lied to me on the phone." Tommy towered over Hank with a menacing look.

Christina intervened. "Listen, guys, this is not the time to air out your differences or measure up. We need to find Emma."

"Yeah, well where is she?" Tommy flopped down on a chair his mutinous attitude unable to hide the tremor in his voice. His jaw set and his eyes narrowed, he waited for Hank to spill his guts.

Once Hank finished recounting the events surrounding Emma's disappearance, he told him. "We hoped you might be able to tell us something about this. Any little detail can help."

"Yeah I know something about this." Tommy got up and rammed his fist on the table which spilled coffee all over the tablecloth.

Christina got up and used a sponge and some soda to blot the stain. Hank figured she did this more to keep busy.

Tommy paced up and down his pain seemingly bigger than he could stomach. "I've told her at least a hundred times not to use this mode of transportation. So, what does she do? Ignores me—like she always does," he mumbled. Turning toward Hank, he pointed an accusing finger at him. "You're the reason she keeps doing this. 'I'm helping Hank,' is what she keeps telling me. 'Helping Hank' is all she ever says these days. Meanwhile, she can't be a kid or go to the ice cream shop, hang out with her friends. She has to help Hank. All you're doing is using her so you can advance your career."

Hank was so consumed with the need to hit the boy in the face, he wondered about those wizards Emma mentioned. He rose slowly and took a grip on his anger by grasping the amount of pain this young adolescent manifested. Hank even caught rebellious tears rolling down Tommy's cheeks. He stared at Tommy straight in the eye. "For your information, Emma loves helping people. She helped many during the last few years."

"Including you, I bet."

"The first one she helped was you, remember?" Tommy's head bent. He remembered. "She can also say no. She has on occasion when she sensed she might not make a real difference."

"Oh, yeah, like she can say no," Tommy argued.

Hank walked around the table to stand in front of him and tilted his head as he told him with assurance, "She can say no," he added his words drawing to a point. "Right?"

Tommy's eyes opened wide as he backed up, embarrassment drawing red on his cheeks while self-conscious eyes marred his handsome features. Hank realized he hit the nail on the head. Without a doubt, this smitten young man had swallowed a whole bunch of noes from lovely, young Emma. In fact, his tantrum showed how fresh the scars still were. "Are you going to help us or not?"

Tommy's bent head gave Hank the impression of discomfiture as Tommy glanced at Christina with worry on his face. He still didn't want to deal with Hank.

"What can I do?"

Hank closed in on Tommy. "You are aware of what's been going on with Emma a lot more than we are. She tells you everything. Think back over the last few months—of anything responsible for causing this to happen—aside from her dad falling into a coma."

Tommy peeled off his jacket and put it back on as though remembering where he stood—his varsity jacket with his last name embroidered on the back.

"What do you say, Carson?" Hank patted him on the back to show he didn't hold a grudge.

"Would you like something to drink?" Christina offered with a smile.

He appeared interested so she gave him some choices and he

picked a coke. He gulped half the soda down before he put the can on the table. "Some asshole showed up in her room a while ago."

Hank glanced at Christina. "Asshole? In her bedroom?"

"This creep Amelia and I met at the bus stop. Surprise, surprise. Found the boy in her room later."

"A boy or a man?"

"Young man, I guess. His name is Hawke."

Christina smiled. "Sounds like Hank." She bit down on a chuckle faced with Hank's raise of eyebrows. "Sorry," she added.

"What about this Hawke?"

"He can appear and disappear. He travels same way Emma does. He came here to retrieve the little oudjat she conjured by mistake five years ago."

"I remember. Emma asked me about this, how to find the owner."

"Yeah, well he found her. He supposedly comes from a better version of Earth. Cocky, and pretty sure of himself."

"A better version of Earth?" Christina mouthed.

"How can we find him, get in touch with him?"

Tommy shrugged. "Have no idea."

"Perhaps using the pendant?" Christina suggested.

"Piece of jewelry is still on Emma's dresser. I spotted it just the other day only the thing doesn't shine anymore. I think the piece is dead."

Hank sighed, a hand wiping the sweat off his brow. "Eloise will be sleeping. I don't want to wake her."

"I can get you into Emma's room if you like." Tommy paused for effect. "Latch on the back door doesn't work. Never locks. Mr. Willis needs to get the lock fixed. Never got around to doing it—just don't tell anyone."

Hank nodded. "Okay, let's do this."

***

The darkness surrounding Emma lightened somewhat, she thought. Or perhaps her eyes got used to the dimness? She now spotted a shadow, an outline of someone nearby. She pondered perhaps these spirits were no longer earthbound and their aura, not bright enough to form a flame or light of any kind remained trapped in this chasm. Without light, how could anyone determine which route to take?

At this moment she realized the only road left to her belonged inside, an inner journey. She took a deep breath, gathered all the wonderful memories she remembered and allowed peace to descend upon her.

A soft cry drew her attention. The sound of someone moaning no, crying, wincing. She opened her eyes and realized she had not budged an inch. Worse, she had no idea how much time elapsed. She refused to allow panic to overrule her judgment. She listened with the intent of discovering where the sounds came from, but she found impossible to pinpoint any particular place. Many sounds abounded now, seeming as though they originated from all directions, and all of them soaked in sorrow. The echo, she thought realizing this may be one entity.

"Who are you?" She yelled out.

No one answered. "Please, I want to help you. Why have you brought me here?"

Her voice repeated a bewildering number of times after each

sentence. *What if I try to speak using my mind?* "Who are you?" She repeated without using her voice.

The crying stopped. *"Who is out here?"* a whispery voice asked. No echo, this time, clear words stuck with the mind to mind conversation.

"Emma. Emma Willis. Who are you?"

"I can't remember. I'm looking for someone."

—26—

TOMMY HELPS

Riding in Christina's older model Civic, Hank, Christina, and Tommy arrived at Emma's house. Tommy got out first and rushed to the back door. "I'll open the front door for you," he said as he ran off. He came back minutes later shaking his head. "Someone had the lock fixed. Maybe Emma's grandmother." He hoisted his shoulders.

Hank's head dropped. "I guess we're done here. We'll need to wait till morning."

Tommy added, "Unless." He ran off to the side of the house where the elm tree stood tall and dark. "Yes!" He said in a loud voice enough to bring Hank and Christina running.

"What did you find?" Hank asked.

"Emma left her window open. I can climb the tree, enter and let you in."

Christina's answer was immediate. "You'll break your neck in the dark."

"Nah, I did this once this week. Like climbing stairs."

"Time to trim the tree again," Hank emitted a sarcastic chuckle. "Come on, Christina, we'll wait by the front door."

Tommy let them in and motioned for them to be quiet. "I think I heard Abigail stirring in the den, and she has good ears."

Hank shook his head. "Abigail is gone. Eloise told me when I dropped by the hospital earlier."

"Great," Tommy rolled his eyes. "We can breathe. Emma's mom won't wake up."

Once inside Emma's room, Tommy showed them the pendant he mentioned. "This thing used to shine, the jewel's mighty signal had to reach all the way to Mars." He handed the jewelry to Hank. "Now, it's dull and dark as though the poor thing died or something."

"So you're saying this might be a transmitter of sorts."

"Yeah, possible."

Christina reached for the pendant from Hank's hand. "Maybe be an on-off switch inside."

"Doesn't open. I tried," Tommy added.

"You will not be able to use this to find Emma," a mechanical tone sprung behind them.

All three jumped, and Christina clutched her heart. "Dr. Manson, you scared us."

Tommy advanced toward him. "Hey fella, how'd you get in here?"

Hank grabbed Tommy's jacket and pulled him back. "Never mind, Tommy. We know this man."

"I came in through the window like you did."

Hank detected disbelief on Tommy's face, but the boy remained quiet.

Hank moved toward Manson. "We need to find Emma. Only, none of us can travel the same way she does."

"This is why I am here. Emma is trapped in someone else's universe." He stared at Christina's opened mouth expression and added, "In someone else's thoughts."

"Can you help her out?" Hank asked.

His head moved side to side, and Hank found his lack of co-operation difficult to believe. "Only humans can enter another human's universe, upon invitation, of course. This one is grim. Dark and cold generated by guilt and regret."

Christina wondered why he understood what went on in this universe but could not enter.

"I can see inside, only I cannot interfere or change things as they are."

"How do we get Emma back?" Tommy blurted out.

Manson ignored him and continued to address Hank. "Only the Pathfinder can release Emma." He raised his chin. "Pathfinder can also set free the errant soul unwittingly holding Emma prisoner, and create a new universe for the soul.

"Thank you," Hank responded. "How do we contact this Pathfinder?"

Manson flicked his hand, and Christina's intake of breath drew their eyes to the pendant she held, shining with a bright light.

"She will find you."

"When?"

"Soon, I hope. Emma's physicality will not endure in the astral world much longer. The empty space around her will create an occlusion of her senses and her soul. She will cease to exist."

Hank approached Fred Manson. "Listen, I don't need you to tell me how you were able to hide the kidney I witnessed you take. I have since come to realize what you can do. I need you to tell me why?"

"Returning an organ to one of your key players, a man whom

they left to die."

"So you're saying they murdered him by removing his kidney?"

"Third rate physicians left him unattended. We stopped him from bleeding to death."

"Why him? Did the physicians realize this man's value? Was the crime malicious? "

"Intent can make mild differences in the scheme of things. Where humans are concerned, intent has no power. The importance lies in the outcome."

"What you're saying is as a police officer, I should be more concerned with the results brought on by fraud, than with the reasons responsible for those who do?"

Manson eyed him with a threat. "I do not have to answer any of your questions. You possess too much awareness of our methods and our world. I am here for Emma."

Hank found his tone menacing, though a glance at Christina's frightened eyes did little to curb his curiosity. He still needed to call on herculean strength to keep silent. When he turned to ask Manson about the worm in his life, the man was gone.

"How long do you think it will take?" Tommy asked with his hands deep in his pocket in what seemed to Hank to be an all-out effort to appear grown up.

Hank reached for Christina's hand as she sat on the bed appearing wiped out with glazed eyes still staring at the stone in her hand. "Should I wear this around my neck?"

She gazed up at him. Hank called on the item with a motion of his hand. She nodded and handed over the oudjat. "Do you suppose we need to stay put?"

Hank shrugged. "I expect we can all go home. This person will find us."

Tommy grabbed Hank's arm. "I want to hear the minute this alien freak contacts you."

Hank gazed up and down at Tommy. Quite brave for a sixteen-year-old adolescent—his heart fastened in the right place. "I will call you."

***

Something woke Hank from a sound sleep. He and Christina left the nightlight burning, but the vision he caught came from the jewel Christina left on the desk in their bedroom as the glow painted the outline of a slight, yet beautiful woman.

Hank first thought his mind might be trapped in the web of a dream since he became unable to move a muscle. Christina slept beside him unaware of his struggle to rise or his fight to find the words to talk to the woman standing a few feet away. Her back to them, she examined the jewel she held in her hand.

Many questions pressed against him, though only one fashioned itself in his mind, loud and clear, "*Emma is in trouble.*"

He caught a sharp intake of breath as she turned to stare at him. "*How are you aware of this?*" She waved her hand, and he regained the use of his legs. He sat up in bed. She read his thoughts, same way Emma did, Hank thought. "*She disappeared tonight on her way to my house. We were warned she is in the astral world trapped in someone's thoughts. She's in corporeal form.*"

"*Who is your source of information?*"

Hank hesitated. He wasn't sure the term would make a

difference. He decided honesty to be the best policy. "*A Dev-ronair. He cannot enter the human's universe. He said only the Pathfinder can. He reactivated the oudjat.*" Hank tried to keep his sentences short and hoped the woman could hear them.

The woman walked away from the desk into the glow of the night light. Striking, Hank thought, with limpid cerulean eyes impossible to describe.

This time, she spoke the words, "Are you certain of the term you mentioned? Devronairs don't mix with humans—at least not on an individual basis."

"This one is here to help."

"Their whole race is here to help. However, they have their own agenda and don't concern themselves with mere humans unless this becomes an utmost urgency."

"What is your name?"

Christina tossed and turned beside him. "Hank?"

"My name is Columba," the whisper brushed his ear.

Hank turned on the night lamp beside him. He found the room empty. He got up and checked the state of the oudjat which provided irrefutable proof of Columba's visit. Not some feverish dream his worried mind concocted, Hank recognized the encounter did take place, and the alien stood where he did now, mere minutes ago.

He picked up the pendant which Columba once again deactivated, and Hank realized she hurried to help Emma.

In bed, he watched Christina sleep. She'd spent hours tossing and turning, worrying about Emma before finally dozing off. Still, even though he wasn't about to wake her to reassure her, he couldn't wait to share his encounter with the woman he loved.

Grateful for the love in his life and the joys this life brought him, he still wondered about the next version of Earth and, of course, the optimal version of his planet of which he'd just caught a glimpse. Somehow, the look ahead to a better world provided him with a strange sort of wonderment and an odd brush with humility. Manson secretly admitted he needed to worry more about results and less about intent or purpose. Perhaps intent, like beauty, lay in the eye of the beholder? If so, this meant purpose might change color with each one who glanced at any deed, creating false realities in a myriad of strange colors. Hank drifted off with the thought of Emma being rescued and the promise of the magnificent future which lay before him, both beliefs putting a smile on his face.

***

Emma no longer tried to communicate with the spirit in the cloud. She realized the task pointless. This spirit had likely wandered for a long time, and the soul appeared empty of memories of days on Earth.

Instead, Emma spent her time generating positive, soothing thoughts of home and on the beautiful things she looked forward to accomplishing. She also used her mind to call out to Columba in the hopes the Pathfinder might locate her.

Only the present seemed to exist in this realm. Unable to focus on the length of time she floated within the chasm, events appeared to be current evolving in the moment or in an instant. Her arms were getting weak, though, and she wondered why.

On and on she sensed the lament and the cries. Questions were thrown her way she could not answer. So when she caught the sound of her name, she didn't quite believe her ears. The voice became clearer.

"Emma, I'm here to release you."

"Is someone calling me?"

"Columba. You're trapped in your grandmother's universe."

"Columba! Thank God. Are you talking about my Granny Dottie?"

"Yes. First I will need to point your Granny's thoughts to another universe, one where she will be happy and remember only the pleasant lives she lived."

"Please be careful. My dad might be trapped in here somewhere, but I can't find him."

No answer came, but Emma actually witnessed the fog clear and the blue dome return, and while she searched the immediate area for her father, she met up with Columba.

"How did you find me?"

"This is what I do, one of the reasons I'm here on this Earth."

"There must be millions of other souls like my granny, trapped in a universe of regret and sadness."

Columba nodded. "We liberate those we find, souls we are able to reach. Do not worry about the others. No concept of time exists here, and once the reunion takes place, they will find joy and fulfillment."

"I thought people moved on to better versions of Earth."

"The majority do."

Words did not express Emma's gratitude. Tears rolled down her cheeks as she thanked Columba for her kindness. When she opened her eyes, she didn't recognize her surroundings. "What about my dad," she remembered to ask.

She turned her neck slowly to read the time on the clock and happily remembered today was Friday. She didn't need to get up in the next half hour. Good thing too, because for some strange reason, her legs and arms did not move. She didn't recognize the room and wondered if her surroundings were part of some other universe, one from which she might never wake up.

***

At seven o'clock on the following Friday morning, Hank in no hurry to answer the phone awoke to the memory of his vision of beautiful Columba and Emma's disappearance. He reached for the handset on his night table. "Hank," he answered in a voice hoarse with sleep.

"Eloise," Hank caught the tears in the voice and felt the bottom fall out of his world. "Don't tell me Emma isn't back."

"She is. Only I can't wake her. I took off her shoes, shook her, called out to her—nothing. Not a grunt or a stirring. She lies there, motionless. Should I call for an ambulance? She might be in a coma."

"And tell them what." Hank's heavy sigh and fist slamming into the dresser drawer woke Christina. "Listen, does she have a pulse. Is she breathing?"

"Yes, she is breathing. She has a pulse. But, Hank, my husband is breathing and also has a pulse."

She sounded hysterical and about to lose her cool. "Eloise, Christina and I talked to someone from the astral world last night, from where your daughter travels to and from, and they assured us they were going to bring her home. However, because she spent more time in the astral world with her body than is usual, they also mentioned she would need a chance to heal, to rest. Give her until tonight, please."

"If Emma hasn't recovered by dinner time, I will need to call for an ambulance, Hank. I apologize for being so testy, but Emma is the most important ..." She could not finish her sentence as tears took over.

"Is Emma all right?" Christina asked sitting up in bed.

Hank nodded. "Okay, Eloise. Before you take any drastic measures, let me know. I can do this without drawing media attention." He hung up the phone.

Hank took time and effort to give Christina all the information about the previous night's events.

"Why didn't you wake me?"

"I tried. I couldn't even move until I began talking to Columba with my mind, the way Emma taught me." Columba's beauty will not be easy to forget, but the how and the where recollection was already fading.

Once he related what he remembered, Christina eyed him curiously. "How beautiful—on a scale of one to ten." Her eyes narrowed as she waited for his answer.

"Unfair. The woman doesn't fit any of the scales. Her beauty is more from within, I think. I'm not even sure anymore."

Christina kissed Hank's lips. "I'm just glad she's not from Earth, at least not from this Earth. I would hate the competition."

"You are the only woman I love, Christina. Since she is not you—no comparison is possible."

Christina loved his answer as she stretched her tired body

against his, wrapped her arms around his neck, and poked her tongue in his ear something she knew drove him wild.

—27—

VISION GONE

*E*mma tried to stir and open her eyes, wake up to her surroundings, but her arms and legs did not respond—the only part appearing alive and well being her mind, her brain no longer scrambled with someone else's frantic pleas and questions she never answered.

She thought of Hawke and wondered if this sensation of being suspended in time was what he experienced to cleanse away the years he'd spent on Earth. Simultaneously, Emma worried about her mom saddled with so many concerns in her meager life and who did not deserve to suffer because of her daughter's mishaps.

"I'm so sorry, Mom," she attempted to whisper. When she did, she remembered the massive crypt of regret and sorrow dug around her grandmother's soul and opted to tell her mother how much she loved her instead. "Thank you, mom, for taking care of me. I love you so much."

From a distance, Emma caught the sound of someone calling out her name. On the third try, she turned her head, and caught sight of her granny Dottie—beautiful, young and so very different from the grandmother she remembered.

"You must save your father, my sweet one. He needs your help. He did not find his way back. You will need your pendant's light to recapture his essence."

During this time, Emma witnessed her mother's call to Hank. "Hank, Emma stirred. And, she whispered she loves me. Faint, mind you, but I managed to understand some of the words. She even turned her head."

The echo of her name repeated numerous times. Her mother's excitement on the phone left the last advice of her grandmother's words distant and fuzzy. "You will need this to align the stone."

"What do you mean the light of my Oudjat? I don't understand," she breathed.

"Emma, you're home, in your room."

Emma opened her eyes and sensed her own cheeks damp from her mother's tears. Eloise sobbed as she pressed herself against her.

Emma couldn't move to push her mother away, yet she wanted to escape. "I need to go back," she whispered.

"No," Eloise shouted. "You must stay grounded, or we will lose you again for good. Hank said you needed to stay out of that place for now." Eloise moved back and began to cry when Emma realized herself unable to shape a single reply.

Emma discovered she could not go back to the astral world. She seemed to be trapped in her room. Sleep soon overtook her feverish thoughts, and as she felt herself drifting away, she hoped her granny Dottie would repeat the rest of her sentence.

Hank walked into Emma's bedroom, and found Eloise with both arms around the bedstead about to collapse. He ran to her, offering his arm for support. "Can you walk?"

She nodded, looking up at Hank. "I heard your shoes coming up the stairs, and I tried to get up to meet you."

"Sorry about my running shoes. Didn't take the time to remove them."

"Never mind the shoes," Eloise cried. "Emma is here, but she said she needs to go back. I lost her again."

Hank held on to Eloise's arm as he walked with her, and didn't let go until he helped her get comfortable in the chair. He stared at Emma and released a big breath. Taking her pulse, he turned toward Eloise. "Don't worry. She didn't go anywhere. Emma's asleep. I'm no doctor but look at the way she's turning her head. You would not see movement if she were elsewhere."

Eloise got up gently and took a few hesitant steps toward the bed. "This is true. I also detect slight blinking of her eyelids. Thank God!"

"Thank you, by the way, for giving her a little more time," Hank said. "I'm glad you decided to allow your daughter another good night's rest before calling an ambulance.

Eloise stared at Hank with guilt coloring her expression. "I was on the phone with the hospital earlier when I noticed Emma toss and turn her head."

Hank couldn't believe Eloise was about to contact the authorities without first talking to him. "What did you say to them?"

"Nothing. They left me waiting on the phone and I never got to talk to anyone."

Hank sighed, visibly relieved. "How long since you've eaten?"

Eloise shrugged. "I can't remember."

Hank moved away and keyed a number on his cell pad. "Sweetie, I need your help. Emma is sleeping, but Eloise needs to eat and rest. I can't stay. I have to be at the office."

"It's Saturday," Christina said. "I can be at Emma's place in ten minutes. I'll be glad to help Eloise care for Emma. But why do you need to go to the office?"

"Believe me, sweetheart. I would much rather stay put. Such an overwhelming air of duplicity and betrayal at the office. I swear, Christina, seems as though everyone is lying. I can't tell who is telling the truth anymore."

"This is a time when you need Emma's help."

"Can you look after things for me here? I'll be back in an hour. I promise."

When Hank took his leave of Eloise, she said, "I didn't mean to eavesdrop, but I hope this is not inconveniencing Christina. I would hate to impose on her generosity. She is such a kind person."

"You caught one side of the conversation." Hank took Eloise's hands in his and smiled. "Christina is pleased to help you both, and she will be here soon."

He walked toward the door and glanced back at Eloise. "To care for Emma, you'll first need to care for yourself. Emma would not be pleased to wake up and find her mom in poor health because she worried about her daughter."

***

Hank contacted Tommy first thing on his way to work. Yes, Hank considered this might be too early on a Saturday morning, and the boy might be asleep, but Hank realized Tommy waited for news of Emma.

He tried his house first, and his father said Tommy was at football practice. Then he called his cell with the intention of leaving a message. Only, Tommy answered, mumbling a quick question. "She back?"

"She is, and she is sleeping. So enjoy your game and don't worry. Everything is back to normal."

Hank hung up realizing Tommy interrupted his field training to answer his phone, anxious about Emma and recognizing Hank's number. He too enjoyed access to his private cell phone.

Arriving at the precinct, Hank released a grateful sigh. Most of the administrative staff he frequented during the week would be elsewhere. The parking lot was indeed less congested. He entered the building by one of the back doors and walked toward his office.

Midway there, he stopped and scanned both sides of an adjoining corridor. Down the drab passageway, as dull as other hallways leading to most of their corporate offices, he hung a left and hurried to the second door on his right.

In front of the door stood a large bay area where two desks faced each other—help for the Director of Internal Affairs. Of course, no personnel members worked on a Saturday at this early hour. In sixty minutes or so, a designated person would be at their desk. For now, Hank took full advantage of the solitude around the office.

No surprise, Hank found Andrew Watson's glass door locked. Hank plucked a bump key out of his pocket, one to which he filed the prongs. Hank slipped on a rubber O-ring around the neck to make a small space between the tumbler and the key. He drove the key inside the lock and tapped on its head with a mini screwdriver as he veered the key to the right. Using a rag in his pocket, he turned the door handle without any problem.

He locked the door again once inside. A flashlight by his side, he kept the noise to a minimum—clueless of what he hoped to find. Perhaps something out of the ordinary or at least discover the origin of all the deceit lurking in their offices these days.

Dressed in black jeans and black sweater, he searched the available drawers first trying to ascertain if the material he read appeared relevant or not.

Hank pulled on two more drawers inside a metal armoire along the wall—both locked. He took out a smaller key and repeated the process he'd done for the door. He located a small notebook with numbers scribbled on each one of the pages, matched to initials on top of each sheet. Without any basis to establish relevance and reason, Hank shoved the notebook back in the drawer. He nevertheless took the time to jot down a few of the combinations.

He continued to the second drawer and found an envelope with Barbara Leclerc's name scrolled on the front flap. He pocketed the mail worrying time might run out and whoever due to be on duty might find him in Watson's office.

He peeked outside the glass door, and his heart sank when he spotted Celia, one of the administrative assistants setting up shop and launching her computer earlier than expected. Worse than being trapped in Andrew's office, Hank could not find a single place to hide should she decide to come in for whatever reason. For the nth time this morning, he wished for Emma's help.

He punched Christina's number on his phone, praying she

would answer.

"Hank, where are you? You promised you'd be here in an hour—now it's more like,"

"Yeah, well, I'll be here all day if you don't come rescue me."

"What?"

"You need to come to the precinct and ask to speak to Celia Warden. They will get her for you, and when she comes ask her about … I don't know. Security for your kids' last outing or something."

"She's not the one who takes care of this."

"I understand, sweetheart, but I need her to step away from her desk. I've broken into an office next to her station, and I'm trapped inside."

"Hank!" she remonstrated. "The things you have me do." A marked sigh later, she added. "Now I understand a little better how Emma feels. Okay, I guess I can think of something. I'll be at the precinct in fifteen." She continued, interrupting Hank's next sentence saying, "By the way, Emma is awake. I gave her some juice and a little cereal. She can move her arms, but she says her legs are still too weak to stand on."

"Ah, such a relief. Please hurry. If Celia needs to come into this office, she'll find me. Nowhere to hide." He ducked beside one of the filing cabinets and waited what seemed like an eternity. He made sure to close all the drawers, unable to lock them without a proper key. He also made sure to wipe his prints off everything he touched. He spotted Celia pick up her phone and leave her desk. He ran out closing the door gently and sprinted toward his office.

Glad for the familiar setting, his heart pounding like jungle drums, Hank forced a couple of deep breaths to calm shaky nerves and sat down to read the letter marked with Barbara's name. As an afterthought, he rang Christina's phone. "I'm out so you can pretend this is an emergency call and leave. Thank you. Love you."

He hung up before getting an answer. Flipping the envelope on its belly, he glimpsed Barbara's seal, the green and red dragon head, and the slit in the sticky substance across the neck of the beast meaning Andrew read the letter.

He feared what he might find. Many of Barbara's lies over the past few weeks now lay with their guts exposed. Like the one where she mentioned not informing Andrew Watson of their suspicions. This current Barbara differed so much from the woman he worked with for many years. Integrity and fairness usually dubbed as her middle names, he didn't recognize her behavior anymore.

He remembered Luigi and his dual personality. The man he met on the day he bought Christina's engagement ring and the man he ran across at the restaurant, the one who swore they never met. Both were very different people, yet appearing to be the same. Had Emma not taught him about wizards, he would not be the wiser despite all their differences.

The letter read: A brief note of caution. Be careful when addressing Hank Apple. He seems to be under the strange impression you and I are responsible for his recent failure at nabbing Dr. Fred Manson and making the charges stick.

He and Bill Frost are working together under this very assumption. I managed to give him the slip, for now, informing him I brought Cyril Platt into the fold. Of course, you and I understand Cyril Platt is scheduled to die and will never be part of this elaborate charade.

Thank you for agreeing to meet me next Tuesday morning.

I will give you vital information on a long existing police matter, one which will shed light on much of Apple's success. This information will floor you. It is a delicate subject you will need to keep secret to take full advantage of the situation.

Hank could not believe his eyes, especially when she finished with a quote from Scripture: *From the lips of children and infants, you have ordained praise because of your enemies, to silence the foe and the avenger. B.L.*

The letter fell to the floor as he dropped his face in both hands, shaking with anger and sorrow. Why did he take so long to figure this out? The worm circling the apple. Now, his biggest wish: to discover wizards had taken over Barbara's person. Even so, wizard or not, Emma's secret might in a short time become public knowledge if Barbara proceeded with her plan. "Emma, more than ever I need your help," he mouthed aloud. Now he wanted to find the courage to leave the office and pay Emma a little visit.

He tucked the letter away in his vest pocket, locked the door and left.

On the way home, Barbara's message kept flashing in his mind. What did she mean by Platt, scheduled to die? *Does he have a terminal disease? Or are they planning to kill him?* Fred Manson warned him about the worm circling the apple. Did he mean Barbara? Or did he refer to wizards and their plundering ways?

When the distant sound of a horn caught his attention, the noise blared in his ears, rapid reflexes moved him to slam on his break. He got out of his car and searched the area around him. Nothing and no one—except he held up traffic, and one driver brandished his fist out the window, the car behind him inches from his back bumper.

He apologized with a shrug and drove away still searching the area for the irate motorist who honked him out of his thoughts. He almost caused an accident. He needed to calm down which was when he remembered Emma's words. Whenever he became overwhelmed with a strange sense of anxiety or inexplicable apprehension, to take a mental assessment of the people he loved. He slowed by the curve in front of Emma's house, stopped and closed his eyes, picturing the woman he loved and how much he needed her.

Hank still needed several minutes to settle his thoughts and gather a smile. The fear lifted. The wayward musings blew away as though sucked up by a big wind. The bounce returned to his step while walking up to Emma's front door.

He hesitated, a firm grip on the handle. He might be an unwelcome presence in the Willis home with Emma still recovering from a trip she agreed to take to visit him. Wasn't like him to feel responsible for those events. Once more he closed his eyes and thought of Christina. Yes, she would grab him and insist he go home with her if only to let Emma rest, but he would do his job and stop worrying about imposing on everyone around him.

One of the reasons for his success in his career had to do with minimizing his concerns over people's sensitivities. Hank performed at his best when he took charge and got things done—a bull in a china cabinet, Christina often said.

Before he made up his mind to go inside, the door swung open, and he contemplated the attractive face of the woman he loved.

"I thought I heard you drive up. What are you doing standing on the front stoop?"

He entered, still a little bashful of his surroundings, in particular with those brown doe eyes fixed on him. "How did you manage with Celia Warden?"

"I never went inside the precinct. I pulled into the car park when you called, so I doubled back."

"Guess she needed to step away from her desk. Plain luck— has to happen sometime."

"What's this about you breaking and entering in someone else's office?"

Hank put up both his hands and shook his head. Remembering his thoughts of her in the car and how they dissipated the odd sensation creeping over him, he walked over to Christina and took her in his arms. Softly, he brushed her lips with his and proceeded to devote some time to a deep, delicious kiss.

"Wow, you sure know how to turn a girl's head," she whispered against his cheek. "Which is why I almost hate to say this, but Emma wants to see you." She made a grimace. "Oh, and Eloise ate, I rounded up a few things she had in the refrigerator and made her a chicken salad. She is lying down in her room. A couple of hours rest will do her a world of good."

"You, my future wife, are a veritable angel." He smiled. "In fact, you should go home. I'll see what Emma wants. Won't be far behind." He kissed the tip of her nose.

—28—

Emma's Wings Clipped

Her head propped against a few pillows, Emma caught the beautiful day outside her window, yet she couldn't stop the tears from streaking her cheeks. Home and whole again, what purpose did she serve? Her powers seemed to be gone—the very powers Emma cursed most of her life.

From her encounter with the Devronairs, she wondered if she might come from somewhere other than Earth, but she couldn't fathom from where else she might have originated, or if they even spoke the truth. As far as her life tottered along, the loving union of a gentle woman and a go-getter father conceived Emma and she followed the tradition of a long line of powerful women—the only truth she beheld until someone gave her specific proof of the contrary. Her biggest problem now stemmed from not being able to use her powers. The ones she needed to help her dad.

Her Granny Dottie provided an explanation, but she didn't catch the whole message—and she failed to reconstruct the few sentences no matter how many times she ran the words through her mind.

A soft knock on the door had her wipe the tears with her sweater's sleeve. "Come in."

Hank walked in, appearing big and burly though he tried to

tiptoe and stoop somewhat to shrink his size. "Christina said you wanted to see me." He walked toward the bed. "How do you feel?"

Emma swung the blanket off her legs and dragged herself to the side suspending her legs off the bed. "The last three times I tried, I couldn't stand," she said.

Hank stood in front of her offering his support, and she tried again, holding on to Hank's arm.

This time, with Hank's help, she managed to wobble to the window and took a deep breath as she let go of his arm. Grateful she could now stand, she breathed in the gentle breeze blowing the white lace curtains to the side.

"All you need is patience, Emma. You can't expect a miracle. You need time to heal."

"The opposite of what Einstein said."

He smiled and waited for her to finish.

"He said: 'I foresee only two ways to live your life. One as though nothing is a miracle. The other as though everything is a miracle.'"

"I stand corrected, and I applaud the way you are living your life." Hank smiled holding out his arm as she turned to make her way toward the bed.

Emma pinched her lips not to cry anymore—awash with too many tears in the past little while. Instead, she walked unaided and sat on the edge of the bed dropping her face in her hands. Sobs took over, sobs about her loss of friendship with Tom, sobs about her dad, about her mother's pain and her grandmother Abby's anger.

"Emma," Hank cooed. He sat on the bed next to her and put an arm around her drawing her close. "It's going to be okay." He rocked her gently trying to soothe the pain away. He reached for a tissue on the nightstand to hand to her.

Forever grateful for a friend like Hank, Emma considered herself responsible for doing away with the tears and the pain. Both weighed on her in an unproductive manner.

"Mom said I have you to thank for bringing me back. How did you do that?" A few hiccups followed her words and she swallowed them, refusing to wallow in self-pity.

"Long story." He smiled. "Manson came to your rescue. Showed up here in your room."

"How did you find out about the oudjat? How did you get into my room?"

"Tommy. He told us about Hawke, about the pendant and he was with us when Manson showed up in your room. Manson reactivated the oudjat. Christina brought the pendant over with us, and after a while, Columba came to the glowing pendant. When Columba showed up I couldn't move or speak. I remembered the telepathy you taught me, and I told her what Manson mentioned about you being trapped."

"Wow, seems as though everyone came to my rescue. I'm so grateful." She couldn't finish, the pesky tears returned, bringing along with them a terrible sense of failure.

"Emma." Hank's tone sounded helpless, and she took pity on him.

She swallowed the lump sized pain in her throat and explained. "Even my granny Dottie tried to help me. Only I didn't grasp what she said. Mom sat beside me, and I didn't understand whether her words belonged to a dream or if I still roamed the astral world. I missed most of what she said I needed to do to bring Dad back."

Hank got up, pacing in front of the chair. "Can't you find her again?"

Lips pinched she shook her head side to side. "I tried to go back since I woke up and I can't." She took a shaky breath. "I invoked the little sentence, assumed the proper position. I even asked Christina to bring me granny's diary to go over the steps again—nothing." Emma made two fists staring down at her feet.

Hank pulled the chair closer to the bed and took her hands in his. "Sweetie, I bet you this has to do with the fact you're too weak."

Emma shook her head.

"Sure. This might be like your legs? You weren't able to stand before, and now you can walk."

"I don't think so, Hank. I don't seem to be able to connect."

He sat back in the chair his eyes on the window. He chuckled. "Swear you won't tell anyone?"

"What?"

"When I pegged you as being lost in the astral world, I called Manson and got a disconnected number. Oh, he showed up afterward. Don't ask me how or why, but for a while, before I alerted Christina and please don't tell her?"

"I won't Hank, I promise."

"I sat down in a quiet area, in the dark, helpless, goddamned frustrated. You needed my help, and I couldn't reach you. I mean, it's not as though I can jump in my car and race to go find you— the convenience store, remember?"

"I remember," she said with a smile. "Go on."

"I figured since you taught me how to perform a little telepathy maybe I might be able to reach the astral world and save you somehow."

"You didn't try, did you?"

"Yeah." He chuckled. "I sat down in the living room and whispered the little sentence I witnessed you saying a couple of times, holding my stance, my breath until I gave my square noggin a doozie of a headache. Meditated too hard. After this though, I could sense everything, even movement in the dark—of course after ten long minutes of focusing on one thought, staring at one point, you're bound to go a little crazy. But the fake movement, whatever you want to call this, scared the hell out of me. What if I projected myself and couldn't come back.? I wouldn't be of any help to anyone."

Emma bit down on the nervous chuckle. "Yes, I understand. I know what you mean. Often, reaching for lofty goals scares us into not attaining them." She got up and walked slowly to granny Dottie's little bench by the window. "I worried I'd never see you guys again. Perhaps this is why I can't return to the astral world. I am scared." She stared at Hank. "In a way, I am lucky. I became aware of these powers when too young to understand how impressive and dangerous they are. In fact, for years I kept complaining about how they interrupted my whole schedule, my life with my friends and with my family. To me, this all became a game. Now they're more like loose matches in my pocket."

"What?"

Emma laughed at Hank's round eyes and dropped jaw. "My father always used to say whenever he wasn't sure what advice to give to his weird daughter, 'Whatever you do, never walk around with loose matches in your pocket. They'll start a fire faster than you can call for help.' He'd smile and muss my hair. These days, my daddy's expression of loose matches in my pocket seems to apply to my powers. This novelty of fear didn't exist back in the carefree days."

"Yeah, I understand. Innocence is bliss. You can't let fear stop you, though. If you do, the wizards will create much more chaos. You're the only one who can see them, who can fight them."

"I'm sure I'm not the only one, the only one we are aware of, for now." Emma walked back to sit on the bed. She grabbed her hair and gathered the strands into a ponytail she tied at the back with a knot in her tresses. "I need to go back there don't I?"

"Not today you don't. What do you remember of your grand-mother's words?"

"She told me Dad can't find his way back. He's lost. She said I need to use the light from my oudjat to recapture his essence."

"Columba's pendant shone before she turned off the light."

"Yes, but mine never did." Emma glimpsed Hank about to add something, and she hurried to explain. "I tried to find an on and off switch. Nothing. I thought maybe I need to shine a light through the stone or on the stone."

"She didn't say anything else?"

"Yes, she did. Only I missed the first part of the sentence. She said, 'You will need this to align the stones,' whatever that means. I can't figure how to align the stones."

"Where is your pendant?"

"On the dresser."

Hank got up and walked to the jewel sitting in prominence on top of Emma's jewelry box. He picked up the pendant and rolled the jewel over to check for a mechanism of some sort. "The only thing I find strange or different about this pendant is how the black stone on top seems to be separated or raised above the other stones. I spot a distinct circular ridge surrounding the small stone."

"I noticed this too. And I thought maybe a fissure existed into which I could stick something to turn it, like a latch perhaps."

Hank ran his big fingers around the stones. "Maybe some sort of swivel bezel. The small channel 'round the stone appears smooth, though." He sighed as he put the pendant back on the dresser. "The piece is quite beautiful, and a little heavy?" His eyes questioned her.

"It's weight never bothered me. Most of the time, I forget I'm even wearing the oudjat."

A knock on the door surprised them both, and Emma invited the person inside.

Tommy, a little intimidated by Hank's presence entered nonetheless. "Your mom said you were better. She told me to come up."

"I am. Thanks for all your help, by the way. Hank mentioned how you were able to point him in the right direction."

Tommy stared at Hank and smiled. "Yeah, glad you're back."

He didn't appear as though he knew what to say, or perhaps Hank's presence inhibited the moment for him. So Emma thought she might include Tommy in their conversation. "I told Hank about the dilemma with my pendant not having a light."

Tommy rolled his eyes. He addressed Hank. "When the other oudjat died—lights off, Emma wondered why no lights ever shone from her pendant. I told Emma she would need to consult a gemologist—the only way to find out about the stones and what they can do—if anything."

Hank shook his head. "Not a bad idea, you could ask Luigi." The grin on Emma's face warmed Hank's heart. Still, would she be able to trust Luigi?

Tommy added, "You wouldn't have to tell him what the pendant can do. You say the jewel is a family heirloom, and your late grandmother once told you how you should be able to align the stones somehow, and you were curious to find out how to do this."

Hank smiled at Emma. "Sounds like a plan to me."

Tommy stuck out his arm making a fist and Hank understood this was a show of friendship Tommy extended. When Hank did the same, Tommy pumped Hank's fist. "This is what I'm talking about," Tommy added.

Hank glanced at Emma. "Don't worry, I'll make all the arrangements, or better yet, I'll ask Christina to make the appointment with Luigi. You kids have fun." Hank walked toward the door.

Emma asked. "Hank, didn't you need to talk to me about something?" Emma swallowed the small chuckle rising inside her at the appearance of Hank's raised finger and raised eyebrows. He meant for her not to read his thoughts.

"Not today I don't."

Once Hank was gone, Tommy came closer and sat on the chair pushed up against the bed. "Ok, now that the dick's gone, how do you really feel?"

"Don't understand what you have against Hank. He's aware, intelligent and a decent human being."

"Sure. Hank's okay, I guess. My biggest beef is the way he uses you for the good of his own career."

"I see more his calls for help as a show of respect for who I am and what I can do. Most men of Hank's caliber would scoff at my powers or deny the very idea of them because they don't understand them."

"True. Or some people might want in on some of the action. I guess Hank never asks for anything personal. He intends to get the bad guy anyway he can, of course. I just don't relish you being in the middle. Bugs me."

She smiled, comforted by his support. "So, Mom tells me you left the dance to come straight here Friday night. Sorry to interrupt your evening."

"No interruption. Amelia's mother picked us up. I had her drop me off at Christina's place."

Emma's concerns involved the evening's turnout. She didn't dare ask.

"At least one good thing happened on Friday night. I don't think Amelia's a ditz anymore. She's actually a very nice person."

"I'm glad," Emma breathed looking down at her feet.

"I also discovered once I suspected you were in trouble, I couldn't ditch her fast enough. Minutes with her arms around my neck became hours."

"So sorry I ruined your first date with Amelia."

"No. You didn't ruin anything. This was our second date, and now, I understand what you meant." Tommy got up to sit beside her on the bed. "You were right all along, Em." He paused as though searching for the words.

Emma ignored her first impulse to move. She remained where she sat with their legs touching, with Tommy's hand placed gently on her own. "What do you mean?"

"About waiting. No kiss passionate enough, no squeeze tight

enough. No kind of physical contact with anyone could ever give me the satisfaction and the thrill I experience from being in your company."

He murmured his last words, and when she stared at him, she spotted tears in the corner of his eyes. He smiled, so she did too. He came closer, and she didn't run this time or scold him. Instead, her eyes magnetized to his open mouth, she closed her eyes preparing for the kiss she feared as much as she desired.

Emma first welcomed the gentle breath from Tommy's sigh, and when she sensed the pressure of his lips on hers, she responded with a slight pressure of her own. A soft moan escaped her mouth as the kiss endured, and she was disappointed when Tommy pulled back.

"I'll wait a lifetime if this is what you need." He fingered the soft tear on her face and smiled. "I'll be here when you're ready." He jumped off the bed and walked toward the door.

He turned before walking out and gave her a small wave. The slight wave reminded her of the long-ago Tommy, her friend and confidante and their childish customs. A few moments ago appeared older Tom, a would-be lover and a young man ready to sweep her off her feet. She raised her hand and waved back.

Lying down in bed, filled with a warm sensation while her heart performed its own little dance, she wondered if the fact she still pictured Tommy as an eleven-year-old boy sometimes turned out to be the reason she couldn't dig out any romantic emotions for him. Well, the excitement she just experienced depicted her all grown-up and proved to her she might develop passion for this new and more mature version of Thomas Carson. The thought brought her newfound peace, renewed courage, and an unrepressed smile.

—29—

HAWKE IS BACK

Hank and Christina invited Maria and Matt over to their house for brunch Sunday morning. Hank needed to consult with Matt about his current problems.

Matt chugged the last gulp of his beer and rubbed a hand over the top of his head. An onyx ring on his right finger had turned before he applied the gesture and Matt scraped his head as he ran the hand against his bare scalp. "Frickin' shit. I'm not used to this ring Maria got me. My bald head is all scratched up. The damn ring keeps turning on me at the oddest times."

Hank spotted the red welts on his friend's head but remained more preoccupied with Emma's pendant, and with the stone they needed to turn. Christina had secured an appointment for them with Luigi on Monday morning, and Hank looked forward to this.

"What a mess," Matt added. "This means since Barbara never contacted Cyril Platt, no one is conducting an investigation on the two names Manson gave you."

"Too right."

"So why does she want to send you to Miami? Doesn't make sense."

"I suspect the wizards want me out of the way. The evil bastards must be trying to create problems for Emma. I'd bet real money they discovered her powers over them."

"Question is how to get Barbara back to normal?" Matt paused, his eyes narrowed in thought. "Can Emma do this?"

"She's not sure. She'll need to find a way to separate the evil from the human."

"You said positive thoughts kept them at bay, right?"

"Yep. Emma understands how to bring back someone wizards took over. But to separate the wizard from the person without causing anyone harm is something I'm not sure she can do."

"Did you discuss this with her?"

"No. Emma's been through a lot these past few days. I'm meeting with her, later on, today."

"Hey," Matt shouted. "This means Bill Frost's suspicions of Barbara were right on, bro."

"True," Hank breathed. "But what made him doubt Barbara of all people?"

"Maybe he put a tail on her."

"Yes, but why would he think to have her followed? Barbara is the paradigm of honesty and integrity. Something tipped him off. I worked with her for many years, and I needed a slew of lies on her part to suspect her. Worse, Emma taught me about the wizards and what they can do to disrupt a person's demeanor, and still I took forever to spot the discrepancies."

"Don't make this a big deal. You're too close to her to believe what's going on."

Hank shook his head. "No. Something in Bill's tone when he spoke to me, as though," Hank hesitated.

"What?"

Hank eyed Matt. "Almost as though he was aware of what is

going on. From wizards to …"

"Don't say, Emma. He can't be aware of Emma's powers."

Hank stared at Matt, and for the first time since he met him, he caught Matt flinch. "He mentioned an old newspaper article about Patrick Willis' help to find Boleslaw five years ago and how Willis now lay in a hospital bed, in a coma."

"Oh, my God. How would Bill learn about Emma? Impossible I tell you."

Maria planted herself in the middle of the room. "Enough you two. Brunch is served, and I cannot wait to dig in."

***

Later the same afternoon, alone at home, Emma stood by the living room window waiting for Hank to arrive. Her mom visited her dad at the hospital with her aunt Franka. And after the awkward conversation over the phone with Amelia, who spent thirty minutes complaining in the whiniest tone possible about Tommy's decision to dump her, she welcomed any distraction to remove the memory of her best friend's tears. "I don't understand, Emma. We kissed, we danced, and we hugged and hugged. Everything went super well. Tommy said he liked me a lot."

Emma remained silent. Understanding meant exercising patience and kindness while she allowed Amelia to vent her troubles. Though Tommy tried to explain his sense of loyalty toward Emma, she still doubted his intentions would endure. At sixteen-years-old, a handsome buck and star quarterback on the prowl, Tom Carson's choice of girlfriends abounded. So, Emma didn't hold her breath, although the episode in her room did leave her breathless. Tommy stirred something in her, an emotion she had no time or desire to explore right now.

When she observed Hank's car pull up the drive, she hurried to the door she opened as he reached the veranda steps.

"Hank, I've got great news," she told him with a big smile.

"I need some about now," he said his tone irritable. As though realizing he still churned dark thoughts inside his head, he smiled. Entering the hallway, he added, "I meant I hope you can brighten my day a little."

"My powers are back. I went to the astral world."

They stood together by the door once Emma locked it.

"Wonderful, Emma. Did you locate your Granny Dottie?"

"No. I tried to contact Columba, to solicit help to find my granny. No luck."

"Is this strange or not? Does their absence mean you aren't connected?"

"No. To find a particular soul in the astral world is difficult. Their image or residual image is not always present or even the same."

Hank removed his shoes this time. Both walked over to the divan in the living room, and he sighed as he sat next to Emma. "Here's my news." Without preamble, Hank gave Emma the letter he found in Andrew Watson's locked drawer.

Emma sat down beside Hank reading the letter twice. She placed the single page on her lap and dropped her face in both hands. "Hard to believe someone is about to give my secret away." She straightened on the edge of the sofa and took a whiff of her fingers. "Wizards wrote this letter."

"Honeysuckle?"

"Yeah, the odor is strong, but here is the worst." She stared at Hank. "Did you open this letter? The seal is broken."

"Andrew Watson did. Can you help Barbara?"

"I'm not sure how to help her, and soon, more people will find out about me."

"Can't you do the same thing you did for your uncle?"

She shrugged. "Jimmy fought a losing battle, but he nevertheless fought them. With the proper incentives, bringing him back became easy. When wizards took hold of my dad, and I bent close to his ear asking him to picture the people he loved, he did, and the wizards left him, but this was also when the coma ensued."

A fearful sigh escaped her as she sat back into the cushions. "They merged with Luigi the day you went to pick up Christina's ring. I don't know Luigi, not enough to create a powerful incentive to bring him back or separate him from those creatures. Even if I did, he might just fall into a coma. I don't understand what I'm supposed to do, and there's no one around to explain."

"Nothing in your grandmother's diary?"

Emma kept her eyes riveted to the letter in her lap. "My powers are beyond the realm of those of my ancestors." She handed Hank the letter. "I'm not quite sure why. All I understand is now nothing prevents the whole world from finding out who I am. Even if we manage to stop Barbara, Andrew Watson read the letter."

"Our saving grace is the message is not specific." He got up to pace. "What if Andrew Watson is also under the evil influence, which would explain why she says they realize Platt is scheduled to die."

"Yes," she breathed. "I follow. This would mean once they're back, depending on how long they were under, they should forget everything that happened."

"This would mean quite a rehabilitation of all they've done and said over the last few weeks or months, even. Can you help either one of them?"

"I don't think so. At this stage, the wizards are not fighting with them. They are using them at different intervals. From what Hawke told me, the evil needs the human body to spread. If they inhabit them too long, the human dies and then they have to start again."

"So they did try to rid themselves of your dad and your uncle."

"Yes, I believe they did this on purpose. I couldn't understand at first why wizards would even bother with them. My father and uncle aren't critical to their plan other than killing them to scare me into not interfering with their design."

"I guess they're on to you." Hank hesitated. "Are they responsible for trapping you in the astral world?"

"No. Was due to another matter." Emma hesitated. "Listen, Hank. Do you want me to check on Barbara wherever she is, and see if I can spot the creatures?"

"Yes, but only if you promise not to wander off again. None of us would be able to sustain another blow like the one we received Friday—you missing and lost in a place where no one can reach you."

"I won't. I promise." She smiled and sat back into the sofa, her arms crossed on both shoulders. She would only project herself to obtain a better idea of what went on with Barbara.

Leaning against the cushions, she pictured Barbara Leclerc as she remembered her. She didn't need her location. The Universe would send her to meet with her wherever she may be.

"Wait," Hank called out to her.

Emma turned around and came back to her living room. "You're lucky you caught me."

"Please don't alert anyone to your presence. You have no clue what these devils are capable of, and no one will be there to help you."

She hesitated, thinking she might be able to find a way to extricate Barbara from their hold, but then glimpsing Hank's forehead slashed deep with worry lines, spotting the terrified look in eyes pleading with hers for reassurance, she agreed. "Okay. I'll gather as much information as I can and come right back." She squeezed his arm. "Don't worry, I'm only going there with my mind."

When she first encountered the haze of astral world, she met with a familiar voice greeting her from inside the big blue dome. "Hawke," Emma smiled, happy to see him. "You're free."

"Yes, I'm returning home to Earth Optimal for a while. Fear not, I will be back fighting the fights which need to be fought." He came close to her, and his eyes peered inside her soul. "Columba mentioned your brush with the Devronairs. She also mentioned your entrapment in the tentacles of someone's sorrow."

"Yes, she demonstrated great kindness when she helped to release me. She also took care of my granny and helped her on her way toward better memories. The only thing is I need her help, my granny's help, so I can figure out the last sentence she came back to tell me—something on how to recapture my father's essence."

"I want to help, Emma, but Columba is the one to show you how to draw the most out of your oudjat."

"You think this was what my granny tried to tell me? How did you find out about the oudjat?"

He tilted his head giving her a raise of his eyebrows. "Still don't get I can read all your thoughts."

"Of course." Emma hesitated. "Does this mean you can read all my thoughts, even the ones my memory can't recover?"

"Yes, but I can't, not anymore." Hawke smiled as though trying to lighten the mood, but Emma considered his feeble attempt at ignoring her request similar to the strange comportment she witnessed from the Devronairs. He knew her secret, yet feigned ignorance.

Emma did not own the luxury of delving into this mystery. In the blink of a moment, Hawke disappeared, and she found herself in a dark, quiet room.

Had to be a bedroom, Emma thought. She wondered why Barbara kept the room so dark. The day had begun with clouds in the sky, but now the sun beamed, and a warm breeze caressed those enjoying the day outdoors. An aromatic zephyr filled with the scent of flowers and the promise of summer had tickled her face with delight when she walked around the old elm tree less than an hour before Hank's arrival.

Emma's eyes became accustomed to the dimness around her, and she spotted a figure sitting on the bed, hunched over what appeared to be a framed photograph. She moved in closer and recognized Barbara Leclerc, still in a bathrobe and crying out loud as she spoke to the photo she clutched with both hands.

The honeysuckle odor seemed faint, but no doubt in Emma's mind wizards had attached themselves to Barbara at one point. When? They appeared to be absent for the moment even if the damage they caused remained, evident in Barbara's pain.

Emma remembered Hank's description of Luigi when he and

Christina bumped into him at the restaurant, embarrassed and confused. If the wizards were riding Barbara Leclerc often, they might have turned her life upside down without her being the wiser as to how or why these changes occurred.

She also remembered Bill Frost's wife, Jeannie, sobbing in front of her baby, Madeline, the day she visited the Frost household. Emma didn't spot any wizards, but perhaps they attacked Jeannie instead of Bill creating an imbalance in her life.

Tears began to trickle at the sight of Barbara's grief. She decided to leave. Nothing left for her to do but to inform Hank of her visit.

—30—

THE JEWEL

When Emma and Hank walked into Martin and Son Jewelers, even as early as nine in the morning, the place brimmed with customers. Both attendants served clients as did Luigi.

"What are the odds of Luigi being overtaken by wizards once he gets his hands on your oudjat?" Hank stopped to ask.

Emma turned to stare at him raising her shoulders as she did. "No idea," she whispered. "You would need to fight him to grab the pendant."

"Right. I'll be ready to jump Luigi. Send me a signal if you suspect anything."

Emma bit her lip not to laugh outright at Hank's dire expression as she pictured him jumping on Luigi. She tried to shake the urge, but her shoulders moved up and down as laughter overtook her. She wiped her eyes and apologized. "Sorry, Hank. The picture you painted made me laugh."

"Yeah, right." He rounded his eyes which made her chuckle even more.

She flipped the tissue into her sweater's pocket just as Luigi sailed toward them.

"Sorry, so sorry. I didn't expect so many people today." He

bowed, extending his arm for the two to follow him. "We'll go to my office. More privacy."

Emma and Hank stared at each other. So far, so good Emma thought. No wizards on the horizon. They jogged to catch up to Luigi. He appeared in good form, his business thriving.

Luigi closed the door behind him. "So, let me examine this piece of yours, Emma," he said with shortened breath.

Emma took the pendant from around her neck to hand to the jeweler. Silence prevailed as he scrutinized the piece. The rush disappeared from his demeanor. He seized a hand lens and proceeded to inspect the pendant with more precision.

"Where did you get this?" he asked the slow manner of his voice suggesting disbelief.

He dropped the tool to stare at Emma, waiting for an answer. "Family heirloom," Emma told him with a little shrug. Luigi's tone gave her the impression of being chastised. She didn't steal the piece. "The Eye of Horus was handed down from my grandmother."

"I'm going to need my best loupe," he cooed. "This pendant is unbelievable." He rummaged around in his tool chest. "Do you even realize what this jewel is worth," he murmured as though to himself.

"No. My granny never said."

Luigi's right eye looked big as he stared into the loupe to examine the eye of Horus.

"This pendant's background is genuine Jadeite. I'm sure of this. I would need to do tests to ascertain if this is Imperial Jadeite, but I'm confident of Jadeite in no uncertain terms."

"Similar to fake jade or something?" Hank asked.

Luigi's eyes bulged out of their sockets as he stared at Hank. "Jadeite is many times more precious than jade—a rare composition of sodium, aluminum, iron, silicon and oxygen, found mainly in Myanmar."

"Where?" Hank asked.

"Burma, next to Thailand." He once more applied his eye to the loupe and inspected the other stones. "In 1997, a small Jadeite necklace sold at Christie's auction for ten million dollars."

"What?" Hank's turn to appear stunned.

"Of course, this pendant is only a fraction of the Karat weight of the necklace in question. Still, this jewel might fetch anywhere from five hundred thousand to over a million dollars at such an auction—perhaps more in a private sale. The stones for instance. The first and biggest stone is a pink diamond. No doubt about this, and one of the rarest diamonds in the world. I can't even begin to tell you how much this is worth. The gray stone, maybe musgravite from the taaffeite family, which is another precious stone. This little stone on top is a black opal. Most valuable gems come from New South Wales, no doubt."

Emma noticed Luigi sounded breathless. Her pendant excited him in an endless way, and she regretted showing him the jewel.

"Of course, as I mentioned, I will learn more once I run some tests."

Hank grabbed Emma's pendant out of his hands. "The pendant is not for sale. And no one is going to run tests on this."

Luigi's smile disappeared, and his eyes narrowed. "I don't understand. Why are you here?"

"Luigi," Glad Hank was on her side, Emma used her friendliest smile while taking the jewel Hank handed her. "We need your help to figure out how to rotate one of the stones. My grand-mother gave me these instructions, yet I'm not sure how to do this. I thought you might be able to tell me."

He reached for the pendant. "May I," he asked casting a cautious glance toward Hank.

"Of course," Emma handed him the necklace.

After he had stared at the stones for what seemed to Emma like a long time, he put down his loupe and tried to explain. "Most unusual setting. I believe a swivel ridge may be fashioned between the black opal and the stone underneath." He picked up his loupe and handed the glass to Emma. "Pick the loop up with your right thumb and index finger. Proceed to rest the lens on your other thumb to steady your hand."

Emma followed Luigi's instructions but still needed his help to steady the loupe.

"Take a look at one side of the small ridge underneath the opal. You will notice two minute puncture marks. Might be key holes to allow the stone to turn, yes. Feasible."

Hank asked. "What kind of instrument would she use as a key? Do you sell this type of tool?"

Luigi's broad smile returned. "Impossible. No."

"Why not?" Hank's suspicious tone produced a chuckle out of Luigi.

"Here, take a look, detective. You'll understand."

Hank took the loupe and the pendant from Luigi. "Name's Captain, by the way."

"I stand corrected."

"All I see are two minute punctures, and there seems to be," Hank twirled the loupe to better his view. "A ridge, a tiny one, inside the punctures."

"Yes! Good eye, Captain." Luigi spoke with confidence. "I believe several prongs are lodged inside each hole." He turned toward Emma. "A key had to come with the pendant, I'm sure. Otherwise to fashion one, we would need to separate the stone from its setting and even doing so, I don't know about recreating something so small. You would be considering a new setting, and this would be costly, and risky for the jewel."

Emma slipped the pendant around her neck finding difficult to hide her disappointment.

"I'm sorry, but anytime I've worked with heirlooms, I found myself at a loss when I needed to replace certain parts with more modern ones, which are not quite in keeping with the piece's authenticity I'm afraid."

Hank gave Luigi the nod. "Thank you for your time. And I wouldn't mention the worth of this pendant to anyone if I were you. This has to remain confidential, you understand."

"I understand, Captain. I will not divulge this to a single soul." Turning toward Emma, he added. "Should you ever want your jewel appraised or sold, please, keep me in mind."

"I wouldn't go to anyone else, Luigi."

He bowed from the waist and walked while still in a crouched position to open the door. He swiped the air with his right arm as an invitation for them to leave.

"Thank you." Emma could not get her expression to appear grateful. Cracking a smile all the way to her ears weighed a ton.

Silence on the way home prevailed. Hank honked at anxious drivers cutting them off. He also threatened to pull out his cherry and teach someone else a lesson. Yet, he kept to himself and didn't offer any feasible solutions to her problem as he liked to do. And even though Emma did not wish to interfere with his thoughts, she caught the depth of his worry for Barbara gelling in his mind like black tar and liable to lead him down a road of no return.

"Please don't obsess about Barbara. Your attitude will only serve to make things worse for her and for you," Emma said tentatively. She didn't wish to upset Hank even more.

He turned, but softened his expression. "I'm going to assume your observation can be attributed to your brilliant powers of deduction, and are in no way due to your powers of mind surfing."

Emma chuckled, rewarding Hank's effort to replace rising anger with glibness. He remembered to lighten up not to attract the evil they feared. "Good news is I believe I found the solution to our problem."

"What do you mean?"

"You might not remember the chest my granny Dottie made for me to celebrate my eighth birthday. Just a square box she shaped and smoothed while she attached hinges at the back to fasten a cover. She painted the little chest trove in a mixture of oranges."

"You're right. I don't remember this."

"I used the box when we first met, during the days of Boleslaw. A year after the incident, my grandmother Abigail gave me a very expensive one to replace the little box. She meant well. The old box became too small to keep all my souvenirs. Still, I refused to throw my granny's gift away, which my grandmother wanted me to do. She even called me a hoarder when she helped me clean my room a few times which is why I decided to hide Granny Dottie's gift in the big chest at the foot of my bed—not to throw it away by mistake."

"How is this our solution?" Hank threw her a glance.

"Box is locked with a unique key hooked to the bottom. A key my grandmother told me she found amongst one of her ancestor's belongings." She smiled, raising her eyebrows at Hank. "Where the key's bow normally would be, are:" She waited for him to connect the dots.

"Two small prongs," he breathed, smiling as he did.

She nodded, unable to curb a broad smile. "Only thing I need to figure out now is if the key works, and what to do with the key once I figure out the mechanism."

"Can you imagine if your grandmother had thrown this away?"

"My grandmother would never discard anything belonging to her ancestors. However, this sounds like something I might have done."

Hank's unmarked car allowed him privacy from his office, but a call came through on his private line. He hit the Bluetooth attached to his ear since only a select few knew the number. "Hank."

"I can't talk," he recognized Matt's voice. "Barbara and Andrew have called a special meeting, and they are looking for you."

"Who told you this? They weren't supposed to meet until tomorrow."

"Bill Frost called to warn me."

"Why didn't he call me?"

"Beats me, but you need to haul ass to the office, ASAP. Barbara is planning a press conference with some big announcement, and Bill states she is not herself."

"First I have to drop off Emma."

Emma placed a hand on Hank's arm to reassure him. "Leave me behind the precinct," she whispered. "I'll fly home. I need to retrieve the key."

As he turned into the second precinct, the very place he did not wish to be while accompanied by Emma, he repeated his conversation with Matt. "Are you sure you will make it home all right?"

"Don't worry about me. Make sure Barbara does not broadcast to the world anything about my powers. I'm too young to be burned at the stake." She smiled to relieve the moment.

"Matt is headed toward the precinct and Bill is on his way. We'll take them by force if needed."

"I carry all the faith in the world in you, Hank." Saying this, Emma stepped out of the car and walked toward the darkest corner of the lot to disappear in a matter of seconds.

Hank ran out of the car he parked near the rear entrance and stopped when he heard someone call his name. He spotted Bill running toward him as though springing out of nowhere. "Where's your car?"

"I parked down the street."

As Hank resumed his walk toward the door, Bill grabbed his arm. "Don't go in the building. Tim called in a bomb threat."

Hank stared at him searching for the wizard in his eyes. "Are you crazy?"

"Do you know any other way to evacuate a police station?"

Hank thought Bill seemed healthy, but he sniffed to catch a scent of honeysuckle in the air around him, something he could not do if his life depended on it.

"Or any other way to prevent Barbara and Andrew from giving away Emma's secret to the press?"

The comment secured Hank's attention. Hank turned toward him, stunned enough by the words to cease his siege on the precinct. "You know?" Then he chastised himself for being too trusting. "What do you mean?" he rephrased cautious of spilling Emma's secret to this FBI representative.

Bill smiled. "You'd be surprised of the extent of my knowledge."

"Who are you?" Hank breathed, shocked to his core.

"A working stiff, same as you."

"No way. You're not from here—from Earth—are you?"

"Of course, I am."

"Earth Optimal?"

Bill backed up, his eyes showing stunned surprise of Hank's awareness. "Turns out, Manson is right. You are too aware of what's going on around you, at least for your own good."

"You're a Devronair?"

"No. But you're right. I'm not from here. Doesn't matter where I come from, where Tim and I come from. We'll deny this if you tell anyone. If you try, we'll make sure they put you away for a decade or so."

"So, you did find out about Emma."

"We found out this morning. Fred gave us the mandate to protect her, and to prevent her information from leaking out to the media—at all costs."

Bill's statement confused him. "Someone told me, Devronairs don't bother with humans in an individual way. Why would Fred care about Emma—at all costs? Does Fred plan for you to remove Barbara Leclerc and Andrew Watson if necessary?"

"Nonsense. I have no idea where you received this information, but your Intel is wrong."

"The Pathfinder informed me."

"You met the Pathfinder?" Bill's round eyes expressed his surprise.

"Yes, Columba."

"Where are you from, not from here I'm betting?"

"Yes, I'm from Earth—Refuse," Hank painted a sarcastic smile on his face. "And I'm going inside. There's no need to harm Barbara or Andrew. Emma can spot the wizards, and she can remove them."

"Impossible. No human, optimal or otherwise can recognize wizards. Neither can Devronairs."

"Can you and Tim do so? What are you called, by the way?"

Bill gave Hank an enigmatic smile and refused to answer, and Hank figured the FBI agent preferred covering his ass and say nothing. "As far as I am concerned, no species can detect the bloody creatures."

The commotion around the precinct disrupted their conversation as employees and policeman walked out of the building. Passersby surprised by the turmoil slowed their movement to swarm around the area like flies hoping to catch a nibble of the situation at hand. Their curiosity heightened, they lent a deaf ear to the cry of policemen, who through loudspeakers urged them to back off and walk away in other directions.

"What the hell did you do, Bill?" Hank spotted her, Emma standing between two cars. Dressed in black from head to toe with her hair tied behind her back, she indicated with her index finger she planned to go inside. She wore a smile on her face, and he found himself hoping she discovered a way to help Barbara and Andrew, at least rid them of the evil creating such havoc around them.

"What I needed to do to protect your protégée. You're welcome, by the way."

"You want to help, follow me inside." As Hank was about to follow Emma, Hank caught Tim coming toward them, as though materializing out of thin air.

"Don't mind him," Bill stated. "He's going to stop the press from interfering."

"How?"

"Not your concern right now."

They both ran into the building through the back entrance, Hank not sure of which direction to take. Then he heard Emma's voice telling him they were in Barbara's office. "She and Andrew both realize the bomb threat is a ruse, but they can't convince anyone else to stay."

"At least, Barb's Intel will turn out to be right," Hank mumbled. He glanced at Bill, whose eyes were blank, and he realized he didn't overhear Emma. He ran toward the office Bill following close behind.

—31—

Precinct Evacuated

Hank yanked the door open and saw Emma suspended in mid-air and giving him the nod. "Place reeks of honeysuckle. The key fits, by the way. And I did try to twist the opal on my oudjat. The only problem is I'm not sure which way to turn the stone, but I will do my best."

"What is the meaning of this, Apple? Barging into my office like this." Barbara seemed incensed with him. Appeared as though Barbara and Andrew did not locate Emma.

Before he made time to reply, Emma positioned the small key into the stone's setting and gave a slight twist toward her right. A trail of soft blue light jetted from the opal, a ray Emma realized no one else detected. She pointed the beam toward Barbara and watched her fall to the ground in slow motion, like a marionette when someone lopped the strings.

Hank ran to her lying on the floor, but Andrew stepped in with an abnormal amount of force, and pushed him back hard enough for Hank to bounce against the wall. "Stay away from her," Andrew shouted his eyes riveted and dark. "I'm not sure what's going on here, but you're responsible for this." He indicated Barbara's body on the floor.

"Emma," Hank called. A few seconds later, Andrew lay on the

floor beside Barbara.

Hank rushed to check each of Andrew and Barbara's pulses. "Barbara's out cold, but she has a pulse. Andrew," Hank hesitated. He took in Emma's panic stricken expression and kept the verdict of Andrew's death to himself.

"Oh, my God." Emma took thirty seconds to retrieve her body from home and materialized in the office. She acknowledged Bill Frost with a nod, uncaring if the FBI agent noticed her. "I didn't do anything different, Hank. I swear."

Bill approached Andrew and checked for a pulse. "He is fine."

"What are you talking about I didn't detect a pulse." Hank stared at him.

Eyeing Emma, Bill answered. "Sometimes, if they are inhabited by those creatures too long, nothing remains since the spirit has passed. They die the instant they are separated."

Emma approached Bill. "So, Devronairs take life while you give life back. Where are you from?"

"As long as it doesn't interfere with a Devronair's plans, we can give back a human his or her life."

"Will he recover?" Emma asked.

Bill nodded. "In reality, giving back someone's life means returning this entity's soul." Bill smiled.

"Seraph." Emma smiled. "You're from the Celeste Dynasty, two Galaxies away."

"I didn't realize you might read my scrambled thoughts." Bill bowed from the waist. "For you, sweet Chavah." The last two words were whispered for her benefit only.

As for Hank, on the phone with the hospital, he asked them to send an EMS to the premises.

Tim burst into the office looking for Bill. "There you are. EMS is right behind me."

Hank hung up the phone. "Did you call the paramedics? The attendant said they dispatched a unit to this address." Hank spoke to Bill.

"Tim did. They're at the door."

Hank extended a hand toward Emma. "Come on, kiddo. Let's get you out of here."

"I want to understand how this will turn out because I still need to take care of my dad." She turned toward Bill. "Can you bring him back?"

"Your dad's in a coma—impossible for me to do anything." He stroked Emma's arm. "I'm sorry."

Hank glanced at Bill, and the FBI agent nodded. "They'll both be fine. Tim and I will make sure Barbara doesn't wonder why she is in the hospital. They'll both need to be told what happened, with a certain measure of editing, of course. Next will be a matter of time with sabbaticals, rest to allow them to mend their personal lives."

"I don't need to be factored into this explanation, do I?" Emma asked, concerned and unwilling to be mixed up in the problem.

"No." A barely imperceptible bow of Bill's head accompanied his words. "Your decision. Of course, Tim and I will keep your secret."

"Thank you. I will keep yours." Emma smiled as she allowed Hank to take her by the hand to walk her out at a fast pace toward the rear entrance where Hank parked his car.

Once in the car, Emma asked. "Can you take me to the hospital, Hank? Or do I use my own means to go visit my father?"

"I'll take you, sweetie. Christina told me this morning they moved your dad to Bellevue."

"Yes. Late last night. They phoned my mom early this morning but never asked for her permission to do so. Apparently, they can run more extensive tests at Bellevue."

He hesitated. "I guess you found out about Bill and Tim?"

She nodded. "Amazing how people around us are not who they seem to be. I never realized how many aliens are here, helping us. Yet, we are still staring at a long road ahead of us."

"If you can bring your dad back, and learn how to separate whoever's under the influence of these devils, we'll make great strides."

She nodded. "Wish I wasn't alone to deal with this. I know so little about the wizards, Hank. Andrew would be dead without Bill's intervention."

"Yes, granted. Not your fault, though. This happened because the wizards used the man up. Not much left of him."

"Bill said he can give back life so long as the life doesn't interfere with a Devronair's plans. Who knows what their intentions are, and they pride themselves in removing whoever crosses them, bringing them straight to Earth Optimal. I guess what scares me most," Emma took a deep breath. "I didn't tell you, but," she paused a few seconds.

"What?" Little traffic circulated in the tunnel, but Hank slowed down staring at Emma. "You can tell me."

"They convened a meeting in the astral world of what appeared to be a whole nation of Devronairs. A simple flame represented each one of them." She sighed, staring out the window at the streaks of red lights bouncing off the shiny metal sides and top of the Holland tunnel, courtesy of cars flying through with their lights on, not unlike a bullet traveling through the human body. Gruesome she realized, but this represented her mood right now: vulnerable and expendable.

"Well, what happened?"

Emma hesitated. She didn't want to put Hank in the same precarious position with the Devronairs. "They brought me up on charges, stating I knew too much about their plans, and they scheduled me to be sent to Earth Optimal."

"God! And you're just telling me this now?"

"Never got the chance. This event preceded me getting trapped in my grandmother's web of sorrow."

"So this is what happened." Hank chewed the inside of his lip and the sadness in his eyes moved Emma to touch his arm and reassure him. "Did they sentence you?"

"I read their encrypted thoughts and answered in kind, defended myself by explaining how I might help them. Doing so, made me realize I used my granny's diary as a means to explain what I can do—rationalize my powers." She stared at Hank. "Truth is no one mentions wizards in the diary or how to remove them. I found no mention of other races being here to help us."

"What are you trying to say? Didn't your Granny Dottie tell you what to do?"

"Yes, to bring back my father, not to do away with the wizards." A huge breath later, Emma added, "Somehow during the trial, Manson and the others changed their minds about me in a radical fashion. Shocked me to discover how fast I convinced them to leave me alone and let me help."

"Thank God—good thing, right?" Hank glanced her way with

a big smile. Emma spotted moisture in his eyes. "Trial is not what's bothering you, is it?"

"You witnessed Manson's level of arrogance, right?"

"An understatement, I grant you." Hank confirmed.

"More than arrogance. Anger almost, ill will toward humans, at least the people on this version of Earth."

"Go on."

"Well, not so much what they said, more like a feeling. Devronairs told me, now that they understood who I was, they would allow me to continue here, on Earth Refuse, and they would also call on my help now and again."

"Of course, now they understand who you are—your powers—and what you can do for them."

"Maybe. Manson's arrogance melted like ice on a hot day. His attitude changed and became one of respect and appreciation."

"Grateful for your help, of course."

"Grateful or not, we were warned about what they do with meddling humans. When they first pulled me into their meeting, Fred appeared so adamant."

"Manson? He doesn't decide, does he?"

She shrugged.

They arrived at the hospital, and Hank showed his pass to the parking lot. He veered the car as close to the door as possible and turned in his seat to stare at Emma. "You're not suggesting you are like them."

"No, of course not. I would remember same as Bill and Tim do, and as do the others we encountered."

"Did you think of asking what he meant?"

"I did." Hand on the door handle Emma stared at Hank as

she explained. "He shook his head, and I read in his encrypted thoughts if I didn't remember who I was or where I came from, he would not presume to remind me—not the exact words, I'm translating."

"From what language?"

"Encryption, I guess." She smiled as she tossed a shoulder.

"Well, this explains the confusion. You misunderstood Manson's gratitude which stems from the help you can give them. You can't be anything else than who you are. Not without knowing, right?"

Emma smiled not the least bit relieved, but needing to erase the deep frown running across Hank's forehead. "Of course, Hank. You're right about their gratitude—palpable. And, your explanation makes a lot of sense. They do know where to find me from now on, and how to use my help." She opened the door and walked toward the hospital's entrance.

"Wait, I'm going with you."

Emma stopped and waited. In a hurry to see her dad, she stood by waiting while he parked the car, happy that Hank wanted to tag along.

The landmark hospital resembled a small city its front entrance shaped into a tall glass structure, and she pondered she would first need to locate her dad's room in this daunting maze so she might attempt to bring him out or another, more complex maze.

Hank caught up and hooked his arm into hers his tall presence giving her courage.

"I hope Barbara is alright," Emma whispered as they entered the huge lobby. "Perhaps you should go visit Barbara later to make sure she's not too disoriented when she wakes up."

"Bill and Tim volunteered to do this, remember?" Hank showed his pass at the front desk and asked for Patrick Willis' room. They were given the room number and told to go to the third floor, East wing.

"I'm worried, Hank. I'm not sure how to work the oudjat. Perhaps, I made matters worse."

Hank walked fast, and Emma almost jogged to keep up. Acknowledging her words, he stopped and grabbed her sleeve to make her face him. "You're alone doing this impossible job, using some method a spirit mentioned to you in a dream. You can't find any instructions anywhere on how to operate your pendant or how to remedy one situation or another. You need to give yourself a break."

He waited until she nodded.

"Emma, you insisted we all remain positive, chase away all negative thoughts to avoid falling prey to these wizards. Emma, sweetheart, you need to practice what you preach."

"Of course, you're right." Emma shifted her feet as well as her way of staring at the heavy burden of doubt.

"Think of this. By being strong and positive, you'll find ways to improve on the use of the pendant. Yes, your first attempts are shaky. It's understandable. But you'll master your oudjat's powers a lot faster if you stay confident in your skills."

Emma smiled up at him. Hank often found the way to her heart, the means to motivate her. She loved this about him. "Thank you. You're quite right. I have to stop whining and start to be more trusting."

"Come on, the elevator is here."

Hank and Emma found the room door open, and Emma tiptoed

in as though not to disturb her father. Or perhaps her hesitation dealt with the place inundated with light. With the curtains drawn back, views of New York and the East River shone in spectacular fashion.

The contrast of life dancing around her father with familiar sounds and light while he lay motionless in a deep coma, contributed to creating this sudden shyness in her.

Hank spoke first, but a mere whisper, he too seemingly wary of entering the room. Of course, Emma realized the big lug standing beside her hated doctors and hospitals. In fact, Hank concocted all types of sound reasons to avoid being in a hospital. She squeezed his fingers smiling up at him, grateful he fought his bugaboos to help her conquer hers.

"How do I do this?"

"Try the same thing you did at the precinct."

She took in a big breath and got into position to twist her pendant. "Bill's not here to bring him back if something goes wrong."

"You're in a hospital. Your dad is monitored. Anything happens they'll be here in a heartbeat."

"Don't you think it's strange the door was open?"

Hank's raised eyebrows and his pointed stare urged her to stop stalling. Emma nodded and gave the oudjat a quarter turn to the right, as she did for Barbara and Andrew. She directed the same blue glow toward her father and waited. Nothing happened.

Both heard footsteps coming down the hall and so Emma retrieved her key and replaced the pendant inside her sweater.

"Are you family members?" a nurse asked with a smile.

"I'm his daughter. Any sign of improvement?"

"No. I'm sorry. We're going to run a few more tests."

"What if you can't find the problem?"

"Next step would be to find a long-term care facility for him. So far doctors are stumped. But don't worry. We've got one of the best medical facilities here." The nurse lowered the top of his bed. "I'm afraid you're going to have to come back later. Nurses are coming to take him for observation in a few minutes, and I have to prep him."

Hank wrapped his arm around Emma's shoulders and led her away.

Emma managed to keep the tears at bay while Hank drove her home in silence. Coming into the house to her mother's cheerful greeting, relief struck Emma that she'd never mentioned to her mom about bringing her dad back. "I'm going up to my room to study, mom."

Once she closed the door, Emma lied down on her bed unable to prevent sobs from overtaking her. She'd tried with the pendant, her last ditch effort and she failed. Her dad did not wake up. Lost somewhere in the astral world, he seemed unable to find his way home, and she didn't know how to help him.

She dried her eyes, blew her nose, and picked herself off the bed. Exhaustion still made her legs shaky as she walked to retrieve her school bag. Not fully recovered from her extended stint in the astral world, the morning's commotion didn't help.

Emma needed to prep for an exam due at two o'clock, two hours to study. She spread her math tomes on the bed, a copybook full of notes and tried to concentrate. Instead, she fell asleep.

—32—

MATH EXAM

*E*mma awoke to her mother's strained voice. Eloise shook her lightly to get her to respond. "Emma, Tommy and his dad are downstairs. Your exam is in less than forty minutes. Would you like me to drive you instead?"

"It's okay Mom, I'm up." Emma jumped to her feet and grabbed her books to dump them in her bag. She ran to the mirror and gave her hair a few strokes of the brush. She also dabbed a little eyeliner over and under her lids to hide the red from the swell of her tears.

"Are you alright, honey?"

"Yeah, sure, Mom. Just a little tired." She smiled at her mother and gave her a kiss and a hug, grateful she took Mondays off.

"At least, you used most of the morning to study," Eloise answered unaware of her daughter's latest antics.

"Yep," Emma called out as she ran out the door to the waiting car.

"You look lovely," Tommy said keeping an eye on traffic ahead. His father sat in the passenger seat. "I'm surprised you didn't call me this morning for help with Bull Randal's notes. I spent an hour with Amelia over the phone. The bull actually made a mistake in one of his examples, confusing even me."

"Pure luck, I didn't get to the error." Emma wondered how she might gather her thoughts to pass the exam.

In a large auditorium, the Board demanded seniors sign in at the reception area. Since the Board assigned math exams according to grade level, students sat in designated sections to help with the supervision involved.

Rules also demanded all students leave their cell phones and electronic devices behind. Emma left her cell phone at home. As she walked toward the specified section, she heard her name called. She looked up and caught Amelia sitting six rows back a big smile on her face and waving at her. Naturally, the farthest seats from the podium, in any section, filled first so Emma now took her place in the second row from the front. She lost track of Tommy. A year ahead of them in math, Tommy wrote his test in the room next door.

Emma, glad to collapse in any seat, her legs still not stable, deposited pens, pencil, and scientific calculator on the desk. She knew not to write inside a booklet distributed earlier until asked to do so. So much ceremony went into these Board exams, the provision to countermand cheaters almost greater than the measures deployed to evaluate a student's learning curve.

The supervisor responsible for their section was one of Emma's favorite teachers, Miss Linsey, and though kind, she would not assist with any math questions.

The teacher raised the handbook and asked them to fill out the first section with their name and student ID number.

Emma did as told, her hand shaking as she did. She worried all the math she ever learned left her brain, and she might not be able to solve anything.

Miss Linsey asked them to go ahead with the exam, specifying three hours were allotted for the test. The teacher also mentioned the school allowed students to leave two hours into the time allowed. She smiled as she sat behind the desk.

Emma stared at the first question and wondered why the answer appeared on the page in a grayed-out manner and all the details explaining the reason for the response accompanied the solution in the same watermark mode. The board is giving an example, she shrugged

Emma stared at the professor in front, at some of her classmates on each side of her, but stopped short of turning around to gaze at Amelia. Well, if they wanted to give away the first question, she would take those free marks granted in the margin. When Emma found the same exact grayed out area giving the solution to her next problem, she raised her hand to ask for Miss Linsey's help.

The teacher walked over, and Emma asked why the answers appeared to be written for questions one and two.

Miss Linsey's puzzled expression convinced Emma she did not understand her question. "Emma you can use the blank paper to do your calculations, but you must transcribe your work on this sheet." She smiled, unable to spot the watermarked answers Emma indicated.

"Thank you. I will do this." Emma's turn to smile. As Miss Linsey strolled down the alleys, she glanced at the next five questions and discovered the answers were also provided. She didn't understand how this might be possible. Emma felt dishonest for recopying the answer on the sheet in the same format. She also wrote down some of the theorems she recognized and soon found her confidence returning. Emma wondered if these answers might be the work of wizards attempting to make her fail math? No honeysuckle odor around her.

However, to make sure, she redid math problem five to which she remembered the answer. The watermarked answer agreed with hers, and was correct.

When she finished, she looked at the clock and realized only one hour had passed. Glancing left and right, she caught students scratching their heads, sweating, some making balls of sheets of their work paper while others spent their energy erasing their penciled answers.

With one whole hour left before being allowed to leave she thoroughly reviewed each question and solution to ensure no notable mistakes.

Emma did not understand what transpired with this exam, and though grateful, she sensed a little unease creep up when she considered people might think she found a way to cheat the system. Yet, if she told anyone how she obtained the answers, no one would believe her. She wondered if Bill Frost played a hand in this, for the help she gave him and shook her head in disbelief. Perhaps Fred Manson had toyed with her test. She dropped the idea, too ludicrous to entertain. Fred Manson, a well-oiled machine, followed only the orders Devronairs gave him. In fact, only a few people were aware of her exam today, and none of them possessed the power to alter a test.

One hour later, Emma walked out of the auditorium and for an instant she became conscious of all eyes on her. Out in the hall, Emma searched for Tommy. Unable to find him anywhere, she headed home.

Emma sat on her bed realizing she needed to prepare for her

science exam the next day, but could not muster the courage to do so. Her mother had not returned from visiting her dad at the hospital, and she didn't have the heart to cook anything for supper.

The phone rang. Her cell indicated Tommy.

"So, how did you do?" he asked without a greeting.

"I'm sure I did well. First one out, and the exam seemed rather easy." Emma had no intention of admitting to anyone about the answers being provided for her.

"Dumb luck. Mine happened to be difficult. I needed the full three hours although I'm sure I did well. Amelia called me in tears. She thinks she flunked the exam."

"She's dramatic. She'll come out fine, you'll see."

"Looks like you've come full circle," Tommy added.

"What do you mean?"

"Remember in grade three, you were an ace in math. Don't know why or when you lost your confidence."

"True, in a way. I lost my nerve the year the curriculum introduced fractions."

"What are you talking about? You're the only person I met who can do fractions in her head."

"Yeah, but by the time I mastered them, they introduced algebra and calculus. Takes me a little longer than anyone else to understand, I guess."

"What I said, full circle."

Tommy's words of a full circle struck Emma's mind like an echo, and she wondered why. "Can I call you back, Tom? I am about to go fix myself a little something to eat."

"Who do you have tomorrow?"

"Reynolds—science."

"Ah. You need to cram. I'll call you later tonight."

Truth be told, Emma did not feel the least bit hungry. Her main preoccupation with the term full circle waylaid all other thoughts. She picked up her oudjat and the key to make the opal turn. *What if I turned the gem full circle and held the position for a while. This might provide a beacon to help Dad find his way home.*

The thought gave her renewed courage, and while the idea cheered her up, the earlier mention of food grumbled a noisy protest in her stomach. She remembered she hadn't eaten since morning.

She decided to reheat leftover spaghetti, and add a little salad for her and her mom, after which Emma would crack the books and review the material she needed for her science test in the morning, not wanting to go to another exam unprepared. Later tonight, she would sneak into her father's hospital room and attempt to guide him home.

***

FBI agent, Tim O'Rourke peeked into Barbara's hospital room and whispered to his partner. "Is she sleeping?"

Bill Frost nodded. "I mind-swapped with her and discovered she is quite aware. She knows about Emma's powers and so it was easy to bring her up to date on everything."

"You didn't tell her why we're here or who we are, did you?"

"No. Mentioned the wizards and the fact our powers were similar to Emma's. Also confirmed she would no longer be attacked by these creatures—her sole preoccupation to find the means to mend her life back to normal." He checked on the woman resting in the hospital bed. "I also told her Hank Apple was aware of the situation."

"That's more than I can say for the man in the next room. He's out of the woods, physically I mean, but far from Barbara's spiritual development. Unaware of anything and everything, he succumbs to primal forces around him. I needed to keep any words I said to him short and brief."

"Lack of a well-developed spiritual personality. How did you communicate?"

"Verbally." He shrugged. "Explained he suffered some sort of cerebral virus and the attack influenced his decision and robbed him of his short-term memory. On the plus side, he doesn't remember anything Barbara told him about Emma."

Tim O'Rourke approached Bill and faced him. "Hey, did you know Apple asked me what we intended doing about Rabbi Minsk and that politician?" Tim scratched his head as the name escaped him.

"Kirk Assany. How is this possible?"

"I tried to feign ignorance when he asked, but he found me out. He got angry, so I asked him how he discovered those names. He admitted Fred Manson gave him the information."

"Well, well. Devronairs must be feeling the pressure of time." Bill shook his head. "We need to round up those two with enough evidence to break their ugly chain of despots—before our friend Manson shuttles them out of here."

Tim smiled. "My thoughts exactly. Putting these guys away will go toward stopping the thefts. Sometimes, Manson and his kind don't understand you can't always remove a canker by lopping the thing off. Makes the disease spread. Hank also said Fred told him once Minsk is removed, the thread will come undone from Miami."

Bill smiled. "Thank you, Fred, although I suspect what he meant is once we pull on the thread from Miami, the route will disappear." He walked toward the door, Tim on his heels.

"Which confirms our tactic: to round up all their routes and do enough damage to crush their activities for good." Tim stopped and eyed Bill until he turned toward him.

"Why all this trust in Hank Apple? Why didn't Fred tell us?" Tim once more took up Bill's long strides.

"We work with Hank. In normal circumstances, our man Hank would have no choice but to share, but Barbara tainted us with such mistrust. Wizards mucking up the plan, as usual, nothing to do with Manson and his band of merry men."

The two Celestials walked fast, and when they turned the corner, they disappeared from view.

***

Emma landed in her father's room dressed in black and prepped to leave at a moment's notice, the hour much later than she wished. Her mother returned home without the usual bounce in her step, eyes red and lids swollen. Doctors mentioned her father's condition needed to improve soon, or he might encounter brain loss if and when he recovered. Emma spent some time at home reasoning her mother into hoping for the best and staying positive. Emma sure didn't need an attack of the wizards on her mom.

A single nightlight affixed to the far wall took responsibility for keeping the room from total darkness. The blinds remained open, and though neons streaked the night sky in abundance, Emma found making her way around the room difficult.

She avoided bumping into a makeshift table laden with syringes, thermometers and other tools she did not recognize. Moving closer, she spotted the book her mother read to her father, lying on one of the nightstands. On top of a commode, the flickering lights indicated the beat and drone of the life support machine keeping her father's vital organs functioning until his nervous system healed enough to support his body. A mask covered most of his face, but she could still spot his eyes and there seemed to be movement in them.

She took the key out of a small pocket in her back satchel and removed the oudjat from around her neck. She gave the stone a full turn of the key and at once, a bright yellow light beamed on her father. The golden stream appeared to illuminate the whole room, only she realized no one spotted the formidable ray—her dad the only person needing to discover the light to follow the sunny glow home.

She sat on one of the straight chairs at the foot of the bed. She didn't trust herself in the comfy sofa near the window wall. Any softness under her and sleep might take her.

Emma kept her arm supported on the chair's armrest and the oudjat directed toward her father. Little sound occurred in the corridors, and from the brightly lit clock on the wall facing her, Emma kept track of time.

Eyes on the timepiece with the big Roman numerals as the second's needle sped along fast, right to left or left to right, she pondered. Unlike the minute or the hour needle, this one reassured her time indeed passed.

Did the big clock hypnotize her with the spinning needles or did she fall asleep? Emma might never understand how or why she caught the smiling expression on her dad staring at her through the haze of clouds.

"She said you would find me, bring me home. I waited, with more patience than I ever dreamed possible." he chuckled.

"Dad! Who said?"

"Your granny Dottie. We shared a nice long chat, and she is wonderful. Thank you for bringing me home, my sweet daughter."

A rough hand on her shoulder shook her hard. Emma opened her eyes and stared at the nurse's angry features looking down at her. "What are you doing here at this hour? How did you get in?"

Emma straightened in her chair. "Someone took pity on me and let me in. I have exams during the day, so this is the only time I can see my dad."

Another male nurse stood by her father's bedside. "Looks like you came at the right time. He's awake."

Emma got to her feet and spotted her oudjat on the floor, the little gold key still attached. She snatched up the pendant to slide the jewel in her pocket. Taking two full steps to her father's side, she spotted him opening his eyes. The nurse removed the mask, and he smiled at them. He tried to talk, but instead closed his eyes and went back to sleep.

"Looks like he is going to be alright," the female nurse said to her with a big smile. "The doctor will be here soon. I suggest you go home and come back in the morning. He will need his rest tonight, as will you."

Emma nodded. She touched her father's hand, the one tied to

the bed with an IV running through, and she knelt beside him rubbing her cheek against his hand, wetting his skin with her tears. She rose and wiped her nose and eyes with a tissue the nurse gave her. "Thank you. You'll take good care of him, I am sure." She smiled, turned, and walked out to find a dark corner. She would fly home.

—33—

HOSPITALS

In her euphoria, Emma wished she might share this good news with someone and the thought brought her to Tommy's house. She circled the place and found a light on in his window at one thirty in the morning, which meant he studied for tomorrow's science test. She peeked through the glass to make sure Tommy worked alone, and she caught him sleeping with his head resting on his arm leaning on the desk.

She entered and whistled a soft tune. Tommy stirred and lifted his head. Before even spotting her, he whispered, "Emma?"

Her heart skipped a beat, touched by the place Tommy afforded her in his thoughts. Tommy Carson, a faithful friend who never passed judgment, never stared at her with disdain or shame or anger like most of the people in her life did at one point or another. "Yes."

He pivoted his chair to stare at her, his eyes still sleepy. "What are you doing here?"

She smiled from ear to ear, unable to curb her enthusiasm. "My father's back." Only, when she began to explain, she broke down into tears.

The sound of his chair rolling back shattered the silence, and in one giant step, he encircled her in his arms. "Oh, Emma. I'm so happy for you."

Emma unable to speak sobbed on Tommy's shoulder for the next few minutes and took the tissues he gave her until the waterworks stopped. "I'm sorry. Such a relief." She took in a deep breath and glanced at him. She smiled as she fingered a few of his own tears rolling down his cheeks. "You are the first person I wanted to tell," she whispered, biting her bottom lip.

He cocked his head, and Emma read a question in his eyes. Tipping her chin toward him, he bent his head, bringing his mouth close to her face, enough to brush her cheek with a kiss. He retreated to stare into her eyes, and when she smiled, he bent his mouth to touch her other cheek with a soft kiss.

He stayed with his cheek pressed to hers his mouth touching the lobe of her ear. "I don't want to do something tonight we'll both regret tomorrow," he whispered.

Surprised by his restraint, Emma backed away the same question in her eyes.

Tommy took a deep breath, one he expelled in an unsteady fashion on her forehead, as though chasing nerves away. "Part of me wants to take you in my arms and make love to you until morning, never even stopping to catch my breath. Another part is holding me back, and I think this has to be the stupid side of me, too dumb to seize a precious moment."

"I understand. Believe me, I do."

"You, Emma?"

She nodded.

"I must be stupider than I thought." Even those words don't shake the resolve holding me back. I think my restraint comes from the fact I'm in love with you, Emma. I'm almost seventeen years old"

"In another six months." Emma smiled.

"And I already found the woman I want to spend the rest of my life with."

"Tom," she interrupted him. "You will meet lots of new people in college and university. Something tells me in a while I will become nothing other than a childhood memory for you."

He shook his head vigorously. "No. This feeling, you don't understand which means you don't share, at least not this way, takes over my whole being—renders all other feelings pale and unimportant. Even if I came to cherish someone else, no one would ever be unique enough for me to have and hold all my life—only you."

Emma noticed his shoulders deflate a little. She wanted to kiss away his troubles but didn't know how to do this without hurting him more.

"I see other girls, and while all of them display certain qualities and offer the potential to be loved, they are not you. Never will be. I'm in love with who you are. I want to protect you. I want to spend my life with you. And, I will wait as long as it takes for you to love me back." He smiled and kissed the tip of her nose.

She clung to him. "Kiss me like you did Amelia," she whispered, waiting while holding her breath.

Emma witnessed the deep breath Tommy took, the look of pain that crossed his brow. She figured him sensing the torment of an unfulfilled desire, a kiss leaving him only the brief, sweet moment of a caress with the woman he loved, never to be repeated. Her selfishness surprised her when she became more coherent and the euphoria left her body.

When he bent his head, she backed away with tears glistening in her eyes. "I'm sorry, my beautiful friend. I do love you, Tom. Perhaps not the way you love me—yet," she added as she prepared to travel on the astral wave. "I will make falling in love with you, one of my life long goals, Thomas Carson," she added in his ear before hugging the wind to travel home.

As she arrived in her room, she continued out loud, "When I do, my love will last forever."

***

The next morning, Hank paced the lobby at the hospital waiting to take Barbara home. The doctors had just released her this morning, and pulling the overnight bag her daughters brought her, she followed Hank along the winding corridors.

"They're letting you walk out of here?" Hank asked surprised to see her walking unattended.

"Are you kidding? I threatened the hospital with a law suit if they didn't allow me to leave here on my own two feet." She smiled at Hank. "Cooped up in that little room, I almost went stir crazy." Barbara stopped as she looked up at Hank. "So, what actually happened to me? And how long did this occupation last?"

Hank realized his giant steps forced Barbara to a small trot. He slowed down and answered with a question of his own. "I thought Bill explained everything to you?" He didn't want to give anything away.

"Explain," she mumbled. "If you can call what Bill told me an explanation."

Hank tugged on the handle of Barbara's case to haul for her.

"Don't bother, Hank. Bag's holding me up right now." She chuckled, and Hank thought she wanted to lighten the mood between them.

"What did he tell you?" Hank asked. Barbara's turn to hesitate, so he added. "Bill can perform some of Emma's tricks?"

She nodded.

"True. At least, this is what Mr. FBI told me. You should also be told Emma is the only one who can spot the wizards—that we know of."

"My God! We are in deep trouble."

Hank pushed the latch of the main door. "Car is parked the last row. Wait here, I'll bring the car around."

"I'll walk with you. Does me good to walk. How can we prevent these wizards from hurting anyone else?"

Hank stopped to stare at her. "We can't. We'll need to work on people, one at a time if we must." He hesitated before resuming his walk. "Were you able to straighten things out with your daughters?"

She smiled. "Coma brought them around. All forgave me when I lay there like overcooked broccoli." She chuckled. "The doctor explained I'd suffered from a severe hormone imbalance which affected everything I said and did in the last little while."

Hank resumed his walk toward the car. "Neat little package. I'm glad. No one deserves to be brought on this sort of ride."

"Last thing I remember is you giving me the names of Kirk Assany in North Carolina and Rabbi Minsk in Miami."

"Don't worry I'll fill you in on the rest. Only we never accomplished much with these names since you decided to bring the matter to Cyril Platt."

Silence prevailed as Hank unlocked the car with his remote and helped Barbara into her seat. He stowed her bag in the trunk. When he took his place behind the wheel, he glanced at her and took in the deep frown on her forehead. "What's wrong?"

She shook her head releasing a deep breath. "I don't ever remember speaking to Cyril about this or anything else."

"You didn't."

"Thank God."

His hand on the key, Hank couldn't hide the hesitation crossing his brow.

"What?" she asked tugging on his arm while holding her breath.

"I read somewhere that you told Andrew during your transformation you hadn't spoken to Cyril because the man was scheduled to die."

"My God! I have no idea why. Looks like I'll need to contact an old friend."

"Give the matter a few days, right?" Hank smiled patting Barbara's hand. His attention back on the road, he negotiated a left hook to carve his place in traffic, his mind already on the rest of his day.

After dropping off Barbara, Hank took on his next port of call. Out of one hospital, he found himself driving toward another hospital, this time, to support Emma. Hank disliked hospitals, abhorred being on the premises—the overpowering scent of medicaments pumping through the vents as the only air anyone breathed, the drab walls no matter what color of paint they dabbed on to enliven the place. He hated the implication stating behind every door lay someone who needed mending or fixing or happened to be too old or too sick for anyone to rescue. People waiting to die—or worse, asleep in one of those narrow cots in excruciating, debilitating pain praying for the right to die.

Patrick Willis celebrated being out of his coma, and Hank thought a personal welcome might please the family. He drove fast, too fast, but the thought of reaching his destination suddenly occupied his whole mind. He realized this behavior to be out of character for him—a warning perhaps? A huge truck appeared before him the massive vehicle swerving out of nowhere a few feet in front of him. Wizards took over, the bastards.

In the Holland Tunnel at this busy time of day, to avoid this truck he needed to slam on the breaks and slide into the left lane at once. He reacted fast enough to avoid the collision, ignoring the painted sign STAY sprayed in bold letter throughout the lane and yanked the wheel toward the left while his car deviated close to the side of the tunnel. At least, Hank's ploy allowed the car coming up behind time to adjust his maneuvers.

The small car did, the driver sitting on his horn as he zoomed by. Hank didn't take the luxury to respond. In fact, he wanted to stop and release the demons still giving him problems. Instead, Hank kept his mind on Emma while he drove at a more reasonable speed, at least to keep up with the other drivers. He called out to her for help wondering if she might hear him. Would he be able to reach the hospital without another occurrence? He kept his mind on Emma and all the noble work she set forth.

When he drove into the hospital parking lot, he recognized that the thought of Emma had helped him arrive in one piece. Slumped over the wheel of his car, he hesitated to be amongst other people. Armed with thoughts of Christina, the love of his life, all the blessings he found in the last few years, he managed to leave the sanctuary of his vehicle, walk inside the massive Bellevue Hospital portal and head toward Patrick Willis' room wearing a smile.

He renewed his commitment not to be ruled by petty things. The big moments he would handle. However, he sometimes needed a workaround formula to master the silly things in his life.

Finding the room door open, Hank walked in grateful the place buzzed with happy faces. Emma and Eloise, Franka and little Martha, Abigail and even Tommy stood in the room for a visit. Patrick, propped up in bed, appeared to enjoy the commotion revolving around him.

Hank caught Emma's glance and concerned expression. She sensed something different with him.

"Hey, the police is in the room," Patrick exclaimed. "Everybody behave." He laughed as he extended his arm to shake Hank's hand.

"Good to see you're feeling better, Patrick. I'm sure everyone's told you how worried we all were."

"Yeah. I feel sorry you people made such a fuss about this, though I am grateful you didn't give up on me." He stared at his daughter, and Emma took her cue to come closer. He grabbed her hand. "I don't remember much about what happened. Lose a little more of the dreams with each passing hour. Still, I know somehow you're responsible for bringing me home, Emma. Thank you," he said squeezing her hand.

"Dad, you did this on your own. This is the hundredth time I'm telling you."

"Sorry, honey. Didn't mean to make you uncomfortable." He turned toward his wife. "Somehow, I remember this woman reading to me. Don't you think this is strange?" This last question Patrick addressed to Hank, and he waited for an answer.

"Well, I read somewhere about how coma patients who recover can recall movements people made around them." Hank smiled. "Christina wanted to come, but she's volunteering today at the community center. She'll be here for the night shift."

Patrick shook his head. "Tell Christina not to bother. Eloise is taking me home tomorrow morning."

"So soon?"

"Yeah. Doctor says I've warmed up the bed long enough." He shrugged. "Besides, they can't find anything wrong with me, and they poked around enough to last a lifetime, another weird memory hanging over me." He imitated shivering with disgust.

Eloise handed him a glass of juice. "Patrick doesn't trust twenty-first-century medicine," she said to Hank.

Emma stared at her mom and dad. "Sorry, I need to go. I'm writing another exam in an hour. And I'm hungry."

Patrick glanced at her. "How was your science test?"

Emma didn't tell anyone answers were given to her, ready for her to transcribe. She figured she might be the one doing this: projecting the information lodged in forgotten corners of her mind onto paper since this happened to be information she studied, but could not remember under the pressure and fatigue of the moment. "Easy, actually. I'm sure I did well."

"Good, good. What's on the menu for this afternoon?"

"English."

"English!" Patrick smiled. "You should pass with ease."

"I'll take you home," Hank said. "Can I give you a ride somewhere, Tommy?"

"Nah. My aunt's picking me up in front. She works here. We're going to lunch together. Kind of hoping Emma might be able to accompany me."

Emma seemed surprised. "Your aunt from Connecticut? Your father's sister?"

"Yeah."

"You never told me she worked here. Kind of far to commute twice a day."

"Forty-five minutes or so."

"Well, thanks for the invitation, Tommy. Only you have no exam today, and I do. You have the leisure of taking the bus home."

Hank spotted the eyebrow toss Tommy threw Emma. Tommy knew she could fly home in seconds, and although most of the other people around the room also realized the same thing, Tommy remained silent.

"Come on, kiddo. I'll get you some fast food and drop you off at school."

Hank saluted everyone, and with his hand behind Emma's back, he piloted her out of the room and into his car while anxious to address the subject on his mind.

—34—

HANK & HONEYSUCKLE

mma was the first one to talk as Hank drove in silence. "I caught the slight odor of honeysuckle when you entered my father's room, Hank." She glanced at his rugged profile waiting for him to mention something.

"Is the scent still present?"

"No. honeysuckle's gone. What happened?"

"Don't know. The first thing I realized I drove like a maniac. I barely had time to avoid a fifty-three-foot truck looming in front of me. Appeared out of nowhere." He took a deep breath. "I'm glad you told me about the wretched smell. I worried Fred Manson and his troops might be trying to cut short my time here." He stared at her while stopped at the light. "Knowing as much as I do."

"Wizards to be sure. You need to be careful, Hank. I can't lose you, and these awful creatures are not only sneaky, but they are also desperate."

"Didn't you say they only nest somewhere once?"

"Yes, if you fight with them and win, they can't come back again. However, when wizards sneak inside someone and monopolize this person's actions, but leave on their own, they are able to return." Emma turned toward Hank, once more concentrated on the road ahead.

"What does this mean if you're the one chasing them away? With the oudjat for instance?"

"This is not an exact science, not one I am familiar with in the least, but since I'm driving them out with the oudjat, which is like fighting with them or pushing them away, I don't believe they can return."

"Hope you're right. How do I know if the creeps left on their own or if I managed to shove them away?"

"What did you sense when you first encountered them?"

Hank hesitated. Then he shrugged as he admitted, "At first I thought only seconds passed when I spotted the big rig in front of me. But, by the time I realized I drove too fast, and I acted out of the ordinary, I'm sure more time than what I imagined went by. The odd sensation of not being in charge, of not being alone lasted for a few minutes at least. If wizards are shy of being discovered or worried about not being able to return if we fight them, this might explain why the bastards left."

"Well, you're right. Seems as though the wizards didn't give you the time to fight with them, but you did become aware, which is excellent and the reason why they left."

"In other words, they might return."

"Yes," Emma whispered. "The good news is you became aware of them almost the instant they invaded you. What were you thinking before all this happened?"

Hank's furtive glance came with a crooked smile. "How I hate hospitals."

Emma patted the firm shoulder beside her. No need for words of caution. Hank's tone told her he understood too well what had started the debacle with the wizards. "How is Barbara?"

"Doing well, considering how the bastards used her. She is a little upset our investigation reached a standstill."

"Remember when you asked me to spy on Barbara? I told you I caught her crying in the same manner as Bill's wife, the way Jeannie cried during my visit?"

"I remember." Hank let out a noisy sigh. "The good news is she says she made peace with her family." Hank pulled into a fast food restaurant's parking lot. "Will this do?"

"Sure, you can go through the drive-thru. Might be faster."

Hank gave their order and continued to the open window. "What do you suppose brought on those crying sessions?"

"I suspect a little depression occurs when the wizards leave a person. A hormonal imbalance perhaps."

"Which means Jeannie Frost suffered the same thing as Barbara did at one time or another."

"Yes. The thought came to mind. Not sure if Bill even realizes this. We will need to warn him."

Hank paid for the two burger combos and moved to an out of the way area to park. "Speaking of Bill." He paused waiting for Emma's attention. "No clue as to how I'm going to work with him now. We hold our usual meeting day after tomorrow and don't know what to say to him or even how to behave around him."

"You behave around me without being self-conscious every day. And your knowledge of what I can do is extensive. I don't see the difference."

"Well, first off, you promised me you wouldn't attempt to read my thoughts or probe my mind without permission. Bill made no such promise. And, he's an alien, not from this earth. I'll need to censure what I think around him—not an easy task for a human."

Emma chuckled as she swallowed a mouthful of her fries. "Don't worry. Bill and Tim might not even be able to read our minds. Most of these aliens come to Earth with a unique purpose to fulfill. Away from their environment, they can't always perform as they normally do. A lot of interference caused by our atmosphere impedes their actions, not to mention the communication problems brought on by our primitive moeurs. They didn't know about me until Fred briefed them."

"I understand. Still, not relishing this type of situation."

"Why not talk to him about this, clear the air. He'll be happy you took the first step. While you are discussing this with him, you might want to mention his wife Jeannie's problem with the wizards, and how to inform Jeannie to prevent them from returning. He'll be grateful. He'll learn to trust you with assuredness."

"Yeah. You're right. Bill did go all out for Andrew."

"How is Andrew, by the way?" Emma was afraid to ask. Yet, she owed Bill a debt of gratitude for bringing him back from the dead.

"Not faring as well as Barbara, but he'll recover." Hank squeezed Emma's hand dipping into her fries. "Not your fault. You helped get him out of the hole."

"What's wrong with him?"

"Memory loss is his biggest problem. Doctors say he might recover with rest and time out." Hank wiped his hands and shoved the rest of his food in the bag. "Where do I drop you? At home or at school?"

"Home. I can pick up my books and leave when I'm ready."

"You're not going to eat your burger?"

"I"ll refrigerate the hamburger for later. I'm never super hungry before an exam." She glanced at Hank's high brows. "Don't worry. This kind of meal is best eaten reheated." She laughed at his cross-eyed expression as he put the car in gear and drove away.

Emma, grateful Hank never asked how she would get to school made up her mind to fly to her exam, of course. She hoped she might bump into Hawke. With all the trouble she caused him and his sister, more so since Hawke's union to his betrothed ended thanks to her, sometimes, she wished she never conjured the second pendant.

Yet, without the second pendant, Hawke or his sister Columba might not be in her life. Both taught her about the wizards and helped her to accomplish her mission,

Emma paused as she closed the refrigerator door. What mission? Ludicrous, she thought. Too much melodrama tainted her life right now, and she longed for the days of spending hours on the swing tied to the old Elm out back, for lazy summer afternoons riding her bike while trying to keep up with Tommy. "Wait for me," she'd yell at him in the distance. He'd stop and pretend to check something on his bike while waiting for her to catch up.

Preparing to fly to school, Emma thought of her dad at the hospital, still confined to his bed yet as bombastic as ever, and smiled. She sympathized with some of his angst and frustration. As an adult, life became so much more complicated than the world coloring her surroundings as a child.

In her elementary school catechism, she learned how man lost paradise because of partaking of the tree of knowledge, the science of good and evil. Did this mean human knowledge might be the actual culprit for steering God's children away from their destiny? Perhaps the sort of data and all the hidden traps about this information gave a man and a woman the illusion of God-like finesse which in time created the rift between parent and child.

As she hooked her book bag around her shoulders, she considered how this division perpetuated itself in each teenage youngster vying for independence. With the dawn of knowledge, or at least the presumption of awareness, came responsibilities, the need to conquer freedom, and in most cases, the great divide which fostered loneliness and frustration.

Through the after haze, she pictured the smile on her father's face when he admitted how he'd patched things with his mother. Even though he remembered little of their conversation, Emma witnessed the happiness in her father's demeanor. Her Granny Dottie managed to forgive and love him wholeheartedly. Deep down, she considered this should also be true of the Infinite Creator. Emma believed the Creator might wait for his children stuck in the realm of Earth Refuse to be ready to merge with the others, ready to love again. Although, perhaps sublime love meant giving the smallest creature freewill to pursue their dreams without interference—no matter what the consequences.

This would explain the Devronairs' feverish actions on Earth— like one-track minded creatures avid of realizing their dream of Nirvana. Even the Celestial quadrant from so many light years away accepted the challenge of coming here to help. Emma considered others might also be present, proving her theory—the Creator did not interfere with the freewill of humans, aliens, or whoever decided to rectify status quo.

Perhaps the exigence of a deadline did exist, and no matter what happened they would need to respect the time allotted to straighten their world and rid the place of fear and greed, thereby shaking the Earth free of wizards. After all, for all alien races and billions of universes to share Heaven in peace and harmony, perhaps the Creator's children needed to show how they could band and work together toward a common, unselfish goal.

Emma did not encounter Hawke in the astral world. She dropped down in one of the washroom stalls disappointed and dreading the loneliness enveloping her. Emma imagined she may never see Hawke again. He said he would return to help with the battles, but she may have caught sight of his last farewell to her.

During her English exam, Emma discovered why she viewed the answers in watermark on most of her questions. The answers came from her own memory, from the material she studied. The blank pages reflected the faint impressions of what Emma read. She discovered the reason for the answers her mind produced during her English test. Since the subject matter came easily to her, she didn't take the time to cover the last two chapters of her book. The last couple of questions had to do with the matter in those chapters. The answers were not provided for her. She extrapolated an answer for two of the questions, but the last one on her exam dealt with a statement and a particular date on which the report originated. She guessed at an answer.

Ironic, she smiled. She would get a higher grade in math and science than she would in her best subject, English. Presumption of knowledge arose to taunt her again. Best to give an all-out effort to all matters equally, and not presume she understood one more than the other. Perhaps this was the actual fault, she reasoned as she later brought her exam to the waiting pile at the front desk. Drawing false conclusions from the little knowledge earthlings did learn. Much more happened around human beings than anyone might ever imagine. No wonder everyone got it wrong now and again.

In the corridor on her way out, Emma bumped into Christina.

"Christina, what are you doing here?"

"Hank told me you were writing an English exam. Someone was kind enough to show me the way."

Emma caught Christina's hesitancy as she bit her bottom lip, glancing left and right. "Is there somewhere we can talk?"

"Sure. Follow me."

Emma led the way to the indoor gym on the main floor in the east wing. The two women needed five minutes to reach the area, walking fast and in complete silence, yet the gym was the one place Emma realized would be empty at this time of day. Whatever practices might be held would be done so outdoors.

Emma ended the jog taking refuge in one of the darker corners between the basketball nets and the seats, underneath the rafters. "What's wrong, Christina?" Even as she asked, a little out of breath, she suspected she already knew the answer.

"Something's wrong with Hank." Christina took a deep breath, lowering her tone of voice. "We had a terrible fight last night, in fact, we never go the distance in any fight. Usually, Hank or I will give in and apologize or give each other a hug. This is our second time around, you understand. We learned how arguments and petty differences will drive a wedge between us."

"Yeah, I can imagine." Faced with Christina's frightened expression, Emma asked, "What makes you say he was acting out of character?"

"Well, he shocked me with his short temper, and by the way,

he lashed out at me as though he resented me for no reason. We decided on an August wedding—a small affair at our local church with a few friends. Now he wanted to postpone this in light of everything that's happened to Barbara and Andrew. I mean I realize he's fond of Barbara, but I still can't understand how this might infringe on our personal life."

"Well, you're right. Precinct affairs should not impede on your upcoming nuptials, except we're talking about Hank and his utter devotion to his career." Emma preferred not to blame the wizards for Hank's predicament. Smart enough to spot them earlier that day meant he might detect them while fighting with Christina.

"I went to sleep on my side of the king-size bed, crying, and reasoning somewhat like you are now. Only this morning, when I brought up the subject of our wedding date he didn't remember the argument or the ensuing fight we shared."

Emma's mood deflated as fast as the huge breath she expelled. "Wizards. I find this odd. He sensed them this morning while driving to the hospital. They almost rammed him into the back of a truck in the Holland Tunnel. Later, when he reached my father's room at the hospital, I detected the honeysuckle scent on him."

"God, Emma. What am I going to do?"

"Nothing we can do, except catch up to Hank once he is under the influence," she added under her breath.

"And hope he doesn't fall into a coma when you chase the buggers out of him," Christina added aware of what Emma accomplished with her dad and the others. "Can you do something to prevent this from happening again?"

"Sorry," Emma answered holding Christina's hand to give her courage. "And since the wizards only visited Hank a few times, he won't fall into a coma when I battle them with the Oudjat." She hesitated. "Call me the minute you suspect their presence."

At home, Emma paced her room after she called out to Hawke and Columba. She needed more precisions on how the wizards operated. Yet, her calls remained unanswered. After a while, she considered they might not be able to help her having never experienced them first-hand.

Instead, she curled up on the floor, and using the foot of her bed as a backrest, she scoured her granny's big book of magic powers handed down through the many generations of elders.

She remembered Aurora affording a couple of chapters to time travel, her logic being if she were able to go back in time to help Hank, she would use her oudjat to fight the wizards of the previous evening.

However, either the day's toll rendered her too tired to comprehend the meaning of Aurora's words or her great grandmother's arguments were too technical to sink in. She found she had to read all the paragraphs dealing with locomotion and the time segments more than once and to no avail.

She put the book down and made sure to turn on her cell phone. If she got a call from Christina, she wanted to be ready to go.

—35—

Help At Hand

*E*mma woke up to the high pitch whir of a lawn mower nearby. When she opened her eyes, disorientation set in when she didn't recognize her surroundings or gauge the time. She realized she fell asleep on the floor with her head propped on the diary. Still grasping her cell phone, Emma glanced at the clock on her bedside table. Asleep for more than three hours, she wondered why her cell phone didn't wake her.

The sound of sixties' music playing on the radio downstairs reassured her. Her mom made them supper.

She remembered Hank needing help, and she scrambled to her feet checking the recent calls on her phone worrying she missed Christina's call.

No calls from Christina, but she paralyzed staring at two calls from a number she knew well. A private number handed out to very few people.

Imagining the worst, her legs gave away and she dropped on the bed trying hard not to focus on the dark images forming in her brain. Hank called her, in dire need and she didn't hear the phone. Why not? When she checked, she realized she clutched her cell too tight on the one side that mattered and lowered the sound to nothing.

With a shaky hand, she punched in the keys to her voicemail and listened to both messages he left her.

"Emma. You're either screening, or you're still in your exam. I need your help. Wizards are popping in and out of me, and I don't know how to keep them away because I'm not sure when they arrive and when they leave."

The conversation ended abruptly, and Emma worried about Hank's life.

When she checked the next message recorded a mere half hour ago, she hoped Hank would tell her the moment lapsed, and he managed to fight the wizards off.

"I just entered St Michael's Church. I'm straddling dark corners. I don't want father Steven to see me. I figure these bastard wizards won't want to stick to me in a place like this. But, I don't think my plan is working."

Emma couldn't believe the frightened tone in Hank's voice.

"I believe more of them are fighting to get inside me now, more than a single one. Please help me. Wizards are getting stronger, and I'm running out of places to hide."

Emma wiped away the tears streaming down her face. At least she knew where to find Hank. As Emma got ready to fly to St Michael's, she replayed the last part of Hank's message.

"Oh, and Emma, when they leave your body you need a good cry, but it's a primal urge similar to when you wake up from surgery or when unconscious for a while. Maybe, the wizards don't leave. Might be they take us with them when they fly away, a little piece of us at least, which is why we can't locate our way back."

Emma grabbed her phone and prepared to leave remembering all the small flames she glimpsed when traveling down the murky corridors of the astral world to find her dad. She wondered about the fires and whether they were remnants of human spirits. What if the flames represented people who could not find their way home, like her father?

When Emma reached the church, she crouched behind one of the pews at the back and caught Matthew Logan running down the aisles on the west side, where streaks of sun poured through the clerestory's stained glass windows. Emma got up and covered the distance between them by cutting through the nave. "Matthew," she called out with a whisper. Yet the echo in the tall nave carried her words while amplifying the sound.

Startled, Matthew stopped and turned to face her. Then he signaled for her to hurry toward him.

When Emma reached him, having to go through rows of pews, she caught him kneeling on the ground tending to Hank who lay unconscious.

She couldn't prevent the sharp intake of breath stamping the silence around them like a cry of despair or the tears that came rushing out unstoppable. "Is Hank okay?"

Matthew took off his jacket to bundle and prop under Hank's head. "I detected a pulse, faint, but steady."

Emma wiped her eyes with her sweater's sleeve. "Matt, can you make sure no one comes here?"

He redressed and nodded. "What are you going to do?"

"Not sure yet. But I am going to try to bring Hank back."

Emma crouched beside Hank to sit next to him on the cold flagstone floor to be as close as possible while being invisible to other passersby who might wander inside the church.

She took her oudjat from around her neck and positioned the

small key she now kept on the same chain. She rotated the opal a full turn toward the right. Emma spotted the ray of golden light beaming from the jewel, she directed the light toward Hank.

They waited in silence. Matt sat in one of the pews, as inconspicuous as the big man could be, darting his eyes now and again toward the main and side entrances of the church.

A few people did enter, but stayed on the left aisle of the nave, in front of the pulpit. While Emma waited, she wondered if Hank even knew he needed to go toward the light. When she saw more people enter the nave, she worried a service might be planned, and she hoped Hank might find his way back sooner than later.

The wait became the tricky part since she had no way of testing her theory or whether the pendant worked or not.

Twenty minutes later, the sound of sharp heels echoed throughout the nave down their aisle, and Matthew sprung to his feet to check the main entrance. Emma glanced back and spotted Christina running toward them.

Matthew cautioned her to be quiet, and she eyed her surroundings as though just now realizing she ran inside a church.

Emma found her dark eyes stricken with terror. When she approached them, Christina bent to be at Emma's level. "God, I got a weird message from Hank. Please tell me he is all right and you can help him," she pleaded.

"I'm doing what I can, Christina. We need to be super quiet not to draw anyone's attention. I'm not sure how long this will take."

"What are you doing?"

"Directing the Oudjat's light toward him so he can find his way back to us."

Christina nodded and sat beside Emma, and grasping her arms

around her folded legs, she rested her forehead against her knees, the tremor in her shoulder demonstrating she cried for the man she loved.

Another twenty minutes went by, and the church filled up, but on the other side of the nave, close to where the priest would say Mass.

A strange scream came from Hank, right before he opened his eyes. Matt stood and helped raise his head and torso from the floor. "Can you walk?"

Hank nodded. "No harm in trying." Then he spotted Emma.

She smiled at Hank, putting away the key and slipping the pendant around her neck. She watched Matt labor to help Hank up on his feet. He didn't look solid, and she remembered her own weak legs when she spent some time in the astral world. "Where were you?"

Christina came toward him and wrapped her arms around him. Hank cautioned her. "So happy to see you sweetheart, but I'm going to need help getting to a seat. My legs are weak and useless."

Matt slipped an arm underneath his shoulder while Christina held up his other side as much as she could and both helped him to the first pew they found. Hank sat down and hauled a deep grateful breath.

Emma stayed in the aisle staring at him and hoping he remembered part of the journey he took.

He nodded smiling at her. "Fog all around. Fog deepened whether I moved forward or backward. I opted to stay put. I remembered about the light."

"You fought them."

"Yes. I won. Only when wizards leave you, seems as though

they take with them fragments of our essence. Maybe this was how I got lost."

Christina kissed his cheek. "What was the scream we heard, just before you opened your eyes?"

Hank kissed Christina's lips and stared up at Emma. "I followed the light, even when the fog got deeper, I followed the goddamn blessed yellow light, but then I got to a precipice and literally had to walk off the edge to keep following the light. The beam happened to be way down below. Scared the bejesus out of me."

Christina laughed and squeezed him with all her might. "I'm so glad you're back." Christina stared into Hank's eyes. "You said you fought them—the wizards. Does this mean, they won't return?"

Hank turned toward Emma with the same question in his eyes.

Emma smiled releasing a deep breath she never realized she held. "This is precisely what this means."

Christina extended her right arm for Emma to join them. "Thank you, my wonderful friend for bringing my man back to me."

Five minutes later, Hank hobbled down the aisle supported by Matthew and followed closely by Emma and Christina.

Outside, Christina stared back at the church and mentioned, "Hank, would you prefer getting married here?"

Matthew turned toward Emma. "I can give you a lift home, Emma."

Hank intervened. "Very sweet of you, Matt, but Christina and I live a few minutes away. We'll drop her off." He turned toward Christina answering her first question. "If you don't mind, I like the Basilica. The great church is closer, plus I'd rather not be reminded of the close call I escaped." He smiled, now standing on his own two feet, and inviting Christina to walk beside him. He laid an arm across her waist.

Matt prepared to take his leave. "Thanks again, Emma. If you ever need anything, anything at all, you call me. I'll come running." He gave her the thumbs up and sped in the other direction his hand still waving for Hank and Christina's benefit as he ran to his car.

"Are you going to drop me off or should I fly home?" Emma asked waiting for Hank's answer.

"I'm driving you home, of course." Hank gave her what Emma referred to as a 'dah' rise of eyebrows and she chuckled.

In the car, Hank mentioned how he spotted a lot of those white and orange flames littering the fog. "What do you suppose they are? They can't all be people who are waiting to get home, can they?"

Christina drove so Hank turned in the passenger seat toward her, and with his arm resting against the back of his seat, Emma sensed him relaxed enough to discuss the matter.

"Best to talk about this now. You will lose your memory of the place in a couple of hours."

"Not a bad chunk of change to forget. So, what do you think?"

She shrugged. "I'm not sure. Hard to say. We know so little about these wizards, and it's too easy to jump to conclusions. I suspect one day we might discover how to defeat them, one way or another." Emma gave him an apologetic expression.

"I know you're doing your best, Emma. If it weren't for you, a few of us would not be here anymore." Hank smiled and stretched his hand to muss her hair. "Don't give up on us, sweetie."

—36—

AUGUST COLORS

Glancing around her after closing the front door, Emma walked to the curb. Summer was winding down, visible in the days getting shorter and in how the trees were laden with a full and cumbersome load of leaves and flowers. Most of her friends satiated on outdoor sports and vitamin D and C considered themselves ready to tackle the new term coming up in a few weeks.

The loud toot of a horn made her jump out of her skin. She shook her head, narrowing eyes attempting to scold the driver responsible for the jolt causing her heart to skip a beat. Of course, August became the month when the DMV handed Thomas Carson a valid permit to drive a car without the aid of another driver. This meant his omnipresence at her house now made her address his address, forever bursting with crazy suggestions of places they might visit together, and more than willing to drive her anywhere she wanted to go—anytime.

Emma scooted into the passenger seat, deciding not to attack his impatience full front. She learned how annoyance in a young buckaroo his age had more to do with raging hormones than a genuine need for haste, and to ignore the infraction: hands down best method to assuage the fire.

"Sorry for the horn," he said with a chuckle. "Didn't mean to make you jump, but a little jolt of reality appeared necessary. You don't want to be late for Christina. You are the maid of honor."

"Christina doesn't need to be at the church for another hour, Tommy."

"Well, you might need to help her with her dress or whatever it is you gals do. I mean, I've seen those dresses, low cut in front and dipping in the back. You'll need to make sure she doesn't put the dress on backward. That would be a little too revealing if you get my meaning."

Emma caught loud, boisterous laughter going on in her head, only she wasn't laughing, the exasperation of Tommy's fun at her expense wearing her down. She searched the perimeters but found nothing out of the ordinary. "Tom, I just came from Christina's house. I have just helped her with her dress, her hair, and her bouquet. She's fine, except now, if you take me to her place, we'll be waiting for an hour before we leave for the church while she is having her makeup professionally done."

"Professional makeup? You're kidding."

"No, I'm not. The makeup is for the pictures at her house, and at the church."

"Where's Hank?"

"Staying with Matt and Maria. Christina doesn't want Hank to peek at her wedding dress before the ceremony."

"So why didn't you say this?"

"I tried to tell you on the phone, but you hung up before I finished. I barely had time to make it home, help my mom with her hair, and grab a little something to eat before you parked at my door trying to take me back to Christina's house from where I just came." Emma stared at him with a smile, if only to show Tommy no hard feelings.

"Hum, this is a pickle," he stated as he stowed the car keys in his pocket and sat back in the seat.

"Would you like to come in and I'll make you a sandwich?"

"Sure, that'll work." He smiled and took a look at her dress and her hair. "You are lovely, by the way. No need for professional makeup," he chuckled.

"Thank you."

Tommy got out of the car and escorted Emma into the house. "By the way, who's doing Christina's makeup?"

"Her mother. She arrived from Miami last night, with a friend, and I find she is quite capable."

Both teenagers walked inside in time to catch Patrick Willis crawling around on his hands and knees searching for something he lost. "I was putting on cufflinks when one of them fell and rolled somewhere. I can't find the damn thing. Hate cufflinks. Your mother is making me wear them."

"Where is Mom?" Emma asked.

"She's upstairs fixing her hair."

"Dad, her hair is excellent."

"Yeah, well, a strand came loose at the back, and when I tried to pull the mesh out of the way, the whole hairdo tumbled down to one side."

Emma rolled her eyes after letting go of a huge breath. "I'll go help her. The mesh belonged with the hairdo, Dad."

"Here Mr. Willis." Tommy held one side of the sofa up in the air. "Bet your cufflink rolled under the couch. Have a look."

"Ok, but make sure you don't drop that couch on my back,

young man."

One hour later, a little group of thirty people stood inside one of the smaller round apertures of St-Patrick's Basilica in Newark. Emma allowed her eyes to roam with love over the little group made up of the favorite people in her life. At times, even though her family acted a little nutty, she loved them—in spite of their flaws, and why wouldn't she like nuts as squirrelly as she happened to be?

By now, both her father's cufflinks hung on his cuffs, and she'd repaired her mother's hairdo handled by her dad's clumsy hands. Tommy sat next to her, for once not in the driver's seat of his car, his hands to himself and on his best behavior. More to the point, two of her most beloved friends stood in front of God and their friends, facing the prettiest décor of flowers Emma had seen in a long time. There to pronounce their vows to love each other until death separated them, Emma hoped this would not be for an insanely long time.

The same laughter she heard in Tommy's car echoed through her head. She searched the rafters and found him, sitting on one of the beams only visible to her. *"Hawke! Where have you been? And why are you laughing so hard?"*

"The bride is not wearing her dress on backward, I see."

The unexpected comment drew laughter from Emma. In fact, the laughter she attempted to hold back shook her. She managed to muffle the sound, but tears of mirth poured down her cheeks as she tried to wipe them away as fast as they poured.

"Why are you crying," Tommy whispered. "This is a joyous occasion."

"Tears of happiness," Emma managed to utter. Then she eyed the area where Hawke had appeared, but he was gone. For some reason, the fact Hawke never strayed too far away bathed Emma in a delightful peace. She understood he could not interfere in her life, but tingles warmed her when she realized he cared enough to show his face every now and then, even if his gesture was more to laugh at her and her predicament.

Christina's dress flowed in white pleats around her like a soft cloud. Gathered at the bust, the white sheath rendered her petite figure as lovely and as a vaporous as an angel. Her nut-brown hair tied upward sprouted delicate tendrils which framed her face under a crown of flowers.

As the priest pronounced Hank and Christina man and wife, she caught Barbara sitting two rows over wiping her eyes. She sat beside Martha Tyler, Christina's mother. Even retired Captain Ken flew in for the occasion, alone but in good spirits. The informal wedding allowed best man Matthew to sit beside his girlfriend Maria in the first row, and the maid of honor to sit with her family, which included her aunt Franka, her uncle, Jimmy and little Martha. Even Abigail Tichy accepted the invitation to attend, wearing an expensive, blue sequined dress. Christina invited Amelia and her family, and autistic Josh attended, also in good spirits.

Every now and then, Amelia glanced to her right and smiled at her and Tommy, although Emma understood Amelia's smiles were aimed more at Tommy. He pretended not to notice and refused to look her way.

When Christina and Hank kissed as man and wife, Emma's heart soared faced with their absolute serenity. She closed her eyes sensing the profusion of love between them. Emma found herself wishing she would one day experience this rich emotion with someone of her choice, although for now, she preferred living with the mystery. In fact, she enjoyed the innocent days in her young life. Grown-up time would be upon her soon enough. Emma designated the present-day interval as a time to fantasize about her future.

—37—

GIVING THANKS

*E*mma relaxed after a big meal pondering on how different this Thanksgiving dinner happened to be. Turkey Day rolled around this year with earth-shattering changes. Eloise and Patrick cruised around the Caribbean Islands for the holidays. Franka, Jimmy and little Martha flew down to Disney Land with Abigail, while Emma, Hank and Christina spent Thanksgiving dinner with Bill Frost and his family.

Her parent's decision surprised Emma. Of course, they invited her to come along, but she sensed this trip was long overdue for her mother and father to relax away from home and all their usual cares.

Emma realized this excellent dinner also served an unusual dessert: an excuse for the men to huddle and work on their long-term projects. Why else would Bill extend his invitation to include Tim O'Rourke and Matt Logan with his fiancée Maria?

The women sat around the outside patio on this freakishly warm November day. Emma watched Jeannie's eldest, Brittany, who turned thirteen years old a week ago, walk away holding each Christina and Maria's hand as she led them through a tour of hers and her sisters' redecorated rooms while five-year-old Caroline skipped in front of them.

Emma didn't have the heart to move after the big meal she enjoyed. Besides, she appreciated Jeannie Frost's company. In fact, the two women became fast friends that day in August when Emma took the time to coach Jeannie on how to handle the wizards. Yet both busy with bustling schedules, they didn't often spend time together and missed each other's friendship.

"Where is your young man, today? I told Bill to include him in the invitations."

"Not to worry. Tommy spends Thanksgiving with his dad and his dad's sister in Connecticut."

"I didn't mean to pry."

"Of course not. A fair question." Emma smiled. "Brittany is such a beautiful person," she said. "Inside and out."

"She is," Jeannie said with a smile. "The three of them are."

"Yes. Sweet little Madeline fell asleep in her plate of turkey and mashed potatoes. How cute was that?"

"A devil of a time cleaning her up. All she wanted to do was nap."

Emma gazed at her friend admiring the soft, elfin qualities about her. She hesitated, which prompted Jeannie's question.

"You want to ask me something?"

"More curiosity than anything else. So you tell me if you think I should mind my own business."

"If you need to understand about Bill and me, I wouldn't mind talking to you about this. With anyone else the discussion is forbidden, of course."

"Well, I always wondered about your origins. Surely you're not from Earth, this Earth."

"I come from Earth Optimal. Bill helped my parents and my

brothers settle there, and I was born on Earth Optimal shortly afterward. Bill and I met through the course of his travels."

"So there is a lot of age difference between you and Bill," Emma commented with surprise.

"Bill is Seraphim. We say Seraph for short. When they attain maturity, they stop aging. When he suggested I come here to provide him with cover, my father insisted we do this formally, through marriage, an Earth Optimal union which is the only one I understand."

Emma remembered Hawke's explanation of Earth Optimal marriage. "So, you gave birth on Earth Optimal, I imagine."

"Yes, of course."

No wonder she appeared young and like a child herself. "How were you able to have Madeline there? I thought travel to Earth Optimal wasn't possible with Columba's oudjat still in my possession."

"Seraphs don't need a key to travel through portals. They use a single thought. Bill brings me with him whenever I am homesick."

"Must be difficult on the children, living and going to school here. Do you worry about Earth—this earth's contamination?"

"Children are home schooled. I agreed with the requirement of their school that they attend one month out of the year to fulfill board exam needs and such. This also allows them to pick out the differences between the two places."

"Let me guess. The month they attend school is June, right?"

"Yes." Jeannie hesitated then admitted, "They're not really home schooled. They go to school on Earth Optimal and I spend most of my days there with them."

Emma understood a little better why their house on this Earth didn't need furnishings.

"What about Tim? He is not Seraph also, is he?"

"From the Celeste Dynasty, but he comes from a different planet within their Galaxy." Jeannie rose to search the area around her to make sure they were still alone. "Tim is a hybrid—angel and man. He holds the same powers as an angel, but sometimes craves the pleasures of a human."

"Our Earth?"

Jeannie nodded her eyes depicting the secrecy on the subject. "His father is Throne in the hierarchy of angels, but his human mother died when he was five. So he was raised on Shiloh by his Angel father."

"I didn't understand when Fred Manson talked of hybrid children. The picture is beginning to form in my mind."

"My children are hybrids. Brittany can transport, the same way Bill does—half angel and half human. She's the one who transports us all to Earth Optimal when we need to be there. And at her young age, Caroline is quite the healer."

Emma thought of her own experience with fear and sadness, and of Jeannie's brush with the wizards. "Still it doesn't take much to be contaminated on this Earth?"

"You're right, of course. Bill has formed a protective shadow around them to thwart any unworthy experience on this Earth. And, when they attend school or visit the family over there, they forget this place."

Emma remembered Hawke's words. "Cleansing while they visit, right?"

"Right." Jeannie appeared surprised by Emma's comment.

"Do many other types of hybrids exist here on Earth?"

"Well, I am not allowed to divulge anything which does not pertain to me. I should not have said anything about Tim. However, I can tell you to watch your step with Fred Manson. I caught in a gust of wind how Fred intends putting you to work for his legion of Devronairs. They can be demanding, and one must not cross them."

Emma caught the laughter of Brittany and Caroline returning with Christina and Maria. She thanked Jeannie for the information and appreciated that Jeannie, who did not normally allow such confessions, had taken the time to confide in her.

As for Fred Manson, she refused to think about his legion of tireless workers. Emma needed this day of giving thanks to endure a while longer.

And the Story of Emma Willis continues …

Emma Willis III, I Can Help You, will find Emma in the prime of life at age 20. She will come across new situations, new friends, and of course, be surrounded by all of her beloved friends and family.

As usual, the problems at hand will force her to discover solutions to help the many people in her life. In turn, her big heart will awaken to new horizons and more powers than she could have imagined.

Sometimes great souls are called upon to do great things, and friendships may be challenged. Emma will power through the obligations with grace and determination.

Look for Emma Willis I, I Can See You, and your collection will be complete ... for now.

Joss Landry

If you have enjoyed this book, please so kind as to leave a review.

Reviews are important to authors as they allow them the feedback they need to continue their work. Writing can be a lonely process. However, putting a smile in someone's life is its own reward!

Thank you for your kind support.

About the author:

Joss is a mother and a grandmother who enjoys thinking outside the box by writing fiction. She and her husband love to travel and these escapades to other countries, the look into different customs are what feed her imagination for the books she has already written:

Mirror Deep,

Exhale and Reboot, a Novel,

Ava Moss,

What About Barnum? coming soon, and many more to come.

Julie Kahn

www.ingramcontent.com/pod-product-compliance
Lightning Source LLC
Chambersburg PA
CBHW051220120726
47905CB00004B/1199